STILL LIFE

Also by the author

SHADOW OF A SUN
THE GAME
THE VIRGIN IN THE GARDEN

DEGREES OF FREEDOM: THE NOVELS OF IRIS MURDOCH
WORDSWORTH AND COLERIDGE IN THEIR TIME

Editor: THE MILL ON THE FLOSS (*Penguin*, 1980)

STILL LIFE

Antonia Byatt

CHARLES SCRIBNER'S SONS

NEW YORK

First published in the United States by Charles Scribner's Sons 1985.

Copyright © 1985 A. S. Byatt

Library of Congress Cataloging in Publication Data
Byatt, A. S. (Antonia Susan), 1936–
Still life.
I. Title.
PR6052.Y2S7   1985   823'.914   85–14323
ISBN 0–684–18577–6

1 3 5 7 9 11 13 15 17 19 H/C 20 18 16 14 12 10 8 6 4 2

Printed in the United States of America.

ACKNOWLEDGMENTS

This book was written with the help of an Arts Council Bursary, for which I am very grateful. I am also grateful to Monica Dickens for a matter of plotting about which she knows. This novel could not have been written without the help of the London Library and Douglas Matthews, its Librarian. My editor at Scribners, Laurie Schieffelin, has been understanding in every sense of that word. I am grateful to Will Vaughan and John House for talking to me about painting, to Jacquie Brown for typing accurately at unnatural speed, and to Michael Worton for some felicitous French and more particularly for aesthetic sense and general encouragement.

I am grateful to Little, Brown and Company, in association with New York Graphic Society Books, for permission to quote from *The Complete Letters of Vincent van Gogh,* and to New Directions Publishing Corporation for permission to quote from *The Cantos of Ezra Pound.*

For Jenny Flowerdew

May 4, 1936–October 11, 1978

Talis, inquiens, mihi videtur, rex, vita hominum praesens in
terris, ad conparationem eius, quod nobis incertum est, temporis,
quale cum te residente ad caenam cum ducibus ac ministris tuis
tempore brumali . . . adveniens unus passerum domum citissime
pervolaverit; qui cum per unum ostium ingrediens, mox per aliud
exierit . . . Mox de hieme in hiemem regrediens,
tuis oculis elabitur.

Bede, *Historia Ecclesiastica Gentis Anglorum*

"Such," he said, "O King, seems to me the present life of men on earth, in
comparison with that time which to us is uncertain, as if when on a winter's
night you sit feasting with your ealdormen and thegns—a single sparrow
should fly swiftly into the hall, and coming in at one door, fly out through
another. Soon, from winter going back into winter, it is lost to your eyes."

Les mots nous présentent des choses une petite image claire et usuelle comme celles qu'on suspend aux murs des écoles pour donner aux enfants l'exemple de ce qu'est un établi, un oiseau, une fourmilière, choses conçues comme pareilles à toutes celles de même sorte.

Marcel Proust, *Du côté de chez Swann.*

J'essayais de trouver la beauté là où je ne m'étais jamais figuré qu'elle fût, dans les choses les plus usuelles, dans la vie profonde des «natures mortes».

Marcel Proust, *A l'ombre des jeunes filles en fleurs.*

Les substances mortes sont portées vers les corps vivants, disait Cuvier, pour y tenir une place, et y exercer une action déterminée par la nature des combinaisons où elles sont entrées, et pour s'en échapper un jour afin de rentrer sous les lois de la nature morte.

G. Cuvier, quoted by Michel Foucault, *Les mots et les choses*, p. 289.

STILL LIFE

POST-IMPRESSIONISM: ROYAL ACADEMY OF ARTS, LONDON
1980

He signed the Friends' Book in his elegant handwriting: Alexander Wedderburn, January 22, 1980.

She had said, peremptory as always, that he was to go early, straight to Room III, where "the miraculous stuff" was to be found. So here he was, a distinguished public man, also an artist of a kind, stepping obediently through Room I (French 1880s) and Room II (British 1880s and 1890s), on a lead-gray morning, into the pale gray, classical, quiet place where the bright light shone and sang off pigment so that the phrase "miraculous stuff" seemed merely accurate.

On one long wall hung a row of Van Goghs, including an Arles *Poets' Garden* he hadn't seen before but recognized from small photographs, from charged descriptions in the painter's letters. He sat down and saw a bifurcated path simmering with gold heat round and under the rising, spreading blue-black-green down-pointing vanes of a great pine, still widening where the frame interrupted its soaring. Two decorous figures advanced, hand in hand, under its suspended thickness. And beyond, green green grass and geraniums like splashes of blood.

Alexander was not worried about whether Frederica would turn up. She was no longer in the habit of being late: her life had schooled her to temporal accuracy, perhaps to being considerate. He himself, at sixty-two, felt, not quite accurately, that he was now too old, too settled, to be put out, by her or by anyone else. He thought with warmth of her certain approach. There had been a pattern, an only too discernible repetition in the events and relationships of his life into which she had ruggedly refused to fit. She had been a nuisance, a threat, a torment, and was now a friend. She had suggested that they look at Van Gogh together, setting up another form of repetition, deliberate, contrived, and aesthetic. His play *The Yellow Chair* had first been presented in 1957; he did not like to think too closely about it, as he did not like to think too closely about any of his past work. He stared at the serenely impassioned garden made out of a whirl of yellow brushstrokes, a viridian impasto, a dense mass of furiously feathered lines of blue-green, isolated black pot hooks, the painfully clear orange-red spattering. He had had trouble finding an appropriate language for the painter's obsession with the illuminated material world. He would have been lying if he had recorded only the more accessible drama of the painter's electric quarrels with Gauguin in the Yellow House in Arles, the distant necessary brother who supplied paint and love, the severed ear delivered to the whore in the brothel, the asylum fears. At first he had thought that he could write a plain, exact verse with no figurative language, in which a yellow chair was the thing itself, a yellow chair, as a round gold apple was an apple or a sunflower a sunflower. Sometimes he still saw the brushstrokes, as it were, in this naked way, so that any more metaphorical thoughts of this garden had to be undone, the idea of black wings to be stripped from the painted leafage, the vulgar idea of blood splashes washed off the notation of geraniums. But it couldn't be done. Language was against him, for a start. Metaphor lay coiled in the name sunflower, which not only turned toward but resembled the sun, the source of light.

Van Gogh's idea of things had also been against him. The yellow chair, besides being brushstrokes and pigment, besides being a yellow chair, was one of twelve bought for a company of artists who were to inhabit the Yellow House, the white walls of which should blaze with sunflowers as the windows of Gothic cathedrals blazed with colored light. Not only metaphor: cultural motif, immanent religion, a faith and a church. One thing always linked to another thing. As the *Poets' Garden*, a decoration for the bedroom of the "poet Gauguin" was more than it seemed.

Arles, 1888

Some time ago I read an article on Dante, Petrarch, Boccaccio and Botticelli. Good Lord! it did make an impression on me, reading the letters of those men.

And Petrarch lived quite near here in Avignon, and I am seeing the same cypresses and oleanders . . .

There is still a great deal of Greece all through the Tartarin and Daumier part of this queer country, where the good folks have the accent you know; there is a Venus of Arles just as there is a Venus of Lesbos, and one still feels the youth of it, in spite of all . . .

But isn't it true, this garden has a fantastic character which makes you quite able to imagine the poets of the Renaissance strolling among these bushes and over the flowery grass? . . .

The youth of it, Alexander thought. I thought I was world-weary then. In July 1890, two years after writing this, Van Gogh had shot himself inefficiently in the groin, and had died slowly. In 1954, Alexander, a time-obsessed man, had read the centenary edition (1953) of the *Letters*. He had himself been rising thirty-seven, and when *The Yellow Chair* was put on, had passed that age, was older now than Van Gogh, as he had, in the 1940s, realized that he was older than Keats. He had felt, perhaps briefly, the power of the survivor. What nonsense. The eternal youth of Provence. He thought of thick, fat, hot motorways carving up that land. He turned his attention to the timeless fields of wheat and olives.

She made a kind of progress up the Palladian marble stair. A painter stopped to kiss her; a journalist waved. John House, who had organized the exhibition, came almost leaping down the stairs, accompanied by a smallish woman in a pine-green tentlike coat. He also kissed Frederica and introduced the woman, fumbling her name, as "a colleague" and Frederica as "Frederica—you must forgive me, I never know what name you're working under, women these days are so protean." Frederica did not attempt to ascertain the fumbled name, having given up interest in stray new people until it was clear that they were of real concern. She assumed wrongly that John House's colleague was an art historian. The colleague looked at Frederica with an apparently absentminded scanning attention. John House spoke of the history of the gathering of the images, an emptiness here (Jacob wrestling the Angel), an unexpected illumination there. Frederica listened attentively; went on and signed the Visitor's Book. Frederica Potter, Radio 3 Critics' Forum. She negotiated a free catalog. She made her leisurely way toward where she had told Alexander to be.

An old woman, armed with a Sound Guide, became quite excited and pulled at the arm of another, "Hey—look at that—*Winston Churchill* painted that, the . . ."—carefully—"*Cap d' Antibes.*"

Frederica dipped round her to stare—Claude Monet: "Au Cap d'Antibes par vent de mistral." A whirl of blue and rose, formless formed plungings of water and wind. "To paint," she remembered from Proust's description of fictive Elstir, "that one does not see what one sees." To paint light and air between ourselves and objects.

"I said, dear, *Winston Churchill*—." The second woman tugged free of the clutching fingers. "*Not* to be mentioned in the same breath with . . ." she said, looking nervously from Frederica to painted signature.

The arrested water shone and danced. In the catalog John House quoted Monet's description of the painted light around the snowy haystacks as an enveloping veil. He also quoted Mallarmé. "I think . . . that there should be only allusion . . . To *name* an object is to suppress three-quarters of the enjoyment of the poem, which is created by the gradual pleasure of apprehending it. To suggest it, that is the dream . . ." It was not a view of things with which Frederica was entirely in sympathy; she liked naming names. But she looked briefly down, dazzled by the flowing skin of worked and delicate color; the blue and rose tourbillons of the mistral on the sea, the prismatically sliced frosty nimbus round the mysterious squat stacks. She scribbled words, notes, in the margin of her catalog.

Daniel bought a ticket, and paid for the hire of a catalog; he wasn't sure why. He had come, he believed, because he needed to discuss certain administrative problems with Frederica. He was aware that she believed he was in need of art. Under his arm he carried a folded newspaper with that day's headline: PEACE MOTHER DIES. He was raw to bad news, more raw as he grew older, which was not perhaps quite what he had expected. He saw and did not see the paintings. There was a field of poppies and corn which reminded

him only of small and large, faded and ghostly, versions of Van
Gogh's *Harvest*, which he had seen repeated in endless hospital corridors, waiting rooms, school offices. He had seen these ample fields,
as he had seen Cézanne's geometric brown-and-green undergrowth
in more than one mental hospital dayroom. Odd, he thought, considering that Van Gogh himself had died mad and despairing in such
surroundings. Not serene, overexcited, these fields. Daniel's patience
with the nervously ill was not what it had been. Although he was
eleven years younger than Alexander, Daniel too was in the habit of
thinking of himself as a survivor, a battered and grizzled survivor.

Alexander saw her coming toward him. A dozen or so schoolgirls
were dutifully filling in Xeroxed, handwritten, one-word-answerable
questionnaires. Alexander, always a connoisseur of garments, realized
that Frederica had changed her style, that the clothes the young creatures were wearing could be described as a parody of the clothes
Frederica had worn at their age, and that Frederica's new style was
not unrelated to this shift. There she was in a conventional two-piece
suit, fine dark wool, muted geometric pattern in greens and unexpected straw browns, caught in at the waist—still very thin—to give
the effect of a bustle, the skirt long and straight to the knee. She had
ruffles (not swashbuckling) at the neck and the small velvet hat
could, but did not, support a veil. The pale red hair was in a figure of
eight chignon at her neck, reminiscent of one of Toulouse-Lautrec's
fine-drawn café habituées. Fifties *and* post-impressionist, thought
Alexander, connecting. She came up and kissed him. He remarked
on the dress of the young. She took the point eagerly.

"My dear, I know. Pencil skirts and batwing sweaters and spiky
stilettos, tottering with their hard little behinds sticking out, and all
that red *lipstick*. I remember when I thought lipstick had gone forever, a dream of painted excess, as I thought paper taffeta had gone
forever, in Cambridge, when we all took to glazed cotton. Do you
remember?"

"Of course."

"Do you remember the eclectic sixties—when we went to the
National Portrait Gallery—*everything*, from swamis to major gen-
erals and majordomos too. These are so serious and uniform. More
and more of the same. More of *me*."

"Lèse-majesté. And you? You have reverted to type?"

"Oh, I'm in my element. I understand the fifties. I couldn't do the forties bit at all, padded shoulders and crepy things, ugh, and page-boys—I think it must have been purely Oedipal; those were my *parents'* things, dammit, what I was getting away from. This is my scene."

"So it is."

"And *now* I have money."

"In our new austerity, you have money."

"In our new austerity, I am old enough to have money." They saw Daniel advancing.

"Daniel doesn't change," said Alexander.

"Sometimes I wish he did," said Frederica.

Daniel did not change. He wore the same black clothes—baggy corduroys, heavy sweater, working man's jacket—that he had worn through the sixties and seventies. Like many hirsute men he had thinned a little on top where once his black fur had been extravagant, but he had a plentiful and prickling black beard, and his body was still compact and very heavy. He looked, in this setting, a little like some painter. He saluted Frederica and Alexander with his rolled newspaper and said that it was cold outside. Frederica kissed him too, reflecting that he was dressed like a man who smelled dirty, but in fact didn't. Alexander smelled, still, of Old Spice and a sort of agreeable toastiness. His smooth brown hair was as thick as ever but shot now with needles of glittering silver.

"We must talk," said Daniel.

"First you must look at the pictures. Take time off."

"I keep trying. I went to the King's Carol Service."

"Good for you." Frederica glanced shrewdly at him. "Now, *look at the pictures.*"

Gauguin's *Man with the Axe*. "One for you," said Frederica to Alexander, still skimming the necessary accompanying print. "Androgynous. John House says. No, Gauguin said. Do you think?"

Alexander considered the decorative gold body, itself a repetition of a body on the Parthenon frieze. He saw a blue loincloth, flat breasts, purple sea with coral tracings lying flatly on it. He was unmoved, though the colors were rich and strange. He told Frederica he preferred his androgynes to be more obscured, more veiled, more *suggested*, and directed her attention to *Still-Life, Fête Gloanec*

1888 in which various inanimate objects, two ripe pears, a dense bunch of flowers, swam across a bright red tabletop rimmed with a black ellipse. The picture was signed "Madeleine Bernard," and Alexander told Frederica that Gauguin had flirted seriously with that young woman, had characterized her, as was fashionable at the time, as having the desirable, unattainable androgynous perfection, complete sensuality combined with unattainable self-sufficiency. Frederica informed him from the catalog that the vegetation was supposed to be a jocular portrait by Gauguin of Madeleine, the pears her breasts, the dense flowers her hair. "You could read it another way," said Alexander, interested now. "You could read the *pears* as androgynous in themselves, as partly male."

"And the hair as other hair," said Frederica loudly, scandalizing a few bystanders, amusing a few more.

"You like to *work* for your images, don't you, Alexander?"

"It's age," said Alexander, peaceably, untruthfully. They were beginning to attract a penumbra of gallery goers, as though they were offering a guided tour.

They moved on to the *Olive Pickers*. Daniel's mind was elsewhere. He remembered a straight mass of red-gold hair, in cold King's Chapel, more golden than foxy Frederica's, slowly settling onto a collar as the pins released their grip. He saw a mass of freckles—sometimes melding into sixpenny-sized brown patches of warmth—moving over the hard frame of cheekbones and brow. The sexless voices rose in the cold. "Unto us a Boy is born." "Herod then with wrath was filled." The voices played with the slaughter of the innocents, treble and descant hunting each other, while she bowed her head, unable to sing in tune.

The olives had been painted from the asylum at St. Rémy in 1889.

As for me, I tell you as a friend, I feel impotent when confronted with such nature, for my Northern brains were oppressed by a nightmare in those peaceful spots as I felt one ought to do better things with the foliage. Yet I did not want to leave things alone *entirely*, without making an effort, but it is restricted to the expression of two things—the cypresses—the olive trees—let others who are better and more powerful than I reveal their symbolic language . . .

Look here, there is another question that comes to mind. Who are the human beings that actually live among the olive, the orange, the lemon orchards?

Frederica and Alexander held a discussion of natural supernaturalism. Daniel looked at the pink sky, the twisted trunks, the silvery leaves, the rhythmic earth streaked with yellow ochre, with pink, with pale blue, with red-brown. Olives, Frederica agreed with Alexander, could not *not* recall the Mount of Olives, the Garden of Gethsemane, in the day of Van Gogh the pastor's son, the lay preacher. As the cypresses must always, differently, mean death. Daniel asked, for politeness really, why Van Gogh had been mad, was it just that he was driven? Alexander said that it may have been a form of epilepsy, exacerbated by the atmospheric-electric disturbances of the mistral and the heat. Or you could make a Freudian explanation. He felt guilty toward the child who had not survived, for whom he had been named. He had been born on March 30, 1853. His dead brother, Vincent Van Gogh, had been born on March 30, 1852. He was in flight from his family, his dead alter ego, his uncertain sense of identity. He wrote to Theo "I hope you are not a 'Van Gogh.' Essentially I am not a 'Van Gogh.' I have always looked upon you as 'Theo.' " Daniel said he could not see the pain Frederica said was in the olives, and Alexander, still lecturing, said that Vincent had objected to paintings of symbolic Christs in Gethsemane by Bernard and his *compères*, had torn up his own, had made do with the olives themselves. He told Daniel about the terrible St. Rémy painting of the blasted tree, about *noir-rouge*, and Daniel said that it was odd that these orchards should be all over the walls of other asylums now, to cheer people up. The trees stood under their haloes of pink and green strokes, small flying things, solidified light movements or saccades of the eye, brushstrokes, pigment.

To Emile Bernard, St. Rémy, December 1889
Here is a description of a canvas which is in front of me at the moment. A view of the park of the asylum where I am staying; on the right a gray terrace and a side wall of the house. Some deflowered rose bushes, on the left a stretch of the park—

red-ochre—the soil scorched by the sun, covered with fallen pine needles. This edge of the park is planted with large pine trees, whose trunks and branches are red-ochre, the foliage green gloomed over by an admixture of black. These high trees stand out against an evening sky with violet stripes on a yellow ground, which higher up turns into pink, into green. A wall— also red-ochre—shuts off the view, and is topped only by a violet and yellow-ochre hill. Now the nearest tree is an enormous trunk, struck by lightning and sawed-off. But one side branch shoots up very high and lets fall an avalanche of dark green pine needles. This somber giant—like a defeated proud man— contrasts, when considered in the nature of a living creature, with the pale smile of a last rose on the fading bush in front of him ...

You will realize that this combination of red-ochre, of green gloomed over by gray, the black streaks surrounding the contours, produces something of the sensation of anguish, called "noir-rouge" from which certain of my companions in misfortune frequently suffer ...

I am telling you about this ... to remind you that one can try to give an impression of anguish without aiming straight at the historic Garden of Gethsemane ...

Daniel thought about dead Ann Maguire who, like Anna Van Gogh, the Dutch pastor's wife, had named a younger, hopeful child for a dead one. (Though in Van Gogh's case, the names Theodorus, Vincent, Vincent, Theodorus, appeared and reappeared from generation to generation, the cultural parallels to certain persisting aspects of the family face, a heavy brow, an intense blue eye, a cheekbone, a nostril.) In the churchyard in his last parish a family in the English 1870s had tried to name a son Walter Cornelius Brittain and had buried three, aged five, aged two, aged one month, interspersed by variegated dead daughters, a Jennet, a Marian, an Eva.

In August 1976 a car, containing an IRA gunman, possibly already dead, ploughed onto a pavement and killed three of Mrs. Maguire's children, Joanne, eight, John, two, Andrew, six weeks, leaving one son, Mark, aged seven. People had been shocked, by numbers as well as by gratuitous death itself, as people will be, and Mrs. Maguire's sister and a friend had founded the Peace People, whose brave beginning and sad end will not be chronicled here. Ann Maguire had borne a second Joanne, in New Zealand, from where she had returned, unable to bear cultural transplantation. Although the papers referred to her as the Peace Mother she had not been active in the Peace People. She had brought a case for legal compensation for her dead children's lives and for her own suffering and one of her few recorded public utterances was to call the first offer of compensation "pitiful." The day of the hearing of her second case she had been found dead. Daniel had pieced the story together from the radio: "with throat wounds. Foul play was not suspected," and from conflicting newspapers. "With hedge-cutters." "With a carving knife." "With an electric carving-knife" "by her side." Her motives, the coroner was to say, were "not completely easy to understand." Daniel, who had become a specialist in wild blows of chance, thought he understood some of it.

He had not prayed for Ann Maguire. He was not that kind of priest. He had metaphorically shaken a large fist, impotently, at some looming energy-field and got on with his work, his work.

He followed the other two into the dark shadows of the room housing the Low Countries. On the far wall, nuns ascended and descended a cool gray stair in winged white caps. The Lauriergracht in Amsterdam was gloomed and glittering. Mondrian's *Evening* was somber and cloudy. He liked these. Like Vincent, although he was unaware that Vincent had remarked on it, he had "Northern brains" and responded biologically and spiritually to tones of black, donkey brown, varied grays, touches of white in dark. "One of the most beautiful things done by the painters of this country has been the painting of *black* which nevertheless has light in it," Vincent had written from Holland. Xavier Mellery, the painter of the nuns, was described in the catalog as "creating a light which is the negation of that which envelops our immediate visual experience of things; it is rather the interior light of your mind . . ." Daniel was used to such language; it was his daily, or anyway weekly, pabulum. He knew about the light shining in darkness and had come, for reasons completely different from Alexander's desire for exactness, specificity, to mistrust figurative language. He never now made a sermon from a metaphor, nor drew analogies; he preached examples, cases, lessons. But he liked the black Dutch paintings; they were, so to speak, on his wavelength.

He cornered Frederica.
"You said you'd news of Will."
"A postcard, yes."
"Where this time?"
"Kenya. On the way to the Ugandan famine, I think."
"Hippie," said Daniel.
"Helping out," said Frederica.
"What *use*—comparatively—is a chap like that, wi' no training, no medical . . . no . . . ? Another mouth to feed. It makes me wild."
"I think he *is often* useful, in his way. You judge him so."
"He judges me. Judging runs in the family."
"It does," said Frederica.
"Once," said Daniel, "I was in Charing Cross Hospital, someone's kid had taken an overdose and died, they pump them out there regular as clockwork but this one's liver couldn't take any more. Anyway, there I was, going up this endless corridor, thinking what to do about the mother, who blamed herself—wi' *reason* mind you, she was one of those soft suckering witch-women, but that made it worse, not better—and there was th' trolley wi' the dead girl on it, sliding by me—sheet right over, porters in those soft theater boots and floppy plastic bathcaps—and when they'd got past me and were turning in't door, the first one looked at me from under his plastic frills like, with my own face. I was shocked for a minute. Got all his hair tucked up in that thing, you see—otherwise, he's not so like me, not *strikingly* so. 'Hi,' he said. 'Going about your father's business, are you?' So I asked him what he was up to and he said he was going to and fro in the earth and walking up and down in it, and then he pushed th' trolley in, and I went in after, and the mother began her howling and shrieking, and Will said, 'Well, I'll walk off and leave you to it.' And I said, 'Where are you going, then?' And he said, 'I told you. To and fro.' That was the last I saw of Will."

The nuns ascended the stairs in a perpetual cool silence.

"Quoting scripture for his own purposes," said Daniel.

"That was rather funny, I thought," said Frederica.

"Anything on the postcard about coming back? Any plans?"

"No."

Sometimes she wished Will would not write to her at all, if he would send no messages to Daniel. Sometimes she told herself the postcards, or exercise-book scrawls, *were* messages to Daniel, but one should never, she considered, ignore surface meanings in favor of implications, and the damned things were addressed to her, to Frederica.

"Oh, hell," she said.

"Not to worry," said Daniel. "I'll push off. I'll see you."

"You haven't seen the *pictures*."

"I'm not in the mood."

"We were going to have coffee in Fortnum and Mason's."

"No, thank you all the same."

I

ANTE-NATAL: DECEMBER

1953

I

It was written over the entrance, gold letters on purple gloss on red brick. Gynecology and Obstetrics. Inside the archway an archetypal hand, the first of a series, pointed on a placard. Ante-Natal Clinic, First Right. It was dark in there.

She rode up and chained her bicycle to tall railings. She was six months pregnant. The bicycle basket sagged heavily on the front mudguard. From it she took a string bag, in which was a paper bag containing knitting, a wrapped lemonade bottle, and two heavy books. She went in.

The central reception area was red tiled, walled most of the way up also in dried-blood-red tiles, high windows way above eyes. At a table sat a royal-blue sister with a crimped white turret on her head. In front of her stood twelve women. Stephanie counted them and joined them. She looked at her watch: 10:30 exactly. Twelve was not good. She wedged the string bag between her feet, took out a book, held the paper up to the dim light.

A fourteenth woman pushed through the swing doors, past the thirteen, addressed the sister.

"My name is Owen. Mrs. Frances Owen. I have an appointment."

"So have all these ladies."

"At ten-thirty, with Mr. Cummings."

"So have all these ladies."

"Ten-fifteen," murmured one or two.

"But—"

"Now if you just take your place you'll be seen in your turn."

"I—"

Mrs. Frances Owen stood behind Stephanie. Stephanie lowered the book and murmured, "Block bookings. Some of the sisters are less efficient so they just heap the notes up and the last become first. It's a nice calculation, whether to arrive early or late. Best to get the first first appointment. Nine-thirty. Except the doctors are often late."

"It's my first time."

"In that case they'll keep you longer, taking details. The queue goes round you."

"How long?"

"Better not to think."

"I—"

Stephanie read William Wordsworth. She had decided to read through his poems, slowly and thoughtfully, in these queues. There were three problems with this: the weight of the book, increasing nakedness as the examination wound from stage to stage, and failure of concentration, owing to painful legs and a general pregnant incapacity to finish sentences, her own, Wordsworth's, or Mrs. Frances Owen's. Who was now quiet.

She read.

A slumber did my spirit seal.

The book often opened here.

I had no human fears.

Ordinary words, in an extraordinary arrangement. How did one recognize what was extraordinary? She shuffled forward, manipulating the string bag with sensible shoes. In her turn she came to the sister, who extracted a folder with Orton, Stephanie Jane, EDD 4. 13. 54 on it, from a pile on her left, transferred it to a pile on her right, and permitted Stephanie to sit on a brown canvas-and-metal tube chair for another half hour.

> She seemed a thing that could not feel
> The touch of earthly years.

Seemed. She looked at the women. Hats, head scarves, bulky coats, varicose veins, bags, baskets, bottles.

> I had no human fears.

Once her heart would have leaped up, just at the rhythm. Now its own rhythm was strained and sluggish. Inside her, unperceived, another quick rhythm fluttered, perhaps synchronized. She dozed, open-eyed, looking up at slits of light. "I am sunk in biology." The phrase pleased her. "Sunk in biology." It was not a complaint. Biology was very interesting. She had never imagined it could be so wholly voracious of time and attention. She read slowly.

> No motion has she now, no force.

On the contrary, too much and not her own. They called her name. She went into the corridor, hurrying as though she did not know very well that she was simply being transferred to another waiting chair, that the urgency of their voices bore no relation to the speed of their, or anyway her, movements. Mrs. Owen spoke behind her.

"I've got terrible pains in the back."

"It's the standing and these chairs. They'll get worse before they get better."

There was a disagreeable note of clergyman's wife in that. A jolly, sympathetic delimiting of response. She must not make that particular sound. The church was beset with choirs of false voices. She did not want to speak. The antenatal queues were, apart from the baby who fluttered and arched, her nearest approach now to privacy.

"Do you want me to get someone?"

"Oh, no," said Mrs. Owen, already aware that doctors and nurses were not there to be pestered. "I'll manage." Stephanie held up the heavy book again.

The antenatal clinic proper, beyond the red mouth and throat of reception, was, like the whole maternity wing, part of a military hospital added hastily at the beginning of the last war, in anticipation of hosts of wounded soldiers who had never come there. It was on one floor, temporarily walled, a repeating H shape of corridors and slopes with dismal bright blue paint. Stephanie and Mrs. Owen, clutching notes, bottles, knitting, Wordsworth, turned left and right and were greeted by a fat nurse who put their bottles on a tray among jam jars with cellophane frills, various medicine bottles, a gin bottle, and a large ketchup pot. They were shown into cubicles with inadequate curtains, where they were told to strip completely and put on the clean toweling gowns in there. Stephanie's gown had a cheerful beach look, orange and poster-blue pajama or deck-chair stripes. It reached her mid-thigh, would in no way meet over her jutting belly, and had no belt. She was used, but not reconciled, to such indignities. She gathered up Wordsworth and the string bag. She could hear Mrs. Owen being castigated for not having turned right and left, instead of left and right, to Hematology, seeing as it was her first time. They spoke as one speaks to distracted children or incapable old people, who do not look or listen.

"My back hurts," said Mrs. Owen, "And I—"

She was hurried away slowly to Hematology.

At one end of the cubicle room was a set of scales before which another long queue was forming. There were only two chairs in the whole place for at least a dozen women, many now uncomfortably unsupported by girdle or bra.

The scale platform was occupied by a woman so huge, so grossly hung about with mounds and protuberances and pendant ledges of fat that it was impossible to see where there was a baby, or how large, or how high it was. She laughed, as the fat will, while nurses gathered and tutted over the sliding weights. She was diabetic and a cause for concern. Nurses liked gallantry and real problems. Wordsworth read differently among so much, so various flesh.

No motion has she now, no force.

Wordsworth was a man speaking to men. He had said so. One would need to know things—technical things—about speech, about why and how rhythm worked, about selection of nouns and word order to explain how he could state with finality, so that the words for it were *his* words—simple truths. Her education had hardly started.

Mrs. Owen returned. Her face was very white above her very brief, neatly closed gown. There was a moving line of blood along the inside of her leg.

"Mrs. Owen!" Stephanie pointed. Mrs. Owen had an elaborate hairstyle piled incongruously above her thin nakedness. She bent to peer down. She stammered.

"Oh, how embarrassing. Oh, dear. I kept trying to ask them, was a bit of bleeding all right, and the pains, but there wasn't the opportunity, and it really wasn't *this much* . . ."

She made a deprecating, apologetic gesture, gave a small cry, and fell over. A great deal of blood pumped and washed over the clean tiled floor. Stephanie called, "Nurse," and almost immediately there was a lot of efficient rubber-soled running, a trolley, heaps of towels and swabs, subdued chatter among the women. The doctor emerged from the frosted-glass cubicle beyond the scales. Mrs. Owen, now chalk white and motionless on her trolley, was wheeled behind curtains. There was more running. Stephanie was fetched away, divested of her gown, arranged on a hard high couch under a cellular blanket. Even here, one could wait a long time. Stephanie propped Wordsworth against the hard ledge of the bulge.

> She neither hears nor sees
> Rolled round in earth's diurnal course,
> With rocks, and stones, and trees.

To name the whole earth with three nouns, that was authority. Rocks and stones and trees. The rhythm formed by the reiterated "and." Everything, even if named, was part of the same thing. And the one complex word among simple verbs, diurnal.

A young doctor came. He probed her hard, tough sides with reasonably kind fingers. He pushed a stethoscope into her softness and listened. He did not meet her eye: this was usual.

"Well, Mrs. Orton, how are we?"

She could not answer. Tears were running all over her face.

"There are traces of sugar. Are you sure the specimen was taken on rising? Mrs. Orton, what is the matter?"

"The English. Are so damned. *Polite*. For hours and hours we stand—with no girdles—in cold drafty places. That woman. That. Mrs. Owen. Lost her baby—I know—because—because no one would let her tell them. Because I wouldn't. Because nobody here—"

"Don't be hysterical. It's bad for the child. Your child."

She sniffed, wet.

"She would almost certainly have lost it anyway." It sounded as though he was conceding a point.

"But not so *foolishly*."

This slightly unusual speech pattern seemed to enable him to address her directly. He came to the head. He peered at her wet face.

"Why are you so particularly upset?"

"I didn't listen. Nobody did. We taught her to stand in line."

"You would think anyone in that state would have been clever enough, sensible enough, to get out of line."

"I truly doubt it. This place puts you in line. You stay in it. You stand for *hours*, without a girdle, because of block bookings and not enough chairs. Two chairs for all those women. Standing *hurts*. This place changes you. I told her myself not to think. Doctors are busy."

He looked automatically, by association, at his watch. It was true, he was busy. He had seen Stephanie before, but perhaps only once. He remembered her vaguely—blonde, curved rounds, placid, no trouble, always using "the pregnancy" as a reading desk. He didn't think that was quite right, but hadn't formulated why.

"Your baby's fine," he said. "Just fine. Strong heartbeat, a good size, nice position, coming along fine. Your weight's good, no problems. Do stop crying. It does no good. Pregnancy is an upsetting time for some people. You must try and keep calm for your child's sake. Please. Look—if you're upset, go and have a good talk with our social worker, a good—"

"I don't want a good talk. And I seem to *be* a social worker most of the time. Unpaid. I was trying to take time off. I don't—I thought I could read Wordsworth and forget about the damned queue."

"Yes. Now, if you'd just swing your legs down." She considered apologizing and did not. She did not feel angry with him; she could imagine how it was for him—woman after woman after woman, all the same, all different, weeping on occasion for fear, boredom, pain, frustration, humiliation. How could he take on all that, much of it irremediable, at ten-minute intervals? He was a very young man. He could peer professionally down his speculum into her vagina, but he blushed when his eyes met hers. However, she should not apologize for her tears. He could at least, whatever his personal reticence, have promised to investigate the problem of the insufficient chairs.

Here she did him less than justice. He recognized the chairs as part of his province. On her next visit there were another half dozen.

II

Out in the air identity was partly restored. Businesslike and not languid, brisk and not tearful, she mounted her bicycle. She kept her back rigorously straight. The fetus or baby seemed to like the bicycle; its movement usually, and she felt happily, ceased as hers began. The roads round Blesford were still more or less country lanes, bare blackthorn hedges and deep ditches, with the first few bungalows isolated on their little plots on the edges of little capillary roads. She remembered the lanes in summer, cow parsley and warm leaves, but not, not bodily, her own light movement. Eclipsed is maidenly grace, says Dr. Spock with a curious inversion. Well, that was true.

She braked to avoid another cycling figure: her husband, Daniel, heavy and black, clanking a little because of a rubbing chain guard. They rode along side by side, amicably, both heavy, legs efficiently working.

"Was it all right?"

"No troubles. Longer than usual. How was yours?"

Daniel had been officiating at a funeral.

"Not nice, really. Old ladies from t'home. One daughter wi' three or four kids in tow. Crematorium. Usual anticlimax—old birds standing round a bit o' grass at t'back they'd got lease of for a few hours, wi' a garden label saying, 'Mrs. Edna Morrison,' and a few bunches of chrysanths put in rows. Looked ready to be blown away, the old biddies. But pleased wi' themselves because they were still on their pins and not slid away into eternity. There was no tea, thank God. T'home doesn't run to one, and t'daughter only wanted to get all t'kids back to Sunderland."

"Someone in our queue lost her baby. Just there. On the floor. Fast."

She hadn't meant to tell him that. Daniel was much more subject than she was to gynecological and biological terror about the coming birth. His bike swerved and straightened.

"Does that happen often, then?"

"No, no. Only I felt bad, because she tried to tell me she felt rotten, and I was just trying to read."

He frowned his black frown.

When they got back, the little house was empty. This was unusual. She put on the kettle and built the fire. He sliced toast, fetched butter, honey, cups. He put his large arms around her thick body.

"I love you."

"I know."

They sat side by side on the hearth rug. The fire caught; Daniel held the toasting fork to the grate. A smell of toast began to infiltrate the paint smell that was a perpetual consequence of their attempts to make the place habitable.

"Where's Marcus, then?"

"Hospital. In his own queue. He goes by bus."

"Psychiatrist once a week for half an hour never did any good to anyone. In my view. Though I'd not presume to say what *is* needed."

"Don't," said Stephanie, putting a hand on his knee. "Daniel, don't. Let's have tea together."

"I'm not complaining."

"No. I know."

Marcus Potter, Stephanie's young brother, was living with them, apparently indefinitely. In the summer of 1953 he had suffered some sort of breakdown, or nervous crisis, which had been caused (one view) or exacerbated (a more informed view) by his bizarre relations with the ex-biology teacher at Blesford Ride, the public school where his father, and Stephanie's father, taught. There had been some kind of religious fantasy, and a possibility of homosexual tampering. Those in authority had decided that Marcus should intermit a year of his education, in order to recuperate, and that he should not live with his father, a man of uncertain temper, of whom he had expressed extreme and unreasoning terror. Nobody had said what Marcus *should* do. The result was that he appeared to do little or nothing, spoke minimally, and was increasingly reluctant to leave his bedroom or the house. Nobody had also said how long Marcus should remain in his sister's house. Daniel, a naturally vigorous seeker of solutions, tried to restrain an instinct to shake or confront Marcus with the unsatisfactory nature of this inertia. Daniel had occasional violent feelings toward Marcus, which he suppressed. Bill Potter, the father, was a violent man.

Stephanie saw Marcus, as though they had called him up by naming him, making his way home. The process seemed to cause unnecessary difficulty. He stepped forward and retreated at the little garden gate as though rebuffed by some force field or buffeted by some invisible gale that had no effect on the branches of the little trees and evergreens in the front gardens of the cottages. He carried his long, thin arms crossed protectively in front of him, as asthmatics do. His head, with its dull-straw hair and moon glasses, was down. Stephanie watched him dance or shuffle, two steps forward, one back, almost sideways along the paved path. She felt protective and threatened. Daniel saw her face set.

The door rattled for some time. Marcus was struggling with his key. Daniel suppressed fairly easily an impulse to get up and open the door for him. He turned the toast. Marcus came round the door feelingly, like a blind creature, clinging with fingers to edges and surfaces. Although the front door opened into the sitting room, he was plainly disconcerted to find them there.

"Tea and toast, Marcus," said Stephanie, in the voice she had heard herself use to Mrs. Owen. She disliked this voice very much but employed it more and more. Conversation with Marcus had become largely monosyllabic, which did not help.

"No," said Marcus palely, adding inaudibly, "Thank you."

He began what Daniel thought of as his "creeping" to the back-stairs. The room—dark with small windows—was only half furnished and half painted. Armchairs, little dining table, Stephanie's old, good mahogany desk stood on uncarpeted boards, splashed with paint. There was a big rag-pegged rug in front of the fire, and one or two pieces of coconut matting elsewhere. The walls were papered with very large blue roses, surrounded by dove-gray and silver-tinted leafage. Half of these were partially obliterated by a white undercoat. Daniel never had time—nor, truly, inclination—to make a good job of the painting. He was self-trained not to notice his surroundings. Stephanie had tried herself, but the paint vapor made her vomit, and she had an idea that this might damage the baby. Daniel, quick to notice essentials, had no idea how much Stephanie disliked living in this unfinished mess. She would have agreed with him largely as to what were essentials and inessentials, but the mess depressed her.

Marcus reached the staircase, which also descended into the living-room, and looked vaguely back. He went, less sidling, up, and they heard his bedroom door open and close. No further sound. Daniel took the toast off the fork.

The silence upstairs imposed a silence downstairs. Stephanie watched Daniel, wanting to protect him from Marcus.

"Let's talk to each other. Tell me about your day."

A verbal lot, the Potters, even peaceful Stephanie. Words helped them, apparently. His "day" was better left without conversion into narrative, amusing, querulous, or appealing. A funeral, already described, two drunk tramps, another lecture from the vicar on interfering in the domestic wrangles of his parishioners. He looked at his pale gold wife, her arms folded about her belly.

"Toast," he said, monosyllabic. He gave her a perfectly browned, gold-buttered honey-glistening warm-smelling slice. Sunk in biology, she thought, listening for creaks or moans above the ceiling, listening to the soft stirring in her belly, licking her fingers. She did not offer Daniel this satisfactory phrase.

Listening for Marcus, she heard Frederica's bicycle grind gravel. She came in in a rush, fell dramatically to her knees before the fire, beside her sister, cried "Look!" Stephanie saw small buff papers pasted with white strips.

MINOR SCHOLARSHIP OFFERED NEWNHAM + WRITING + PRINCIPAL +.

SCHOLARSHIP OFFERED SOMERVILLE + CONGRATULA-TIONS + PRINCIPAL +.

"It worked," said Stephanie. "You did it."

In 1948 she had opened almost identical telegrams. What had she felt? A great lightening, even if only temporary, of the burden of her father's inexorable expectations. She had not realized how heavy the burden had been till it was lifted. She felt pleasure only very much later, and pride and self-satisfaction later still, on the brink of departure. She handed the telegrams to Daniel.

"Is that good, then?" he said, not knowing the significance of scholarships. "A definite offer."

"I've won. I've won," Frederica crowed. "I did a Viva in Oxford, just me and all the dons, *all*, in robes and furred gowns, and me with a blackboard explaining Milton's English and Latin words. I've never talked so much *in my life* and they were interested, they were. I got all sorts of things in, *Britannicus* and *Henry VIII* and *The Broken Heart* and *The Winter's Tale* and feminine endings and they didn't stop me, they said go on—oh, and Satan's speech to Eve in the garden —I was in a place of my own—oh, *glory*—"

Stephanie nodded and Daniel watched Stephanie. He knew what he did not know about her, but only as a blank. Once she had had all this. Whether she had unaffectedly cried, "Oh, glory!" he did not know, and doubted. He imagined her wish to go on teaching, for they shared, he and she, did they not, a pastoral compulsion. She filled the cottage with the lost and unhappy. When they were not put off by Marcus's rigid, unfocused stare. He waited for a clue, a reminiscence of her own Viva, but she was silent. Frederica spoke to his thought.

"They all remembered you, Steph. The Newnham dons asked what you were doing. The Somerville ones remembered too. One of the Newnham ones said she'd always hoped you'd come back. I said of course you were *deep* in domesticity and waiting for the baby and she said that was what so many good students seemed to be choosing these days . . ."

"You'll go to Newnham."

"Despite the lovely Viva. How do you know?"

"Well. *He* wanted us to go to Cambridge."

"I might have rebelled."

"You might. But you've got a Cambridge mind. Heavy morals. Grown in. For all the Oxford language-talk."

"They said they'd see me in three years to do my D.Phil. at Oxford. *Imagine.* They asked me what it would be on. I said John Ford. It was the worst moment. They laughed so much, they couldn't go on with the interview. I don't know *why*, still. I don't care. I did it, I did it. I won."

"We know," said Daniel.

"I'll stop boring on. I'm sorry, I talk. I talked too much to the other girls over coffee. I went *on and on* about Eliot's Chinese jar moving perpetually in its stillness, how ironic, and you could *hear* them wishing I'd stop and somehow I couldn't. I'm sorry, Daniel. I need to let off steam. It's only just dawning. I can get out now, can't I? I can get away from Home—and Them—and the weight of it all. I'm free."

"How are they?" said Stephanie.

"Baddish. They don't seem able to get over the Marcus thing—it's somehow dismantled their idea of themselves as parents, you know, good parents whatever, and the Home as a home. Daddy sits a lot, doing nothing and muttering to himself and Mummy's just *retreated* —she never starts a conversation, or asks a question, or—You'd think they'd be overanxious about me, their one remaining child and perhaps they are, but they have miserable ways of showing it. Daddy kept rather obviously bestirring himself to mind about my exams and piling up my desk with secondary stuff I've no time for—I don't want to read literary criticism yet, almost at all, and I'm damned sure he doesn't smother his clever boys with it. My work is *my work* and my ideas are *my ideas* and he ought to leave them alone, I say.

"When these telegrams came I ran down and opened the door to the boy and I showed them to Mummy and she began very bravely, 'How lovely, dear,' and then began to cry and shut herself in her room. Not very festive. So I came here. But I can get right away now, I can, can't I?"

There was a silence.

"How is Marcus?" said Frederica. Daniel and Stephanie gestured mutely at the ceiling.

"He's had heaps of letters. Well, about three, I think. From that man. Daddy shreds them up—I saw him doing it with a *razor blade*, Steph—and burns them. He rang the hospital and told them to stop that man sending letters. You could hear him shouting down the telephone halfway down the road. Then he didn't go to work for two days. Probably the invisible psychiatrist should have a go at *him*."

"And Mummy?"

"As I said. She did say to ask you about Christmas."

Daniel said, "She could come and talk about that."

Stephanie said, "She seems to have stopped coming."

In the early days of Marcus's retreat or illness Winifred had come regularly; Bill had not, partly because "they" had said better to leave Marcus alone, partly because he disapproved of Daniel, the Church of England, Christianity, and Stephanie's burial of her talent among these things. He disapproved with a liberal atheism that produced emotions more akin to seventeenth-century religious fanaticism than to agnostic tolerance. So in a sense, Stephanie was lost to him, as Marcus was lost.

Winifred had sat for hours in those early days on the sofa, next to Marcus, who moved away, and like a parody of a mad religious discipline, abbreviated his answers, elongated his silences, until he had imposed on his mother a similar pattern of behavior.

"I'm doing no good," she said to Stephanie.

"How can we tell?"

"I can tell."

Winifred was not unlike Marcus. Or Marcus was not unlike Winifred. Defeat communicates itself, is handed on. Unlike euphoria, Stephanie thought, considering Frederica. It was odd how glory could not be shared. Frederica, now smoothing and folding her telegrams, would perhaps learn this.

"We s'll have my mum, too, by Christmas," said Daniel, heartily and with edge. "We shall have a real party."

2

AT HOME

Beginnings, ends, phases, terms. Stephanie thought of this phase as the deprivation of privacy, not contemplating the possibility that privacy was gone forever. She was a woman with a young body whose knowledge, biological and intellectual, was defined in clearly marked periods, menstrual, domestic, academic, rounds of flesh, blood, rites, qualifications. The pregnancy was another such, with its set term.

In December came the end of her teaching at Blesford Girls' Grammar School. At the last assembly, where Frederica received, as Stephanie had once received, the School Governors' Prize for Academic Achievement, she was given a leaving present by teachers and girls. Frederica strode grimly up and carried off the Oxford Companions to English and Classical Literature. Stephanie's presents were useful and various: an electric tea maker, with alarm, a set of Pyrex dishes with night-light heaters to warm them, and a layette, knitted and stitched by Upper III and Lower IV, little embroidered viyella nighties, crocheted lamb's-wool matinee jackets, knitted bonnets and bootees, pretty fluffy blankets, a woolen lamb with black stitched eyes and a slightly thrawn neck, dangling from a scarlet ribbon. The headmistress made a long and patently truthful speech about how they would miss Stephanie, and a brief speech about Frederica's outstanding good fortune. They sang "Lord, dismiss us with thy blessing." Stephanie felt tearful, not because she loved the school, but because something was finished.

Wheeling her bicycle out of the school for the (official) last time she saw Frederica striding away in front of her, past the still-unleveled bomb crater, bearing a satchel, a large paper parcel, two shoe bags, and a paper carrier.

"Do you want to put any of that in my bike basket?" Frederica jumped. Her hair flowed lank and forbidden over her shoulders, crimped by the traces of regulation ribbons.

"You shouldn't still be riding that thing. You'll do yourself and the progeny an injury."

"Rubbish. We are balanced and dignified. Give me that bag." They went on in silence.

"Where are you going, Frederica?"

"Somewhere called Nîmes."

"What?"

"Headmistress found it. 'French family desires respectable English girl to speak English to their daughters.' I'm off after Christmas. Nice to have to speak French. Nice to get right away from here. Not sure about the daughters."

"I actually only meant where are you going now?"

"Oh, to perform a rite. You might disapprove. If you don't, you can participate. If you don't fall off that thing."

"What sort of rite?"

"A kind of oblation. Of Blesford Girls' Grammar."

She flung open her mackintosh and Stephanie saw that she was wearing a skin-tight black sweater, wide elastic belt, long gray pencil skirt.

"It's going in the canal. Do you want to come?"

"What is?"

"Blesford Girls' Grammar. Shirt, tie, beret, skirt, ankle socks, and gym kit. I can't put the mac in; I haven't got another. I've weighted this parcel."

"With what?" asked Stephanie, afraid for the Oxford Companions.

"Stones, idiot. I don't drown books. You should have known that."

"Drowning perfectly good warm clothes is an awful *waste*. Some poor girl—"

"I told you you didn't have to come. You shouldn't if you've already turned into a full-time clergyman's wife. Which I wish I could understand how you can bear. Steph, did you *want* an electric tea maker? Do you *want* to rescue these horrible garments, these symbols of pettiness and niggling, for Daniel to give to some tramp-ess? Don't answer. Do come and help. It's only once."

There was nothing remarkable about Blesford Canal. It was decayed and decaying, darkly full of a strange, fine black weed, like tendrils of soot, tipped with faded moss green. Its banks were slipping into it, over falls of broken, dislodged bricks. Little boys occasionally drowned there. The sisters stopped on a narrow bridge over it, near nothing, except a gasholder and a filthy billboard with a Capstan tobacco advertisement. Stephanie leaned her bike against the parapet. Frederica hefted the paper parcel onto the ledge.

"This is a plain rite. No words, no prancing around. I'm a grown woman. I just want someone to know that this—all this *stuff*—has been a burden and nothing but a burden from start to finish and that I feel no twinge of regret at coming out of that place, and that I shall never go back into it, ever, so help me Frederica Potter. No more group life. I won't belong to anything, ever again. I stand for *me*. Do you want to help shove?"

Stephanie thought of the sweet, soft, on the whole carefully made layette. She thought of Felicity Wells, the senior mistress, passionate about George Herbert's poems and Anglo-Catholicism, who had spent a lifetime tempting with these fine things girls from this dirty town. She thought of John Keats, alive in Hampstead, dead in Rome, read in Cambridge, read here, in class. She thought of blackened red brick, chalk dust, shoe boxes, muddy hockey boots, the smell of groups of girls in classrooms.

"Yes. I think so."

"Okay. One, two, three, ready. Over she goes."

The parcel splashed heavily, soughed, and sank in a trail of thick, slow, glutinous bubbles.

"What ceremony else?" said Stephanie, blasphemously.

"None. I told you. This is a gesture that simply means itself and no more. You wouldn't give me some tea, would you, if I come home with you? Would you? I don't want to go back to the house yet, a bit, not yet."

Daniel's mum came. She was not unexpected; she had been coming for months. They had moved from a council flat, Daniel's choice of home, to this partially renovated artisan's cottage to make space for her when she was sufficiently better from her fall and fractured hip. They decorated the third little bedroom for her before they finished their own, putting up a sprigged paper, installing a fat armchair, a fringed table lamp, a satiny quilt and a dressing table with a glass top, all fetched by Daniel from the relinquished Sheffield house. Visiting his mum in hospital made Daniel morose and gloomy, which Stephanie noticed, but did not ask about. He remarked that he had almost certainly brought the wrong objects, except the dressing table, which was alone of its kind. And it was fifty-fifty, he said, that that would be said to be too big, which it was, of course, in that room, taking up far too much space. But it had done that before.

The day she came, Stephanie went up and put flowers on the dressing table, a potted cyclamen, almost maroon in its dark red-purple, a crystal vase, a wedding present, containing asters, violet, cherry-pink, shell-pink. Brave and graceful flowers. When Daniel was at the station, she remembered that the lamp had flickered alarmingly. She tried it, and it flickered. She went downstairs, fetched fuse wire and screwdriver, went upstairs, changed the fuse. She was beginning to tire on the stairs. As she worked a hand, or a foot, hard, protruding, worked its way up under her skin, outside her rib cage. When she heard the front door she was momentarily unable to stand, for inner turbulence. She had meant to open the door, welcoming.

Daniel's mother's voice came in, small, plaintive, continuous, carrying.

". . . last time I ever go anywhere on them British Railways. Any road, you'll have to carry me out of here feet first, I reckon."

Stephanie came down. Mrs. Orton spread like many heaped and plumped cushions in Daniel's armchair. Her clothes, her face, her hands, her glistening rounded legs were many shades of what Frederica later learned from her to call "mohve," like, yet unlike, the innocent bright asters and the cyclamen, which now in Stephanie's mind resembled bruised flesh. She wore a molded oval felt hat, with a deliberate dent at the high point. From beneath the hat poked various sheeplike curls of iron-gray soft hair, with a purplish cast, perhaps simply a glow reflected from the shining expanse of floral artificial silk below. Stephanie, bumping the baby on the chair arm, bent to kiss the isolated, overdefined crimson apple-round of the cheek. She offered tea.

"No thanks, pet. I was just telling our Daniel, I was right put off by what passes for tea on t'railways these days: I couldn't stomach no more. No tea. And I hope you haven't gone to any trouble cooking for me because I can barely keep owt down these days, not after t'hospital, me appetite quite sickened away on me wi' the things they serve up—greasy bits o' beef skirt and nasty little salads wi' half a two-week-old egg and a few outside leaves o' lettuce and a bit o' wet beetroot, no, it was an effort getting it down, let alone *keeping* it down—I can tell you, there was many as couldn't; eggs from t'infernal regions we got for us breakfast as often as not, right stink bombs, but could you get any o' them nurses to have a sniff or give us another i'stead? I don't know what I'd ha' done if t'owd dear in't next bed hadn't a had a daughter as worked in't chocolate factory in York, kept her supplied wi' great bags o' rejects she couldn't bring hersen to eat on her own—funny that—they get put right off, working wi' chocolate, she had a craving for salty things, them roasted peanuts she was always popping in and Smith's Crisps. T'owd dear wasn't up to doing much better by the chocolates, having problems wi' sugar in her water, so I did well out o' that. Until she passed on, which she did two weeks past. Mind you, when our Daniel come in now and then to visit they thowt I was on me way out too, wi't dog collar, and that, dog collars in them places meaning death . . ."

Half an hour later, eased out of her coat and hat, her belongings piled by Stephanie's bed since they wouldn't fit in her room, she said, "You wouldn't have a nice cup o' tea, would you?" It took Stephanie some time to realize that she always refused what was offered at the time when it was offered, whether out of a curious notion of good manners or out of cussedness Stephanie was never wholly sure.

When Marcus came in for supper, two hours later, Daniel's mum was still talking, to Stephanie, who was in and out of the kitchen dishing up vegetables and making gravy, to her son, who moved his weight cautiously from time to time on a dining-room chair and frowned and frowned. She had, during that time, said nothing about man, wife, or child; her conversation was, as it was predominantly to remain, purely descriptive and immediate to herself. About the railway carriage, the stop at Darlington, the routine on the ward in Sheffield General Hospital, two or three obsessively studied old dears and a batch of more distantly hinted ones, Stephanie knew a great deal. About Daniel's mum she knew very little. She thought she had never been so tired.

Marcus backed away from the door once or twice—it was not a very bad day—and made his usual rush in. He stopped in the doorway, confronting the large fact of Daniel's mum.

"Who's this, then?"

"My brother, Marcus. He is staying here." Marcus looked, dumb.

"This is Daniel's mother, Marcus. Who has come to stay."

Neither Marcus nor Daniel's mum spoke. It seemed to Daniel that neither of them had bothered to take in, until that moment, the fact, carefully explained to both beforehand, of the other's presence. Stephanie put food on the table: roast beef, Yorkshire pudding, roast potatoes, cauliflower. The meat had been expensive. She and Daniel were learning about herrings and shin of beef, gnocchi and onion tart. Daniel's mum, wedged in Daniel's chair, watched every movement critically. Marcus wrung his hands. Mrs. Orton addressed him.

"Don't fidget, young man."

He put his hands quickly in his pockets, bowed his head, and made his way sideways to his place at table.

Daniel carved. He expressed his pleasure, in overringing tones, in rare beef. Mrs. Orton said nothing. She cut all the brown edges of her slices away and ate those, leaving a growing, mangled heap of red beef on one side of her plate. She chewed steadily and loudly. Marcus gagged and pushed away an almost-untouched plate. Mrs. Orton told Stephanie how in her day they made right big puffed-up brown Yorkshires and served them separate, with the gravy poured in, before the meat, to spin it out; you had to scrape and pinch in them days. She accepted two more helpings of beef, asking Daniel to cut it from the edges, remarking that bloody meat had always turned her stomach, we all have our different tastes, don't we? She admonished Marcus.

"You've eaten next to nowt, young fellow-me-lad. You've got a peaky look; you could do wi' a bit o' substance. Get it down."

She laughed. Marcus stared palely at his plate.

"Not much to say for 'imself, 'as he? We was brought up to eat what was put in front of us. What do you do wi' yourself all day then?"

Marcus poked silently at the tablecloth with his fork. Stephanie said that he had been seriously ill and was convalescing. This had already been explained in Sheffield, by Daniel. Mrs. Orton showed an interest in Marcus that she had failed to show in Daniel and Stephanie. She asked several sharp questions about what he was ill of and what treatment he was getting. Marcus did not answer. Mrs.

Orton speculated about why this was, speaking increasingly of his illness to Daniel and Stephanie as though he wasn't there. Daniel thought that in a way this was what Marcus had appeared to want, to be present yet absent and unconsidered. In the days that followed Daniel's mum was to elaborate this confidential and blotting-out commentary to an embarrassing extent.

On her way to bed that night Stephanie fell over the cyclamen on the landing floor. She came down heavily, spattering her nightdress with earth, shards of flowerpot, dark streaks of water from spilled asters. Daniel found her there on hands and knees, tears running down her face. There was a listening stillness behind closed doors. Daniel got down, put an arm around her thick middle, hoisted her silently to her feet and pulled her toward the bedroom. She resisted, pointing in angry dumb show at earth, water, petals on the linoleum. She stood and shivered and wept.

"Come on." He burrowed in her drawers for a clean nightdress. "Come on, love."

"Don't mess my things."

"Now, now. When did I ever mess your things?"

He lifted the soiled nightdress up over her unresisting shoulders and head, and for a moment she was naked, bursting breasts, strangely risen navel, arms and legs fragile and ineffectual beside the central weight. Daniel stroked her and dressed her while she wept on. He whispered hoarsely, "Go to bed. My love. Go on."

"I've got to clear all that up. I only meant to make it welcoming and nice. I even thought I'd got the colors right."

"Look," he said. "Look—it's not *that*. She liked them. She believes flowers breathe out carbon dioxide—well, they do—and they have to be put out at night. She always has, ever since my dad was in hospital when he died and the nurses wheeled the flowers out every night. They do, you know. She was only doing what they do."

"She put them jolly *far out*," said Stephanie, childishly.

"Aye. Well, she doesn't bend well. None of us do, at the moment, for various reasons. You get into bed and I'll clear it up."

She got into bed. She listened. Dustpan and brush, taps, back door. He must be digging earth and replanting the cyclamen corm. He was the most thorough man she knew. She heard him come quietly up the stairs; she heard the clink of vase and saucer. When he came to bed, they clung to each other, cold and clean and silent, feeling that even these small movements were overheard. As her muscles slowly nevertheless relaxed the child began its dolphinlike arching and wheeling. In so far as it distinguished between night and day, it was active at night. Daniel, though his ferocious passion for his wife's body included its swollen state, was not a man who could be brought to a close interest in this unseen life. The more it churned, the more he moved away. Even in bed there was no privacy. As for Wordsworth, she thought as she sank into sleep, as for Wordsworth . . . Another unfinished pregnant sentence. She dreamed, not for the last time, that the baby had prematurely got out, like a kangaroo embryo, and was making its way blind and white and tiny up and up the billowing creases of Mrs. Orton's purple front, as that woman talked on and on, shifting so that at every turn the climbing thing was about to be casually suffocated.

Marcus looked at the psychiatrist and the psychiatrist looked at Marcus. The psychiatrist was called Mr. Rose and was, as far as Marcus could remember from time to time, medium in height, medium brown in coloring, and with a medium tenor voice when he spoke, which was infrequently. Sometimes Marcus thought of him as wearing glasses and sometimes he seemed to remember the man's face naked. His room, too, which was one of a series of repeated offices in Calverley General Hospital, was medium brown and medium gray. It had a brown leathery couch, two metal-and-leathery chairs, an oak desk, and pale green walls. There was a filing cabinet and a metal coat cupboard, both battleship gray. On the wall over the desk was a print of Munch's *Scream*. On another wall was a dog-eared calendar with colored reproductions of Great Paintings. This month there were some Cézanne apples on a checked tablecloth. There was a venetian blind, normally down with its slats open. The view it obscured was pipes, fire escapes, a sooty-walled well. Marcus did not lie on the couch. He sat on a chair facing the desk and did not look at Mr. Rose, though he did from time to time tilt his head to measure the angled slices of building and reflected light arranged by the blind.

He had no faith in Mr. Rose's capacity to "help" him. This may have been because he defined "help" to himself as a putting right of something that had gone wrong, a restoration of some earlier, good "normal" state, and he was not sure that such a state had existed or could exist. Normal was what people said some of their actions and relations were, from time to time, and in Marcus's experience, what they said they were bore only a vague relation to their actual forms and configurations. Bill would *say* what fathers and sons, sisters and brothers, boys and girls did or were and would scream quite other definitions or labels. The idea of the boy at school, of the "friend," of the "good sport," of the "bright chap," bore the same kind of bizarrely streamlined relation to real creatures. Marcus thought of normality as a complex pattern on tracing paper, peaks, rounds, interlocking jigsaw parts, which, when slid over the mess of the actual graph or representation of what was, produced a thickened shifty outline, a jigging blurring worse than the original. The attraction of Lucas Simmonds had been that he had appeared to be confidently, unusually, happily "normal," good friend, good sport, reliable leader, bright chap, blazer, flannels, and smiling face. He had been able to appear "normal" because he was abnormal, he was an outsider, he was mad, he saw and desired normality with a piercing vision of what it might ideally be thought to be.

It did not occur to Marcus to say any of this to Mr. Rose. This was partly because he was secretive, partly because, with his own version of Potter arrogance, Marcus supposed Mr. Rose would probably be unable to follow the significance of his reflections, and partly because he supposed Mr. Rose was primarily interested in sex. He supposed Mr. Rose was interested in finding out if he, Marcus, "was" homosexual, and while he would have liked to know that himself, and remembered the one explicitly sexual moment of his relations with Lucas with tremors of disgust and anxiety, he had no wish to go into that with Mr. Rose. He had a deep, consciously formulated desire not to be sexual at all, but did not expect to be believed if he said so. He rebuffed suggestions politely, and allowed long silences to spread in the little room like ripples from some very stony stone descending. Mr. Rose addressed him as if he were younger, simpler, and less capable of thought than in fact he was. This made it easy for him to appear younger, simpler, and less thinking than he was. He thought that he and Mr. Rose bored each other. They connived in a sleepy state of inertia.

This week, prompted in fact by a carefully reasoned, properly concerned letter from Bill, Mr. Rose was trying to find out whether Marcus thought about going home, and if so, what he thought. Marcus said he wouldn't like it, and added that he supposed he'd have to go sometime. Why wouldn't he like it? said Mr. Rose, and Marcus said the idea frightened him, he would be trapped, there was a lot of noise, he just wouldn't like it. *What* wouldn't he like? asked Mr. Rose, and Marcus said unhelpfully, everything, everything, the noise especially, but everything.

The word "home" in fact raised in his mind as they spoke their tedious sentences a mental image that it did not even occur to him to describe to Mr. Rose.

He saw a house, the house, almost the house a child draws in its infant school, four windows, chimney, door, garden path, lazy-daisy looped flowers in rectangular parterres, only this house was also a crudely three-dimensional flimsy box, barely containing something very large and very much alive, covered with rusty pelt, so that every aperture bulged with glowing fur, was pushed outward, cracking, and a claw showed here on a sill, and a ripple of muscle there. And the thing growled and howled to itself in the center of its blind struggle.

The conversation came to a halt, like an unequally overweighted seesaw, at Bill's anger, Marcus's fear. He's always angry, said Marcus. Were you always frightened? said Mr. Rose. Oh, yes, said Marcus. Tell me about being frightened when you were little, said Mr. Rose.

"There was the time I saw the bear," said Marcus unguardedly, remembering the bear.

"Which bear?"

"Not a real bear. I was sitting behind the sofa playing with a kind of milk lorry I had. And they called me, and I crawled out, and there was this huge bear between me and my mother, very tall, sitting up the way they do, as tall as—all the way up to the light fitting. It seemed quite real. I mean, I didn't know it wasn't. I couldn't cross the room. So they came and picked me up, and told me off."

"What do you associate bears with?"

"Oh, the Three Bears. I was always getting told the Three Bears."

Mr. Rose sat up a little. "What did you feel about the Three Bears?"

"Oh well. I don't really remember."

"Did it frighten you?"

"You mean the bears bursting out of the house, shouting out of the windows, chasing the little girl away? I suppose it did."

It was a difficult tale. Too much sympathy was required. There was the lost child, in the forest, peering through windows, knocking at doors, creeping in from outside, trying to find things that fit, food that was acceptable, chair, porridge, bed. Then the bears required sympathy, their warm, ordered breakfast disrupted, their chairs and beds appropriated and messed, broken, used by the intruding child. And then the child, whom he always saw as very peaked and pale, with staring rays of pale gold hair, a spiky, sly little girl, required sympathy in her way, having smashed a chair, dirtied spoons, unmade beds. And then the outburst of anger, and the quick sliding through the window to the outside again from the furious warm inside.

"And the little bear's chair was smashed all to pieces by the little girl. I was sorry."

"For the little girl or the baby bear?"

"I don't know. For both perhaps. For the bear because it was his thing, for the little girl because of the shouting—"

His tone conveyed some contempt for this line of questioning.

Mr. Rose asked Marcus what he thought of when he thought of home. Marcus's mental furniture was meager. He and Stephanie both always won Kim's game, the objects on a tray, but whereas she remembered them for their quiddity, naming and denoting them in language in her mind, he did it with a geometric map and total spatial recall. Home to him was a pattern of relations, lines between chairs, window oblongs, stair numbers with corner segments, whereas she could remember every missed stitch on a tablecloth, scratches on enameled jugs, worn carving knives. Marcus was unconvinced of the persistence of places or things, perhaps of people. For instance, the lavatory at Calverley General never struck him as being the *same* lavatory as he had entered last week, month, or year, but always generically as "the" or "a" lavatory. In the same way he never recognized himself as eating with a familiar spoon from a familiar plate. He never supposed a bus might recur in his life, to be traveled in a second time, with a recognizable darn in its upholstery. The bus lines were mappable, new buses succeeded each other infinitely. Everything was provisional. So home for Marcus was a few dangerous objects that were extensions of people, Bill's ashtray and pipe, Bill's carving tools, his mother's rubber gloves, his bed and the shelf in his bedroom with his model Spitfire. He didn't say this either. He told Mr. Rose he supposed he missed his bedroom. Mr. Rose wished to shake him, and knew this would have been unprofessional. So he yawned, asked if Marcus was using his time in any particular way, looked at his watch.

That night, in Stephanie's house, Marcus dreamed he had gone home and Bill was carving a meal to welcome him. The meat was cylindrical and bloody, and still had the furry skin on. Also, he saw at one end, pads and claws. One of the penalties of talking, or even stubbornly not talking, to Mr. Rose was that afterward he had odd dreams. There they were at the table, his mother in a hat like a helmet, his father carving the bloody paw that was all the food on offer. As he carved, it contracted painfully, still alive, apparently.

Mr. Rose, had he had access to the whole elaboration of this pleasing metaphor, with its roots in folklore and childhood culture, hallucination and dream, might, or might not, have understood something about Marcus that he did not already understand, and might, or might not, have felt able to offer help or advice as a result of this understanding. Marcus told himself that he had muddled up some bears, examined his own dream, concluded it told him nothing he didn't know, and decided not to report it to Mr. Rose. Imaginary bears were not the essence of the matter.

3

CHRISTMAS

The nuclear Potter family had practiced a muted and aimless version of the British family Christmas rite. They had inhibitions about concentrating on what might be called the Dickensian essentials—a great deal of specified food and drink, presents wanted and unwanted, the gathering of friends and relations. They had no available extended family; there were Potters scattered about North Yorkshire who had not been seen since Bill's Congregationalist parents had cast him off for unbelief. Winifred was the only child of dead parents. Their household gods were created, not inherited, and were meager and fleshless. This was partly—in the Dickensian context—because of uncertainty of manners, owing to upward social mobility. They had ideas about respectability and propriety that as intellectuals they despised but as Christmas dinner eaters they endorsed. Daniel's dad, the engine driver, when living, had got drunk in the pub first and at home later; there had been gusto, jollity, somnolence, and regret. Bill Potter took a glass of sherry, and shared out a bottle of sparkling wine. No neighbors called and they visited no neighbors. They were blameless of seasonal road accidents; they were closed in with themselves, more than usual, since no shops were open and no employment was possible except to "enjoy oneself" and wash up more plates than usual, as Frederica frequently pointed out.

They ate frugally; they had learned in the war to make do with the plain, avoid waste, make things go round. Winifred had aesthetic uncertainties. As she had little dress sense, only a vague fear that any hat or dress she chose might be vulgar, so she had no sense of a possible style in which to decorate a house, or even a dining table, for Christmas. She solved the clothes problem with rigorous inconspicuous plainness, and was inclined to solve the Christmas problem, much less successfully, the same way. When the children were little they made paper chains and strings of painted cardboard milk-bottle tops, and these were draped over mirrors. (They were never long enough to cross the room.) When they were little they had a little artificial tree and put out their stockings on Christmas Eve. Neither

Bill nor Winifred could bring themselves to lie about the provenance of the gifts they found in the stockings. This was not really because of an absolute respect for truth but was something to do with their inhibited negative sense of style. They could not be seen telling stories; it looked daft. Frederica, frustrated of magic, took it out on her classmates at a very early age by stripping them ruthlessly of their illusions. This made her neither popular nor happy.

There was no singing, because they could not sing. There were no games, partly because they didn't know any, partly because all five were united, in this if in nothing else, in the belief that dice, cards, charades, were a frivolous waste of time. So, apart from opening presents, they watched each other and waited for Christmas to be over so that they could resume their intense and private working lives.

This year, for Stephanie, had to be different. There was the church, which she helped to decorate with holly, mistletoe, evergreens. There were parish parties. There was the fact of her two families. After thought, she asked her mother to bring the remaining Potters—Bill and Frederica—to Christmas dinner in the cottage. This might, she said, provide a sensible bridging occasion when Marcus could establish some new contact with his parents. Winifred was doubtful. She seemed to have lost some sense that events could be controlled or hopefully directed. Stephanie spoke also, for her almost sharply, to Marcus and told him that the visit would happen and that she trusted him to help with it, to behave well. He seemed to respond and even, to her great surprise and encouragement, took the first active part he had taken in any event for six months, preparing for the feast.

She wanted to make the cottage festive, mostly for Daniel. She spent money they didn't have on green leafage and bought a large, real tree in Blesford marketplace. It was delivered swaddled in raffia, conical and bursting with dark needles. Stephanie unwound it like a cocoon, stroked and spread its spiky boughs, spent time and effort stabilizing it in a bucket of earth with the weight from the kitchen scales. It stood there with its thick different life, blue-green and somber, smelling of resin and forests. Mrs. Orton, who spent every day settled in Daniel's chair, stared, said Stephanie would do herself a damage, and offered no assistance. Marcus, palely flitting past, consented, when asked, to hold the trunk upright with one thin hand while she toiled, tamping earth, lashing clothesline around trunk and branches. Marcus said in a thin voice that the smell of pine needles was nice in the house. Mrs. Orton said they were messy things, got into everything.

Stephanie had a vision of her tree hung with gold and silver fruit and bright with candles. Because she was a plain Potter she wanted her fruit *plain*, not frosted with garish patterns or stenciled with poinsettias. She could find in Blesford only gnomes, dwarfish Father Christmases, hideous antique lanterns. She sat down one afternoon with the idea of coiling gold and silver thread into starbursts on milk-bottle tops. Marcus surprised her considerably by saying why not wire, and surprised her still further by constructing, from fine gold and silver wire, a whole series of stars, hexagons, starry hollow globes, and complex polyhedrons, an abstract fruitage that glittered brightly, weaving threads of light among the dark threads of the needles.

She preferred Christmas to other Christian feasts—a magical tale celebrating birth, a common miracle. Bill had been given to anti-sermons. His children had been lectured on the folly of the virgin birth, the slenderness of evidence for shepherds, star, or stable, with the intensity of Strauss or Renan, as though ascertainable historical truth was a freedom he passionately desired for his children. And it was desirable, or would have been, if his style had been less intimidating, if the proposed freedom had offered a color, light, or warmth to compensate for astral and angelic voices.

Now Daniel was difficult, telling her not to come to the hospital, where he was to be Father Christmas in the children's ward.

"I want to see you."

"Not there, you don't."

"Shall I embarrass you?"

"I'm not in this job to be easily embarrassed. No. I just think—I just think."

He could not say what he just thought, which was that she should be afraid of that place now. As he was himself.

She came.

The farther in your bed was, the worse you were. At the end were cubicles, out of sight and sound. In the outer ward was a silky-white hygienic artificial tree. Those children who could possibly go home had gone. The very sick had been wheeled into spaces vacated by simple fracture and tonsillectomies. Stephanie visited his ward regularly; the perpetual inhabitants she knew.

Two teenage boys, Neil and Simon, with muscular dystrophy, immobilized now forever, propped up side by side with twig-arms disposed lightly on clean sheets and skeletal intelligent faces cocked at unnatural angles, open-mouthed, among the pillows. Anorexic Primrose, thirteen years and seventy pounds, delicate eyes closed against a world she refused to recognize, hands folded white and nunlike, or worse, beneath a sharp chin. Gary, shaven, swollen-skulled, brutal-looking, heavy-eyed with his death burgeoning and forceful under the bones. The mobile lower population of younger inhabitants, staggering Dopey-like in dressing-gowns, trotting in party dresses. Charlie, aged eight with a stinking cancerous hip, who propelled himself flat on his back on a trolley made from a pram base, flipper hands paddling, olive, oval face—too big, all their faces were too big—grinning with flickering contempt as he wound skillfully around Stephanie's ankles, his foul air preceding him, and behind him decay and a whiff of disinfectant. Legless Mike, trundling on tree-stump hip pads, his one arm a long puckered cone. Mary in a pretty pink dress out of which stuck yellow claws and a head and face made by plastic surgeons of grafts ranging in color from vellum to grape-purple. Mary, lashless, browless, lipless, hairless, except for a freshly washed blonde tuft above her left ear. Mary had fallen or been pushed into an open fire, more than once. Mary never had visitors. Sometimes Mary went home, and came back with another scar or suppurating patch. Stephanie picked Mary up—Mary liked to be picked up—and perched her on one hip as she walked from bed to bed. Between Mary and the unborn child was a network of expanded muscles and a sealed drum of amniotic fluid, in which it rested, stretched an unfinished limb, rolled and rested.

Beyond swing doors were the babies: mended hairlips, and small creatures who had had constructed for them by human skill gullet or anal opening or separate fingers with which the working cells and DNA during their gestation had failed to provide them. In an incubator a brown-gold boy, naked and perfect except that both his legs had been broken during his birth, and were now suspended from a delicately constructed pulley and weight inside his transparent container.

A gramophone began with a bang on "Away in a Manger." The nurses and the few mothers who had managed to be available on Christmas Eve sang ragged and loud. Stephanie sang. Mary grunted and Charlie whizzed chuntering past on his low wheels. The gramophone banged a bit more and produced Tchaikovsky. Little girls from Miss Marilynne's Blesford Ballet School did a snowflake dance, little boys (fewer in number) a snowman tumbling dance, melting most convincingly. The gramophone spurted out "Rudolph the Red-nosed *Rein*deer." Bells jangled. Who do you think *that* can be, children, said Sister. And Daniel came in on a hospital trolley disguised as a sleigh with scarlet blankets and silver-paper runners, drawn by hospital porters dressed as polar bears. The ballet-school children ran up to distribute presents. They took these from Father Christmas and gave them to the nurses, who gave them to the hospital children.

There was something not right about Daniel, his wife thought. The Gyn man who usually wore the outfit was thinner than Daniel, so that Daniel's back garments appeared in large and small expanses under and through the red, like coals in a fire. He had left off his clerical dog collar and was losing strips of his white eyebrows, moustache, and beard—the undergrowth, the perpetually springing beard stubble was subversively blue-black. He stumped awkwardly about the ward, asking people if they were comfortable, and occasionally getting answers. He was not really jolly. One or two of the healthier children cried when he came near them; he moved resignedly away on these occasions, as though this reaction were entirely natural. He avoided his wife.

Most of the toys distributed by the ballet children were cuddly toys, pink, blue, and white, bunnies, ducks, bears. No child, Stephanie had observed, will love a random cuddly toy, uninvested with history or personality. What were needed, and were not given, were constructive things, Meccano, Plasticine, things bad for the sheets and easy to lose. A puffed-up snowflake, face averted, tried to offer a woolly bear to Stephanie to give to Mary. Mary buried her face in Stephanie's womb and grunted. Daniel strode up, booted and cloaked, ludicrous and blackly angry.

"Put that child down. You'll hurt yourself."

"No, I won't. She likes it."

"I don't." He grinned horribly at Mary across his skewed woolly mouthpiece. She cringed and began to whimper. "Quite right," said Daniel. "Come on, Steph. We've done our duty."

"What's *wrong* with you?"

He could not say, though he knew. He could have dealt with this decently without Stephanie. Now, seeing Mary's shapelessness goblin-like straddling her thick hips, he wanted her and his child out of there, as though they were vulnerable to these most bizarre manifestations of the random and the destructive. But Stephanie stood there calm and healthy and said he must speak to Mrs. Marriott.

Mrs. Marriott was a refinement of alarm. She sat all day, by the cot of her son in a cubicle. He was a pale lovely baby with a defective liver and dubious kidneys. They had tried surgery and were experimenting with dieting. The child slept, mostly, very deeply. The woman, not still by nature, moved around the cubicle rearranging baby powder, water jug, nappies. She had lost fifty-six pounds in four weeks. When she saw Daniel, shedding red and white fuzz, she said palely that she was afraid now she would lose little Stephen; it was hope that killed you, wasn't it, best not to hope, but what else could you do, sitting there? She felt so useless. He did not know and could not say. He tore off the silly beard and began a sentence about resignation, which he could not finish. He knew that what he was communicating was urgency, irritability, frustrated life and fury, wrong things here, and indeed Mrs. Marriott began hopelessly, her head in a pile of clean muslin nappies, to cry. When Daniel saw his wife coming toward the cubicle to offer comfort where he couldn't, he flailed his arms and drove her away, leaving Mrs. Marriott to cry on, not even telling himself it was good for her to cry, since how could he know, how could he imagine?

The Family Service in St. Bartholomew's came later. It incorporated the nativity play, to which Stephanie thought she looked forward. She had helped enthusiastically with the costumes, making for Mary a trailing blue robe of cornflower taffeta, her own Cambridge May Ball dress sheared apart at the seams, lending or donating bright belts and beads to deck out the three kings, one of whom wore a peacock-feathered turban made of the shot-silk stole she had worn with that dance dress.

The organ sounded. The children came into the church, half skipping, half marching, keeping uncertain step. A big boy and a big girl, eleven-plus age, she stooping with embarrassment, stood at the lectern and read alternatively the brief, fairy-tale bits of Matthew and Luke. Matthew's three kings, Matthew's moving star, Luke's stable, ox, ass, shepherds, and singing angels. The children mimed the tale, serious, inhibited. Blonde, Danish-faced Mary sat solemnly on the chancel steps with a Joseph smaller than herself in a striped toweling bathrobe and a towel tied to his head with plaited wool. He was only too conscious that he had nothing really to do; his hands strayed from time to time above his freckled face to adjust his headgear. A diminutive innkeeper held the flats of unformed hands up to indicate that there was no room in the inn. Smaller children and deaf grannies in the congregation twittered, as each year they twittered, like starlings on telegraph wires, urgent and aimless, look there's our Janet, look at our Ron, there, don't he look funny, lovely, dignified, daft . . .

"And she brought forth her firstborn child, and laid him in a manger, because there was no room for them in the inn."

This central moment was always awkward. Now, as every year, Mary, back to the pews, bottom upended, fumbled in Mrs. Ellenby's old wooden crib and brought out her best and largest doll, smiling, pouting, celluloid, with hard eyes on a metal hinge that clattered open and shut, open and shut, as the wavering child righted herself, thrust it up briefly and apologetically before the congregation, and pushed it back under the blankets. Owing to the permanent rigid curvature of the celluloid limbs, swaddling was not possible, so the doll was swathed in someone's pretty christening shawl. Paper-masked sheep and cows and donkeys huddled in and knelt, adjusting their heads. Three diminutive kinglets, carrying a brass paraffin lamp, a silver sugar castor, Mrs. Ellenby's Chinese enameled cigarette box, bowed, wobbled, kneeled. A flock of small shepherds collected in the nave. Down the aisle came a blond choirboy, in sheet and halo, his pure voice just cracking, accompanied by a very limited multitude of the heavenly host. And on earth peace, goodwill toward men. The parents were moved in a confused way. They were moved by their own flesh and blood acting out the motions of birth and parentage with that mixture of awkwardness, ignorance, seriousness, and imitation that can be observed in the necessary games of mothers and fathers. It is the childishness of Mary and Joseph that moves—nothing to do with the celluloid babe which is always somehow redundant in this set of emotions. Parents are moved because childhood is so swift and vanishing. They are perhaps also more darkly moved by some threat in the law of flesh and blood itself. These small creatures are the future, they are only acting out what they will be. Not only childhood vanishes; men and women, having handed on their genes, are superfluous. To watch this acting is to be marginally caught between times, between roles. Mary looks protectively at the doll; Mary's mother looks, moved and protective, at Mary's childish body and soft face. And time runs on.

Herod appeared in the pulpit—he was, as always, the best actor—stamped a small foot, tossed an imperious forelock, straightened a paper crown, dispatched a token army across the chancel. The slaughter of the innocents was offstage. The large boy at the lectern read about Rachel weeping for her children, because they were not. Stephanie had in other years enjoyed this believed fairy tale; this year her own heaviness, fear perhaps of real birth, prevented her.

They had a nice tea in the rectory, with a yule log iced by Mrs. Ellenby, and like good children did not receive gifts but brought them, wrapped relinquished Dinky toys and woolly animals to be redistributed to Dr. Barnardo's. Daniel told them how at this time God had so loved the world that he had sent his only son to give it life, to be made just like them, so that God might live man's life and man might through him come close to God. God's life and man's life, one life, Daniel said. She thought she would have made a better job of it, not believing a word, just because she was a good teacher.

What enlivened the world? Daniel himself, his restlessness, his impatience. The edge in the blond angel's cracking voice. Her belly, churning. Dark trees. Charlie, Gary, Mary. Did he who made the lamb make thee, her dark mind said, and for a moment she loved nothing and no one. She smiled and distributed cups of milk, little packages of brightly colored, sugared chocolate buttons, like magic beans.

Her mood of hostile detachment persisted through midnight mass, despite the presence of old friends, Miss Wells, the Thones. Mrs. Thone sang loud and clear those loud, chanting hymns that Yorkshire people enjoy, who sing the *Messiah* not with the abandoned full rotundity of the Welsh, but sober and strong, heavy and rhythmically marked. They came partly for the singing, the people. They sang that gloomy invocation, "O Come, O Come, Emmanuel." They sang the Yorkshire "Christians Awake" and "O Come all Ye Faithful" with a mixture of respectability, sober energy, and abandon that always confused Stephanie, who associated the noise both with repressive habits and with unused forces finding an outlet. They stood there, still and dark and hatted in rows. The English are ugly, Stephanie thought, not for the first time. There was a preponderance of middle-aged faces, plum colored, ashen, pasty, pursed into a combination of too much patience, caution, and suspicion. They were not outdoor faces, they were not easy faces. Nor were they suffering faces. They were the faces of people concerned predominantly either with what people thought about their behavior, property, social standing, or with their own judgment of other people's behavior, property, social standing. They were more uncertain than their parents had been about these things. It was a generation that had had to be brave and now did not know how to be peaceful. See the hosts of Midian prowl and prowl around. Their clothes were ugly carapaces, designed to show the quality of the cloth and be decent: wine reds, bottle greens, odd, strident royal blues. She thought of D. H. Lawrence's requirement of tight white trousers and thought most of these shapeless persons would be worse his way. No good to sit under beautiful Italian trees among beautiful Italian peasants and inveigh petulantly against miners and respectable women. She thought instead of *The Mill on the Floss*, that cruel social history of English religion, locating its true center in the Lares and Penates, a dense structure of *things* that defined who you were and what your relation to others was, spotted damask, sprigged china, the graduated expense and display of bonnets kept to be worshiped rather than worn. This had, and George Eliot knew it, little or even nothing to do with Christ's injunctions to his followers, and certainly nothing at all to do with the Incarnation, which was now being celebrated as the congregation sang "Unto us a Boy is Born" as Daniel at the white-draped altar, with its lovingly embroidered white cloth, watched with Mr. Ellenby over the bread and wine. George Eliot, Stephanie thought, was a good hater. She looked long and intelligently at what she hated, with curiosity to see exactly *what* it was, and the necessary detachment to imagine it from within and without, these two breeding a kind of knowledge that was love. George Eliot had loved the bonnets and sprigged china—because she knew them, or because writing them down gave her power over them, made her gentle and generous to their meaning? She tried to relate this sudden vision of the *things* of the pieties of the Dodson sisters to Daniel's mum's instructions about how to cook Christmas pudding, and largely failed.

Stephanie had hopes that the familial Christmas dinner might in some way restore something of the frail threadwork of decency and courteous behavior broken by the earlier violence of her father and brother. Mrs. Orton, bizarrely enough, represented the necessary public presence of an observer who might inhibit wrath, induce politeness.

She would have had no such hopes in the old days, when Bill took pleasure in flouting normal expectations, seemed driven to flare up, to "create" as Mrs. Orton might put it. He had embarrassed Stephanie forever at her own wedding. But those who "create" social terror are vulnerable to those who, ruthlessly or desperately, are capable of creating greater terror. Marcus had embarrassed Bill—as well as hurting him—in a way that outstripped any mischief or shock Bill had ever caused. From what Stephanie had seen of Bill lately, from what Frederica reported, his spirit was daunted, at least for a time. She did not consider, though she could and should have done, that Bill's very real affection for herself might temper any onslaught. He did not like Daniel, or her marriage, and made that clear.

She worked at civility. She made Cumberland sauce to go with the turkey, translucent and clear wine red in little pots, with fine gold strips of peel lying in it. She spent time shelling boiled chestnuts to sit among the traditional sprouts. She rubbed bread and herbs and made stuffing. She built little mounds of nuts, raisins, and mandarins. She laid out bright scarlet napkins. She built a good wood fire. There were cut-glass wineglasses on the table. Stephanie did not like cut glass; she was of the generation that discovered the plain, the functional, the Finnish. But the lines of light glittered on the carved glassy flowers and formed a bright, hazy, enveloping pattern with the triangles of round mandarins, the crisscross of orange peel, Marcus's fine polyhedrons in the tree, the changing firelight itself.

When they came, she saw Bill would not "create." She opened the door to them, crimson faced and breathless from basting the turkey, a butcher's apron inadequately covering a distended Quaker-gray dress. He stood on the doorstep between Winifred and Frederica and seemed so very much smaller than either tall woman that he looked to Stephanie horridly shrunk. He carried several parcels and a box of bottles. "My contribution," he said, perhaps anxiously, to his daughter, who found it almost impossible to kiss him across the barrier made by these objects and her own girth. When she tried to take the boxes he summoned Frederica with a touch of his old asperity and told her to make herself useful. The Potters edged their way in, nerved to meet Marcus, and saw Daniel's mum, lapped deep in flesh and garments in the armchair, flesh overlapping flesh as her chin folded over her folded neck. Marcus was not there. They took chairs—a little too close, the circle, for elegance in the small space. Stephanie offered sherry. A voice spoke.

"Please excuse me if I don't get up. Truth is, I can't, wi'out help. I can just about get down here of a morning and then I'm stuck until someone gives me a 'and up, which they don't want to be doing too often, do they, dear?"

"I'm still strong enough for a tug," said Stephanie, too brightly.

"And how are you keeping, Mrs. Potter? Bearing up, despite troubles? As long as you've got your health, I always say . . ."

Winifred said she was well and looked at Stephanie, sitting near the kitchen. Stephanie she thought did not look well. The gloss had gone from the blonde hair, the face was sharper; however the cheeks were flushed and the body swollen. There were lines around the sharpened nose and indigo shadows around the eyes. And not much color in the lips.

"How are you?" she asked her daughter cautiously.

"Thriving," said Mrs. Orton. "The amount the young can do nowadays—now when I was carrying Dan I was *not* able to get up for days together, me ankles swoll so, and I 'ad dizzy spells, something terrible, but she still gets around on that bike, perky as Punch. You'll do yourself an injury, I say, but she knows best no doubt for there isn't a day but she's off for some long trip or other on the thing. One day last week we 'ad to get us own lunch, me and young See-all-hear-all-say-nowt upstairs, and then I had to bellow to get him down t'elp or I'd 'ave been stuck 'ere in this chair wi'out a sup or bite from dawn to dusk and beyond. But 'e made a bit o' Welsh rarebit after some coaxing. 'E's not as incapable as 'e looks, I've come to 't conclusion."

Briefly, no Potter could speak. Fortunately at this point Daniel came in, humming, from Morning Prayer, taking up too much space, wishing everyone "Happy Christmas" in a clerical boom. He took in Marcus's absence, went upstairs, and came down with the pale boy behind him. Marcus stood on the bottom step. Bill stood up and faced his son. Daniel's mum issued a disregarded injunction to sit down, do. Bill took two steps forward and very formally held out his hand. Marcus, limply, but for a perfectly decent period, took it as it was offered, and then moved on to lay a cold cheek against his mother's. Through Stephanie's mind ran an image of a huge rent, in sail canvas or something like it, being stitched with large, clumsy, visible stitches, but stitched. The next thing was the mutual offering of presents, which she proposed.

The presents were curiously uniform. Marcus received several anonymous shirts and socks. Daniel too was given garments, some he might wear and some he wouldn't, socks, scarf, tie, all of them not black, as though the company had made a preconcerted attempt to cheer him up. Stephanie had miscellaneous pieces of kitchen equipment and bed linen, not a book, although Frederica had all books if you included a book token from Mrs. Orton. Bill had books, and tobacco, and a book token from Marcus with a Brueghel snow scene reproduced on the front, which he turned over several times as though it must contain some message other than "Happy Christmas, love Marcus" written neatly on the dotted line. Stephanie went back into the kitchen to dish up. Daniel adeptly and too obviously converted a reminiscence of his mum's about a joint of pork she had once cooked into a general conversation about Christmases past. They remembered wartime making do. They discussed the new turkey farms. Bill borrowed a corkscrew and opened some bottles of Beaujolais he had brought. Sentence by meaningless sentence they held the occasion together.

In the kitchen, Stephanie struggled with the turkey, bloated and slithering in its fatty dish. Her face glistened with heat and effort. She suffered from an excess of exact imagination. They weighed on her. In all of them some private violence pulled against prescribed behavior. Bill most. If public medical statements have been made about a man's deleterious effect on his son's psyche, there is bound to be anxiety and embarrassment attendant on their meeting. On the other hand, there was the infinite English capacity for underplaying dramas, ignoring situations, pretending things were normal. Bill had had his own small share of this sometimes useful refusal to recognize awkward truths, particularly where Marcus was concerned.

And there was Winifred, who had tried to teach her son her own form of passive resistance to Bill's rage and had only, perhaps she now thought, exposed him to a homosexual religious maniac. She had once told Stephanie, whom she trusted, though it did not come easily to her to make confidences to her daughters, that she was possessed by physical loathing of Lucas Simmonds and of what contact—she was not specific—he might have had with her son. "I wanted to vomit," she had said sharply to Stephanie. "Indeed *I have* vomited." Stephanie did not know how far this revulsion might perhaps include Marcus himself. Marcus found large areas of the world untouchable; Winifred brought herself to make contact with them with difficulty.

Stephanie could feel Frederica's tolerant and arrogant knowledge that she, Frederica, was now tangential to all this. She could feel Mrs. Orton wanting to be noticed, desiring to be liked, preventing these things.

And there was Daniel, who was unhappy or angry, she did not know why. She could hear him being professionally cheerful, caricaturing himself and the cloth, as he did, under stress.

She felt every housewife's fury when the guests could not be got to table and the food was ready. She felt irritable, tearful, contemned. She carried in sprouts and potatoes and smiled and smiled.

The food was eaten. Chewing took over from talking. Daniel sliced the bird's plump breast and pulled tendons out of the lopped legs, fished for stuffing with a long spoon. Marcus caused the first flurry by refusing meat. He did not say, but looked, that the sight of it made him feel sick. Mild Stephanie felt momentary pure rage at his rejection of her good gravy, her dedicated basting, her care. Mrs. Orton took it upon herself, watching him pick at a little heap of sprouts and chestnut, to observe that he had very likely *made* himself ill with being faddy. It was Frederica who retorted, "Plenty of protein in chestnuts," and took another helping for herself.

They all got hotter and redder and shinier and fatter. When Mrs. Orton proposed that they listen to the Queen's speech on the radio, Bill's only protest was to produce a bottle of brandy from his case, open one of his gift books, roll himself a cigarette with gift tobacco, lean back, and stare covertly at his son. Who had his eyes closed in an expressionless face but was still present, in his chair. No, Stephanie thought later, it had been no more and no less than could have been hoped—a reasonable coming together of people close to each other, not by choice, reluctant in many cases. Nevertheless it had, from the first glass of sherry to the momentary blue veil of flame on the pudding, been what she would have called civilized. They had behaved well.

Daniel was unhappy. Stephanie did not understand Daniel's unhappiness because, quick about his attitudes to church wardens, shirt buttons, Bill's fury, the Ellenbys' lazy matter-of-course snobbery, she was unable to catch the shifts of his feelings about herself, or now, about the two of them. She had her arrogance; she did not believe he had fully imagined her physical battle with the turkey, her anger, and shame at her anger, over Marcus's vegetarian gesture. Daniel had in fact imagined all these, and had also adequately encompassed her relief that small talk and eating were proceeding. He knew a lot about English ways of "not speaking." There was more than one couple in his parish who had communicated for years only by note or through neighbors. And beyond married couples there were siblings, parents, children who froze speech forever, from revenge, terror, hopelessness, small hardened stubbornness. He knew what it meant that Marcus should stay in the room while Bill managed for three consecutive hours to make a series of acceptably banal factual observations.

But he was not happy. He thought, he had wanted her, Stephanie.

Not a home. Just her. He wished now he had not given her what he believed to be a very beautiful nightdress, creamy and ruffled. He had seen her look at Frederica's books and had understood what he had half sensed on the occasion of Frederica's telegrams, her sense of loss. He had his own sense of loss—the grim singleness of himself and his job alone in an anonymous bed sitter.

He looked at them all. There were three kinds. The pale Potters, the vanishers—Winifred, Stephanie, Marcus, who effaced themselves too quickly. The flaming Potters, Bill and Frederica, today out-talked by his mother, but capable of endless egocentric parabolas of speech. And he and his mother, heavy, flesh and blood. His mum was a horrible nuisance, no question. And ate and ate and ate: everyone had watched her guzzle, blank pale Potters, birdlike, judging, flaming Potters, fastidious Marcus with his bits of greens dissected and rejected. His child had the weight of all this on it. If it was not born like hospital Mary, it could be genetically fated to resemble his mum, or Marcus, or the awful Frederica. Flesh of these fleshes and blood of these bloods.

He considered the mothers round the table with an almost superstitious wariness. His own, now saccharine and anecdotal about the good old days of his childhood, when he had in fact eaten sardines with a fork out of a tin in silence, day after day, while she slept. Winifred, washed away and thinned down by a lifetime of self-effacement and subordination to these ferocious, pale, or fuming creatures. Stephanie, double, self-contained, so egg-inviolate that Charlie did not frighten her nor Mary shake her calm assurance. What would become of her, of him, of his child? He felt the mothers and the family, as in a different way he felt the hospital children, as a threat. He told Stephanie to put her feet up and went into the kitchen for solitude, where he began purposefully on the dishes. He was joined, which annoyed him, by Frederica. Who had, among other disqualifications, no turn of speed with a tea towel.

She used it initially to fan her face with. She said, "Well, that went off okay."

"Yes."

"Nice to be out in the cool though. Air. I can't bear somnolent groups of people."

Neither could he. He remarked, however, that there was little to choose between kitchen and living room in respect of air, since the oven had been on since dawn. He handed her a dripping plate.

"Good practice. I'm going in a week or two. To be a mother's helper. Not my *forte* but a mother's helper in *French*, at least."

"Very nice."

"I have wondered if I ought to leave Mummy. She's in a grim state. I don't think she finds me much use. Tells Steph things, not me. I'm unnecessary. Just as well for me. I've got to get moving."

"Yes."

"You don't like me much. I've noticed. I didn't for a long time; I was only interested in whether I liked you. And when I decided I did, I noticed you didn't like me."

He handed her another plate.

"I don't spend much time thinking about liking or not liking," he said.

"No. But you can *do* it, without thinking about it. I hope you get to like me. I mean, we shall know each other all our lives. Though I hope we don't go on having family Christmases. I long to be with people I've *chosen*. Are you afraid of defeat?"

"What?"

"Well—you go on—like a bulldozer—like me. Aren't you afraid of being the other sort—the sort that stops and suffers?"

"Everyone has to be that."

"No—look—some people aren't *defeated*. Some are. Look at the people in this house. *You* aren't defeated."

"No?" he said, passing another plate, and regretted it.

"Daniel. You don't feel weighed down, too?"

"No, no. No more than is inevitable, and manageable. You're young enough to be dramatic about everything."

"And how old are you, so wise?"

He was twenty-four. He laughed.

"You should get Marcus out of your house," she said, rattling a handful of cutlery.

"He's unobtrusive."

"Is he? I hadn't noticed. He's an energy absorber, like shock absorbers in cars or astronomical antimatter."

Since Daniel agreed with this he was reduced to silence. Frederica studied him as he dealt with the roasting pans. His waist was huge over the sink, his arms black and hairy below rolled-up sleeves, the mass of his black hair ruffled by effort. The back view of a large man in a small space at the wrong height. She did wish he liked her. But she did not care greatly. Her mind was full of the future, which presented itself as a bright empty space crossed by tracks of her own shining, clear-cut flights, her passage swift and sunlit. There was going to be very little room in Frederica Potter's life from now on for this imposed world of people and chairs you had to have because they were there. It might be all right for Daniel; his purposes possibly included its transfiguration or consecration or whatever words from whatever language he chose to describe it in. But she rejected. She dropped, and broke, one of Stephanie's wedding-present wineglasses. Daniel swept up the fragments.

4

MIDI

When Frederica left for Nîmes she had no real idea of the south. She knew that Nîmes was a provincial city and would have preferred it not to be, seeing "provincial" in terms of the English nineteenth-century novel, not of the Roman Provincia, Provence. Drifting city-ward in her generation, she had really hoped for Paris and bright lights. She had booked a sleeper from Paris in terms of time—"I can't sit up all night"—not distance—"I am going a long way south." When she boarded this train she became involved in an altercation with the sleeping-car attendant, which she enjoyed, because it was in French, and she was able to use her subjunctives and conditionals, and say "si" instead of "oui" at appropriate moments. She lost the argument, which was about her reservation, which was for berth No. 7 in English which the conductor obstinately read as 1 in French. Frederica explained that in France the 7 is crossed but that this is not done in Thomas Cook's in Calverley, N. Yorkshire. The attendant said there was a gentleman already undressing in No. 1. Frederica received no answer to her question about numéro sept, but was given permission to stand in the corridor of the train, which was already sliding away from its platform. She watched Paris rattle past, foreign blocks of lit windows, knots of wire, and she was offered a Gauloise by a compact little man who leaned his elbow companionably against hers on the window rail. She accepted the cigarette as she accepted most offerings, and still elated at the sound of her French being understood and responded to by Frenchmen, volunteered the information that she was going to Nîmes, to stay with a family. She would have told him much more, all sorts of improper things, only to hear the old information newly proposed in new words. She would be lucky, the man told her, to see the south in spring. The maquis smells wonderful. For the first time Frederica's imagination touched at the south. He was going to St. Raphael himself, the man said. He was a traveler. He sold liqueurs, mostly to the hotel industry. He could offer mademoiselle a taste of Cointreau, Grand Marnier, Chartreuse, if she really had no berth.

Frederica replied brightly that that would be very agreeable. This was despite a strong sense that the man was unduly anxious about the outcome of his overture; anxiety is a great destroyer of response, and Frederica had no taste for being closed in a sleeping compartment with a *worried* man. On the other hand, she did not want to stand until dawn, and she did want the French words to go on being threaded together. The sleeping-car attendant came back and announced that by great good fortune he had an empty berth for which the occupant had unaccountably not appeared. He ushered Frederica into No. 7, and stood, perhaps awaiting a tip, which she was unable to offer, being provided only with notes of large denominations. This caused her to close herself abruptly in, without the traveler in liqueurs. And then she was delighted by the solitude of the sleeping car, and forgot him.

She undressed partly and padded about the perpetually shifting floor in stocking feet, suspenders, slip, and bra. She investigated ring hooks, water flask, lidded washbasin. She tried to peer out of the peephole in her blind. A station clashed by so fast she could neither read its name nor discern the pattern of its ironwork. Black masses of bush, or bull, or thatch elongated themselves, howling. She liked that. She liked to be alone in a warm, lit box with the world streaming darkly by. She curled on her bunk, admired her long legs, thought about desire (not for the traveler in liqueurs), read part of *Madame Bovary*, part of *Les Fleurs du Mal*, and all of a novel by Margery Sharp, bought on impulse at the Gare de Lyon. She saw the dawn when it came and pulled up the blind. There in the pale lemon gray were expanses of espaliered rows of strange stumps like truncated Virginia creepers, squat and tough. These large spaces did not rush past but seemed endless because endlessly repeated. Understanding took time. Vines in her mind trailed over trellises, depended from arbors, clung. Around these orderly gnarled wooden roots the cold soil heated almost visibly as the incredible bright dawn advanced.

She dressed carefully, green herringbone tweed suit, pinch waisted, court shoes, very plain, and a complicated face, the tricky little eye-liner triangles at the lid corners almost smudged by the swaying train. She had a sort of velvet cap, from which she had snipped a bit of veiling. She believed cheap clothes could be made elegant by paring them down to essentials. Sometimes this worked, sometimes she looked tarty, sometimes she looked drab. On that morning, descending the steel ladder onto the sandy Nîmes siding in two-inch heels and an inverted tulip skirt, she looked all these things.

The Grimaud family had written to say that they would meet her with a blue Corvette. It was only at this late stage that she began to think about them; they had been a means to an end, Frederica Potter's removal from Blesford and Yorkshire. A large man and a small boy appeared at the other end of the platform; she hobbled on her heels, humping her heavy suitcase, toward them. They greeted her and introduced themselves—Monsieur Grimaud and Paul-Marie. Paul-Marie had un-English shorts, long white socks, olive-brown legs. Frederica ignored him. M. Grimaud swung up her bag, smiling. He had a wide waistline, iron-gray hair *en brosse*, a tanned face with smile lines set round the mouth, a signet ring, gold serpent coiled round bloodstone. He was at ease in his skin. He asked about her journey, and sitting beside him in the car she recounted the mix-up over the sleeper numbers, enjoying, still, hearing herself speak French. M. Grimaud laughed. He swung the car out into Nîmes and beyond Nîmes into the countryside, straight roads with plane trees, cultivated wild land right and left. M. Grimaud explained everything easily, with a French educational fervor and a local passion that Frederica was too culturally inexperienced—and too confused—to place. The lovely light, as they traveled, grew and grew.

The fields here, M. Grimaud said, were fields of lavender, a major Provençal industry. Here she was in the land of the Langue d'Oc, which must be distinguished from the Langue d'Oil. He spoke of troubadours and ancient lords and sang, unembarrassed and unaffected, snatches of song about lavender, about almond trees, about love, in incomprehensible Provençal. Frederica saw the long ridges of dusty gray-green lavender leaves and imagined violet spikes. She saw unshadowed earth in yellow light, more vines, new shoots of what she did not recognize as young maize. Later, traveling knowledgeably south at thirty, forty, full of accrued wisdom about good little places, local food and wine, Cafés Routiers and long-vanished sand dunes, she tried to remember the surprises, only half experienced that day, of that land to her unexpecting eyes. It had seemed, because she was, raw and new, dust and brightness. And the smells, the beginning of the smells of the south, more immediately apprehensible, more durable in the memory, at least when re-evoked. Herbs in rough places, juniper, rosemary, and thyme, which she would have named but not identified, oregano, which she could not even have named. They approached the *propriété* along an avenue lined with limes— *tilleuls*, a word, a name, already in her vocabulary, but now suddenly associated with a solid form and gusts of fragrance. M. Grimaud discoursed on the making of *tisanes*, and made obscure references to Marcel Proust. *Tisane*, like *tilleul*, was in Frederica's vocabulary, the word, not the thing, but it was some time yet before she would understand their connection with Proust, who had entered her consciousness largely through a striking nightmare, dreamed the night before her Oxford entrance examination, which she recalled, as M. Grimaud talked and the scented trees brushed past.

In this dream she had been locked into the school library with an exam paper containing one question and one only: Compare and contrast narrative method in Proust and *Tom Jones*. She knew nothing about either and in the dream wept bitterly from shame and impotence. When she awoke she was further annoyed at having dreamed a category confusion, a man and a book, not realizing that the category error was partly the answer to the uncouth question, since Proust was coterminous with a book as the eponymous *Tom Jones* was not. She was never to think of that dream without some of its investing emotions, shame and irritation, even after a man at a party in 1969 had told her such dreams are dreamed typically by those unlikely to fail plausible and real exams. Then, in 1954, as the car passed under what seemed a medieval or Renaissance courtyard gate, there was Frederica, brooding grimly about a personal failure in a dreamed, unreal competition. In later years, say 1964, 1974, 1984, the first vision of Nozières took on its perfection and primacy, as it is only after the mind has cleared itself of the flow of daily pre-occupation, planning, expectation, that the moment of a death can be known for what it is, and one's life mapped, prospectively and retrospectively, to that threshold. The yard was walled in gold stone covered with clean dust and lichen stains. Hens ran, calling.

Madame Grimaud, short and trim with a well-managed waist, solid hips, and strictly upswept smooth black hair, stood on the doorstep with two cross-looking and awkward teenage daughters, to whom Frederica was to be required to converse. Mediterranean women in black dresses—Frederica's first sight of these—moved around and behind this group. There was a lot of formal handshaking and Frederica, directed in part by the nature of the language, spoke several formal French sentences of graceful gratitude. Inside, at a huge oak table in a stone dining hall, dark walled and tiled, she was given a bowl of hot chocolate, a huge piece of French bread, unsalted butter (again the first) and *confiture aux cerises*. She was conducted up flights of stone stairs with wrought-iron balustrades to her huge room, whose walls were painted a bright dark blue—a color that reminded her of a postcard of Van Gogh's *Starry Night* and even more of the color behind the fleurs de lys on the banners in Olivier's 1944 film of *Henry V*. Its powdery darkness amazed her. No English room was ever dark blue; maybe this was more like Reckitt's blue? The floor was faded blue and tawny tiles. The bed was high, high and curtained, covered with lace and bobbled crocheted cotton. There was a wash hand-stand with ewer, slop bucket, and china washbasin.

The room was twice the size of the sitting room at home in Masters' Row at Blesford. There was neither writing table nor desk, though there was a whole set of heavy, yellow-painted bedroom furniture, wardrobe, cupboard, chest. It was alien. It was interesting. She was excited by so many strange *things*. She was also exhausted. And, to her horror, briefly homesick for carpets, bookcases, small casement windows, man-made heating devices, the familiar, the known.

Later, at least for many years, she was not to see this time as part of her life, and perhaps therefore it need not now be told at length. Frederica's recall of things seen was very much less lucid and automatic than those of Stephanie or even Marcus. Her mind was self-referring and exclusive as theirs were not—impersonal only in relation to the teasing out of the intellectually taxing problem. In the 1970s Ezra Pound's laminated view of vital and moribund cultures, centered partly on Provence, made her see M. Grimaud's easy educating communications about the land, the lore, the language in which she found herself, as a sign of real energy in his community that had been ersatz, or only wished for, in post-Festival of Britain Yorkshire. Bill Potter had his local pride; his evening-class students collected local words, described patterns of social behavior and family inter-relationship with a kind of Fabian zeal, but without the sun-saturated liveliness of M. Grimaud's sense of what was shared and perpetual in his world.

This family, which was not her own, which threw her own, absent and dispersed, into sharp relief, was certainly kind. M. Grimaud was captain of a ship that ran between Marseille and Tunis. He was away for weeks at a time and would return laden with *gigots* of Algerian lamb, jars of oil, sacks of pulses. Madame ran the *propriété*, which was large, and not labor intensive (words that entered Frederica's vocabulary ca. 1960). There were hectares of vineyards—she never knew how many—and orchards of peaches, cherries, melons. There was at least a sufficiency of migrant Italian house and garden servants, who rendered any conventional mother's help more than redundant.

Frederica, who did not even make her own bed, acquired one or two odd skills. She learned to cut asparagus daily, in the wide, ridged, humped beds outside the golden walls, spying out newly poking purple heads, slicing, with a gritty sharp knife, just under the soil. She also learned to assist in the preparation of foods she believed herself, in 1954, to dislike: aïoli, *estouffade de boeuf*, kid stewed with wine, tomatoes, and garlic, *potage de légumes* hand wound through a Mouli, dressed salads made with unknown leaves and fronds, crimson, cream-white, spinach-dark, curly pale green. She turned the handle of the spit when the Algerian *gigots* were roasted, larded with garlic and anchovies, in a kind of oval cage of iron slats in front of a hot fire of vine stumps inside the huge hearth; she sat on a bench inside the *cheminée*, turning the ratchet as it wound down, basting the lamb with oil and its own juices from a diabolical long spoon.

Her one apparent asset, her good French, turned out to be a disadvantage. Marie-Claire and Monique learned little English because Frederica intimidated them and they intimidated her. She rewrote their homework in respectable English but appeared, at that time, not to have inherited the family teaching compulsion, and was unable to explain the principle by which she was altering their grammar and syntax. Thus, although their marks improved, the two girls were not learning. Only much later did it occur to her that this was her failure. Academically self-sufficient and wholly self-centered, she saw their sullenness and ignorance as their concern and their fault. Madame Grimaud treated all this with brisk courtesy, remarking on one occasion that it could at least be said that Frederica was a good moral influence. Frederica saw this observation at the time as a mark of signal failure of insight. Later, in England, it occurred to her that it might have been said ironically, but by then she had forgotten the context and intonation of it, could only remember that it was said under hot sun outside the Maison Carrée in Nîmes, where the air was fluent and the stones shone.

They made courteous and persistent attempts to amuse her. On the second day they gave her a rubber ball attached on a long elastic thread to a wooden bat. She stood in the courtyard, solemnly playing, seventeen, sex starved, muscle-bound, an intellectual shark, at Jokari. She was no good at this. The *domestiques* and Madame Grimaud observed her failure solemnly from doors and windows as they moved about their household works. Frederica was put in mind, *mutatis mutandis*, starting with the intention, of Miss Havisham bidding the

boy Pip to play, of the brewery yard where he had met Herbert
Pocket, which (the yard) irked her, because she could not properly
visualize it.

She was taken everywhere. To the covered fish market at dawn to
buy fish for a bouillabaisse, which held no romance for her for she
had not then read Ford Madox Ford's description of the great bouillabaisse in the Calanques, nor Elizabeth David's description of the color
and patterns of fish on the stalls. She went to the dressmaker with
Madame Grimaud, where there was a stocky replica, adjustable, of
Madame Grimaud's female French form standing headless on a metal
leg. Everyone knew everyone and stopped to speak to everyone. She
thought she remembered lovebirds at the dressmaker, and did remember dark coffee and *langues de chat*. The lovebirds in her mind
fused into a watching parrot, perhaps made by the metal leg. She
visited neighboring *propriétés* and sipped aperitifs from unlabeled
bottles, white port on terraces, in arbors trailing wisteria, under acacia
trees. In two of these families there were young men, sons and heirs
who would inherit the land, unspeaking grave Michel, noisy Dany
with one word of English—"bluejeans"—and an explosive Lambretta churning up pale, clean dust. She had ideas about these two,
especially about Michel, but saw that to them she was invisible, not
quite real, as *au pair* girls frequently, perhaps usually, are. She spoke
a lot, and they turned and congratulated each other on her French,
as though she was some sort of barrel organ she thought, being not
only sex starved but starved also of admiration.

When Monsieur was at home, more cultural and purposeful expeditions were undertaken. They went to a floodlit performance of
Mistral's great Provençal work *Mireille* in the Roman arena in
Nîmes. In the same place, one day, Frederica saw bullfighting. She
had hoped to understand the aesthetic excitement of this pursuit, to
see and recognize the "moment of truth" even if she must simultaneously be revolted. But all she saw was slow, repeated, stumbling,
coughing killings at which she retched in a very conventional English
animal-loving way, which upset Monsieur Grimaud, who was an
aficionado and had been lecturing Frederica on the provenance and
meaning of that word. The place suddenly had its history of blood-
letting to be sniffed, and yet even that was not exciting, maybe

because the Nîmois did not roar for blood as the Romans had, but sunned themselves and discussed finer points of capework. They did, it was true, have an agitated fit of booing and hissing, but this was, M. Grimaud explained, an expression of spontaneous disapproval of Picasso, who could just be made out, small brown face under black beret, at the other side of the arena. The crowd, M. Grimaud stated, thought his art was fraudulent and Frederica, trying in vain to imagine any English football crowd holding any communal view about any modern artist, suddenly remembered the Picasso prints on the walls of Alexander Wedderburn's study in Blesford Ride School. She had been in love with Alexander. Here, distant from home and muddle, she was sure she was still in love with Alexander. She had made, circumstances had made, rather a mess of this love. She did not think he would like to hear from her, or possibly even to think about her. His Picassos had been blue period, the Saltimbanques, a strange boy with a pipe, crowned with flowers. It was odd to sit here, so far away, in sun and shouting, and see the small dark and light rounds of the face of the man who had made those images. His lines are very economical, she said to M. Grimaud, who looked solidly startled at this view and spoke dismissively of women with three breasts, or single eyes, paintings more infantile than those of Cro-magnon man. Moreover, he said, Picasso had discovered and ruined the traditional potteries at Vallauris, which now turned out only nasty ashtrays with distorted bulls and gross doves. He has killed the tradition he loved, M. Grimaud said with contempt. Frederica thought he was being philistine and was later to learn that he was being simply truthful. The drawings of bullfights, however, have real merit, M. Grimaud assured her, which silenced her, since she didn't know the drawings and was sick of the bullfight.

Afterward bleeding bull steaks hung from hooks in butchers' windows, or lay overlapping on white plates. The Grimaud family purchased and cooked many of these—it was customary, Frederica was told. Frederica gagged on hers, nauseated by a memory of the foundering black body as the life left the legs, of the crawling sheet of sticky blood over the shoulder under the pics, of trailing hooves and horns dragged over sawdust. She was later to discover that a certain J. Olivier believed that Vincent Van Gogh's self-mutilation in Arles was an aspect of some bull ritual. The victorious matador, he said, was awarded the ear of the bull, which he would offer "to his Lady or to a female spectator who has drawn his attention." (No ears were awarded on the day of Frederica's visit to the corrida.) So, J. Olivier argues, Van Gogh, vanquished and vanquisher both, cut off his own ear after the altercation with Gauguin and presented it, in his own honor, to the lady, the Arles whore.

The vignoble produced a reasonable *vin rosé* which she drank like water every lunchtime. Unlike Marie-Claire, Monique, and Paul-Marie, she did not add water, believing it to be childish or in doubtful taste to dilute good wine. The result was burning headaches, dizzy spells, and prolonged periods of lassitude that the Grimauds, courteous as always, ascribed to the mistral, to heat, to unaccustomed diet. They may have been glad, since she was turning out to be hard to amuse, that she slept deeply in the early afternoons.

There were no books. M. Grimaud told her how Nîmes had been settled by the veterans of Octavius's victory over Antony and Cleopatra, whose names, Antonin, Numa, Flavien, Adrien, persisted, even today, as did the emblem of the defeat of the serpent of old Nile, the Nîmes chained crocodile. He took her to Uzès where Racine had once come to ruralize, contemplate the priesthood, began to write. Uzès was and is a town out of another time, a yellow town on a gently conical hill, geometric roof on roof, a town that must have been as it now is when Shakespeare wrote *Antony and Cleopatra*. Frederica tried to talk to M. Grimaud about Racine but, although he could quote several speeches, he was more interested in what Racine was and meant than in what he had written. He had a Racine, a Molière, a Chateaubriand. Frederica borrowed also Hemingway in translation, and read about bullfights and the earth moving, which caused her to feel worse, sex starved, desperate for life, and love, and action. She also developed a need for the English language. Madame took her to the city library in Nîmes, a gaunt, dark building with high shutters behind grilles and dusty leather books, ceiling high. There was not much in English: she borrowed the complete works of Tobias Smollett. These were not what she was hungry for, but they were English, and narrative. Narrative is one of the best intoxicants or tranquilizers. They were at least *long*.

Madame then thought of the *vélo*.

On this Frederica explored the unvarying hot flat country. She bumped along furrows between vines, spattered cobalt blue with spraying. She listened to cicadas and breathed the pervasive liquorice that grew locally and was processed in a factory on the Nîmes road. Whenever she fell off the *vélo* she sat where she was, nodding, fumed with wine and drowsy with heat, in a classical furrow, under a pale-bright sky. She decided to become a writer. It was almost inevitable, given the excessive respect paid in the Potter house to the written word, and given Frederica's own mastery of, and intense pleasure in, the school essay, that she should decide to become a writer. Foreign places, moreover, bring out the writer in strangers less word obsessed than Frederica Potter. I do not think the compulsion to *write* about foreign places can be very closely compared to a painter's sensuous delight in new light, new forms, new colors, Monet seeing the Cap d'Antibes in blue and rose, Turner seeing the bright watery Venetian light in Venice, Gauguin in Tahiti. Pigment is pigment and light is light in any culture. But words, acquired slowly over a lifetime, are part of a different set of perceptions of the world. They have grown with us; they restrict what we see and how we see it. I am trying to account for the paradox of the *sameness* of so many accounts, in language, of the strange, the exotic, the new. Frederica will do as an example to illustrate the difficulties of writing about strangeness.

She wanted to set down the southern landscape. Her tradition of looking at landscape was deeply Wordsworthian, whatever intimations she may have had that Wordsworth's language was for his time and place only. Frederica could, in the Lake District, have seen a "Wordsworthian" tarn and been able to render it in Wordsworthian words, and, because these words were known, tested, thought about, she could have introduced minute changes, have seen one little thing he hadn't seen, changed the point of view. There are shepherds in the Andes who have over sixty words for the color brown in the coats of sheep. But they are shepherds in the Andes. Frederica had words for tea-party behavior and shopping discriminations in North Yorkshire matrons. She had a variety of words, and was adding to them, for the structure of a Shakespearean plot or metaphor. She saw these new things, paradoxically, in old clichés. The same Wordsworth, much mocked, thought himself back to an innocent vision, told us that grass is green and water wet because he had reached beyond familiarity to some primal wonder that these things were so and not otherwise, to some mythic sense that he was giving or finding the words for the things, not merely repeating. So also Daniel, walking with Stephanie on Filey beach, had suddenly, out of some metaphorical experience as bodily as breathing, *known* why love was called "sweet" and, as his blood banged, why a beloved was a "sweet heart." So now, more mildly, Frederica saw for the first time that the light was gold, that olives were black and warm, the olive trees were powdery gray, that lavender was a purple haze. But when she saw these things written they seemed, and were, stale, *déjà vu*, derivative.

Frederica was also enough a child of her time to suppose that what she should write should be fiction. "The novel is the one bright book of life," Lawrence had didactically exclaimed and Bill Potter had didactically reiterated. "The novel is the highest form of human expression yet attained." If anyone had challenged Frederica directly as to whether she believed that, she would have argued the toss. But —however Wordsworthian the roots—in the 1950s the recording compulsion took Lawrentian forms. And she had no plot. Or did not recognize those plots she had. And was not primarily in those days concerned with invention.

She tried to utilize Dany and his Lambretta or a speechless Michel and disgusted herself. She was driven back to Alexander, and attempted unsuccessfully to translate that very English poet into a divinity of the olive groves. All that happened was that her sexual needs became painful instead of grumbling and Alexander became unreal in her mind in a bad way. She tried a diary, but it reiterated circuitously and boringly that Frederica Potter was bored and also, to her shame, homesick. She could not see how to see Marie-Claire and Monique, Paul-Marie and Madame, let alone the workings of the wine cooperative, the *réglisserie*, or Protestant Nîmes. She was a good critic, despite her egocentricity, and decided briskly and miserably that writing was not her *métier*.

So she gave up, and sat between the vines in the hot sun, alternately sleeping and working her way through the dusty volumes of *Peregrine Pickle*, bound in crimson and gold leather, with real bookworms making agitated forays from their dark crannies into the heat and light across the extraordinary scenes where Smollett's elderly ladies retained their urine indefinitely to put out putative fires, or sweetened their foul breaths with violet cachous to deceive desired young lovers. She did not ask herself then under what compulsion he had made his plots or constructed his worlds; she accepted them as one accepts fairy tales in childhood.

And Vincent Van Gogh? Provence is as he painted it; we use his images as icons by which to recognize certain things, the cypresses above all, the olives, some configurations of rock and vegetation, the line of the Alpilles, the plain of the Crau, the light itself.

He came, as Frederica did not, with precise aesthetic expectations. He expected to see "Japanese" subjects, the colors of Monticelli, the forms of Cézanne and Renoir, the southern light lauded by Gauguin as a mystic necessity. He saw all these things, as he expected them. He saw also Dutch things in the French heat, bridges not formally different from those in Delft and Leyden, colors in the glare that reminded him primarily of the soft blues and yellows of Vermeer. Also, and simultaneously, he saw what no one had yet seen, what was his to see. Sunflowers, cypresses, olives.

My dear Theo, I wrote to you already early this morning; then I went away to go on with a picture of a garden in the sunshine. Then I brought it back and went out again with a blank canvas, and that also is finished. And now I write to you again.

Because I have never had such a chance, nature here being so *extraordinarily* beautiful. Everywhere and all over the vault of heaven is a marvelous blue, and the sun sheds a radiance of pale sulphur, and it is soft and lovely as the combination of heavenly blues and yellows in a Van der Meer of Delft [sic]. I cannot paint it as beautifully as that, but it absorbs me so much that I let myself go, never thinking of a single rule . . .

Here under a stronger sun, I have found what Pissarro said confirmed, and also what Gauguin wrote to me, the simplicity, the fading of the colors, the gravity of great sunlight effects.

You never come near to suspecting it in the north.

5

MAS ROSE, MAS CABESTAINH

Mas Rose

In the early summer the family went to its summer house, a small pink-washed mas on a hillside in the Basses-Alpes, not far from Mont Ventoux. They took their spiky, useless English girl with them, offering culture, the Côte d'Azur, the Camargue. They took her to the Palais des Papes in Avignon where, on a warm evening, they saw a floodlit French production of *Macbeth*, the Théâtre Nationale Populaire, with Jean Vilar, drawn and romantic, more damned troubadour than Scots butcher, and Maria Casarès, whitely elegant and frenzied, washing blood from her hands while angelic trumpets shrilled from high battlements. Everything rushed forward in strange, denuded fast prose. "Demain et demain et demain."

In the interval Frederica became useful for once and recited to the bored young Grimauds as much as she could remember—and it was a great deal—of the thick, incomprehensible English verse. This brought a new access of homesickness, not for the Yorkshire moors but for the English language, and also for the long days of last summer's play, for Alexander Wedderburn's blown-rose full-blooded verse on the Elizabethan terrace at Long Royston, English summer evenings. As she was telling the shuffling Grimauds that light thickens, and the crow makes wing to the rooky wood, a voice cried above her from the high scaffolding.

"I know that voice. Young Potter. I will not act or suffer at the sword's edge— Not that—I will not bleed—my dear, do you remember?"

This sound was both welcome, and a blow beneath, very strictly beneath, the belt. It was Edmund Wilkie, polymath, to whom in the unlikely Edwardian luxe of the Grand Hotel in Scarborough she had most bloodily surrendered her virginity.

"Wilkie. I can't see in the dark. Where are you? What are you doing here? Excusez-moi, madame, C'est un ami, un ami de mon pays . . ."

Wilkie wriggled into the seat beside her. Here in the Palais des

Papes, as at Long Royston, the audience was on tiers of scaffolding. They had sat together on the other scaffolding and watched the graces dance. Wilkie was the same. Soft, dark, animal plump, exaggerated goggle glasses, a raffish academic.

"Monsieur Grimaud. Madame. Edmund Wilkie. Un ami, un étudiant de psychologie, un acteur. Wilkie, what are you *doing*?"

"What are you is more to the point. I'm staying with Crowe at the Mas Cabestainh. Crowe's French residence. *Very* pretty. Lots of nice people. You've gone all brown and peeling in patches, like a plane tree. Having an exciting time?"

"I'm an *au pair* girl. Everyone is very good to me. We're staying near Vaison-la-Romaine."

"Not far. We could meet. Lots of old friends at Mas Cabestainh. The girl, the beauty, Anthea Whatsit."

"Warburton."

"Yes, her. And Wedderburn. Elevated to producing radio talks. I expect you knew."

"I'd heard."

She was put out. The row of Grimauds, wanting not this chatter but Shakespeare, value for money at last, was inhibiting. She managed, "Is he well?"

"Oh, Frederica. You great fool. He came to see this play last week. Told me and Caroline to come. But dear Caroline's got an almighty hangover, sick as a dog, so I brought him over on the back of the bike to see it again. He's up there."

He gestured vaguely at the upper reaches of seats. The trumpets sounded, thin and clear, for the last act, from the palace's high corners.

"Les anges," said Wilkie, "rayonnent toujours, bien que le plus radieux soit déchu. Is that right? It sounds funny. Can you see him? *There.* I'll be seeing you."

And he scuttled monkeylike up through the rows of seats. Frederica craned upward. A light from a battlement caught, she thought, a white open-necked shirt, a tentative length of lean man, a grave face. *Alexander?*

"Guess what I found there?"

No answer.

"Frederica Potter being nanny to a row of French children."

"Oh, Christ!"

"She seemed very keen on seeing you. Excited you were here."

"Oh, Christ."

"She *loves* you, Alexander."

"Rubbish. A boa constrictor. Always was, always will be. Shut up, and let me watch this play."

Frederica was agitated. She remembered her last encounter with Alexander and failed yet again to understand her own behavior. She had stalked him with infinite care, she had attacked him frontally, she had thrown herself at him and teased him, and finally reached the point of consummation where he was coming to dinner, in an empty house, wanting her. And what she had done was to flee to Scarborough on the back of Wilkie's motorbike. She loved Alexander. Wilkie was only a friend to whom she chattered. She had always loved Alexander. She had an intimation that it had been important to her to have an *impersonal* initiation, in her own control, not overwhelming. But how could she ever explain this to Alexander, who anyway no longer wanted to understand?

"Elle aurait dû mourir ci-après. Un temps serait venu pour ce mot."

Something wrong with that? There would have been a time for such a word.

Alexander's emotions were simpler. He could hardly remember why, or how much, he had wanted Frederica. He referred to it in his mind as a temporary dramaturgical folly. He remembered very clearly that she had made him look a fool. He remembered kicking cornflowers and moon daisies all over the little square garden. He had no wish to repeat any part of the experience.

Tous nos hiers n'ont qu'allumé, pour les sots, une voie vers la Mort poussiéreuse.

Nevertheless, the two parties collided in the dark antechambers of the palace. Wilkie rushed up to Frederica, his bush-baby eyes bright. Alexander hung back. Because the motorbike was tucked cunningly under the very rampart of the fortress, much closer than the blue Corvette, Wilkie was able both to reverse the firm family progress of the Grimauds, and to make it impossible for Alexander not to catch up. Wilkie enjoyed such moments.

"Hello, Alexander."

"Hello."

"Monsieur Grimaud, Madame, Monsieur Alexander Wedderburn . . . un écrivain anglais . . . qui a écrit de belles pièces . . . très renommées . . . un ami . . . de mon père."

Everyone bowed. Alexander, his French less flowing than Frederica's, asked, inveterately good-mannered, how the Grimauds had liked the play. They replied. Frederica interrupted with a comment on the strange effect of the translation on an English ear. Alexander fell silent. Wilkie wrote down Frederica's address. M. Grimaud, interested by these strangers, hoping to amuse their English girl, drew on an envelope a sailorlike map demonstrating the approach to the Mas Rose from Vaison and the Mas Cabestainh. He supposed it was named for the troubadour, very famous and tragic, very Provençal. Courtly love, jealousy, blood, a terrible story. The Mas Rose had no gas, no electricity, no running water, but it was on the mountain, it had a spring, the air was pure, one could see the Ventoux, famous of course for the love of Pétrarque for Laure. He hoped Mr. Wilkie would indeed visit it. Also Mr. Wedderburn. Alexander looked at the stars and shifted from foot to foot. It was impossible for him to mount the motorbike before Wilkie. Frederica too looked at the motorbike and remembered her sanguinary defloration. She plucked Alexander's sleeve. She tried, not successfully, to recall something of the pupil-teacher aspect of their relations.

"Alexander. Alexander. I got into Cambridge."

"Good."

"Actually, I got scholarships at both universities."

"Good. That should please your father."

"He's too upset about Marcus."

"I see."

Alexander looked at Wilkie who deliberately did not see him. Wilkie asked Frederica if she had seen the Mediterranean—the

Camargue—Orange? She told him nervously, one eye on Alexander, how she had stayed with one of Mme. Grimaud's innumerable cousins in Orange, had seen Racine's *Britannicus* and a Cocteau ballet on the same subject in the Théâtre Antique. Imagine, she told him, Aricie in ice-cream pink tights and Britannicus in a weird gold curly wig and a little clattering metal skirt. Very Cocteau, said Wilkie, and Alexander buttoned his head very firmly into his Orphic helmet, thus becoming deaf to Frederica's brightness and absurd to look at, globular white anonymity above the beautiful, clean, white-clothed, untouchable long body. He pulled down his visor and folded his arms.

"Well," said Wilkie, grinning broadly. "It was nice, Frederica. We'll drop in one of these days, you'll see. We'll go for a skinny dip one evening. If you're allowed out."

He pulled out the bike and straddled it, followed by Alexander, who inclined his fat head minimally. They wove off through the theater crowd, bending and bowing together. Frederica wondered if Wilkie had chatted to Alexander about all that blood. It was about equally likely and unlikely. She did not really expect to see them again. At the Mas Rose she hoped every day to see them riding down the white stony hillside track.

Mas Cabestainh

Frederica had wanted, but not dared, to ask Alexander how his writing was going. It was not going well. Life at the Mas Cabestainh was ostensibly designed for the enjoyment and production of art. Crowe had bought the house, gray, bullet pocked, near derelict, for a song immediately after the war and had made it, incorporating its farm buildings, expensively unassuming and very comfortable. It had a large sitting room with an open hearth, a refectory dining room with wooden tables and benches, a small library in which silence was observed. The barns, stables, and servants' quarters had been made into more or less monastic cells in which visiting artists or writers could work or sleep off the night's excesses, alone or together. Alexander had a stable room, white-washed, double-doored, with a yellow wooden bed, a green-shuttered window, a woven rug, a writing table, two yellow-stained rush-bottomed upright chairs, and a bookcase. He spent less time there than he meant to. It was a cell, cool and enclosed, whereas from the terrace in front of the sunlit house one could see, sipping wine, the valley of the Rhône away below, lavender fields, olives, vines. On this terrace there was civilized talk, projects for expeditions, a kind of daily life of the mind for which Alexander, in this not unlike Frederica, had longed in a youth unprovided with games of a serious kind. One project of Matthew Crowe's was that Alexander should write a play for the house guests to act, a play about the story of Cabestainh for whom the house had, in a felicitous conjunction at Crowe's twin predilections for violence and civility, been named.

Guillem, or Guillaume de Cabestanh, or Cabestaing, or Cabestan, had loved the lady of Roussillon, Soremonde, Sermonde, or Marguerite, wife of the seigneur Raymond of Roussillon, who, in a fit of jealous rage, had had the troubadour slaughtered and had served his heart to the lady in a dish. Whereupon, declaring that no less precious food should thereafter pass her lips, the lady had, variously, starved herself to death or flung herself from the window, in which case her blood had forever colored the ruddy rocks of Roussillon. Pound tells and retells this tale, in laminated fragments, in the early *Cantos*.

> It is Cabestan's heart in the dish.
> It is Cabestan's heart in the dish?
> No other taste shall change this.

Alexander was excited by Pound's verse, so fluid, so dramatic, so exact. He was excited by the troubadours, who wrote endlessly varied repetitions of inventive metaphors for love, pain, service. He thought he could write Crowe a parody at once elegant and shocking. It turned out to be unexpectedly difficult.

This was partly because he was anxious about his next major work. He was a writer of the fidgety, costive kind whose works are long in the planning, and meticulous in the execution—only at the very end of a project, when the scaffolding, the foundations, the walls and roof and even the plaster were laid down, did spontaneity and delight take over, in the actual play of, play with, words themselves.

He was not only a perfectionist about the form of his work; he held beliefs, again rigid and inhibiting, about its subject matter. He believed that the English drama would be improved by the deliberate tackling of large subjects, subjects of political and philosophical weight. He was in no way a precursor of "committed" drama—it was, in his case, a question of the scope and ambition of understanding. Too much minor modern art was art about art, inward-looking, narcissistic. Alexander was rattled, disturbed in his habits, by instant fame, by being treated as a major dramatist. His correspondents— agents, theaters, drama groups, journalists, students, teachers—treated him as a major writer and waited to see what he would do next. Given the moral seriousness he had already, these expectations intensified his anxiety about his subject. He toyed with the time of Munich, the decisions and failures to decide that had made the world he lived in. But he felt, in a way that must seem absurd now when the conflict in the Falklands is dramatized repeatedly before it is even over, when the widow of an assassinated president is recreated in large in her lifetime on the epic screen, that these events were too close to be seen clearly, too large and foul and complex to be treated with decorum. He had now formed a plan to write about the falsely sunny period before the Great War. He could parody the poetry of grazing cows and vicarage lawns, fox hunting and romantic love. He could quote trench poetry. But this project too hung fire, impeded perhaps by the conflicting duty to Cabestainh, perhaps by sun and wine, perhaps by distance—English lawns seemed far away.

And then he was partly taken over by a piece he neither intended nor wanted to write and which preoccupied him obsessively, the dramatization of the dispute, in the Yellow House in Arles, between Paul Gauguin and Vincent Van Gogh.

This work had begun, like Frederica's limp tales, as a kind of tourism. He had visited Arles and walked along the Alyscamps. The Yellow House was gone, swallowed by the railway, but the nondescript, indefinite area between nineteenth-century railway and the ancient Roman sarcophagi in their Elysian fields was still there. Van Gogh had divided his painting of the Yellow House with a soft, muddy-brown line, and there still was the soft, muddy raised bank of an irrelevant ditch. Crowe had the new edition of the *Letters*, and Alexander borrowed them to read in bed. He also had a copy of

Gauguin's *Avant et Après*, which recounted the episode in the Yellow House from Gauguin's point of view, patronizing, complacent in its nervousness, making sure the world knew who was the great painter, the great influence, the major man.

The impulse to dramatize the events came out of Van Gogh's descriptions of the "electric" arguments of the two. They quarreled about art. They went to Montpellier and quarreled about Rembrandt. "Our arguments are *terribly electric*; we come out of them sometimes with our heads as exhausted as an electric battery after it has run down." Electricity crackled and flashed in the whole relationship, and in Vincent Van Gogh's body, and brain. Gauguin painted Van Gogh painting sunflowers. "Afterwards my face got much brighter, but it [the portrait] was really me, very tired and charged with electricity as I was then."

Gauguin was uneasy. He woke sometimes and found Vincent standing by his bed. "Between two beings, he and I, he like a Vulcan and I boiling too, a kind of struggle was preparing itself . . ." There followed the Christmas episode of the razor threatening, the severed ear, Gauguin's precipitate departure, the incarceration. In the asylum a kind of dark Christianity repossessed Vincent Van Gogh. The surface of the letters to Theo about Gauguin's defection, the disproportionate interest in the whereabouts of Gauguin's fencing gloves, spoke of an anxiety for Gauguin, a Christian concern. Underneath was rage and humiliation. Vincent himself was afraid of the way madness brought back a religious intensity he had felt and transmuted:

> Well, with this mental disease I have, I think of the many other artists suffering mentally and I tell myself that this does not prevent one from exercising the painter's profession as if nothing was amiss.
>
> When I realize that here the attacks tend to take an absurd religious turn, I should almost venture to think that this even *necessitates* a return to the north.

He was afraid, particularly at Christmas, of a recurrence of his despair and terrible visions.

There was much that was intrinsically dramatic. Vincent's position as scapegoat or demon:

A certain number of people here (there were more than 80 signatures) addressed a petition to the mayor (I think his name is M. Tardieu) describing me as a man not fit to be at liberty, or something like that. The commissioner of police or the chief commissioner then gave the order to shut me up again.

I write to you in the full possession of my faculties and not as a madman but as the brother you know.

And the involuntary malice within the desperate attempts to remain on the safe side of the frontier of madness. If Theo was worried about marriage settlements in the event of death, "why do you not just knife your wife and have done with it?" "Indeed I am so glad that if there are sometimes cockroaches in the food here, you have your wife and child at home." So transparent, so furious.

Alexander became obsessed by the yellow chair, of which the yellow chairs in his own cell were close relations, generic descendants, the rush the same, the back the same, the varnish less lemon and ruddier.

He discovered first that it (like the fencing gloves) had been painted in the wake of the Gauguin debacle and as a companion piece to the portrait of Gauguin's empty chair (*Effect of Night*). Gauguin's chair, an ample, armed chair, was painted in the dark against a lamplit green wall "in dark brown-red wood, the seat of greenish rush, and in the place of the absent a lighted candle and two modern novels." The novels, disposed randomly, had, for Van Gogh, as for Henry James, connotations of French naughtiness. They also, for Van Gogh, represented life. After his pastor-father's death he painted his heavy Bible, in dark light near two snuffed candles, looming over one small yellow novel, Zola's *La Joie de Vivre*. In Paris, learning color, with Theo, he painted the beautiful *Still Life with Books*, a profusion of yellow novels on a clear, brilliant pink ground. (And behind these in the imagination the heavy tomes, eaten away and dusty, of the Dutch still-life masters' reminders of the vanity of human wishes, of death.) Gauguin's chair, *Effet de Nuit*, Alexander came to realize, with its nocturnal color scheme of ruddy browns and murky greens, resembled the iniquitous *Night Café* (and by implication the brothels the two painters had haunted in search of subject matter and what else?, scene of Gauguin's triumphs and Vincent's humiliations). "In the *Night Café* I have tried to express the terrible passions of humanity by means of red and green."

And the yellow chair? Blue and yellow, the opposing colors, clean and upright, no erect candle on its seat but a snuffed out, horizontal pipe, light and cleanliness, bare sanity? The grief-stricken old man in blue of the St. Rémy days sits head in hand on just such a shining chair by a fire with fragile flames. These images had what Alexander desired for his own work and did not have—authority. The man could both paint and name a chair, and bring into play his own terrors and hopes and, behind it, the culture of Europe, north and south, the church itself. The yellow chair was the opposite of the insane messianic visions and voices.

A writer is a man haunted by voices. Alexander walking to and from the water tank in Crowe's kitchen-garden, where balloonlike tadpoles, the size of half crowns, dived and plashed their lips, unable to emerge and metamorphose into frogs, was amused sometimes by the counterpoint that wailed in his mind: Cabestan's heart, Vincent's ear, gassed soldiers' throats, Brooke's poppies, the troubadour's lady like rose and gillyflower, Vincent's irises, jealousy rage and fear, fear jealousy and rage, fear and indignation and pity. Sometimes, before he drank the fourth or fifth glass of Côtes-du-Rhône that would incapacitate him, he thought with guilt of the Flanders fields, with impotence of the forests where wolves ranged, with the sense of temptation, secret delight, and energy welling up from unknown sources of Gauguin's cold bluster, of Vincent's two voices. Mostly he went to sleep, then. Sometimes he wrote verse about colors. He did not think of Frederica Potter at all. He was a man whose personal life, though occasionally exigent, never became a siren song.

The most delightful thing about the Mas Rose was the water supply. It came from a source, a spring, farther up the hillside. M. Grimaud showed Frederica how, by building a slate dam here, releasing a little stone floodgate there, he diverted the clear water into its summer channel, a stone-lined gully that ran down beside the house and along its front wall, passing under slabstone doorsteps. Here they washed Vallauris honey-gold dishes and coffee bowls; here, in running water, they dipped and shook salads and peaches. The house was rosy and set into the hill. Frederica slept in a windowless loft that held her suitcase, a camp bed, and no more. She read at night by flashlight, her own little door open onto the sandy hillside. There was not much air; the roof heat persisted from the day. An army of ants marched ceaselessly under the bedhead and sheared away the edges of her dirty underwear with innumerable mandibles. Owls and cicadas screamed and scraped. Mosquitoes whined and bit Frederica's face into a plump, knobbed, pink parody of itself, giving her an unfair look of the acne from which her dryness of flesh and perhaps of character had preserved her.

It was unfortunate that she had seen Alexander. She lacked his detachment and would not even have thought it morally desirable, believing the Byronic tag, "Man's love is of man's life a thing apart: 'tis woman's whole existence." She retreated into clouded vision, only half saw the Ventoux, the Vallauris potteries, the evening games of boules under the plane trees in the timeless village square. She and Marie-Claire and Monique sat, heavy, sulky, self-absorbed, grace-less, while Paul-Marie darted and chattered like a squirrel after the scaly balls and his parents sipped their white port and admired him.

One afternoon, after she had given up hope, stirring aïoli on the doorstep, Frederica heard the crunch of wheels on stones and saw the motorbike winding down the cliff with its two insect heads swaying in harmony above it. It disappeared behind olives and reappeared lower down the hill. Frederica clutched the oily mortar to her breast. Marie-Claire snickered. The bike drew up in the yard under the tree.

"Dear girl, what *have* you done to your face? I hope we're welcome. What a divine setting. For God's sake put down that mortar, you are ruining the front of your dress. I brought Caroline, now not hung over."

Not Alexander. Of course not Alexander.

Wilkie's girl, as Frederica always thought of her—had he not said, in Scarborough, "I've got a girl, you know . . . ," smoothed blown skirts over thin brown legs and tossed her urchin head free of its case. M. Grimaud came from his vegetable patch up the hill, where, with further engineering of irrigation, he produced excellent tomatoes, courgettes, peppers, beans, and salad. He extended a huge hand and invited Wilkie to lunch.

Frederica wondered whether Caroline knew the Scarborough story, and, if so, whether it was known as a joke or as something apologized for. She was, she thought, glad she was no one's "girl," though Caroline, assured in this position and two years into Cambridge, was intimidating. Frederica felt she looked frightful: the oil was sticky and stiff on her breasts, the sun had frizzed her hair, and the mosquitoes deformed her face.

They ate outdoors—sausages, aïoli, vegetables and salad, fresh cheeses, and new, raw, indigestible Gigondas, inky purple. Wilkie discussed the Camargue with M. Grimaud, whose cousin had a domaine there, asked Monique and Marie-Claire politely what they were studying, and elicited more information in half an hour than Frederica had done in several months. He ate vast quantities of aïoli; his firm, plump chin gleamed with it, like a child's, approached with a buttercup in search of an affinity for butter.

Frederica talked edgily to Caroline. Cambridge—eleven men to every woman. Wilkie—a genius—effortless Firsts—but perhaps still ready to give up and make a career in the theater. "He wants to have his cake and eat it," said Caroline, watching him devour olives and radishes and French bread.

"Most of us do," said Frederica dryly. "What will you do. Marry?"

This was, from Frederica, pointedly rude, but Caroline took it complacently, said, "One thing at a time. *First* thing, will Wilkie go back to Cambridge?"

"I hope so. I hope to know *someone* there."

"What's this?" said Wilkie.

"Whether you'll stay at Cambridge," said Frederica.

"What do *you* think?"

"I hope so."

Wilkie grinned. "I expect I shall."

Caroline sulked a little. This did not spoil Wilkie's party. He sampled brandied cherries and admired the irrigation. He walked among the olives and flirted with Frederica, Caroline, Monique, and Marie-Claire while talking folklore seriously with Monsieur. Before he left, he proposed that Frederica join a beach party at Les Saintes-Maries de la Mer, next week. M. Grimaud said that would be very pleasant for her: he would deliver and collect her, and visit his cousin on the domaine.

6

SEASCAPE

Frederica arrived when the beach party at Les Saintes-Maries was already settled in. At some distance from other groups, in those days not numerous, on that beach, it had arranged itself around bright canvas bags and wicker baskets in the part-shade of a fishing boat. In those days also the boats were unchanged since Vincent Van Gogh had spent one week there in June 1888 and had painted them, red and blue, green and yellow, with colored delicate masts erect, and the slanted, tapering yardarms crossing each other on the pale mackerel sky. Their lines were curved and beautiful; they were more instantly recognizable than the cypress or even the chair. They were probably not much changed since long before Vincent Van Gogh: the Phoenician auspicious eyes, white circled dots, were painted on the high prows then as in 1888. Frederica read the names on these prows: *Désirée, Bonheur, Amitié.* By these words she would remember form and color. Words were primary. She stood at the foot of the bare dunes, gripping a string bag of swimming things and a volume of Smollett.

Groups already formed are alarming mostly. Frederica had not come in expectation of enjoying herself. She advanced on them bravely rather than hopefully. You could see they were English, though how this was, since they were mostly gleaming brown and both elegantly and scantily dressed, it would be hard to say. A pinker skin tone under the brown, and then the pristine, nondomestic look this kind of English had—untouched, however untrue that might be. They rested on elbows, or lay stretched like stars, stomachs in sand, smooth heads together, a brown hand lifting a white cigarette to a rose-painted mouth, and a line of malachite green smoke going up into the air, which was not here the intense cobalt of the plain of Orange, but pearl-cream gold, a heavy air, soft and undulating like the pale sand and beyond it the warm, hazed, sand-green sea. The figures were not hard-edged, like the high boats, but soft patches of bright color, impinged on by soft sand.

Two unknown men wore blue, one with a fawn skin, just deeper in color than the sand, cerulean trunks and blackbird-blue hair falling smoothly over one brow. The other, fatter, with stark white skin shadowed, sat upright against the boat in navy shorts and sky-blue poplin shirt. Between these, gold dark, dark gold, and violent pink, lay Lady Rose Martindale, solid but not fat or formless, indeed very woman shaped, in pink-and-brown striped silk bathing suit, with gold hair spattered softly over the brown flesh of her shoulders and whitish sand speckled on the gleam of her thighs where she had rolled from side to side. Crowe and Anthea Warburton lay parallel, Anthea pale only by contrast with Lady Rose's bright darkness, and with the sunburned red earth color of Crowe, who had the look of a man bronzed against nature by willpower and decisive planning, a man whose ruddiness was made for peeling crimson but who had constrained his skin to stay on—even the thin shiny tonsure—and go terra-cotta. His trunks, largely buried between the rolls of his stomach and thighs, were red-purple, a color neither heavier nor lighter than his achieved flesh color, which jangled the eye. Anthea lay as though dancing on the hot folded sand, the pale, lively hair curved outward on the duck-egg blue towel on which her lovely profile rested, the skin darker than the tossed gold, the marvelous bones picked out by clear-cut shadows and glitter of sweat. Her bathing dress was peacock, rippled green and blue, like waves of an illuminated sea.

At the edge of the circle sat Wilkie and his girl, like photographic negatives, Caroline olive dark in a white bikini, hair and skin black to Frederica's dazzled eyes, and Wilkie, blacker still, soot black, except for the neat, white, exiguous triangle of his genitals, the smiling teeth, light striking off the bright black hair and off the huge butterfly-blue sunglasses, reflecting in their inscrutable surfaces pearly sky and sand and pearly sea. The boats stared with their painted eyes and no one else but Wilkie looked up. Gray ash dripped on cream sand.

She was decided to be agreeable and unobtrusive. Her highest ambition was to be by the end of the day simply acceptable, to have done no rushing or crashing, committed no vehemence.

Wilkie said to Crowe, "Here is Frederica," and the two strange men in blue lifted a limp and a firm hand in silent salutation. Crowe sat up and stared at Frederica. Caroline nodded and produced with difficulty a half sound. Anthea Warburton pushed back a strand or two of hair from her mouth and said, "Hi," in a failing voice into the thick air.

Frederica's quick mind's eye saw what Crowe saw: a figure broomstick thin against the dune, splayfooted in sensible sandals, thin shouldered in the provincial flowered sundress, with its white piqué triangles below the straps, butterfly bowed on the small breasts, plain, yes, but not shockingly or brilliantly plain, smart in Calverley, unexceptionable in Nîmes and Bargemon, dowdy in this company. Her hair and skin were now strangely colored. The long red tresses, which in *Astraea* had flowed deranged on her shoulders while her paper skirts were slit by Seymour's scissors, had in the hot sun of Provence slowly crimped, frizzled, and broken off lusterless. They stood out now in a fat triangular fan, with a ginger haze of split ends. Her skin had at one stage, unusual in a redhead, been almost chocolate-brown and silk smooth, but she was a northern redhead, and had passed beyond the russet and the Negro, back to a strange peeled patchwork, toast-cinder brown, radish-crimson, freckled bone and the translucent gray of flaking skin still shifting. At the end of the play she had declared to Crowe her ambition to be an actress. Crowe had told her to get a new face. This glaring thin skull, striped and quilted with bites, was hardly an improvement. He smiled benign.

"Well, Frederica, I hear you are employed as a nanny. It seems most unlikely. *Do* sit down."

Frederica sat down. They all breathed slowly, some with shut eyes, some with open. Everything there was slow, slow; a long minute went by, and no one spoke.

"Not exactly a nanny," said Frederica. No one displayed any interest in what she really was. Crowe made known Lady Rose, who had been a friend of the Woolfs in their later years and was writing an elegant book on cats, and the fat and thin men, who were Vincent Hodgkiss, a philosopher, and Jeremy Norton, a poet. Crowe lit another cigarette for Lady Rose. Vincent Hodgkiss observed in a tight pleasant voice that it was hard to determine the colors of objects in this light, which seemed opaque, though hot and dry. Frederica said obviously that the sky and the sea and the boats were uncannily like Van Gogh, and Hodgkiss said that of course they would never have seen them in this way before he saw them. Wilkie said it was Alexander she ought to talk to about Van Gogh, and Hodgkiss said Alexander was an excellent example of what he was talking about, the effect of this light, the difficulty of fixing colors. What color would they say Alexander was now, in this light? Frederica could not see Alexander at all; indeed, she had noted he was not there. She stared around and around now at colorless air and sand as though he might rise from them like a mirage. No, the sea, said Wilkie, and she looked out, at the *Stella Maris*, anchored off the coast, and there he stood on the curving prow, pale on the pale sky, with a triangular patch of yellow like a painted sun—Van Gogh chrome, not Renaissance gilt—between his thighs and his limbs creamy brown like the foam on the new cappuccino coffee. And the long heavy hair was creamy too, in the filtered sun, only just darker than the sky. He rode a moment, and then dived into the shifting, opaque water, which ran away from him in rays, like jewels flashing, opals you might call them, emeralds, lapis, rubies, sapphires, as Van Gogh had said of the stars reflected in that same sea in June 1888.

Had she got swimming things? Wilkie said. She shifted her string bag in her rigid lap. "Come on in," said Wilkie. So she stood up, and pulled down her pants, and rolled on her dark brown bathing costume, under her dress, as she had done on seaside holidays, and then pulled that off too. She was aware that this process exposed first her buttocks and then her breasts, fleetingly, to Crowe, who had seen them and more than seen them, already, but not in circumstances either of them, she took it, cared to remember. She walked with Wilkie cranelike on burning sand to the water's edge. Alexander was disporting himself about the boat. Frederica strode into the water, followed by sauntering Wilkie.

She was a reasonable swimmer. She struck out forcefully toward Alexander, which seemed natural, since the boat at anchor was the only thing to swim toward or away from or around on the flat Mediterranean. Alexander now floated near it, on his back, arms outstretched, hair waving under pale green water. She bobbed down and came up more or less inside his embrace, her crimson, browned, and pallid face peering like a floating decapitated head in his direction. He brought knees to chin, turned gracefully, and looked at her, both their chins on water. She stared unwavering. She had a nasty habit of simply appearing and staring at him. There had been a time when he had been with the then-desired Jenny in the back of a car on the moor at Goathland. There had been a time when she had stared from Crowe's knee, before Crowe's study fire, out at Alexander on the Long Royston terrace. And now in the sluggish sea of the Camargue and the mouths of the Rhône.

"So you're here," he stated, with no apparent note of acceptance or annoyance. She stared.

"Are you here long?"

"I was asked to a lunch party."

"I see."

"Do you wish I'd go away?"

"Not particularly."

"Good." Still staring.

"But I wish you wouldn't stare. It isn't nice. I've never liked it."

"I don't mean to stare." She performed a somersault, shook her head, and said toward the *Stella Maris*, "I just like looking at you; that's what it is. As you know."

Alexander's skin crept, possibly with pleasure. To cover this quickening he pointed out, "You've got badly burned. Someone should have warned you. With your coloring."

The black-and-orange skull grinned. "They did. This has taken months and months to achieve. I was a smooth black girl. Then I peeled. I thought I was past it but obviously not. I'm sorry I look horrid."

"No skin off my nose," said Alexander, who veered between the absurdly avuncular, the undignified childish—and something else—whenever he allowed Frederica to trap him into talk. He crawled away toward the boat and swung himself up. He thought of diving off again before she, swimming doggedly after, was up. But he gave her a hand and they sat side by side on the hot wood, pouring seawater, steaming.

"Are you having fun?" said she.

"On the whole. That is, yes. Of course."

"Are you writing?"

"Not as much as— That is, yes. But the wrong things. Or I think, the wrong things."

"What things?"

"Oh, Frederica." He shifted his damp bottom, and the planks hissed. "Come on. Don't catechize people on a swimming party."

"I want to know. I don't see you much. I really want to know. Why did they say you would tell me about Van Gogh?"

"Did they? Well, I could. Perhaps I will," he fatally added, standing up. "But now I'm swimming."

"Can I come?"

"I can hardly stop you."

He dived, and swam, and turned to see her enter the water, neat as a needle, if inelegant. Her curious visage reminded him of something but he could not think what. She looked flayed, or striped. Tiger, tiger. Not that, despite the staring. More simian. There he was, thinking about Frederica Potter, at Les Saintes-Maries de la Mer. He still believed this was an irritating aberration. She bobbed up at his side like a terrier, treading water.

"Are you writing about Provence, then?"

"Not exactly. Not intentionally. Not about Provence itself exactly. Oh, come off it, Frederica, try to *enjoy* yourself."

"I am." She was.

They swam slowly together round the boat. They did not play water games; he dared not. But she came close on a corner as he turned and humped his body to avoid a rope, and under the colorless many-colored water their naked legs brushed weightlessly. It was still there. It was still there, they both thought, she with greed and apprehension, he with alarm, a sense of injury, and an animal redirection of intention. She said something he couldn't catch.

"What?"

"Dolphin-like. You."

"I like dolphins."

"So do I. They sing. Melodious hootings and echoings. I heard them on the wireless."

"Can't you just *be* in a place, Frederica?"

"No. I think. I have to *think*. So do you."

"No, I don't. To my shame, in many ways, I don't."

But he did. He was very tempted to tell her about *The Yellow Chair*. The whole problem, the way the plays had got wound into each other, would interest her; she would see it was a problem. He turned on his back and swam away, jerky and splashing. She swam after, outside the rainbow of his thrashing. Inshore, Wilkie, lying lazily along the water, propped by flickering hands, watched the to and fro of their dancing and circling and smiled to himself. At the edge of the water Wilkie's girl cried out that it was lunch, they were going to eat lunch.

Lunch was good: little cold herb omelettes, raw smoked ham, huge pumpkin-indented scarlet tomatoes, black olives with garlic and pepper, glistening, wrinkled and hot. There was a lot of red wine, Côtes du Ventoux, and a lot of good crusty bread. There was a sharp, fresh goat cheese and rose-orange Cavaillon melons, green-gold like legendary serpents outside, into whose fluted pink hollows Crowe ceremoniously poured pink, sweet Beaumes-de-Venise wine. Sand got into things, of course, and three or four wasps buzzed, straddled and chewed, could be seen chewing, the meat and the fruit. Frederica drank a lot of wine and said nothing, but watched everyone in turn, charged with unsatisfied curiosity as they lay and lazily tossed ideas between them. She did not give their talk her whole attention. Alexander had much if not most of that. He lay in the sun, near Lady Rose and Matthew Crowe, not near Frederica, and seemed intent on the talk, which was mostly talk between Hodgkiss, Wilkie, and Crowe about the perception and representation of color, on which Hodgkiss was writing a paper in aesthetics, and on which Wilkie had conducted his experiment with the rainbow sunglasses. The latter was now staring at the Van Gogh boats and the milky sea and sky through poppy-scarlet lenses, which Frederica thought was perverse, although she wished she had the courage to ask for a moment to put them on, to see all this.

Hodgkiss and Wilkie talked about the nature of color. Hodgkiss's manner displeased Frederica; he had a mannered Oxford voice, elided words, and used the pronoun "one" frequently. He had the voice of a thin, languid man and the body of a stocky, alert one. He had been reading the notes of Wittgenstein, he said, who before his death had been working on the relation between the private, sensuous experience of color and the universal language of color words with which we appear to be able to communicate it. He spoke of a *mathematics* of color, Wittgenstein, a *Farbmathematik*; one *knew* saturated red or yellow, once experienced, as one knew the nature of a circle or the square on the hypotenuse. Crowe put in that the symbolists of Van Gogh's time had supposed there was a universal language of color, a primary language, a divine alphabet of colors and forms. Something like that, said Hodgkiss. Wittgenstein asked if there could be a natural history of color, like the natural history of plants and answered himself that such a natural history was, unlike that of plants, outside time. Alexander said that Van Gogh in his letters in French very rarely made his color adjectives agree with the nouns they qualified. The result was that they could almost be read as *things* more real than the things they qualified, a pattern of eternal forms from another world, not part of the solid world of cabbages and pears—yellow and violet, blue and orange, red and green. Wilkie said it was known to psychologists that certain colors had certain psychological effects: red, and also orange and yellow increase muscular tension and the flow of adrenalin; blue and green slow the heartbeat, lower the temperature. The conversation moved on to the human habit of color mapping.

Crowe said there was an old passage in Proust where he associated letters of the alphabet with colors. He claimed that the letter "i" was red—in Gérard de Nerval's *Sylvie, la Vraie Fille du Feu*, for instance.

Lady Rose immediately said no, no, "i" was ice blue and Anthea said no, silvery green, and Crowe said women's interest in color depended on what color showed their bodies to best advantage; a woman would always decorate a room in terms of her own skin tone and eyes. He asked the others about the letter "i": Hodgkiss said it brought to mind Henry James's simile for the dress of Sarah Pocock, "scarlet like the scream of someone falling through a skylight." Crowe himself said "silver," Alexander said "sage," Wilkie said "inky," and Caroline muttered "green." Frederica said she did not make associations between colors and other systems like alphabets or days of the week. Perhaps, she said to Wilkie, she was color insensitive as she was tone deaf, if he remembered, and he said no, you have little synaesthesia and vestigial sensory responses you don't encourage, that's all.

Jeremy Norton said nothing. Years later Frederica read a poem by him about that beach, a neat poem, orchestrating color adjectives, unmodified, against indefinite objects and asking subtly how language fitted the world. But today she decided he looked too much like a poet to be a good one, a view at variance with her view of Hodgkiss, who looked too unlike what he was, profound thinker, Oxford don, to be satisfactory either.

Lady Rose went to sleep. Crowe lovingly arranged the wheel of her straw hat to cover her face. Anthea kicked the sand with perfect, active little toes, and Wilkie's girl lay down in the shadow of the boat, pulling him down after her, putting an arm over his sweaty waist, claiming. Crowe leaned back and snuffled a snore. Anthea began to oil her skin. Alexander, unusually lively after a meal, proposed a walk, and did not know if he was glad or sorry when only Frederica accepted.

"Have you seen the church, Frederica?"

"No. I don't know who the Saintes-Maries were, or why there are more than one."

They mounted the white dunes and set off toward the town square and church, past a few white cottages. At that time the Camargue had not been invaded by the tourists, who instigated the establishment of mournful-looking groups of tethered, bony horses in American-style corrals, souvenir stalls with gardien hats, and gaucho hats and Texan sombreros, little cotton peaked caps, with Mickey Mouse or pink flamingos on them. Nor had the later overlapping visitation of hippies of the sixties taken place, who had followed the gypsy processions, of which Alexander now told Frederica, and stayed and sung and smoked and loved and shat on the white beaches, so that the pale sand came to resemble road dirt anywhere.

In the sixties any vaguely holy and distant place became heaped and congested with the bodies of the seekers of the holy and distant. Frederica at that time wrote an essay on overpopulation, relics of individualism, the collective soul and Glastonbury. That was before Stonehenge, in 1980, became enclosed in a concentration camp cage, designed to keep people out, not in, and that fence was built before a Frenchman proposed to preserve the crumbling Sphinx by encasing him/her/it in a transparent plastic skin. A world was coming in which it would almost certainly never again be possible to walk quietly, as Frederica and Alexander walked, through the village where Van Gogh tramped and set up his easel in the clean dust.

St. Mary Jacobus and St. Mary Salome, in some versions accompanied by St. Mary Magdalene and in all by their black servant, Sarah, had sailed to this coast from Palestine, Alexander told Frederica, after the death of Christ. They had been miraculously wafted to this place after days without food or water in an open boat. Sarah had joined them through another miracle, a cloak thrown by Mary Jacobus that upheld her feet on the water. Every year the saints—all three—were taken down to the sea and ritually dipped into it; every year the gypsies from all over France gathered to celebrate this bathing and rebirth. The gypsies' patron saint was Sarah; it was thought she might bear some relation in their minds to a deity of their own, an oriental deity, Sara le Kâli.

"Kali the destroyer," said Frederica knowledgeably, who in fact knew little more of this terrifying deity than her name and brief tag. "Goddesses rising from the sea. Like Venus. I see what they mean when they say the Mediterranean countries have never missed out on a female god. It makes a change."

But she was put out—not disappointed but made uneasy—by the images of the Maries in the church. It is an uncompromising fortress-like church, old, high, square, with no elaboration of aisle or transept, bare, which chimed with Frederica's northern sense of fitness, and yet, in its dark, after the bright sun, haunted by things her blood rejected—racks of fragile spiked flames of votive candles, elaborate china and metal plaques, and pictures offering thanks for favors obtained, the smell of old wax and lingering incense muffling the smell of stone. The sacred images of the two Maries leaned out awkwardly from a plinth on a balustrade. Both had sweet, round, pink-cheeked china-doll faces; both were crowned with wreaths of globular white silk flowers, wound with pearls. Both were dressed in silk floss, tinsel and gauze, pink and pale blue. Both smiled thoughtlessly. Frederica was irresistibly reminded of the two dolls leaning lifelessly on the doll's house dresser, staring, in *The Tale of Two Bad Mice*. They were the first such images she had seen—the Grimauds, like many Nîmois, were staunchly Protestant. She looked at Alexander for guidance; he said that the image of black Sarah was in the crypt. They went down.

Sarah was different. Her carved, dark, fine-nosed wooden face had both austerity and arrogance or contempt, something indeed oriental, though her flounces and veils were the same frothy pastels as those of the upstairs saints. Around her burned iron-spiked circles of tapering candles, yellow bright in the dark. Before her lay heaps of flowers—she was the beloved, the tended saint—dying gladioli, eternal silk-blown roses, *immortelles*. Behind her on the altar was a reliquary in which Frederica could see through glass a bone or two—a shin, a forearm? It was like seeing that female body preserved whole in sand in the British Museum, as one feels it should not be, its reddish leathery skin peeling from its temples, crispings of dead gingery hair over its ears. That woman is many English children's first encounter with death, lying there knees to chin, folded, flaking, tendons taut. The thing itself. Image and bones, altar and woman, half doll, half idol, iron spikes, flame light on the smoke-stained roof. Let's get out into the sun, said Frederica, let's go.

After they had left the church they were a little embarrassed. Alexander, who took refuge from awkwardness in the purveying of information, told Frederica about other Mediterranean goddesses.

He told her Ford Madox Ford's delightful story of the portrait-sculpture of Our Lady of the Castle from St. Etienne des Grès. The Virgin, Ford relates, appeared to a young shepherd in the Alpilles who was chiseling a rock, and remained while he carved her portrait. "When it was done she expressed her complete satisfaction with the statue both as a portrait and as a work of art,—I particularly asked the Bishop about that last point.—There at once was presented to the world the final canon of aesthetics." Ford set out to see this cynosure and found her so wrapped and swaddled in lace robes and veiling that he could see no trace of figure or countenance. And then, one day, he came to her church and saw a great gold crown on one chair, billows of lace on another, "two beetle-like old ladies washing something in a pewter receptacle . . ."

"And the image," Alexander quoted, "was a rude, carved piece of reddish rock." A primitive, such as Gaudier-Brzeska emulated, such as the peasant Virgin would have recognized. Cybele and Venus, Alexander said, were worshiped as conical stones. How beautiful, how amazing, Frederica exclaimed, associating the red rock of Roussillon with Alexander explaining Rodin's Danaïde to her with his perfect, respectful, abstract sensuality. Alexander told her about the Venus of Arles, who had been dug up in the Roman circus there, classically graceful with both her arms, holding up the golden or marble apple. He quoted Van Gogh. "There is a Venus of Arles, just as there is a Venus of Lesbos, and one still feels the youth of it, in spite of all ..."

"Ah yes, Van Gogh," said Frederica. Was he writing about Van Gogh?

They sat in a café and ordered citrons pressés and Alexander told Frederica about the importunate play, about the evanescent summer of 1914, about Cabestainh. Frederica said she could not see what he was hesitating about, he *must* write *The Yellow Chair*, it was *alive*, wasn't it? They talked about how to write *The Yellow Chair*, whether to make it stark and classical by keeping the unities, restricting the action to the terrible days of the battle with Gauguin, or whether to make it episodic and epic, to introduce Theo at least and maybe other figures, even the looming pastor from Nuenen. Frederica said to Alexander, before he could say it to her, that there was an intrinsic problem in writing about artists, for how could he dramatize the battle with the colors and forms as opposed to the whore and the rival, the father, the brother, the nephew Vincent Van Gogh? They got excited. Alexander's mind shifted from conflict over his intentions to certainty that *The Yellow Chair* was what he was writing. (Paradoxically the release of tension enabled him in the next week to run up, turn out, patch together, a poetic melodrama about Cabestainh with which the house guests had some civilized fun.)

Was it at this moment that some reciprocal need established an understanding that they two were friends, would know each other for a long part of a lifetime? Hardly then, though it did cross Frederica's mind that sex inhibited talk and that to be talked to by Alexander was a pleasure not readily to be forgone. He did not touch her until the end of the day when he stroked the frizzled hair briefly and said, "Thank you," meaning it. She went home to her windowless attic, sweltered and turned, remembering Ford's red-stone Virgin with intense pleasure, plotting *The Yellow Chair*, remembering the yellow triangle of Alexander's trunks on the prow of the *Stella Maris*. They did not meet again, that summer.

Arles, June 1888. To Emile Bernard.

I spent a week at Saintes-Maries, and to get there I drove in a diligence across the Camargue with its vineyards, moors, and flat fields like Holland. There, at Saintes-Maries, were girls who reminded me of Cimabue and Giotto—thin, straight, somewhat sad and maybe mystic. On the perfectly flat sandy beach little green, red, blue boats, so pretty in shape and color that they made one think of flowers . . .

What I should like to find out is the effect of an intenser blue in the sky. Fromentin and Gérôme see the soil of the south as colorless, and a lot of people see it like that. My God, yes, if you take some sand in your hand, if you look at it closely and also water, and also air, they are all colorless, looked at in this way. *There is no blue without yellow and without orange*, and if you put in blue, then you must put in yellow, and orange too, mustn't you? Oh well, you will tell me that what I write to you are only banalities.

7

A BIRTH

I

April had come in Blesford, to go back a little. The sun was just not cold. There were spring flowers on the altar. Marcus was restive but nobody noticed because of the idea of Stephanie's baby. Stephanie looked calmer and calmer, because this was her nature and because she was almost reduced now to immobility. What had been swimming and floating and turning was now tightly packed and bone grinding, occasionally lurching round with independent force, pushing at the now-almost-inelastic walls of her body with an urgency that left her gasping for breath and dizzy. Now she was not sailing, she was weighted, and trod splayfooted and with difficulty. Living became absorbed in waiting, and she was not waiting patiently. She had lost her autonomy. Something was living her life; she was not living.

She was afraid. Not of the birth itself, which she had thought out carefully, but of peripheral indignities inflicted by hospitals—enemas and razors—over which she wept slow tears now and then. There was no point, she told herself, in fearing birth, which most women endured and most now survived, and which had a fixed term to it, say, forty-eight hours at most. One could set oneself to endure forty-eight hours of almost anything, she told herself. Women at the clinic had shared horror stories, to which she only half listened, of breach birth and ripping forceps. These things were better faced if they came, when they came. She had read a book about natural childbirth —she turned, in her generation, to books rather than to her mother— and had been horrified by the author's accounts of unnatural alternatives. She made no effort to perform the relaxation exercises prescribed by the book. She had always been confident in her self-possession in her own body. She imagined women were not so civilized that they had no natural sense of what to do with things that happened to everyone as imperatively as eating and excreting. If it was natural to relax, she would relax, when the time came. But because of the enema and razor she once told Daniel she would rather the baby were born at home. Daniel looked horrified, said how would they forgive themselves if something went wrong, and added how could she think of the baby being born in the house with Marcus and his mum hanging around. Stephanie saw that these two, in another way, would be as unsettling as enemas and nurses. She could not, out of a kind of *pudeur*, mention enemas to Daniel. She gave up the argument.

Marcus heard her singing. He stood on the corner of the stairs, listening to her singing in the kitchen through a purposeful clatter of pans. She sang "Abide with Me." Potters only had hymns available on the rare occasions when, tunelessly, they sang. Marcus couldn't remember when he had last heard her singing. He came soundlessly downstairs, behind Mrs. Orton's back in the fat armchair.

Her back hurt, and the pain ran around under the weight like one of the iron bonds around the faithful servant's heart in the Grimm fairy tale. She went on singing. Her head had suddenly cleared; she had decided to make bread for Daniel, which lately she hadn't done. She had read all about the upsurge of adrenaline at the onset of labor, and had forgotten it now, because her head was clear. She bent to get out bread tins, and climbed on a stool to reach a jar of flour. The iron band tightened and relaxed as she stepped down. She came to the end of "Abide with Me" and embarked with brio on "Lead Kindly Light." Marcus put his head round the kitchen door.

" 'I was not ever thus,' " she sang, " 'nor prayed that thou'—Marcus, what are you doing?"

"I heard you singing."

"I can sing if I like in my own kitchen. Do you want to help to make bread?"

"If you like," said Marcus, moving in sideways.

"You can start the yeast in that glass bowl. I've got backache. It'll have to be dried yeast. One of those little packets and two teaspoons of the sea salt and about half a pint of tepid water. 'I loved to choose and see my path but now Lead thou—me—on.' " She poured flour into the scale pan, humming, stopped to catch breath, and bent to pull out a large earthenware bowl. Marcus stood over the kettle, concentrating too much on "tepid." " 'I loved the garish day and spite of fears Pride ruled my will. Remember *not* past years . . .' "

She brushed a floury hand across her brow, and pain hit her, pure and clear like a note in music, spreading up and out from the disturbance in the spine, singing, diminishing. She was uncharacteristically slow in apprehension, turned back, after catching her breath, to the flour, to make a well in the center of the mound. Marcus looked at her flushed face and bright eyes uneasily; he sensed disturbance, without being able to define it. No disturbance, in his world, could be good. He stirred the yeast, sniffing its sour, live smell, watching it bubble, like a living creature under mud. It was of course a living creature. He stirred, and it sighed.

"Pour it in here," said Stephanie. They bent their heads together over the bowl, and she stirred with a knife until suddenly the pain pulled again, even clearer, and she caught the edge of the table, feeling this time the powerful pull of the muscles as well, contracting inside her without any signal of will or even acquiescence from her. "Oh, dear," said Stephanie faintly, and looked blindly at Marcus, who backed away. "I think—" she said tentatively. Marcus was now behind the cooker. "I think—" she repeated, as the pain relaxed its clutch and she was momentarily self-possessed again. It was no use trying to get help from Marcus. She walked out of the kitchen and saw Mrs. Orton dozing in the armchair. Mrs. Orton was a woman. Over the last months she had several times recounted Daniel's birth, a monodrama with its single character, brave and persecuted by men, authorities, and inadequate nurses. She was not sure Mrs. Orton could be any help. She said to her, too, "I think—" and Mrs. Orton looked at her blankly, thinking where to start to complain.

"I think I should go to the hospital." Stephanie finished a reasonable, innocuous sentence. Mrs. Orton continued to look blank and even, after thought, informed Stephanie that it wasn't the usual day for the clinic. Stephanie said no, but she felt pain. Mrs. Orton, with an access of cussedness, pointed out that Stephanie wasn't due for another two and a half weeks and that first babies were always late. Stephanie, who had been told this, wondered if she was wrong, and began submissively to go back to the kitchen. Lots of women got odd pains, said Mrs. Orton authoritatively. Marcus in the kitchen looked horrified, opened his mouth speechlessly, closed it in despair. Caught between them Stephanie was suddenly gripped again, pulled almost off her feet. She leaned, clutching the doorframe, catching her breath, one hand feeling her hard side crawl upward. And no show, nor waters broken, stated Mrs. Orton, without asking, determined to deny. Stephanie felt obscenely naked between these two. There would be no help from either. She panted and stood, until she was released again, when she went to the telephone and dialed 999. As soon as she had finished speaking—even a little before—Mrs. Orton began again, informing Stephanie that even if she was right she was silly, she'd have hours and hours to go, she'd be miserable in one of them hospital rooms all day, better wait till things were really on the move ...

Stephanie got herself past her mother-in-law and up the stairs again. She hadn't packed the statutory suitcase. Now she began: nightdress, hairbrush, toothbrush, soap, Wordsworth, *War and Peace, Arabella, Friday's Child.* If Wordsworth was not right, who? She desperately added Eliot's *Four Quartets.* The doorbell rang. No one could be heard opening it. She closed the suitcase, drops of sweat standing on her brow, and couldn't straighten herself for pain, which hurt and twisted this time, rather than singing, because she was at the wrong angle, because she was tense. Grimly, she hoisted the suitcase and descended. Marcus was coming slowly and obliquely round Mrs. Orton's chair. She opened the door and ambulance men came in. She carried the suitcase to them and said she would get her coat.

"This young man will get your coat."

"It's all right—"

"You keep still, luv. This young man'll be happy."

Marcus fetched her coat. The ambulance men asked if she could walk; she said yes and had to be propped and almost lifted. Like other, more ordinary journeys, it was better once begun.

At Calverley General she was helped somewhat forcefully out of the ambulance and put into a wheelchair. Bright-eyed with adrenaline, she objected to this. She wanted to walk, could walk, she said, it was better. The ambulance men said solidly that they were not allowed to let her walk, and pushed her, rattling, up ramps, through long disinfected corridors. Under her chin, in this chair, the peak of her humped belly rose, contracted, subsided. She hiccuped. They came to the labor ward.

The next bit was, as she had feared, undignified. Set to clamber onto a high, hard, shelflike bed, she felt things grind, pull, and tear inside her. Water ran down her legs; a little nurse in a billiard-table-green overall and tight bulbous white cuffs, above the elbows, mopped at this and peered between Stephanie's legs through misted glasses. The glasses, Stephanie noticed with detached accuracy, made her round bunlike face plainer than it need be; they had flyaway gilded wings rising toward her semicircular little brows. She addressed Stephanie as "mum" and did not address her head at all, issuing instructions about undressing and turning this way and that with her eyes and ears on the hard, pale hump. A superior nurse, in pale purple and white stripes, did come round and peer kindly at Stephanie's face while her naked arms were being inserted into a drafty gown of white sheeting, tied inadequately, with some tapes missing, down her spine. She explained about the shaving and the enema, and Stephanie, who believed in good manners, waited until she had her breath and said it was all right, she knew about those. She added that she was afraid of the enema, she was sorry. She hoped that to say she was afraid would, as often happened, make both the fear and the thing feared easier to handle. She wished the nurses were older. Both of them seemed younger than she was, and she sensed a certain tension under their brisk cheeriness. They came with a metal kidney bowl, soapy water, and a very cold man's razor, rolled back the exiguous white gown, and scraped off the pubic fuzz, creating raw patches in the creases inside Stephanie's legs, leaving those parts of her that were not hot and damp cold and damp, interfering—as they were repeatedly to do—with the rhythms of the pain, causing it to jerk and waver rather than to sing severely as it had. They put cold hands, and colder silver funnels, on the ridges and plains of that stretched hump, and Stephanie wanted to cry out, to shake them off, and was too polite to do more than knit her brows. They timed contractions, said she was doing "fine," and administered the enema. Stephanie then felt local inflammation and irritation almost every-where, and also panic fear. Obedient and dripping, she swung herself off the high couch and plodded to the bathroom where the water was running and the lavatory waited. She wondered how, why, if she could not be allowed to go on foot along corridors, she could be left alone helpless in lavatory and bathroom. All sorts of different pains, eddying across each other like curled-back waves at high tide, like choppy crosscurrents in estuaries, tore at her. She sat, waiting for the fury of the enema to spend itself, and wept a little, quietly, in case anyone should hear. There was a kind of relief when the misery in her bowels had died down. Gingerly, she took off the gown, which anyway hung off the front of her, leaving her largely naked. She stepped into the bath, and rubbed the shaved places in warm water, sighing a little, feeling, hearing, or thinking she heard, bones cracking and splitting in her pelvis. The floor of the bath was cold and gritty, possibly with Ajax. She came out fast, too fast, was caught by another swing of pain as she moved her leg over the side and hung, heavy, absurd, trapped, her damp blonde curls sticking to her cheek and the nape of her neck. The nurses came in and supported her, tied up the exiguous tapes, gave her a toweling robe, and put her back in the wheelchair.

They put her in a bare room with a white bed, a bedside table, a chair, a carafe, and a very small white canvas sling on tubular metal struts, which she only slowly understood, as she climbed docile onto that new bed, to be a cot. And it was only when she saw that small cot that she understood for the first time what was happening—that this was not an ordeal that had gripped her to test her, that two people were here. That this was happening to two people. That someone had to get out. That it was inconceivable that the female body could ever be open or elastic enough to allow anything the size of a baby to come out. That nevertheless there must be an end—it *must* . . . The nurses were about to leave her alone in this room. She said with the first agitation she had shown that she must have her books; they must bring her books. Books? they said.

"In the suitcase."

"They don't bring suitcases to the delivery rooms."

"*I must have my books.*"

"We'll see . . . when anyone has time . . . We're very busy . . . four mums came in at once; we're off our feet. Which book do you want, then?"

"All my books. How do I know. The Wordsworth. All of them. Particularly Wordsworth."

"Wordsworth?"

"Poems. If you've time."

"Wordsworth's poems." The green nurse seemed blank. "I'll do what I can," she said, placating.

"How long?" said Stephanie.

"I couldn't say. You're doing fine. First babies always take longer. Try and relax."

They left her alone. To try and relax. With a bulbous bell push on a long furry flex depending from the ceiling, no instructions about when she would need to ring it and when, as the English require, she must be silent and uncomplaining. At first she lay dutifully and stared at the white ceiling, slowly turning her head to take in the fact that it was an unusually sunny day, that small, shining white clouds, light rimmed, were being blown across a blue sky, that she was on the ground floor with a part-open window that looked onto a closed courtyard of grass. She no longer had her watch, which had gone with her clothes; she thought it must be mid-morning, even midday, but was not sure. She thought for the first time of Daniel. She had not told Daniel she was here. This was because of Mrs. Orton and Marcus, who between them prevented any normal converse at all. It ought to have been possible to rely on those two to tell Daniel, but it was not. She began to worry, and then the pain took over. There was something ridiculous about lying there on one's back while it pulled —and something unnecessarily painful. She rolled sideways with effort, inducing rippling cramps. She wished she had Wordsworth. She swung her legs off the bed, in the next lucid interval, and walked to the window. The air was cold and clear and amazingly fragrant. She peered out. All around the wall, under the windows, were wallflowers—small, velvet-brown, straw-gold, rust-colored shabby flowers, and their warm, generous smell moved on the air. She breathed, holding the window frame, and then, obeying some powerful instinct, began to march up and down the room rhythmically, turning on her heel at the walls, head up, nostrils flared. The next pain, when it came, was possible to weave into the rhythm of this tramping, to time between wall and wall and back again. She began to observe it almost from outside, listening to its rise and fall, letting it make its way. The adrenaline, lost with the enema, flooded back. She tried to recall the "Immortality Ode," which was yet another rhythm. The Rainbow comes and goes. And lovely is the Rose. She strode on. When they opened the door she did not immediately stop, and then came to a halt, conscious of their eyes on her flapping gown and naked buttocks.

"Get back into bed, please, dear, now. You shouldn't be out of bed."

"It's easier, walking."

"You'll make it harder for yourself, using your energy up. You'll contract your muscles. Try and relax. Come on now."

"Look. If I use *these* muscles, I relax *those* . . . It hurts less."

"Don't be silly, dear. Get back into bed like a good girl."

She stood stupidly, and the pain choked again like a suffocating net, as it did when they interfered with its liveliness, so that she swayed, and had to be helped to the bed, where they listened again with their silver funnel, put their hands inside her and made notes, while she smiled politely and the pain rustled jagged and uncomfortable and died away. They timed this meager contraction wisely, told her she'd a long time to go, and prepared to leave again. If she felt she needed to bear down, they said, she was to ring.

She had no idea what this need might feel like, or how easy it might be to identify. It was somehow not possible to ask. She did ask if she could have Wordsworth and her watch and was answered as before: they were short staffed, they would try, she was to be good. When they were gone she had lost her sense of her own rhythms, wanted desperately to get out and walk again and yet was afraid of being reprimanded for being a naughty girl. And she had forgotten, or not been given time, to mention Daniel. After thought, she got up on her hands and knees, moaning softly, swaying from side to side. The pain resumed its clear, relentless pattern, and she worked with it, hot and tiring. No doctor had come. She supposed that was all right. The pain gripped like a claw. The day wore on, and she rocked, and then, since no one came, walked some more, breathing very hard. Through the window with the warm sweet flower smell came the sound of someone screaming regularly and on a rising pitch. Stephanie heard herself thinking that it would be helpful, but not English, not good manners, to make a noise like that.

The desire to "bear down," when it came, proved to be unlike any sensation she had experienced, and immediately recognizable for what it was. It had the appalling, uncontrollable nature of severe diarrhea pains but was otherwise different, in that nothing knotted. Something heavy and hard and huge inside her opened her out like a battering ram and the pain was no longer defined and separate from her but total, grasping, heating, bursting the whole of her, head, chest, wrought and pounded belly, so that animal sounds broke from it, grunts, incoherent, grinding clamor, panting sighs. She managed to roll herself back onto the bed, during this, and clutch the pear-shaped bell. Her vision filled with nasturtium pale scarlet, and then with a curtain of blood. The purple nurse returned. Stephanie moaned wildly that it was coming back; the pain, like an incoming tide, abated a little, rippled back, gathered itself and sprang, *heavy*.

She was a woman who had thought about the ambivalence of female imagining of internal spaces. The moon, whatever we believe about its real size, appears to us to be a silver disk about a foot across and two miles distant. The womb, imagined, can appear to be a tiny crumpled purse to hold half a crown, or silent underground caverns, receding endlessly, corrugated, velvet, blood dark, gentian dark. Blood before it meets the air is blue. And the vagina, which grips a tampon securely, which admits a man who can, a large man like Daniel, blindly explore the lost and charged tip of its cul-de-sac, a pocketed shaft with elastic muscles—how can that narrow sheath take a furious blunt block that appears to the perception of inner spaces to be larger than the body itself, to be breaking out as it expands and can no longer be contained? The spine, Stephanie's shrinking mind stated, is a plane, *flat* on the bed, as though by butchery the belly is severed and the flanks fall. Beneath the helpless trunk a whole wall, a box-side of flesh and cracking bone seemed to rear and expand between the bursting thing and the air. There were now two nurses, holding the legs up, peering under. Some relief could be found by moving the feet rapidly in circles, but one nurse slapped these and reiterated the admonition about not contracting muscles. She was amazed at the rage she felt. She wished the women dead for holding her so uncomfortably in an unnatural position. Her head thrashed from side to side. The thing launched itself again against its prison walls and she thought of time. How long was this to last? As long as the walking and singing? She had been wrong. It could *not* be endured. It rose and drove and the brain throbbed and banged, and from somewhere, even as they cried hold back, don't push, she found the desperate energy to end the pain by increasing it, to *tear through* the flesh wall, and cried out, loud, groaning, defeated, as the body split in half and on her soaked thigh she felt, incredulous, a warm wet ball, with its own fluttering pulse, not hers.

Hold back, they said, more urgently, and she found she now

could. Silence flooded back after the bloodstorm; at the stretched entrance they turned small shoulders with careful hands. Push now, they said, and the muscles dictated mildly, push; and the thing slid away, compact, solid, rubbery, trailing, gone. She could see nothing, only feel their hands busy, far away. And then a voice gasped, choked, thin and scratching, and then with a note in it wailed, on a repeated, climbing catch. "A lovely boy," said the purple nurse. "A lovely big boy." The green nurse was pressing the suddenly diminished hump; *push*, she said, and as the rhythm died, the body pushed for the last time and Stephanie heard the liquid slither of the afterbirth. The boy wailed again, and the woman saw, beyond her feet and the stained sheets, the purple nurse carrying the small blood-red body compact on one hand. She closed her eyes and lay back, solitary, surprised to be solitary, to hear the beat of her own life only, after so long.

They brought the boy to her, his small neck and lolling head coming turtlelike out of a hospital gown like her own in miniature. It was not a time, or a hospital, where the child is put immediately to the mother's breast. But, for a space of time, he lay beside her on the pillow and she raised herself a little and looked sideways and down, damp and exhausted.

She had not expected ecstasy. She noted that he was both much more solid, and, in the feebleness of his fluttering movements of lip and cheek muscle, the dangerous lolling of his uncontrolled head, more fragile, than she had expected. His flesh was dark and mottled, and creamy wax and threads of blood clung here and there. Pasted to his pointed head, its overlapping cap of bone already springing apart under the elastic scalp, was a mat of thick black hair. He had a square brow, Daniel's brow, tiny nostrils, and a creased, emphatically large mouth. A clenched fist, smaller than a walnut, brushed a finely curled ear. He bore little, but not no, relation to the furious thing that had breached her. As she looked he frowned, increasing his look of Daniel, and then, as though aware of her gaze, opened ink-blue eyes and stared at her, through her, past her. She put out a finger and touched the fist; he obeyed a primitive instinct and curled the tiny fingers round her own, where they clutched, loosened, tightened again. "There," she said to him, and he looked, and the light poured through the window, brighter and brighter, and his eyes saw it, and hers, and she was aware of bliss, a word she didn't like, but the only one. There was her body, quiet, used, resting; there was her mind, free, clear, shining; there was the boy and his eyes, seeing what? And ecstasy. Things would hurt when this light dimmed. The boy would change. But now in the sun she recognized him, and recognized that she did not know, and had never seen him, and loved him, in the bright new air with a simplicity she had never expected to know. "You," she said to him, skin for the first time on skin in the outside air, which was warm and shining, "you."

11

Daniel came home. He was tired in an irritable way: school visit, confirmation class, flower committee. Inside his door, like paradoxical twin Cerberuses, sat his mum and Marcus, portentously silent.

"She's gone," said his mum in a phrase more usual with funerals. Marcus made an effort.

"The—the ambulance came. It came—oh—in the morning."

"Is she *all right?*"

"I don't know," said useless Marcus, alarmed.

"O' course she was," said his mum. "Perfectly normal pains. I told her not to be in such a rush but she wasn't going to listen."

"Why didn't you fetch me?"

"We didn't know where you were," said Marcus unhappily.

"It's written in't kitchen diary. Wi' phone numbers. *She* knew.'

"She was a bit upset. I'm sorry."

"There wasn't no rush," said Daniel's mum. "First babies always tek a long time. I shouldn't be surprised if it didn't turn out to be a false alarm. First babies aren't early."

"I'll telephone the hospital," said Daniel, looking from her settled fat creases to Marcus's etiolated pallor.

The hospital said it was a boy. Both doing well. An hour ago. They'd tried to get him but he must have been on his way home.

Daniel repeated this information to the people in his house.

. . .

"I told you so," said his mother. "Perfectly all right. Nowt to fuss about." She sounded critical.

"I'll go to the hospital."

"Won't you have a bite to eat first? No sense in hurrying—you need to keep your strength up, now."

"No," said Daniel. He did not add, "Thank you," since the offer of food had in fact been a request to be fed. "You see to yourselves."

"Can I—" said Marcus. "Shall I—? Would you like me to—get anything for you?"

"I'm going to the hospital," said Daniel. "I don't know how long I'll be."

"Not long," said his mum. "They won't let you stay long, you'll see. Now be a good boy, Marcus, and just put them sausages in th' frying pan—and some bread to fry, and a tomato, and put Daniel's in't oven to keep warm."

He had no desire for warmed-up sausages and fried bread and saw there was no point in saying so. He went out, banging the front door. "Get *on* wi' it, boy," said his mum, behind him.

They had cleaned her up and put her in the maternity ward in her own nightdress, in the middle of a row of women. They had taken the boy away. Under the cotton sheet and cellular blanket she felt shapeless, only herself again. It was a moment when it would have been better to be truly alone. Her hair had snapped into tight curls, as it did when it needed washing, or when she was ill. The adrenaline, or glory, had ebbed away, though she held fiercely on to the memory of it. Daniel strode into the ward rather fast, unlike most husbands, who crept or sidled. His presence confused her; she was becoming used to a female world of endurance, diminished vocabulary, chattered conventional confidences. He was whole, and alert, and for some reason angry. She looked at him out of tired eyes. She wished her hair was less horrible.

"Are you all right?"

"Oh yes."

"Was it bad?"

"Not really." She cast a deprecating look round their captive audience. "Not really, not—the process. More all the people, and what they did, messing about . . . It doesn't matter."

He wanted to *know* how it had been. She wanted to tell him about the light, the joy. The women watched. The conversation creaked uncomfortably on.

"It's a boy."

"I know." He brooded. "Nobody *told* me."

"Well, once I got here, I couldn't..."

"Not you."

"I thought they might've—telephoned from home."

"Not them. It doesn't matter."

"No. They've lost my Wordsworth somewhere."

"I'll find it. Do you want anything else?"

"Chocolate. Something *sweet*. I think because I'm tired."

"I'll get that."

He glowered round at the other women as though their presence was their fault. They bent their eyes to their knitting or *Woman's Own*, or simply the sheets. A nurse came up and asked if he wanted to see his son. Yes, he said still obscurely angry about everything, and followed her along the ward and out into the corridor where through the glass nursery wall could be seen rows of linen cribs and the small, naked heads, white, crimson, fuzzy, skin, variations on a human theme. The urgent monotonous screaming of one or two babies could be heard. The nurse pointed through the glass.

"Second from the left in that row, that's yours. He's lovely, isn't he?"

"How can I tell?"

"Well..."

"There's not much to see."

"I'll fetch him out."

She was tired, too. But she went in, and wheeled the boy out, and back into the ward. Stephanie looked at him, afraid that the sense of recognition, of delight, might not have lasted, that the boy might seem different. He was different—he was soaped, his dark hair fluffed up—but the firm little face was as she remembered. She turned her attention to Daniel, who was staring.

"It's funny," he said. "I hadn't thought it. I hadn't thought he'd be somebody."

"No, I hadn't either. I was so surprised when I saw his separate bed. But he is, isn't he?"

"Get him out."

"Are we allowed . . .?"

"Go on. Get him out."

She lifted him, wet and trailing warm nightdress. He blinked in the light and moved his arms, both together, uncertainly. Daniel, frowning, took in the small face. Stephanie watched Daniel.

"They're all the same," said the woman in the next bed, laughing. "Go on, they're all the same."

"Not always. Is he all right?"

"Oh yes."

"You spend so much time thinking something might be wrong, you aren't ready for someone who's all right."

"I didn't think anything would be wrong."

"How can you know?" he said, and returned to his scrutiny of his son.

"He looks like you, Daniel."

"Aye." The thought did not seem to cheer him. "I expect I look like my mum."

"She says like your father."

"I'm too fat," said Daniel. "Always was. He's quite skinny, this boy."

The boy frowned; the man frowned. He said, "What shall we call him, then?"

"I thought of William."

"William?"

They had discussed Christopher, and Stephen, and Michael.

"I thought of it—for Wordsworth. All those hours—when they wouldn't let me have my book—I walked up and down—it made them very cross—and in my mind I thought "William" because of Wordsworth. Could it be *one* of his names?"

"I like William well enough."

The child seemed more separate, now he had a separate name.

"Your dad'll be pleased."

She turned a questioning face up to him.

"Well, I take it his name's William. He can't've have been christened Bill."

"Oh, no. Oh, my God. I didn't think."

Daniel laughed.

"No, truly Daniel, how blind can one *be*? I was thinking—I was actually thinking of keeping him separate—I was thinking of *Wordsworth*, a separate thing, precisely my own life, nothing to do with Daddy. That was part of the point."

"I expect your dad has a fair amount to do wi' Wordsworth."

"Not for me. Perhaps we'd better not call him William."

"It doesn't matter."

"It does."

"It won't do any harm. We can call him William. If your dad chooses to be pleased, that's all to the good, really."

"I wanted him *separate*," she insisted.

He lay there on the bed cover, separate, seeing their faces perhaps, or a haze of light perhaps, or even trailing clouds of glory.

"We could call him William Edward. After my dad as well."

"He must have a name of his own."

Daniel thought. "What about Bartholomew? That's unusual."

"That's for your church."

"William's for Wordsworth."

"He's getting tied into a community and he's only been here a few hours."

"That's human."

"Oh, yes."

They smiled at each other.

Daniel made his conventional telephone calls. The next day Bill and Winifred came, with flowers and grapes. Bill seemed too slight for his overcoat, which bunched round his thin neck above overpadded shoulders. They came at teatime and had to wait for the cot to be wheeled out of its place in the rows of more or less animated pupae behind the glass plate. Stephanie felt at a disadvantage, her hair further kinked, the nightdress barely meeting over her breasts, which had become huge, glistening and hard, the breasts of a Diana of Ephesus or some exuberant Charity. Around them small conversations were held primly in small voices. Stephanie told Winifred about the labor, in conventional words, stages, and stitches. Bill looked at the Wordsworth, which Daniel had pursued and retrieved, riffling its pages, deliberately inattentive. Then the boy was wheeled in.

. . .

Bill pounced on Daniel's son and lifted him out of his nest, holding him up, full-length, to look at. The boy tried to curl up again, made a protesting mew, like a kitten. Stephanie made an ineffectual rescuing gesture and lay back on her pillow. Bill sat down, still holding the child up at arm's length.

"A fine boy," said Bill. "A fine boy. Does he have a name?"

"William. William Edward Bartholomew."

Bill looked down at the boy, up at his daughter, down again. The man frowned, sharp as a pen, and the boy frowned, with his unreal creases in his new skin.

"He has a Potter look. Somewhere round the brow. A tough look. I hope he doesn't turn out too much of a pigheaded Potter, Stephanie. You deserve better."

He looks like Daniel, Stephanie wanted to say, but could not, for it was visibly true—in Bill's arms the boy had taken a look of Bill, sharp, clear-cut, irritable even.

"He hasn't your coloring," Winifred ventured.

"That dark hair always drops out," said Bill. 'You know that. All babies are born with dark hair, if they have any at all. Look at his brows and lashes, there's the clue. Ruddy, I'd say."

The boy suddenly condensed all his volatile face into one red patch with a hole in the center and let out a cry of fury.

"Please," said Stephanie, putting her arms out.

Bill jiggled William, who went purple and shouted even louder. Bill gave his grandson to Stephanie, and said, "Don't you think the lashes are ruddy?"

But the lashes, fine little lines, were colorless except where wet tears caught the light, and the brows no more than a thickening of down on the skin.

The Potters left when Daniel came. Bill leaned over Stephanie and said quietly, "I take it kindly, you know—his name. I'm honored. I'm moved. One's children—and their children—are all the immortality one has, of that I'm sure. And names mean more than you might suppose."

Stephanie kissed him, her heavy, burning breast against the scrubby nap of his overcoat.

The next day, surprisingly, Marcus came.

Stephanie was beginning to feel ragged. Her hair by now was gluey, and underneath she was sore and blood encrusted. Her belly, which had had its moment of feeling small and empty, now seemed pointlessly huge and shapeless. It sagged when she walked to the bathroom, feeling the grind of the pelvic bones, the soreness at the base of the spine, the pull on fine skin of those hot alabaster breasts. Her separate self was taking a battering, ground between two communities, the ward and the family, both, it seemed, intent on forming her and William to their own rites and classifications.

The trouble with the ward was that although it put you to bed—and in those days confined you to bed—it was so constituted that it precluded rest or sleep. This was partly owing to the nurses' military-seeming routine. The night staff brought morning tea, noisily, at five in the morning, whether or not it was wanted. The time between this tea and the very early breakfast, under the aegis of the incoming day staff, was broken into small, sleepless segments by bedpan, face washing, the baby's feed. After breakfast came bed making, a douche of antiseptic in hot water, baby bathing. The gray night was only a series of arrivals of wailing bundles from the nursery for their midnight feed, a series of piercingly whispered conversations about what to do with babies who would not drink, but lay apathetic, slept stonily, or worse, tugged their sharp gums furiously aside and continued howling.

Nurses both mitigated and increased that natural fear of, or perhaps for, babies that comes with their birth. They mitigated it because they could always reduce the loose and slippery wriggling creature to a neat bundle, turn a nappy into a securely fitting garment without driving the curved pin into the convex belly or florid umbilicus. They could fix the feebly gesticulating arms to the sides with a flannelette version of the swaddling band. It was true that babies seemed consoled to be thus immobilized, as though freedom alarmed them. Nurses could raise gulps and hiccups of gas out of distended stomachs. Nurses could convert a slimy, smelly, twisting mass of flesh to a sweet-smelling mummy or papoose.

But they prickled with rules and moral terminology. Babies must feed steadily for the prescribed ten minutes—no more, or mother's nipples would be sore, no less, or they might not put on. Nurses would pick up their tiny captives, slap cheeks, manually purse quivering lips, apply the child like a leech to the static mother, rub the little muzzle across the nipple as though they were training puppies or kittens. Infants who did not respond to this treatment were castigated for laziness. Those who asked to feed frequently, or enjoyed sleeping in their mothers' arms, were designated "spoiled" and frightful warnings were uttered about not letting these helpless human scraps get the upper hand. Nurses dehumanized babies. There was no mystery in the eyes of William in the hands of a cross nurse at two in the morning—only an animal blankness, an animal greed, an animal apprehension.

The mothers were as sloppy as the nurses were rigorous. The nurses smelled of baby powder and surgical spirit and antiseptic; the mothers smelled of menstrual blood and stale tobacco smoke and perfumed talc and sour milk, which congealed stiffly on pads of gauze inside the little shutters in nursing bras.

When Stephanie went into the lavatory there were always two or more who stood, elbows resting on the sani-pad incinerator, cigarettes stuck to patchy lipstick, flesh protruding between the padded buttons of flimsy nylon honeymoon dressing gowns. They had their hair down, literally and metaphorically; they talked endlessly of surgical and obstetric disasters, a chatter of fear and gloating, licensed and domesticated here, full of details that most, if not all of them, would have bowdlerized in any pub.

Most of them, owing to a geographic chance, were wives of warders at the bleak Calverley Prison. Their husbands, rattling chains of keys, marched in at visiting hours almost in a formed squad. The wives of these men had also a communal gossip about rumbling violence, unmentionable offenses from an enclosed and stereotyped world that cast a dark and nasty light on the other disaster chatter. All the wives talked with a kind of communal anger about men. Their present discomfort and indignity were something done to them by men. They talked of things their own man had "made" them do and shared the satisfaction of knowing it would be some time—even if only a brief time—before they could be "made" to do more. They had "fallen for" their sons and daughters; those very few who thought of breast-feeding did so because they had heard it prevented precipitate falling again.

Stephanie, a good curate's wife, talked to the silent and the sad—from a woman whose child was resolute in refusing sustenance, to a girl who had been cruelly settled in there after the birth of a stillborn daughter. This one too was addressed by the staff as mother or mum.

Her own mother was reticent. When she came alone, it was Stephanie who said, "Wouldn't you like to hold him?" realizing that Winifred had watched Bill dandle William and had made no move to touch him herself. Winifred, invited, lifted the child timidly but easily, fitted him to her body, and touched his cheek, his hand, his chilly foot, with a delicate finger. He slept quiet. Stephanie thought that she could not remember her mother *laughing* with them as children. Nor did she ever play, though she did, dutifully and with pleasure, instruct. Something was there—seeing her with William made it clear what it was, a steady gentleness, a complete concern. She was going to add calm, but did not. Winifred's steadiness was not calm. It existed, and had always existed, in spite of considerable fear. She held the child now with love and fear. Fear of what? Of Bill? So Stephanie had always assumed, but it seemed to her now that her mother lived, bravely enough, in a state of perpetual fear that was almost certainly much older than her marriage to Bill. Social fear was part of it—those meager and niggling fears that she, Stephanie, had detected in the Christmas congregation, thinking of the rigid lower-middle-class social forms of *The Mill on the Floss*. But it was more than that, and more, too, than fear of Hitler, who had focused her own propensity to fear in childhood. (She had once dreamed that Bill and Winifred were in a deep pit or quarry, taunted from above by the frenetic moustached little figure, spouting foreign wrath, brandishing a cleaver, and had realized, in her dream that they, her own natural protectors, were wholly helpless, wholly in his power.) Winifred did not expect much, Stephanie thought, did not expect enough, a human modicum. Why?

"He looks very comfortable with you."

"I hope so. I've had practice. They are frightening at this age, don't you think—so vulnerable?"

"He can shout."

"Does he shout a lot?"

"Not really. Not as much as most. He seems to know what he's doing and gets on with his feeding."

"Marcus didn't shout. He was a very placid baby. If placid is the right word."

"Maybe he should have shouted more."

"Maybe."

Winifred was ready to suppose that any and everything she had done for her son had been somehow wrong. She had loved him too much, or wrongly; it must be so. She put a hand on the warm loose skin of William's head and said, "I keep asking myself if I could have—done things differently."

Don't, Stephanie thought. "People just *are*—what they are. I don't believe parents *make* their children. Who made Marcus's maths?"

"It might have been better if we—Bill—had let him get on quietly with the maths."

"It might. But the maths is *odd*, no matter how you look at it. Do you see what I'm saying?"

"Marcus is odd."

"Yes."

"Stephanie—how will he *live?*"

Stephanie did not answer this question, because Marcus was suddenly and silently there, on the other side of the bed.

He wore his school mackintosh—a little too small—and carried a crumpled paper bag. He took a step toward the bed and a step back and bent his head awkwardly so that all Stephanie could see of his expression was light reflected from the lenses of his glasses.

Winifred stiffened. Stephanie said, "Get a chair, Marcus. There's a stack by the door. Come and sit down."

"I'm all right."

"You make me feel uneasy, *hovering* like that."

Marcus shifted away toward the door. He returned, holding at arm's length before him a metal tubular chair that shook as he lowered it to the ground. Stephanie and her bed were between him and his mother.

"Look—" said Stephanie. "Here he is. William Edward Bartholomew."

Winifred turned the baby toward him, held back the cot blanket from his face.

"He's—very small."

"Big enough," said Stephanie.

Marcus stood awkwardly up again, put out a finger, touched the small cheek.

"He's cold."

"Their skins are always colder than ours."

"Is he—all right?"

"Perfect," said Stephanie sadly, looking from Winifred to Marcus to William. These were indeed the pale Potters. Marcus's eyes met Winifred's and what passed between them was fear.

"Are you all right, then, Marcus?" said Winifred.

"I'm fine," said Marcus palely. "Really, I'm fine."

Winifred, perhaps surprisingly, held out the child. "Here. Hold him. Your nephew."

Marcus pulled his head and neck into his shapeless coat and flung his arms protectively around his body. "Oh no. I couldn't. I might drop him. I might—"

He did not elaborate what he might do.

They had all, Daniel, Stephanie, and Winifred too, been in some way afraid of Marcus's encounter with the child. They had a primitive sense that he might like some bad fairy "overlook" William, or by sympathetic magic infect him with fear.

"Give him back to me," said Stephanie, almost fiercely. Winifred relinquished him speedily, as though he might be safer not with her as well as not with Marcus.

Marcus too had been afraid. Like Daniel, but with less precise imagination of possible flaws, he had been afraid something would be "wrong" with William. On his way in he had peered through the glass wall of the nursery, seeing with a kind of shock the little creatures in their boxlike repeated containers, pink blankets, blue blankets, repeated crossing metal struts of legs. Angry or desolate babies awake, flushed dark rose or blue gray under their thin skins; sleeping babies, neatly bound, had the bloodless wax paleness of death. Or so he thought. The anonymous rows alarmed him.

The sight of the particular baby in his own mother's arms disturbed him. She looked, in that first moment, happy and still. And on her face was a look of concern and warmth he had thought of only in the context of himself, and only as an inadequate screen against the blast. He felt fear—of the boy, for the boy?

Stephanie laid the baby on the bed and unwrapped him. He opened slaty eyes and looked out.

"Can he *see* me?"

"They say not. They say they can't focus for some weeks—the muscles of their eyes aren't strong enough. I think that's not true. I think he sees me. I think psychologists in clinical conditions can't be able to measure very well *what* they see."

Marcus, timidly, brought his face nearer those dark eyes.

"I always thought you could see me," said Winifred to him, gently.

"I'm sure I could," he said, with a plain certainty that arrested her movement.

"But he won't remember what he sees now," Stephanie said. "The first thing I *remember* is having cut my leg and having it washed in the bathroom—sheets of blood, and blood and water, and clear water, and yellow iodine—do you remember, Mummy?—I remember the colors and the smells, blood and water and iodine, and I remember the mirror glittering and I could hear somebody crying and crying and then I realized it was me, and the memory ends."

"There were so many cut knees," said Winifred.

"What's your first memory, Marcus?" Stephanie, firmly normal.

"I think it must have been a pram. I remember a square of light— and a kind of black ribbed frame on three sides—and something— maybe more than one thing—wavering or flickering in the light, across the light, across the square of light. I was lying and watching these long things waving like whips, like the edge lines of waves—and I thought—well, not exactly *thought*—it came to me—how do I know anything more will ever happen? I mean, it seemed to have been like that forever—and it was going to go on being like that forever. I can't explain."

"I used to put you to sleep under the ash tree."

"In a blue knitted coat and hat," said Stephanie, "with big pearl buttons."

"Maybe it was the tree," said Marcus. "Maybe it was just out of focus."

"I loved that tree," said Stephanie.

They all remembered, and did not say, that Bill had put weekends of furious energy into cutting down the ash tree, a wild tree, a fast-growing tree, too big for a suburban garden.

Marcus and Winifred left together. Outside the hospital they stood side by side in silence. Winifred had so long a habit of silence that she could not now call up one word to hold or release her son.

"Well . . ." she said.

"Well . . ." he said.

"Marcus—"

He looked at her directly, gently, helplessly. Something in him was different. She identified it; it was a concern for herself, useless enough, helpless enough, born of fear.

"Do you have any thoughts . . . ? Marcus, what will you *do*?"

"I must think—I know I must. I know I must do *something*."

She wanted to cry out, "Come home." "Come back?" "Just start again," and was filled with self-doubt, the rising fear. If she had so cried out he would have come, willingly enough, unhappy where he was, afraid of what he was doing. But she feared—to damage him, to frighten him, to do the wrong thing.

"What does Mr. Rose say?"

"He says I need occupation. He says I could get a job in the hospital library. Pushing a trolley."

"That might be a good thing?" Meekly following his lead.

"I don't know. I don't *like* hospitals. All this is incredibly tedious."

"Marcus, I—"

"I'll see you. I'll see you here." He edged away. She did not call him back.

.   .   .

Daniel brought his mum to see the baby. In her fat hands he underwent another transformation and became, not Daniel now, but infant Daniel, Daniel helpless, malleable, greedy. Stephanie, weak with postnatal depression, was gloomy. If Potters had made her feel that William was just a link in a complex and possibly faulty genetic chain, Mrs. Orton, crushing him against a pillowy purple breast, made her feel briefly that he was not, never had been, flesh of her flesh. Mrs. Orton made gobbling and suck-kissing noises at him. His head quavered, unsupported. He was vanishing, hot and helpless into her body.

Daniel said, "He doesn't look very comfortable, Mum. Give him here."

"Rubbish. He's ever so happy. Aren't you, my pet?"

Tears swam in Stephanie's eyes.

Picking him up at the end of these days, too sensitive, she smelled, touched, and tasted his peregrinations from one set of hands to another. A child must be recognized by his smell; consider lost lambs in February calling urgently from every part of the compass on windswept fells, consider the silly sheep trotting under their swaying integument of matted wool, sniffing with hard bony noses under black kidskin, rejecting, pushing away, trotting, finding. The lamb's face buried in its mother. Consider the human child, washed but not overwashed, the malt-biscuit smell of the soft head.

After a day's visiting William's heat was wrong; he was sweaty with other people's sweat, damp in nappies other people had clutched. He became limp and rubbery, not live and stretching. His smell was obscured by others, someone's sweet lily of the valley, someone else's cigarette smoke. One day he had a sticky lipstick kiss, cerise on the small plane of his brow. Stephanie laid him on the bed, making white muslin triangles for him, weeping soundlessly, sheets of hot tears over slippery cheeks. This is usual. She shook out his small nightdress and picked him up. He made small contented, vaguely speaking (anyway not calling, not complaining) noises. She saw him through her tears, rainbow hazed, in the light from the reading lamp over her bed, composed. Daniel had brought spring flowers—Dutch irises, pale violet-blue, streaked yellow, golden daffodils, King Alfreds. The nurses would take them away, but not quite yet. Their soft, earthy-airy smell crept through the disinfectant and synthetic *muguet*. Their stems were stiff pale green tubes, their leaves awkward spikes in a vase.

The child opened his eyes and turned his head from side to side and saw light. He saw light as through water, or it could be said that he saw the air as a thick, translucent medium, so that the wide swath of light that scarfed and followed his slow-moving gaze was streaked and stroked with delicate repeated dashes and flashes of pale violet (from the irises) and chrome yellow (from the daffodils). Light was like the close roof of a sphere within which he lay. There arched over this a band of the clear yellow-gold. Between these lay, though he saw them as a ceaselessly moving stream, a band of parti-colored streaked flashes, gold over violet, violet over gold.

As he turned his head among this glory he saw two spaces of pale brightness, shifting shape, and a third behind. They bent toward him, larger and milder and creamier in color, a warmth he knew, the pale, constant warmth of his mother's face, surrounded by the brighter yellow gleam of her hair, and behind that arch over arch, thin light over live moving rounds, the halo of the circumscribed light of the reading lamp. These circles shifted and yet held shape in the sphere of what he saw. They were washed with newness, but he was too young to be surprised, too simply learning to measure joy.

The light, modulated by his tears and the hazy matter of his eye, was a warm light, with the soft light of the flowers spread and diffused in it, though it is not possible for me to say whether he in any way associated synaesthetically the ideas of warmth and light, one necessary to him, one new to him. The particles he saw in the flowing waves of light were streaked with the colors of the flowers, mauve, lilac, cobalt, citron, white-gold, sulphur, chrome, though of course he could not name or distinguish these divisions of light, as he could not see the lip of the iris, the frilled trumpet of the daffodil.

If he had been capable of simile, which he was not, he could have said that the glistening particles he saw were like overlapping transparent fish scales. Or he could have said they were like delicate quills, arching back to feathery trails of waving light in plumes. Or like small, curving, repeated candle flames. Or if he looked, not vaguely but with particular interest on the pale, central moving form that was his mother's face, then the light particles ceased to stream over him and became variously concentric, spiraling, either rays and little flames moving in and out of that warm center or little lines of light focused like flower petals, like magnetized needles, on the massed gold and violet shadows of hair, eyes, mouth. He could have said that the circle of the face was like the sun or the moon, lighting the colored air, but he had no geometry and no idea of a circle, no vision of any world and no idea of sun, moon, or stars. He had watched lightless amniotic fluid and now he saw the light. Who can possibly say if those parts of the brain that become the rods and cones of vision had any precognition, any preparatory dream of light, in that darkness, before it flooded in?

Art is not the recovery of the innocent eye, which is inaccessible. "Make it new" cannot mean, set it free of all learned frames and names, for paradoxically it is only a precise use of learned comparison and the signs we have made to distinguish things seen or recognized that can give the illusion of newness. I had the idea that this novel could be written innocently, without recourse to reference to other people's thoughts, without, as far as possible, recourse to simile or metaphor. This turned out to be impossible. One cannot think at all without a recognition and realignment of ways of thinking and seeing we have learned over time. We all remake the world as we see it, as we look at it. If William did not, it was because he was new, he was barely used to horizontal and vertical framing patterns, he was not separate from his mother. He would learn to name colors much later than things; young children can name "red" but often learn "blue" only as a blanket term for all colors not red.

Later we distinguish: shades and hues, names for these things. I wrote in the color words—mauve, lilac, cobalt, citron, sulphur, chrome—out of an equal delight in the distinction of colors and the variety of words. Communication is a partial and incomplete business. I know that for some readers these words will call up clear images on an inner eye; they will in some sense "see" purple and gold, whereas others will not. No two men see the same iris. Yet Daniel and William and Stephanie all saw the same iris.

Even the innocent eye does not simply receive light; it acts and orders. And we always put something of ourselves—however passive we are as observers, however we believe in the impersonality of the poet, into our descriptions of our world, our mapping of our vision. Vincent Van Gogh was no naïf painter. What he had to understand about pigment and geometry, the relations of colors and the behavior of light, was taxing and terrible. He feared falling into a "metaphysics of color" when he contemplated the "terrible battle" of the complementaries violet and gold in his paintings of sower in Arles and reaper in St. Rémy. He ordered his world of raw and sophisticated vision with the mapping, the patterning of his brushstrokes, with the more primitive sense of touch.

In September 1889 he wrote:

> What a queer thing *touch* is, the stroke of the brush.
>
> In the open air, exposed to wind, sun, to the curiosity of people, you work as you can, you fill your canvas anyhow. Then, however, you catch the real and the essential—that is the most difficult. But when after a time you take up this study again and arrange your brush-strokes in the direction of the objects—certainly it is more harmonious and pleasant to look at, you add whatever you have of serenity and cheerfulness.

(It was like him to insist desperately on serenity and cheerfulness, which are not always, not even mostly, what he added.)

The brushstrokes in *The Sower* are almost tessellations; the sky flows with them, the furrows of purple earth run away from the central heavy gold sun, the sower scatters seeds of gold light which are brushstrokes in the pattern onto the dark morning clods. They are thick and solid; they are the movement of light over things, of the eye over things. In *The Reaper* Vincent's later spiraling forms are everywhere, curling and linking the white-hot furnace of the cornfield, the blue figure of the man, the purple mountains, the green air, into one substance, his vision. He radiated brushstrokes in a self-portrait from his own eyes like twin suns. It is new and the opposite of innocent; it is seen, and thought, and made.

8

A L'ECLAT DES JEUNES
GENS EN FLEURS, I

Newnham was in those days outside, but not far outside, Cambridge University proper. It had the proportions and atmosphere, with its Dutch red-brick gables, its corridors, landings, solid banisters, and mansarded attics, of a comfortable country house. It had a civilized garden with roses, herbaceous borders, shrubbery, sunken pond. Frederica's room, austere and ladylike, looked out over this garden. Frederica was aware that the college was an agnostic foundation, which pleased her, though she was mainly ignorant of the struggles on behalf of women, the anxieties about Fellows in Holy Orders, the anguished battles of principle with God, the church, and the university that had inspired Sidgwick and the other founders. Returning to Newnham in the 1970s Frederica saw it as beautiful—graceful in scale, civilized in space, humane.

In 1954 there was agitation against all things Victorian—except possibly George Eliot, sanctified by that Cambridge authority Dr. Leavis, who had nevertheless declared Trollope and Dickens unworthy of serious consideration and supported T. S. Eliot's image of Tennyson and Browning as poets whose thought was inferior or nonexistent, whose sensibilities were hopelessly dissociated. In 1954 there were strong moves to pull down Victorian railway stations with their red pinnacles and turrets. There was savage mockery of the Albert Memorial. Beauty was the severe uncluttered line of Georgian terraces. The future was with Le Corbusier's austere, regulated floating environments on stilts. High-rise flats going up outside Calverley had raised in Frederica a sense of excitement, expansion, freer life. Newnham represented a dowdy *Gemütlichkeit*, crossed with a pseudo-medievalism, damnable in its arched gateway. This aspect reminded Frederica unfortunately of her father's place of employment, Blesford Ride School, also an eccentric agnostic foundation for misfits. Newnham's mildness, its femininity even, set it apart in Cambridge. Behind it lurked all the restrictive horrors—now, since the loving recreation of televised big novels, since Laura Ashley, so charming—

of Victorianism, table legs with skirts on, chaperons, Duty, and respectability. It was a setting for cocoa, toasted crumpets, tea parties. Frederica wanted wine, argument, sex.

She sat on her neat bed and thought not of how to decorate but of how to contradict the prettiness of her surroundings. Some casually thrown sheets of plain, brightly colored cloth. A modern lampshade? Sculpture? She put out some black Vallauris mugs on a yellow tin tray and a photograph of several people, some in farthingales, doublets, and hose, some in shirt-sleeves and flannels, sauntering among the clipped yews and vanishing alleys of Long Royston.

She saw Cambridge in that first year as a garden full of young men. She knew that there were eleven men for every woman in the university (and had not been told about the presence and advantages of *au pair* girls and Addenbrooke's nurses). She ascribed much of the dullness of her earlier life to the absence of men. It is true that she had always lived on the perimeter of a boys' school. It is also true that the boys—perhaps reduced by her father's ferocity, perhaps unnerved by her own vehemence and fluency—had always seemed a dull lot. But at Cambridge they would be clever and interesting and be able to overpower her in argument and listen to what she said. They would be her friends. She would belong.

She was, despite having loved Alexander and having gone to bed with Edmund Wilkie, remarkably ignorant about how most people lived, remarkably unprovided with ways of distinguishing between one young man and another. She had very few terms with which to categorize them and for some time—to return to the analogy with the South Americans who specialize in adjectives to describe the colors of cows—she distinguished them largely on only two counts, intelligence and good looks. Here, of course, she differed from those of her contemporaries, who came from the world of debutantes and gossip columns, who were armed with a very large vocabulary to indicate acceptable and unacceptable behavior, appearance, provenance. Frederica would have liked to have had a sense of style and knew she had not—not yet. Her ideas about good manners were derived from Jane Austen, Trollope, Forster, Rosamond Lehmann, Angela Thirkell, Waugh, Lawrence, and many other useful and nugatory sources. Her image of Cambridge was partly gleaned from Stephanie (who had talked more about literature than life), and partly from the smart chatter of Wilkie and his girl. Beyond these and more powerful were two conflicting yet related images of a way of life. There was the Cambridge of Ansell in *The Longest Journey* in which thought and cows coexisted in harmony, were indeed (unlike Tennyson and Browning), somehow undissociated. And there was the Cambridge of Lehmann's *Dusty Answer*, a place of violent, suppressed, hopeless female passion and carefree golden young men. It is a town thick with words, wrapped in shining folds of words, alive with the history of words, and she never walked past the cows across the Cam from King's without hearing: "The cow is there. She is there, the cow. Whether I'm in Cambridge or Iceland or dead the cow will be there . . . It was philosophy. They were discussing the existence of objects." And in the same way, going through Trinity Great Court, she heard, "Trinity Great Court mourned in the sun for its young men." Though the dead young men were more fictitious than the cow, and the original of one, at least, was said to be happily striding about Cambridge still, discussing cows, and young men, and literature, and Cambridge.

In the first week she was invited to tea by her first two young men, who signed themselves Alan Melville and Tony Watson, informed her that Edmund Wilkie had said she would be interesting to meet, and entertained her in a brown utilitarian room, smelling of generations of stale powdered coffee, games shirts, and tobacco, in the Peas Hill hostel behind the Arts Theatre. They turned out to be self-assured and to have a style of relentless lack of affectation that it took her some time—and some further researches among other varieties—to place. They served her strong tea in thick white mugs from a brown pot with a knitted tea cozy. There were doorsteps of bread and jam and a fruit cake. Alan was slight and blond with a Scots voice and a navy sleeveless pullover over a checked viyella shirt. Tony was dark and burly and curly, and had an obviously home-knitted or anyway hand-knitted cable-stitched rust-colored polo neck. Both had baggy cord trousers. Alan was reading modern languages at St. Michael's. Tony was reading English at King's. On this first occasion Frederica was not aware of the categorizing importance of finding out where they had been to school and, more simply, of whether they had done their National Service or not. She did find out that they were in their second year and wrote for the university newspaper. The cream-colored, smoke-stained, gloss-painted walls were decorated with a series of photographs of girls—girls in punts, girls on bicycles with gowns billowing behind them, girls lying in long grass, girls staring over wineglasses lit dramatically by flashlights. They explained that they wanted to write up Frederica for the newspaper—Wilkie had told them about *Astraea* and her academic brilliance—a Profile of an Interesting Fresher? Alan took good pictures, as she could see. Would she?

Of course she would. It was, and also was not, a propitious beginning.

She liked them. They drank pints of espresso coffee together in the new coffee bar, from shallow, sloping glass cups. They had beer, and Frederica had cider, in various pubs. (Tony was very good at categorizing beers. Frederica could not manage to like beer, though in this company it would have been helpful. It was tepid and bitter and sloshed chilly in her stomach.) They asked her what she thought about various things, and Frederica, excited by their interest, said what she thought and added some things she hadn't thought much about, or hadn't thought at all, for effect. Sometimes they wrote down what she said, and sometimes they did not. She classified them both as "moderately good-looking" (other words in this set were handsome, beautiful, pretty, elegant, attractive . . .) and both as "rather clever" (as distinct from intelligent, brilliant, intellectual, smart, wise, thoughtful, complex, knowing, knowledgeable, percipient, sharp, quick . . .). Clever was a Cambridge word as well as a word in Frederica's older world of schoolteachers and exam successes. It had connotations of quick-wittedness and sharpness that the more neutral "intelligent" lacked. Tony spoke approvingly of D. H. Lawrence's decency, intelligence (as opposed to Bloomsbury cleverness), and vision. It was a habit of mind and morals she associated with her father. It took her longer to find out that Scots Alan was an excellent scholarly medievalist (not only Scottish Chaucerians and ballads, but European painting and sculpture). He also knew a lot about Lewis Grassic Gibbon and James Hogg, neither of whom Frederica had heard of. They were both, they said, socialists, and could cite Ruskin and William Morris, about whom again Frederica knew nothing. Since Frederica assumed that all decent people naturally voted Labor, this meant less than it might have done. She also assumed, wrongly, that they both came from lower-middle-class serious homes, as she did.

Their *Varsity* piece appeared under the headline A FORCEFUL FEMALE FRESHER. It was accompanied by two of Alan's photographs, one of Frederica, gowned, book laden, in Newnham gateway, scowling (the sun was in her eyes), and the other curled in the leather armchair in Tony's digs, wearing a tight sweater, tight trousers, little black slippers, hand on hip, hand under chin. The first looked angular and contemptuous, the second provocative in an unripe way.

There were headings: FREDERICA ON CAMBRIDGE WOMEN. FREDERICA ON ACTING. FREDERICA ON SEX.

It was more like the *Daily Express* gossip column—which Frederica had never seen—than the serious journalism that Tony claimed to be his intended career.

On Cambridge women Frederica was said to have said that Cambridge was a marriage mart, that women were less ambitious and enterprising than men, that clever girls had difficulty in being truly feminine.

On acting, she seemed vaingloriously to have said that she wanted to have a go at Lady Macbeth, Cleopatra, St. Joan—the demanding roles. Asked about Elizabeth in *Astraea* she had said that while it had been a marvelous opportunity she wasn't sure that the future of English theater lay with the verse drama, and the play was static. Alexander Wedderburn was a *marvelous* person and she was happy to reveal that his next play would be very different indeed from the period nostalgia of *Astraea*. Acting in *Astraea* had been incredible fun and everyone had let their hair down.

On sex, she had said that effective contraception would naturally remove the *raisons d'être* for many of our ideas about chastity, fidelity, and so on. Especially for women.

Her hopes for the future: to be a successful actress, to meet really interesting people, to work in the arts, in London. Not to teach. She had just got out of a school and had no intention of ever going back. She wanted to marry a don, or someone in the serious theater, or perhaps a journalist. She hoped to do well in Tripos but work was not the main reason for coming to Cambridge.

On reading this Frederica, a shrewd literary critic, felt dismayed, then outraged, then panic-stricken. She had been made to sound disagreeable and conceited, and worse than that, disagreeable and conceited in a set of predictable undergraduate clichés. Huge public embarrassment loomed, not for the first or last time in her life, but at a time when she was peculiarly vulnerable; all here was so much a show, so trenchantly judged. She considered weeping, and did wipe away some wet mascara from hot, red-rimmed eyes. She considered getting on her bicycle and going to tell Tony and Alan what she thought of them for exploiting and mocking her. She was restrained partly by a memory of Beau Brummell in a Georgette Heyer novel telling an embarrassed heroine never to admit a fault. Much of the piece's vulgarity was her own. There was nothing in it she could claim with certainty not to have said, except possibly that she would like to marry a journalist, which she would not. Several of the sillier-looking things (about women and the marriage mart) had been quotations from Edmund Wilkie's Caroline, repeated out of a nervous wish to hit a Cambridge note she now greatly regretted.

She considered the problem of Alan and Tony. How far had their vulgarity, as well as hers, been unwitting? Was it malicious? She liked them. She had thought they liked her. Obviously she annoyed them very much in some way, though she found it hard to believe they had set out to destroy her, as she had at first supposed. It seemed unintelligent, when she thought clearly, to suppose that the style of their journalism was the final truth about them that should override and cancel the sense of excitement she felt over their talk about Morris and Lawrence, or the way she had been moved when Alan showed her a postcard of a fifteenth-century French ivory Virgin. She herself was vulgar and clever and arrogant and frightened, uncertain of tone and well-meaning. She would suppose they were no less complicated than herself. She would not sum them up, and perhaps they would do her the same justice.

She also thought: I can do better than that. There are things someone could have written—even about me, even out of those things I said—that would not have been clichés.

The profile nevertheless had several lasting, mostly deleterious effects on Frederica's Cambridge life, some of which she ignored and some of which she never knew about, or did not ascribe to it.

One immediate result was that she found it hard to make friends with other women. She had never found it easy; she categorized women far too quickly as schoolgirls or debutantes. She shared supervisions with a very young, very shy, very academic girl from a not very academic school who expected to be lonely and rejected and was resigned to continuing in this state. The Newnham dons had hoped Frederica would bring her out of herself. They were perhaps misguided by memories of Stephanie. Frederica ignored this girl, which annoyed the dons, who had themselves taken note of the *Varsity* article and of Frederica's views on sex in particular. They treated her with caution and reserve; Frederica, used to irritating and opposing teachers, found nothing unusual in this.

Men were different. Those repelled by the article she did not meet. There were many others, as she had foreseen. Cambridge consisted of many small worlds, some of them interlinked, or partly overlapping, some almost hermetically closed. A woman, perhaps particularly a notorious woman, and partly notorious for promising ideas about sex, could move between world and world more easily than a man. There was a price to pay, as there would be a price to pay for her continued friendship with Alan and Tony. But she was greedy for variety. She had a great deal of energy. She was prepared to pay.

One thing she did not, in the end, do, was live in the Cambridge theater world as she had dreamed of doing. This was one of the closed worlds, perpetually excited, with ambitious plans for the future and a gossip that reached out into the real world, or a part of it. They knew what they were doing and what they thought; their manner suggested openness and warmth, darling, they said, and love, in every other sentence. Frederica did the auditions at the Amateur Dramatic Company and recited her party pieces: the Duchess's proposal from *The Duchess of Malfi* and her own, or Alexander's, tower speech from *Astraea*. Edmund Wilkie sat in the shabby stalls in the dark tiny theater and told her she wasn't the best, or the next best they'd seen, but he thought she was safe. She played Cassandra in Giradoux's *Tiger at the Gates* in a Nursery production of the first scenes of that play. It was not a bad part for a static actress who knew what she was saying, even if she did not manage to create any tension between herself and the others on stage. There was a party after this in the Club Bar where distinguished old members could be seen talking to the rising generation. There was elegant Julian Slade whose *Salad Days*, with the Coronation and *Astraea*, came to represent in Frederica's mind the innocence of that time, the grown-up singing children in their swinging skirts and nice pullovers, the expectation of a happy-ever-after all the more possible and imaginable because the failures of their parents to be happy-ever-after could be attributed to the accidents of Hitler and the war. "What will there be on the news," Frederica had asked Winifred, one day in 1944, listening to casualty figures and planes shot down, "when we've won the war?" And Winifred thought and answered, "Oh, I don't know. Cricket and things like that." Before *Salad Days*, in direct line, there had been *The Importance of Being Earnest*, cucumber sandwiches, and the nursery world of *Peter Pan*, cricket, and things like that. The days of *Salad Days* came to seem, in retrospect, the last days of brightly lit stages and clean costumes.

There were theater men, there were men, met in or outside lectures, who borrowed sheets of paper, offered coffee in the espresso bar, introduced her to their friends. There was one group of such men, a small band of close friends with whom she took to having tea after Shakespeare and coffee after Modern Poetry, with whom she came to play games out of anthologies, dating lines and stanzas of poems, she who had never played. What she loved about these was that they gave her a first sense of belonging to a group, an easier sense, for her as she was, than the hothouse endearments of the theater people, or the intimacies of Newnham bathrooms. For these she dared to cook, producing, in Newnham, her first—cold, clammy, gelatinous, horribly superfluous—spaghetti. For these, it must be recorded, she, Frederica Potter, darned and ironed shirts, hanging her head humbly when one of the latter blew out of her bicycle basket into the Cam when she was carrying a sheaf back over the Garrett Hostel Bridge to their owner, who had been in the navy and was quite capable of ironing his own shirts and mending his own socks. In return they bought her cinema tickets and talked to her and to each other in front of her—about Yeats and Auden, Leavis and Shakespeare, Herbert and Donne. They did this with pleasure—they enjoyed these things intensely. They also enjoyed jazz and racing cars, both of which Frederica found boring. When they talked about these things she watched and judged them—quite attractive, pretty but unattractive, too clean looking, abrupt.

Sex was a problem, and partly a threat. Frederica observed that these friends were happier, livelier, and much more interesting in groups. She liked to go to the Arts Cinema with three or four of them and walk back through Cambridge arm in arm and talking. But she found herself the object of pacts and agreements made without her knowledge. Invitations generally issued ended in her being left alone with one or another of them. Or one would be chosen—not by her— to walk her home; the others would go back to their colleges, and she would find herself ranged with the black-winged, double-backed bird shapes outside her Porter's Lodge in the half-light. It was here that the National Service distinction on the whole made itself felt. Some of the older ones knew what to do with their hands, how to open her mouth, even how to make her ache briefly with desire. There were the unattractive who, close up, became concentrated, sharp, insistent. And the attractive ones who imagined or dared nothing beyond a chilly kiss. Frederica felt excluded from something by these maneuvers. She stood there and was kissed and imagined the lost little band companionably discussing her, and their friend's progress, or lack of it, with her.

She met a medical student at a Newnham tea party who surprisingly invited her to a tea dance in the Dorothy Café. He was a big man who did not waste words. Frederica, standing up with him at teatime in a swirling black skirt, wide suede belt, batwing sweater, and little gold silk scarf, found herself physically happy. She stepped, skipped, swooped, laughed, pressed her breasts up against him and then her hips, laughed again, drank tea. Next week they danced again, and the week after that, after the dancing, they went back to his rooms and he took off her clothes, produced a tube of contraceptive jelly and applicator from his bathroom, and made love to her. He was expert in the sense that he knew how she was constructed, had firm hands, and went on for what, at that stage, she thought of as a long time. He did not speak to her during these events. Afterward he politely offered her what she took to be a shaving towel. She felt almost relaxed. He had been in the army in Germany. He had a habit of uttering sentences beginning with "Girls . . ." as though all girls were the same, and different from him. She had the sense that she was one of a number of girls he was observing and practicing on; she didn't mind this, since she was observing and practicing on him. After taking her to a college dance he observed, "Girls can be frightfully good at choosing clothes and still make an awful mess of evening dress. I suppose they don't get enough practice and so can't see so well what they look like." Frederica, whose one evening dress was a rather angular green taffeta halter neck, did not ask if he included her—she could see he did. He elaborated. "Most girls either have knobby collarbones or are fat just above the breasts. Most girls get divided up into the wrong sort of segments by these strapless jobs. Makes 'em squat and bunchy, d'you see?" Frederica saw. It was perhaps his interest in the female body that made him the most imaginative lover she had met. (This is not claiming a great deal.) She continued to go to the Dorothy, and bought herself a tube of the jelly and an applicator of her own, in case.

Toward the end of her first year, Frederica also came across the upper classes, having caught the attention, at a party given by an acting cousin of his, of a nervous and very rich young viscount ("fairly bright," "physically insubstantial") who took her to two or three parties consisting largely of his relations and people he had been at school with, a country-house weekend and the Magdalene May Ball. Frederica was excited very simply by this—the English are what the English have been, and her head was full of romantic novels, Brideshead expectations, unfulfilled, and the desire to move beyond Blesford. All Winifred's children had inherited her social terror in one form or another; Frederica dealt with it by pretending it was immoral and beneath her. But in sweet Freddie Ravenscar's company it struck. She felt her buttons, her long and short gloves, her shoes, her turns of phrase, her lack of the right acquaintance and relations being as remorselessly weighed and found wanting as her French grammar, her Latin scansion, her verbatim knowledge of Shakespeare had on occasion been weighed and valued. In revenge, or reciprocally, it was from sweet Freddie that she first learned to diagnose male sexual terror. He knew how to bring her the right things to eat at parties, to hold her coat, to order dinner and a decent wine in the Union. If he found himself alone in a room with her—or worse, faced with the good-night kiss in all its public vulgarity at the Porter's Lodge—he trembled with what she slowly and incredulously discovered to be respect for her sex, its purity, its delicacy, its mystery. All these words he brought out in a strangled whisper over dinner in the Dorchester where he took her to dance. "You are so *brave*," he said, by which he meant, though neither of them knew it, "You talk a lot, as though we were the same species." He had a nanny, of whom he talked a lot, and a mother, who remained simply two words, "my mother," until he took Frederica home to be glacially summed up as a predatory social climber. He had some sisters, who appeared regularly in the *Tatler*, and were busy just being ladies. He truly thought women were good and bad and that good women were somehow dirtied by being touched and would resent it. He would not categorize Frederica as either, although his mother could and did, by her standards accurately. He said in a punt, "I think I am in love with you," and Frederica pretended not to have heard, relying on his courage being inadequate to repeat it. She had done this more or less successfully with other men on other occasions. It was, it has to be said, his title and his inaccessible world that held Frederica's interest in sweet Freddie. And, after a time, a mixture of pity and terror—pity for his abject need, terror of his unmanageable, unlearnable, rigid exclusive world. And greed. Frederica liked knowing how things worked, even at the cost of blushing for her clothes and having no acceptable small talk. It was also Freddie who was responsible for introducing Frederica to Nigel Reiver. But that was later.

9

A L'ECLAT DES JEUNES GENS EN FLEURS, II

By the summer of 1955 Frederica was confident and inventive about categorizing people. She was able, for instance, to invent generic labels for her by-now-fixed friends, Alan and Tony. They were, she decided, respectively a chameleon and a fake. The names came to her during a week when she was briefly in rooms with two very different novelists. Alan persuaded a friend of his at King's to include Frederica in a tea party at which E. M. Forster would be present. Tony insisted that she accompany him to a meeting of the Literary Society to be addressed by Kingsley Amis. The tea party came first.

In many ways Frederica had no wish to meet Forster. She was afraid it might spoil for her the sentences about the cow, or the opening of *Passage to India*, both of which she saw as in some way her property, because she had so exactly measured the verbal felicity with which they were put together. There was also, more privately, the matter of the vision of nothing in the Marabar Caves that she had suffered, and recognized, and previously had no name for. She—and Alan and Tony and Edmund Wilkie and Alexander Wedderburn—were now living furiously in a world the novelist said had changed beyond recognition or discrimination in his fiction. What could she have to say to him? Or he to her? All the same, it would be interesting, if not to meet, to be able to say one had met, Morgan Forster.

The tea party was in rooms overlooking the main court, across to the chapel. The novelist sat, small, old, secret, benign, moustached, in a chintz-covered armchair. Whoever inhabited the rooms had spread a tablecloth and there were scones, homemade jam, cucumber sandwiches, China tea, china teacups. Frederica touched Forster's hand and returned to a chair half behind a bookcase to watch. The young men—these seemed very young—had a mixture of public school good manners and a kind of prompting greed for reminiscence she was later to recognize in television interviewers. The novelist spoke of punting, of how time had seemed slower in his Cambridge. He wore furry tweed and his waistband was high toward his armpits. Alan—

who had, Frederica had slowly discovered, a rough background of struggling to survive among Glasgow teenage gangs, who could tell, at discreet moments, hairy stories of bicycle chains, flick knives, knuckle dusters, savage wounds—had brushed his blond hair into a gleaming cap and handed sandwiches assiduously, saying, "Sir," in a Scots way that made Frederica imagine a severe upbringing under an exacting dominie. There were only two women at the tea party. Alan had certain ways, certain mannerisms, that appeared only in male gatherings, or as now, almost male, a certain charming laugh, a kind of humbleness, too. Frederica could not help remembering how the conversation about the cow had been destroyed by the interruption of the female sex. She drew back against the bookcase.

After ten minutes, Forster went to sleep, and remained asleep throughout the rest of the party, which was conducted in hushed and reverent tones while he snored gently and easily. He seemed content. Frederica was brushed by fear of failure, fear of confinement.

The man sitting on the floor next to her had a Polish name— Marius Moczygemba—and a light, clear, classless English voice, which in those days meant not transatlantic, nor yet Liverpool, nor yet adjustable Cockney, but a clear BBC voice with no syllable elided or lost. It was a lovely voice, and he used it to tell Frederica how to say her Latin grace elegantly in church Latin, an Italianate Latin much softer and pleasanter than school Latin with its w's and hard c's. He said he believed she was a famous Cambridge figure; he would like to talk to her, also to paint her portrait since she had an unusual face. "I studied painting before coming here. I think I shall be a painter. I shall be a better painter with a good classical education, don't you agree? Perhaps I should study philosophy. Or do you think English?" Frederica asked what sort of painting he did and he said it was indescribable, but not English Romantic. She must come and see it. She said she would like that. He was a little man, lively, self-contained, very attractive—not only because of the voice.

The novelist woke up, apologized without embarrassment, ate some cherry cake, smiled vaguely on all of them and padded slowly, carefully, away. Walking home across the Backs to Newnham in the sun, Frederica puzzled over the relation between the Marabar Caves, her dark brain's image of moving flame, curling worms, nothing, and

exact language and a man's life in Cambridge with its restrictions, its
scones and irresistible afternoon sleep. Cambridge was, she thought,
not a good place for writers. For readers, yes. How to live? She asked
herself this, often. She thought of Lawrence rootlessly quarreling
with women in New Mexico. She thought of Stephanie in Blesford.
She put up her head and jutted out her chin with generalized
determination.

Tony insisted that Frederica come to hear Amis speak at the Literary Society because *Lucky Jim* was an "important book." Frederica
was to read *Lucky Jim* four times—once because someone had lent
it to her, once to see what Tony saw in it, once because she was ill
in bed, read very fast, and had got through everything else, and once
because she was writing an article on fashions in contemporary fiction. On the first three readings she found it not at all funny and
couldn't see its "significance." On the fourth, which took place after
her brief Cambridge time, and after the invention of the Angry
Young Men, she was suddenly reduced to tears of helpless laughter
by the sheet-snipping episode. By the time of the article she was
able knowledgeably to place Jim Dixon's horrible face pulling,
mockery of Merrie England, practical jokes, and infantile rages as
part of what was known as the "limited revolt" of the intellectuals
against the benign and humdrum welfare state. She was able to
compare this "limited revolt" with reactions to a family structure
known as the Power House, in which the principles and even practice of the parents are so liberal, so rational, so acceptable, that any
necessary rebellion against their authority must take the form of
absurd gestures, petulant or violent. She felt she knew something
about the Power House. She might have been saved from trivial acts
of revolt only by Bill's rages, which were a legitimate cause of revulsion. This understanding did not—in the long run—make her any
more tolerant or admiring of Jim Dixon.

On all four readings Frederica felt a very simple sexual distaste for
Lucky Jim. There was a nice girl, whose niceness consisted of big
breasts and a surprising readiness to find the lunatic Dixon attractive
and valuable, and a nasty woman, who was judged for bad makeup
and arty skirts as well as for hysteria and emotional blackmail. This

character was the object of violent hatred: "Dixon wanted to rush at her and tip her backwards in her chair, to make a deafening rude noise in her face, to push a bead up her nose." Frederica had once had a bead up her nose, as an infant; she remembered the pain. Then there was an old lady in a cerise hat who, Dixon believed, should be crushed like a beetle for delaying a bus on which he was riding. She might have accepted this accurate description of the cruelties of the frustrated imagination but was amazed that so many of her friends found Dixon to be some kind of moral hero. They took to studied rudeness, pranks, and face making. Tony explained to Frederica that Jim was the decent man, the common man, the scrupulous man, making his honest stand against the snobbish pretensions and cliquish frivolity of Bloomsbury aesthetes or *Brideshead Revisited*. Frederica had on a first reading taken *Brideshead* as a satirical attack on the Roman Catholic faith, but she had also been moved by it. If you were going to set up childish irresponsibility as a model of innocence, she supposed she would rather have Charles Ryder and Sebastian Flyte in the garden from which they would inevitably be expelled than the elementary-school antics of Jim Dixon. Both were perpetual children, the one Peter Pan, the other Just William. Frederica had rather hoped to encounter not boys, but men.

The novelist himself, when he spoke, appeared handsome, fresh faced and engagingly unaffected. He was properly self-deprecating (which Cambridge liked) and not concerned to make too much of the important of literature (which Leavis's Cambridge was more ambivalent about.) Later the undergraduates who listened equably enough to his deliberately light insistence that the novel was primarily entertainment were to treat Colin Wilson, author of that existentialist outcry *The Outsider*, with contemptuous and ill-informed savagery. Humor was acceptable and existential passion was alien and suspect. Mr. Amis praised Fielding's good sense, deprecated the excessive seriousness of *Mansfield Park*, and spoke of the saving grace of comedy as a way of destroying pretentiousness. Frederica was not immune to the deadly seriousness with which the charge of humorlessness could be leveled against anyone who caviled at this view. She became cross, partly because she had gone there intending to become cross. Beside her, Tony, wearing a checked woolen scarf tied like a working-class muffler, sat in his donkey jacket, laughed when the novelist put down a question about the novel as a means of "expressing oneself," and asked a question about Amis's view of the value of literary studies in universities. The novelist said he was against pompous and earnest interpretation and in favor of teaching people to recognize, read, and write clear and flexible English. Accessible to everyone, said Tony the socialist. More or less, said Mr. Amis, who was still far from feeling the need to advocate educational exclusiveness.

Outside the English faculty Frederica got into an intemperate argument with the others about the moral usefulness of deflating humor. Tony spoke of popular decency and scrupulousness. Frederica launched into a speech about how the whole business made her more sympathetic to Matthew Arnold and High Seriousness. She said pompous and pretentious were words you should always look twice at, in case you could substitute better ones, like serious, or responsible. "Judging *styles* isn't necessarily judging morals, is it?" she said grandly, waving her arms. "Hooper in *Brideshead* gets nastily mocked for his accent and his hair and not knowing about the moral style of Brideshead. I don't like that; it's unjust. But it's *really* just as bad that Lucky Jim mocks Bertrand Welch for saying "you sam" and wearing a beret and liking art, and abroad, and English history, isn't it? Jim is *so sure* he knows what a nice and nasty skirt for a girl is, and what's more, that nice girls are in nice skirts and nasty ones in nasty ones. In twenty years anyway the nice skirts'll be nasty and the decent skirts'll be something else and we won't be *wearing* any makeup or else we'll be painted like savages, and all his nice discriminations about Christine's choice of lipstick as opposed to Margaret's will be unintelligible or antiquated. And I don't think it's nice or funny to *hate* old ladies for wearing squashed cerise hats."

She was going on. Frederica never knew when to stop talking. She was tapped on the shoulder by an unknown man who said urgently, in a singing Welsh voice, that he found what she had to say very interesting, very amusing, very *serious* too if she wanted that, he'd like to talk to her but not now, could he know her name and college?

"She's Frederica Potter from Newnham," said Tony. "She argues about everything." "And I'm Owen Griffiths from Jesus," said the Welshman. "Secretary of the Socialist Club, and you're Tony Watson, Trevelyan Watson's son, and you write clever stuff in *Varsity* and *Granta* and share your dad's hope for the revolution, but not yet, like St. Augustine and repentance, don't you?" "Something like that," said Tony, squaring up a little, while Frederica tried unsuccessfully to sum up the stranger, whose loud, singing voice was either humorlessly intense or self-confidently mocking, she was not sure, could not tell. He was physically a contradiction too, black and broad and craggy, yet liquid, with dark moving eyes and a mouth that was either fluent or loose. "I'll call on you, girl," he said, and moved away.

It was Owen Griffiths' not-so-casual introduction of the name Trevelyan Watson that enabled Frederica, affectionately enough, to classify Tony as a fake. Trevelyan Watson was a 1930s Left Book Club man of letters who had inherited and renounced a baronetcy, whose books included *Literature for Everyman, The Chartered Thames, Decadence and Revolt* and *Another Tradition*. He lived in Chelsea. Tony had been sent to Dartington, that expensive and very progressive public school, a fact to which he never referred, as indeed, he never referred to Chelsea, allowing it to be thought that he came perhaps from an artisan family in Battersea. His working-class teapot, dripping toast, racing bicycle, shirts, boots, socks, jacket, haircut, were the products of loving research. Considering these, Frederica had further thoughts about the strange relations between the niceties of human perceptions and creations of style and the discriminations of the moral and political life. Did she recognize the glimmering of a later obsessive subject, *her* subject? For now, it was in terms of Tony's fake class origins that Frederica was able to define Alan as a chameleon. Tony she saw as a work of art, not a lie—he simply made it hard to *ask* direct questions about his home life, or his early life. Frederica was later to come to see Trevelyan Watson's house too as a Power House: Tony could not refute his father's beliefs, only reproach him by adopting the style, the attitudes, of the workers he admired, studied, and did not resemble. Frederica was both amused, and offended, by this prevaricating presentation of self.

As Bill's daughter she believed in some kind of truth here too. She was what she was, as wool was wool, and the north the north, and nylon nylon.

Alan, the chameleon, *was* working-class, and would say so, if asked, though he created situations in which he was not asked. Owing to his toughly delicate good looks, his health, his blondness, his truly classless Scottish accent, he could respond with skill to the behavior of those around him. In the pub with Tony he was the real thing, the working-class beer drinker. With groups of musical (usually Christian) medievalists he became a mixture of Scottish pedantry and scholarship with clear aesthetic pleasure. With those interested in painting he became easily knowledgeable and very delicately precious. In the King's homosexual context, Frederica was to notice, Alan could shape-shift back and forth, as seemed to be desired, from working-class roughness to a kind of well-bred (Scottish) Greek athlete at ease in the world. He had canny eyes: Frederica caught him, once she had realized that his shifts were interesting to observe, thinking how or who to be. Later, he became too skilled to be seen doing this. He was her good friend, and she had no idea who he loved, or slept with, or wanted.

If she had more sympathy with the chameleon than with the fake it was because she concluded that women were naturally driven to that state. She had too tough and inflexible a sense of her identity to be as good a chameleon as Alan Melville. She did not intend, as she began to suspect he did, to make a career of it. She tried, in a small way. She said "darling" and "love" to the theater people. She tried to adjust her clothes to the preconceptions of sweet Freddie, though some things cannot be done without money. (He was shocked by a pair of elbow-length nylon gloves she had, which he had supposed might be old lace.) She talked about "value" to the poetry friends and slickly and cynically to Tony and Alan. But only in bed—or on sofas, or in punts, or hand in hand on the Backs—did she truly practice being a chameleon. She gave back as much—or more often as little—as was offered or expected. Her greed did not express itself in bed as it did in conversation. She copied and followed, she did not demand. She was unaware that this was all she did. She awoke once from a dream in which she was a grass meadow, held to the earth by myriad grass roots through her hair, fibrils painlessly incorporating her skin in turf, a Gulliver being absorbed by Lilliput, and over the meadow leaped, slowly, exhaustedly, rhythmically, similarly, a procession of pale yellow frogs, long legged, mostly flaccid, a spurt, a heavy-breathing rest, a floppy spurt, one after the other after the other . . .

This may seem to be a chill and clinical account of a time that was, was perceived as, rich, confusing, full of emotion. The language with which I might try to order Frederica's hectic and somewhat varied sexual life in 1954–55 was not available to Frederica then. She had the physical and intellectually classifying adjectives, but she did not believe herself to be primarily conducting research but looking for love, trust, "someone who would want her for what she was." And she had thought very little about the feelings or expectations of clever boys or clever young men. There were many things, however many beds she hopped in and out of, however many cheeks she demurely brushed, that she was not fitted to understand. She came, after all, not in utter nakedness but cocooned by her culture in a web of amatory, social, and tribal expectations that was not even coherent and unitary.

She believed unquestioningly, with part of herself, for instance, that a woman was unfulfilled without marriage, that marriage was the end of every good story. She was looking for a husband, partly because she was afraid no one might want her, partly because she couldn't decide what to do with herself until that problem was solved, partly because everyone else was looking for a husband. (It is curious, but true, that the offers she received in no way changed her fixed feeling that the sort of woman she was was essentially not wanted as a wife.)

She believed, with a mixture of "realism" and resignation, that women were much more preoccupied with love than men were, more vulnerable, more in pain. There were imposing tags in her mind. "Man's love is of man's life a thing apart / 'Tis woman's whole existence." "He for God only, she for God in him." "I claim only this privilege for my sex—you need not covet it . . . this distinction of loving longest when life, when hope is gone." She was conditioned to desire to be abject. This desire was reinforced by the behavior of Rosamond Lehmann's heroines and of Ursula Brangwen (whom some other part of Frederica was ready to despise heartily). And there was the knowledge gleaned from agony columns, where abject women asked for help with the indifferent, the unfaithful, the only-wanting-one-thing, the other women's husbands.

The Frederica who had fled to Scarborough with Wilkie rather than go to bed with Alexander might be described as instinctively in revolt against "whole" (overwhelming) love, though she would have said she was afraid of failure, embarrassment, bloodshed. The Frederica who conducted experiments in sex in Cambridge was look-ing for an ideal lover. At one level. At another, she was conducting a battle with the whole male sex. She often said, "I like men," as one might say, "I like strong cheese," or, "I like bitter chocolate," or "I like red wine." She came to pronounce that each relationship was what it was—dancing, sex, talk, friendship—as many as there were men. This was true, and she believed it, but it was not the whole truth. Her behavior was more dictated by generalizations about men, or Men, than she was at first aware.

Men had their group behavior. Together they talked about girls as they might talk about motorcars or beer, joking about breast measurements and legs, planning campaigns of seduction like army or teenage gang maneuvers. For these men women were better or worse, easier or more rarefied sex. Simply. Frederica did the same, at first half-consciously, then with deliberation. She judged and cate-gorized men. Quality of skin, size of backside, texture of hair, skill. Men discussed whether girls would or wouldn't. Frederica furiously categorized those men who could and couldn't. If men wanted "only" one thing, so could, and would, and did, Frederica Potter. She took some pride in the fact that there was no one who could feel able to refer to her as his girlfriend. She preempted the planned, staged, pur-chased (with curry, with films, with wine) seductions by immediate acquiescence or unusually direct and candid rejection. These habits took some learning and there were moments when she lost her nerve, even wondered if she were cheap, or a tart. (Fast would have been a good word for her but came from another decade.)

There were men who wanted *her*, or seemed to, who sent letters quoting "the not-impossible She," who asked delicately if she saw them as perhaps special. Here Frederica's confusion was at its height. She believed that she wanted to solve the marriage problem. To find a true mind, with the rest of course added. But she also wanted not to be like her mother's generation, free and powerful only during this brief artificial period before concession and possession. She felt contempt for the suitors, which protected her from taking them seriously, or allowed her to remain abject—in her own mind—before the not-impossible unknown. She prevaricated and cheated, shared them with other women and neither felt nor appeared to feel jealousy. (This was owing to egocentricity: she simply could not *imagine* men in the company of other women.)

It should by now be clear that Frederica was more than once both cruel and destructive. In extenuation it can be argued that she had not been led by custom or by cultural mythology to suppose that men had feelings. Men were deceivers ever, the bad ones, and masterful, the good ones. The world was their world and what she wanted was to live in that world, not to be sought out as a refuge from or adjunct to it.

She might have been instructed by literature. She had read endless descriptions of the shyness and desperation of male first love. But whereas she recognized the humiliation of Charlotte Brontë's Lucy Snowe, of Rosamond Lehmann's brave, doomed girls, and the death of the heart, from some fund of ancient knowledge, she did not recognize, or believe in, the professional coquettes or pure young girls, or mysterious animal presences of the male novels. None of these were anything to do with Frederica Potter, who was brisk, businesslike, interested in but not obsessed by sex, and wanted to make friends of the creatures if they would have it. Women in male novels were unreal and it was beyond Frederica's comprehension that young men might suppose she was any or all of these characters. So they battled, the men to be hopelessly devoted, Frederica to be abject and/or free, and were puzzled and hurt. Frederica was shocked and startled when one young man burst uninvited into a tea she was making for another and smashed a teacup with a poker. She categorized long and deeply considered love letters as parts of a campaign and ignored them.

When one desperate man whom she found unexciting, apart from an encyclopedic knowledge of Thomas Mann, burst into tears and said she was mocking him, she could only stare, become wholly silent, and go home.

She was afraid of confinement. The new Queen and the Duke of Edinburgh visited Newnham, and the Duke, surrounded by hair-dressed academic ladies and gowned, demure-looking girls, asked the senior student jokingly, "Do you ever get out of here?" And Frederica felt rage—rage that he could ask, when she herself was never in, had so much life, was so free, much more free, she innocently imagined, than he would ever be.

The word confinement reminded her of Stephanie. She had seen her, and met William, the summer before coming up to Newnham, just after her return from France. William sat up, his plump extended legs balancing his swaying trunk, and looked at her under his fine black hair and long black lashes, smiling vaguely and secretly, his glance flickering over and past her.

"Hullo, baby," said Frederica, putting out a finger. Stephanie never took her eyes off the boy, never let her attention stray beyond six feet from him. Stephanie told Frederica that she was already expecting another one—conceived, she said, in a moment of release when they thought Marcus might go away. She had felt unconfined, she had actually said. It was a funny way of proving it, Frederica thought, part of her sensuously attracted by William's same yet different flesh and dark eyes, part terrified of him, of Stephanie's bodily content and fatigue, of the process of confinement.

NORMS AND MONSTERS, I

I

Daniel's vicar, Mr. Ellenby, retired, and was replaced by a much younger man, Gideon Farrar. Daniel might have hoped to be moved from Blesford himself on this occasion, but was not. He had met Farrar at a diocesan gathering and told Stephanie that he was known as a live wire. Since Daniel himself had also been qualified with this ambiguous name, Stephanie thought he might have been expected to approve of him, but sensed that he didn't. She went to hear his first sermon, aware of the anxiety and even meager anger of parts of the congregation around her. He had moved things: the sentimental Victorian crucifix was gone from the altar, the branched candlesticks had been replaced by plain square wooden candle holders; the embroidered altar cloth by snowy austere linen. Stephanie, who had disliked the epicene body and sweet half smile of the hanging god, was surprised at her own resentment of his whisking away. She wondered if the new broom was about to sweep away also the very ugly embroidered carpet in the sanctuary, made by church ladies to commemorate the fallen, in military colors, khaki, air-force blue, navy, camouflage. She wondered if, if this went, she would miss it too.

Gideon Farrar, about ten years older than Daniel, was a big man with a presence he enjoyed. He had a square, spade-shaped, abundant beard, streaked and hatched-corn gold and premature silver; the slight curling foot of the spade made him resemble the King of Hearts. He had, under the winged flow of moustache, a large mouth with many different smiles. He wore plainer vestments than Mr. Ellenby, with modern, abstract stitching. He preached a sermon on personal relationships, including his own with his congregation. It was delivered with warmth and energetic friendliness; the preacher's roving eye regularly caught the eye of now this, now that, eager or reticent parishioner.

"Today, on my first coming to you as your parson, I want to talk to you about three meanings of the word person, personality. I want us to think about the second person of the Trinity, Jesus Christ the divine man who is most truly a person in every sense, with whom we have our most important personal relationship. Secondly, I want us to think about modern interpretations of the old sense in which the parson—the word *means* person—was taken in the past to be the personal, the representative man, *persona exemplaris*, the representative of the *personal nature* of the community or parish. And I want, thirdly, to consider the contribution of the new science of sociology to our thinking about personal relationships. For this science—especially in America—sees our social relations in terms of what it calls roles, prescribed dramatic parts—and our enactment of these roles as, say, father, pupil, executive, skilled craftsman, social worker, wife, parson, or whatever. These roles are also given the name "persona" —the word derives from the name for the masks worn by the actors, the *dramatis personae* of ancient Greek tragedy. "One man," as Shakespeare most truly said, "in his time plays many parts." Our roles may conflict. The qualities required by society of a good parson or a good father or a good citizen may put conflicting strains upon us we are unaware of. We, as Christians, secure in our relationship with the perfect, not partial, personality of Jesus Christ, who was all things to all men, may scoff at the insights of this new science, which tells us that our personalities are created by institutions, by history, by the expectations of others, that we *are* our masks. We should be wrong to scoff . . .

"I should like to speak to you for a moment about the revolutionary ideas of Pastor Dietrich Bonhoeffer, who, as you will all know, was imprisoned in Auschwitz for his part in the plot to overthrow Hitler and was executed in April 1945. Bonhoeffer confronted fearlessly the fact that our society has found it can do without God, in science, in politics, even in morals. He learned as a Christian to *welcome this development* because it puts us, as Christians, in the position of Christ himself in an alien and uncomprehending world. In our *personal relationships* we may find Christ . . .

"As your parson I am not your representative. At most I am a *persona*, a mask, representing the history and institutions of the church, things which can be both a strength and at times a wall between our selves and the living truth. These roles have a useful function. But they must not be confining cells—beyond and through them I must be a man among men, I must come to you as a man among men.

"I would urge that we meet, in humble exploration, *outside* this special building as inside it, to discover our personal relations in the world as in the church. Sociology and psychology have much to teach us about the relations of men in groups, and we must learn from their insights. The family is the primordial group; what we are with our family influences profoundly how we shall behave in other groups, and in Christ's family. I have formed the practice of having simple family meals with my parishioners which are *real* meals, not sacraments, not symbols, in our *real* homes, to break bread and wine, to discuss and discover. I hope you will all join me."

The Ortons were invited that Sunday to one of Gideon's "agape" or "family" meals. His wife, Clemency, telephoned and explained that *everyone*—Daniel's mother, Stephanie's brother, the baby—should come. Marcus said he would rather not go. Daniel said that Marcus would go. If he was going to live in his (Daniel's) house, he would do as the household did. Marcus made no reply to this except to retreat upstairs. But he was ready, on the turn of the stairs, when they came back from church to collect him.

Something had happened to the dark Victorian rectory. It smelled of new paint, which was mostly lemon yellow and white. Walls had vanished, and small, stuffy, private rooms had disappeared. The old drawing room and the old dining room were now joined by a large arch and light shone through from the road to the back garden, now resembling a children's playground. There were circular chairs in clear colors—geranium, peacock, lemon—on spiky black metal legs. The thick Turkish carpets were gone and the floors were covered in pale rush matting; gone were the polished mahogany and glass-fronted cabinets, and in their place were a stripped pine refectory table, long benches, a pine dresser with Finnish tumblers and Denby stoneware, pine green inside, matt white outside, with ears of wheat on them. There were white linen curtains spattered with gold and silver irregular discs. On the walls were the Picasso child holding a dove, a Chagall cockerel, some Miró playfulnesses. The windows remained what they had always been—heavy, suspicious northern shutters against the outside world. It was perhaps the windows that made the scale seem paradoxical, a Swedish barn condensed into a suburban house. In Mr. Ellenby's day the rooms had seemed large, high, and cluttered. Stephanie reflected on the human propensity to require things to be as they always had been, to resist change. The clutter had depressed her and its vanishing alarmed her.

Clemency Farrar had the same pleasure in her own physical presence as Gideon. She had a silky black ducktail haircut, a curl over a white brow, a brilliant scarlet sweater with a black and scarlet skirt, and black and scarlet china beads. She was clean and bright. There were four children, who stepped forward like a ballet to shake hands: Jeremy, Tania, Daisy, and Dominic. Jeremy had Clemency's slight bones and blue-black hair with Gideon's mouth and wide eyes. Tania had long black plaits and dark skin. Her eyes and mouth were apparently Chinese. Daisy was black, black as soot and with an unreflecting texture, a flat, East African nose and tight, not glossy, black curls. They wore more or less matching bibbed trousers and polo necks, like a team uniform, and were very clean. They seemed near in age, possibly less than a year between each pair, and about ten years old.

Clemency held her arms out for William and exclaimed over his beauty. Gideon found an armchair for Mrs. Orton and admired her hat. Two teenage girls in aprons appeared and were introduced as young people from the grammar school anxious to meet—is it Marcus? Marcus. Marcus, please go and help Jacqueline and Ruth to carry in the dishes. We all help with our family meals.

"Watch 'e don't drop t'dishes," said Mrs. Orton. Gideon laughed.

They sat round the long table and ate. Gideon and Clemency provided a kind of commentary on both the things to be eaten and the people present. It was rather, Stephanie reflected, like reading a novel in which everything was there because it signified something, not just because it was there. In the center of the table was a featureless carved wooden angel, a polished sphere on top of a regular cone, with a gilded halo and wood-wafer wings spread in half-moons, like a conceptual child dancing. They had carrot and lentil soup, with warm brown rolls.

"Wholesome food," said Gideon. "Earthy food. I make the bread. Clemency taught me of course, but I flatter myself I do it better. It likes my roughness, the dough; it likes to be hammered before it's proved. The baker will sell you yeast."

"I know," said Stephanie, who made good bread.

The wine was in a brown jug. At the family meals, Clemency said, bread and wine were always offered, as a normal part of things. The children had a little wine in water.

They had baked ham, baked potatoes, baked spiced apples, green salad. The stylized ears of wheat were repeated on white round after round. Marcus refused the ham.

"Are you a vegetarian?" Gideon turned his attention from his carving.

"No, I don't like meat."

"There are days—when I seem to see into the life of things—when I wonder if I should eat meat. Mrs. Orton?"

"*I'm* not faddy."

"And there are days," carving vigorously, "when I feel—I will not shut me from my kind—God for his good reasons made us carnivorous; men have eaten meat together throughout time . . ."

"When they could get it," put in Daniel's mum, receiving her pink rounds, honey crusted, clove pierced.

Gideon laid down his knife, picked up his beaker, broke his roll, significantly. The teenage girls thoughtfully chewed their bread. It was very good bread. Marcus turned his potato round and round with his fork and then did the same to his apple. One was an imperfect oval, and one a squashy and punctured sphere. Also, the red transfer on the white plate did not match the green one as it should, so that the wheat ears appeared double and overlapping, not mimetically three-dimensional. He pushed the apple over the pattern and cut the end off the potato. Mrs. Orton was scrambling ham into her mouth, frowning with concentration. Gideon addressed her.

"I believe passionately," he told her, "in nurturing the extended family. It is a privilege to have you all—including you and small William—with us. It is good to see you settled among your people, with your own place, offering something to the family. Too many parents become unwanted when their useful days are thought to be

over. We have weakened the fabric of our society. It is a great
mistake."

"So it is," said Mrs. Orton.

Marcus thought: she is *no* use. She hopes he will offer her more
ham. She does not want to be of use. She eats. This ordinary spite in
Marcus could have been said to be an indication that Mrs. Orton did
in fact have her uses, and would have been so adduced by Gideon,
who was shrewd enough, had there been any sign that Marcus was
thinking anything. But there was not.

Clemency told Stephanie about her family.

"I was an only child, so I believe passionately in family life. I do
family counseling—I trained as a social worker before deciding to
marry Gideon. We are so very fortunate in our own family, which is
so much a unit."

Stephanie could find no way to ask about the racial origins of the
young Farrars, but was told.

"After Jeremy was born, Gideon and I talked about the population
problem and decided it would be wrong to bring more children into
the world when there were so many in need. So we adopted. Tania
comes from a mission in Malaysia, where the Chinese—she's Chinese
—are not very well treated, I'm afraid. And Daisy's mother went
back to Africa when Daisy was born, to be married into an African
family, and left Daisy with relatives, who found they couldn't support her properly. It was a case of an extended family taking on a
task it could well have performed in the country it came from, and
finding it impossible in our closed society. And Dominic's parents
handed him in to a London church one Christmas—they'd dressed
him in a *lovely* romper suit and shawl; they cared very deeply for
Dominic, but it was quite impossible for them to look after him. So
we all came together to help each other. Tania is quite unusually
gifted at gymnastics. Daisy is very musical. She plays two instruments.
And Dominic is our natural comic—a born actor, his teachers say.
We hope for great things. I like to put on family entertainments in
the church where all the children can give of their best together. Do
you do much of that in this parish, Stephanie?"

"The nativity play," said Stephanie.

"We will do something really *marvelous* for the Harvest Celebration. William is too little to do anything but listen, but you must certainly bring him along. And I suppose Marcus is too old. But the Youth Fellowship . . . Gideon is very keen on youth . . ."

They ate apple pie with cream and Wensleydale cheese. The girl next to Marcus said to him, "What are you doing for A level?"

"I was doing history and geography and economics." She did not question the "was."

"I knew your sister at school. Awfully brainy."

"Stephanie?"

"Frederica. I meant Frederica."

"Oh, Frederica. Yes."

"I'm doing biology. And botany and zoology."

Marcus rearranged some slices of apple more intensively so that it looked as though he'd eaten more than he had.

"Why?" he asked.

"Oh, well. I'm good at that sort of thing. I like looking into how things live. You can get quite excited about the life cycle of the rabbit, or about ant heaps."

"Can you?"

"Don't sound so cynical."

"I'm sorry. I didn't—I meant—I really only meant, can you?"

"Makes a change from people," said the girl.

Marcus hadn't looked at her, and didn't. He had no idea what she looked like, how tall she was, even, or whether she was Jacqueline or Ruth. But he suddenly felt rather pleased to be negotiating an ordinary conversation.

"What will you do then?" he asked.

"Grow things. Horticulture. Forestry. Maybe farming. Grow things. You could be happy doing that."

Marcus ate some apple and took a bite of cheese.

"What will you do?" said his unseen neighbor.

"I've no idea. Growing things sounds better."

"Better than what?"

"What I—what I was—"

"You can't say it's better if you don't know what it's better *than*."

"Oh, yes, I can," said Marcus. He still did not look at her. Gideon said he and Stephanie would wash up. There was a shared family rota and it was his go to wash up.

In the kitchen the paint had been stripped from the cupboards, and there was a new scrubbed table. It had been papered in pale sprigged paper and tiled in blue and white vinyl, but the room remained obstinately dark, a place where servants had lived enclosed lives. Gideon put on an apron and crouched over the sink like a keyed-up motorcyclist. His sleeves were rolled up, his shirt collar open. As Stephanie walked backward and forward with plates and dishes, he made her aware of the closeness of their hips in the small space. She pulled in her new waist, thick over her old waistband. He looked briefly at her breasts; her dress was tight under the armpits. His beard over the dishes was lively and opulent. He gleamed.

"Tell me about yourself," he said.

"There's what you see. I have a husband, and a baby, and a mother-in-law and a brother. That keeps me busy."

"It should. Are you sure it really does?"

"I should explain that I am not a Christian. Daniel and I understand each other. I help wherever I honorably can with his parish work."

"You didn't answer my question."

"I thought you might be asking how I fitted into the parish."

"No, I wasn't. You interest me. You hold something back."

And that, she thought, was an old line; she had heard that before. She turned her back to him, reached into a random cupboard to stack plates, to look away.

"I have my privacy."

"I understand that." His voice was resonantly intimate. "But you must allow me some curiosity about *you*—not Daniel's wife, William's mother, Marcus's sister, not yet the helpful spouse of the curate of this parish. All those are roles."

And this too, she thought, watching him watch her.

"I used to teach."

"A different role. Do you regret it?"

She had been brought up, and subsequently trained, to answer questions exactly.

"I miss the talk. The books. Working with books."

"You must not forgo self-fulfillment. That's a bad habit of women."

"I am quite happy."

"No, I think not. I sense an emptiness in you. A habit of self-denial."

She turned on him. "You are embarrassing."

"That's better. I wanted a direct response. Something personal."

"I believe in ordinary good manners, Mr. Farrar."

"Oh, yes, in general, I do agree. But we are going to work closely together."

"I told you. I am not—"

"Not a Christian. In our secular world Christ has many incognitos. It is not our duty—it may not be our right—to break them."

She made nothing of this remark. He caught her shoulders as she passed again, turning her to face him.

"Friends, Stephanie?"

She could feel his will.

"Naturally, I hope," she murmured vaguely. The gold eyes considered her buttoned front. He patted her hair and let her go.

Afterward she was puzzled by how much this usual conversation upset her. It was simply a crude version of the routine pass. It had stated, "I say you are interesting because you attract me." Or, "because I am the sort of man who is attracted to all, or almost all, personable women." Gideon had displayed a not unusual clerical combination of personal conceit and intrusiveness. In some cases—not, she thought, this—clergymen acquired the conceit and the persistence to cover a primary shyness. It was their role. In Farrar the sexual push was—as in Daniel indeed—the product not of insecurity but simply of abundant energy. She was ashamed that she had responded at all. She had needed to be told she was still a woman, and was ashamed to need—at all—to be told in this way. And he had made her say what she felt: that she missed the books.

11

During the weeks that followed, Daniel was surprised and even shocked by the degree to which he himself missed Mr. Ellenby and his certainties. He joked (to Stephanie) that the parish had lost King Log and replaced him with King Stork. But, standing in the church after services, he became aware that both he and the building were changed by the replacement of Mr. Ellenby's profound belief in the mysteries of the Christian faith, the God-given and God-directed order of morality and history by Gideon's emphasis on personal relations. Daniel was ill at ease with the "personal." What Mr. Ellenby had seen as Daniel's interference in the private lives of his parishioners Daniel saw as a *practical* ordering of resources of help. He did not require affection, let alone love, from those he helped; he did put a great deal of imagination and consistent effort into helping them sensibly. Gideon was a man, Daniel saw, whose religious needs sprang from an overpowering desire to exact and bestow affection, contact, warmth. He did not know whether it was a failing or a virtue in himself that he feared and mistrusted this.

When he was alone in the church he thought out what it meant to him, a house where no one lived, a building made to represent an idea of the nature of things, a place where certain phrases, certain prayers, certain confessions of faith, had been repeated and repeated over the centuries, a building where a community had been more alive to its common life than to the individual need of men and women. It was heavy and stuffy and confined; it represented order and authority. In the days of Mr. Ellenby, to whom transcendent truth, order, and authority were living beings, Daniel had been able to afford the luxury of being the rebel, of questioning, in his secret mind, the sources of his religion, of human morals. In the new dispensation, where an almost anthropological vision of the source of morals in the life of the family seemed to inform Gideon's thinking, Daniel found himself regretting the commandments, authority itself. He loved his wife terribly, and his son with protective fear, his mother with a sense of shared blood and tribal responsibility. These loves in themselves would not have led him to universal "love" if there was such a creature. His sense that the old must be comforted, the sick relieved, the useless made useful, came from a need for *order* so profound that he had needed the authority of Holy Orders, a form that sanctioned his dogged use of his life to restore a little order to the muddle and limpness and fear we make of things. Mr. Ellenby had believed *for* him, for Daniel. He had often sat in this church and thought: in another society I would as easily have been a Buddhist priest, a Hindu, a Moslem. What he believed and said he believed every day in the creed was what, in Sheffield in the mid-twentieth century, had been the available and thus the right form to believe. Now, under Gideon, this compromising doubt seemed dangerous as it had not. The church seemed vacant, the altar merely a table, the words (more often extempore, less regularly repeated) less authoritative, more dubious.

There was in St. Bartholomew's the usual group of devout old ladies whose life seemed truly to center in that building. They had never much liked Daniel, who had paid, in their view, insufficient attention to jumble sales and coffee mornings. They had then felt he was subversive. They had clicked their tongues over his brusque closings of conversations about what was and wasn't done; they had criticized his dusty shoes and his preaching vehemence. Now, however, they clustered about him after communion, their faces under their fierce hats a mixture of helpless fear and impotent anger. They asked what he thought would be changed. They asked what Gideon really *believed*. They asked what would become of those who had simple faith and hoped for reward in the life to come. Daniel could not have claimed to love these women, but he did know them, he had watched them, he knew how they held to the repetitions, the rituals, the assurances, the habits of the parish.

Gideon had once or twice referred to them as dragons. He saw them as part of what the church had become, what he wished to overthrow, to make new, to take out into the world. Daniel, looking around at them one Sunday shortly after his first agape meal, saw them as survivors of a threatened cult, clustered for comfort, fantastically crowned with red Phrygian cap, a wreath of corn daisies on a purple turret, a feathered plume on a felt helmet. A stiff smile spread in a frail-skinned face round large, robust, very white false teeth. A pinched mouth trembled in disapproval among radiating lines of wrinkles. Not dragons, not even witches: old. They spoke wailingly and disagreeably as a chorus and he felt himself, briefly, imagining their sense of loss and ransack, to have come out of the dark, out of dusty corners, to be peering and blinking at the church swept clean of cobwebs and lace, vestments and God the Father, candles and the flames of the Holy Ghost.

Gerry Burtt waited for Daniel in a dark corner of the church until even these ladies had left, and then sidled out and plucked the departing Daniel by the sleeve.

"Can I have a word? You see I'm Gerry Burtt."

Daniel did not see. Gerry Burtt made an effort.

"In't papers. Nine months back."

Daniel thought, and failed.

"I were acquitted. That weren't right. *She* were found guilty."

"Oh, yes. Barbara Burtt."

"Aye."

Daniel remembered. It had been a local *cause célèbre*—a young couple, married just in time, accused of the murder of their six-month-old child. Gerry and Barbara Burtt. The child had been beaten, burned, starved, and finally smothered. Crowds of women had howled outside the assize court in Calverley as the figures of the parents were rushed in, blindly muffled under blankets. In the public gallery they had hissed and shaken with rage. A good lawyer had got Barbara Burtt to plead guilty to infanticide. Gerry, who had maintained that he was responsible for none of the sores, welts, burns, on his daughter's body, who had been described as "a little slow-witted" by his counsel, had been jailed for neglect and was now out. His wife, Daniel remembered vaguely, had been recommended for hospital treatment.

"Mr. Burtt. Tell me what I can do."

"Nowt, I expect. Nowt."

He was a thin creature, more boy than man, with a pallid little face covered with dots, spots, and whole continents of ginger tan, mapping his unremarkable features with a lively and apparently alien colonizing stain. He had pale blue eyes, pale, pinkish, slightly crushed stubby lashes. He sat next to Daniel in the church, in a back pew, and slowly, over half an hour or more, produced a few sentences.

"I feel right sick. All t'time. I don't want to go on. I can't work,

I can't do owt, I've got nothing. I can't speak, not in't pub, not to me family. I'm that sick." He repeated, with lifeless insistence, that he was sick. "I don't like mysen. I mek *mysen* sick."

Daniel asked about work. He had none. About his family.

"They don't want to know. Rightly."

The easy phrases stuck in Daniel's throat. How could he use words like forgiveness, like repentance? He said, "You must want to go on. You came to the church."

Mr. Burtt scraped the church paving stone with a metal-tipped boot.

"Maybe I came to—to give up—to give mysen up. I don't know. Maybe I came because of *her*."

"Your wife?"

"*Her*. I tell you—what I came to tell you—is, what I can't abide. What I can't abide is, if they let her out. If she come back. If she come near me. If I'ad to set eyes on her again, I don't know what I'd do."

"Is it likely that they will let her out?"

"I dunno. She wants to see me. They think I—I don't know."

"Tell me more about her."

"She were no better than an animal. No, worse. They look after their own. She were lazy. You can't know how lazy. She never got out o' bed. Never got out o' that one 'orrible nightie. Never cooked, you know, never warmed owt up, for hersen nor me, nor—t'kid. T'room was all filthy cups and packets o' things—cornflakes, cream cakes, chocolate, them sort o' things, peanut butter she 'et out o't pot."

"Sometimes people who sleep like that are ill."

"She couldn't abide the kid because she couldn't sleep. Never opened th'curtains. It were all to keep it quiet. She kept it quiet."

"Did you try to help it?"

"No. No." His sullen, staring face screwed up briefly. "It were *part of her*, do you see? The smell there—dirty bed, stinking nappies, filth all over—it were all *part of her*, like. T'kid were in the midst of it. With the same smell, it had, her smell."

"It wasn't happy. It was in pain."

"It were quiet. Whenever I come home, it were quiet. It were best quiet. If it stirred at all she'd be raving and screaming and banging like a mad thing. She had energy for raving and screaming." He paused. "It hadn't much voice at the best o' times."

"Perhaps she was ill. Needing help. Women do, after babies, most women."

The watery eyes met his, under the camouflage of freckles.

"They all say that. What I think. What I think is, some are wicked. Just wicked. She were dirty and wicked. I come here—to church—I come, because in church you can say it were *wicked*, what happened to 't kid, what she is, what I done. Or didn't do, any road."

He had come for judgment. Daniel sighed.

"How old is she?"

"Eighteen."

"A child."

"Oh, no. She were never a child. She meks me sick to my soul. She'll come back."

Daniel could not bring himself to urge Gerry Burtt to forgiveness.

"Sir, I come to you for help. For mysen. Help for mysen."

He exhaled a sour smell of despair, from mouth, armpits, trousers.

"If you can't see her, you shouldn't. It would do no good. Perhaps you should go away from her. Find work."

"Who'd want to gi' me work?"

"Come and have a pint, and we'll think about work."

Judgment was still required, still waited for.

"You know you should have protected the child. Cleaned it. Got a doctor."

"It were horrible too. It were—not right—covered in sick, lying in filth."

"All the more reason."

"I were frightened of it."

"It was little and helpless."

"I know," said Gerry Burtt. The oily skin under his eyes exuded damp drops. "Who would think a man could be such a poor thing as I was? No one can see how I could'a *let* it happen. You can be a fool, a right fool, just a helpless fool, sir."

"Oh, yes," said Daniel. "You can."

·   ·   ·

They drank a pint in the public bar of The Bag O'Nails that night and on various later evenings when Gerry Burtt appeared unannounced in the church. Daniel sat with his coat collar turned up, so that his presence might appear to be friendship, not charity. (This was one of the habits for which the old ladies criticized and disliked him.) He thought about Barbara Burtt, of whom he had no clear idea, and of the dead child, Lorraine, of whom he had less still, wounds, stench, enforced silence, no one there, no one there. He considered getting in touch with the authorities to find out what they believed Barbara's state to be, whether or not Gerry was justified in fearing her release. He did not do this because he felt that Gerry needed him, trusted him to take his word, to treat his fear as real and important, his moral horror as moral horror, not displaced guilt, though it was that too. "I come to you for help. Help for mysen." He found him temporary work wheeling loads of rubble from the site where Gideon's new youth club was to be built. He could not imagine what Burtt had been like before all this. All he communicated now was fear and loathing. Such things can be catching.

When he came home after one of these conversations in The Bag O'Nails his wife was sitting at the table feeding William, who was reclining in a small carrying chair. The house was now scattered with William's property, much of which consisted of small plastic objects in geometric shapes and primary colors: a round sky-blue dish, a yellow bucket with a white lid, a blue bath on white folding legs, a scarlet beaker, a series of round and square and triangular teething rings like huge primitive coins, or jewels, on fine chains or silk cords. On the table were various bowls of hot water containing blue Heinz tins of jamlike smeary stuffs. These were as muted, as bland or murky in color as the plastics were bright. Gray-green apple puree, yellow-green mushed peas, fawn milky cereal, cloudy orange juice. William himself presented the same contrast in colors and textures: his chair was peacock and white stripes, like circus tent canvas; his suit was buttercup yellow, and all smeared and spread with sticky fingers and masticated biscuit droppings and spat milky residues. There was a smell of milk and a warm, malty smell and a nappy smell and a disinfectant smell. Stephanie was putting something greenish into his mouth with a spoon, and William was letting most of the green run out again, moving his lips and tongue in random bubblings and suckings. One sticky hand held Stephanie's pale hair; one snatched at the patient spoon. Stephanie's face was streaked with slightly glittering, stiffening threads of drying food. Daniel held all the images in his mind for a moment, the stale smells of Gerry Burtt, the empty church, the old smoke and beer in the public bar, and the contradictory, cloying competing smells of his child's daily life, the bright things, the films and ridges and overflow and mess among the bright things.

"Gideon came in," said Stephanie.

"What for?"

"I don't know. He wants Marcus to go on a nature ramble with his Young Christians."

"Do him no harm."

"He may not want to go."

"He'd better. Better do something."

"You feed William; I'll make you tea."

His son looked at him with beady black eyes when Stephanie stood up to go, and opened his mouth to protest. Daniel spooned up some apple and pushed it into the incipient noise. Much spluttered out in droplets. The round tongue curled around the rest, spoon shaped, and sucked. Daniel felt every man's pleasure that apple was becoming baby, that fruit was going into flesh, that the curled pads of fist and finger, neck and cheek, were almost visibly expanding. The little black eyes looked into his. The mouth opened like a bird's. Daniel touched the warm head, the hair that was his hair and bent his nose to it. William smelled right, under all the alien muddle, sweet and sour. He smelled human; he smelled of Stephanie, of Daniel, of himself.

There were times when Daniel, cycling through Blesford, imagined his home as a very small place with very bright, soft light, secret inside closed windows, warm and private. Inside this thick, safe shell was order: his wife sitting by the fire, the child washed and fluffy-haired, the things on the table wholesome, a warm teapot, hot toast, solid sweet honey, the bright simple cleanness of William's plates and dishes, his oilskin table mat with a cheerful picture of all the single-minded creatures in the House that Jack Built, gnawing, killing, chasing, tossing, milking, kissing, marrying, waking, building.

And there were nights when he lay in bed, listening to the child making that terrible stirring sound, the broken, coughing, irritable sound that came before the howl and felt, after weeks of broken nights, that his house in the half-light was flimsy and overcrowded, undermined by whisking rats, blown through by gales that found crannies and made rents. At such times he heard his mother turn every few minutes on old bedsprings, the almost soundless brushing of Marcus's bare feet on his frequent nightly trips to the bathroom. His memory of the living room was sagging plaster, damp ceiling, unfinished paint over stained wallpaper, nappies in green-gold slime in their yellow bucket, grime on the windowpanes, closing him in. He said to Stephanie, one of these bad nights, hearing them all breathe and William starting up like a motor bike engine, "It's like living with a dragon, breathing smoke and flames and roaring out."

"I'll walk him."

"No. Get some sleep. I'll walk him."

And he paced the house, a heavy man in his socks, clutching his small son to his chest, one whole human body no wider than his own solid trunk, from soft crown to tiny, flexible feet. He paced his small space, measuring the limits of the downstairs room, door to skirting board to door, humming hymns, repressing the small flailings of the fists and ankles, willing the baby into quiescence. He walked with love, watching the heavy flutter of the fragile eyelids. He walked with rage, balked by the walls he met, by the uneasy sleep of the inhabitants, by his own love.

II

NORMS AND MONSTERS, II

At first, when Marcus left, Winifred had simply shut up his bedroom. Then, when he did not come back, she took to cleaning in there, during the day; hoovered, cleared shelves, put away old toys forever. Then, as he still did not come, she did more radical things, recovered the eiderdown, made new, plain curtains, and last, which should have been first, repainted the walls, which had been duck-egg blue, in white, the door, which had been cream, in white. She made the room clean and uniform and empty. In the day she often sat there, at his desk, looking out over the little garden at the rugby field beyond, where other boys ran, or circled arms round waists, stamped and struggled, a huge, headless circular crab. She thought, those boys are normal boys, and asked herself, what is normal?

She stopped when Bill came in, and came down to cook. There was not much cooking for only the two of them. Mostly they sat in silence. That would probably have happened anyway, Winifred considered. The talk had been Frederica, proclaiming, boasting, complaining, reciting, inciting, and Bill, hectoring, lecturing, questioning, disputing. Now, over the little meals she made, Bill read. He read fat books: nineteenth-century novels and works on psychoanalysis and psychiatry. It was possible that he did not see what he ate. He had been in the habit of complaining about his food and now did not. Winifred increasingly cooked the same weekly menu, chops one day, bacon the next, kippers, two days of roast lamb, two of spam and corned beef. She substituted bread for potatoes and tinned beans for most vegetables. She no longer made puddings; there was fruit, and three dwindling pieces of cheese, replaced as they became crumbs and then gaps. While Bill read, Winifred thought. She sat very tense and rigid while thinking, so that sometimes at the end of meals her fingers hurt where she had gripped the knife, her jaw hurt where she had set it.

She thought in an energetic, jarring way inside her stillness about her life, her home, her husband, her possessions.

The possessions that particularly attracted her attention during these silent meals were small objects with very limited functions. She considered daily the butter dish that exactly held a standard half-pound block of butter, the little butter knife with its blunt blade, the teapot stand in faded green pink and gold, the cheese dish, its wedge-shaped lid ornamented with brown floppy flowers, its handle a twisted pottery rope, the egg cozies in red felt, the pickle fork, a miniature trident, the small silver things, egg cups, toast rack, sugar tongs, brush and pan for removing crumbs from the tablecloth. These last had to be polished and were so intricate that the polishing always left traces and unattained streaks of iridescent tarnish. She had been pleased to acquire, to be given, most of these things, she remembered sourly. They made her life appear to correspond with some ordered, ideal form, some series of ceremonies to which the proper utensils lent authenticity and grace. Someone in a pottery had enjoyed twisting the cheese-dish handle. Someone had been pleased with the fine arch of the toast rack, an upturned boat shell, and had not considered the doorstep slice, or how to reach the little ring handle if the rack was full.

One had an idea of what one's life was going to be, of a home, of being a mother. Being a wife was more complicated, good and bad wives varied; there was room for argument and redefinition. Bad mothers, unlike bad wives, were all the same: negligent, improvident, self-regarding, indolent. Good mothers were also all the same: patient, comfortable, selfless, steady. In taking on being a mother she had assumed it would be done wholeheartedly and properly. It was her life, she *was* a mother. Being a good mother meant letting go at the right time. Stephanie had gone to Cambridge with her goodwill. Frederica's flighty rejecting chatter about the horror of "homes" had been determinedly tolerated. But Marcus's flight brought terror. The home was not a home if he screamed and wept at the thought of returning to it. And she? She had recently realized that there was something in being a woman, a mother, in late, in tiring middle age, that almost *automatically* alarmed and irritated others. She remembered having, in her youth, been irritated by those she then saw as old, or aging women, almost irrespective of their characters. She had not thought about it much, then, but did now. It was hard to cause fear and despondency involuntarily.

These cheese dish and egg cozies seemed swollen and grotesque. She thought of them as thick and saw their places on the tablecloth darkly and hotly, absurdly, outlined. She herself seemed to herself swollen and grotesque. She was besieged, or, it would be more accurate to say, infiltrated by the menopause. Her outer surfaces were sore, dull and dry. Inside she felt her blood course thinly and jerkily, her bones growing brittle, her irritable vision weakening. She had an idea of herself, which was not quite accurate, but became obsessive, as having once inhabited her body easily, not *noticed* that she was seeing clearly, walking painlessly, turning her head rapidly without dizziness or nausea. Now when she turned it fast, what she saw, or worse, the act of seeing, smeared the air between her and the objects, closing her in, making them problematic and threatening. There were the hot flashes. There was the paradox that she felt everything thinning, diluted, enfeebled, and yet heat could rise inside her as though she was boiling, an old witch in agony on her pyre, while she sat and looked at Bill reading, with the table set between them. The heat was not only blood or boiling fat; it was rage, to which she was wholly unused, causeless and loose, though she watched Bill, who was always angry, and took a humiliated, secret pleasure in accusing him for it. There she sat, a handsome, still, silver-gold woman, upright and judicious looking, and saw herself in her mind's eye as a raging volcano of overflowing flesh and cracking bone, dead hair, dull eyes, numb fingers, monstrous.

One day she looked at Bill, judging him, as she judged him daily now in a silent rush, making up for years of suspended disbelief, of retreat. An image came into her mind of a gaunt dog, living in a hovel with a drunk old man, kicked, beaten, bruised, starved, yet lying down to howl and pine, having to be dragged away when the horrid old man fell over and broke his neck. It had pined to death and had to be shot, or it had been nursed to health; she could not remember which. She must have read it somewhere. She saw it so clearly—food cooked in a tin pail, a roof with holes in, the dog scuffling for crusts, going hungry, the man's repentance after his drunken rages. Words like faithful and loving had been used. Of the dog. Winifred felt contempt for the dog and a more considered contempt for those who used human words for virtue for its behavior. It was its nature to accept blows, to attach itself. It should be neither praised nor blamed. And she?

She cleared up after him when he went out. She made Marcus's room new and white and clean. She cleaned Bill away. His cigarette stubs in grimy ashtrays nauseated her. She scrubbed the ashtrays. She shelved, randomly, heaps of books she would once have circumspectly moved aside and dusted. She washed his clothes as soon as they were dirty, or even before. If he noticed, he did not speak. She rubbed and twisted and ironed his shirts with cleanly loathing. She watched herself doing this as though it was, if unexpected, nevertheless a part of the manifest destiny she had taken on. Once, a pile of letters and papers slid by accident into the wastepaper basket and she left them there.

She heard him crashing about, searching, and said nothing.

Several times he said things like: "I can just about work. Not well. The life's gone out of my teaching. I bore the boys."

"And me?" she heard herself shouting. "And me? What do I do well? What?"

She was quickly quiet.

"You," said Bill, "look after . . ."

"What?" she shouted. "What?"

"Don't shout."

"How *dare* you say that to me? How dare *you* say that to me?" Bill's face creased into age. He said what he always said.

"You know I don't mean it. You know it's just something that happens."

"He couldn't bear your shouting."

"Oh, my dear, I know."

12

BEHOLD THE CHILD

It was agreed that Stephanie should have some time to herself, to work. It was agreed, largely by Daniel, that Daniel's mum and Marcus would mind William while she did an hour or two in the Blesford public library. This was the advantage, he explained, of the extended family. In fact Marcus felt simply afraid and Daniel's mum said she hoped Stephanie wouldn't be long, would be back well before the next feed and would tell Marcus if owt was to be done about supper. Stephanie felt that she was being accused of desertion by some powerful representative of motherhood. In fact, at William's age, Daniel had often been left for long periods while Mrs. Orton visited neighbors, or went down to the shop. Mrs. Orton said she could surely have read a book with all of them *in* the house, and Marcus then said breathlessly that they would be all right. Stephanie got out an old folder, her Oxford Wordsworth, her schoolbook bag, and set out for the library.

A period of acute discomfort followed for all of them.

Stephanie found it physically hard to pedal her bicycle away from the house. She felt held as by a long linen binder, such as mill children had worn to work machinery, to the shape of her son in his woven basket, one fist in his small ear. She seemed to hear, to feel, to smell, powerful calling sounds, rufflings of the air, odors, which wanted her back, insisted that she must return. She put down rational foot after rational foot, with difficulty.

Marcus went upstairs and shut himself in his bedroom.

Mrs. Orton settled in the armchair, opened *Woman's Realm*, turned up the radio, drowsed.

William heard the radio, turned a little, scratched the bridge of his nose with a flung fist, and let out a small wail. His own voice startled him further; he drew a breath and called, a quavering note.

Marcus came out, stepping as on eggs, listened.

William called with less conviction.

Mrs. Orton called, "Yung man, yung man, the babby's crying."

Marcus did not reply. Mrs. Orton banged with a nearby book on a table. William, hearing this, shouted. Marcus crept to the top of the stairs.

"Yung man, you must lift him. See what th' matter is."

"Perhaps he will go back to sleep."

"Not much chance o' that."

Marcus opened Stephanie's door and went in. The shuddering wicker basket was beyond the white-covered bed, near the window. William's shrieks now had an indefatigable rhythm, as though to breathe were to howl. Marcus approached. The little body, its blanket kicked back, was twisting hotly. The face was amorphous and many colored, from anemone-pale to a rich angry purple. Marcus bent down and picked the baby up, as he had seen Stephanie do, under his arms. He came up quickly, lighter than he looked, alarming in his scrappiness. He held his breath, gentian, for one long terrible moment and then let it out in a high lament. Holding him gingerly, protuding flat on his back before his chest, Marcus edged his way to the stairs.

He paused to adjust the little body to the descent. His eyes met the dark angry eyes. The baby was somebody. Helpless, enraged, he seemed nevertheless not beseeching but tyrannical.

Marcus went down two or three steps. And then more.

"That's no way to hold a babby," said Mrs. Orton, from her chair.

In the library, Stephanie laid out her books. Never before had she attempted to work without the outside sanction of an essay to write, an exam to pass, a class to prepare. There were two formica tables with metal legs among the shelves of fiction, politics, household, gardening, mother care, philosophy books.

The other fixed inhabitants were all men. Two tramps, one reading a newspaper, one behind several heaped volumes of the *Encyclopaedia Britannica*. One in a laddered mud-colored sweater—one in a black, undertaker's overcoat. A very neat, very old, very small man with a magnifying glass in a tremulous hand and a heap of works that gave no clue to his avocation: *A History of English Trees, The Origin of Species, The Open Society and its Enemies, Home-Grown Herbs for Everyone*. A thin, student-seeming youth with a mathematical textbook.

Two or three housewives, or apparent housewives, standing and chatting near the fiction shelves.

She decided to read the "Immortality Ode," just to read, clearly. She had the vague idea that if she could pull her thoughts together she might be able to write a Ph.D. on Wordsworth for the new university. She felt panic. She had with some pain cleared this small space and time to think in and now thought seemed impossible. She remembered from what now seemed the astonishing free and spacious days of her education the phenomenon of the first day's work on a task. One had to peel one's mind from its run of preoccupations: coffee to buy, am I in love, the yellow dress needs cleaning, Tim is unhappy, what is wrong with Marcus, how shall I live my life? It took time before the task in hand seemed possible, and more before it came to life, and more still before it became imperative and obsessive. There had to be a time before thought, a woolgathering time when nothing happened, a time of yawning, of wandering eyes and feet, of reluctance to do what would finally become delightful and energetic. Threads of thought had to rise and be gathered and catch on other threads of old thought, from some unused memory store. She had snatched from Marcus and Daniel's mum, worse, from William, whose physical being filled her inner eye and almost all her immediate memory, barely time for this vacancy, let alone for the subsequent concentration. She told herself she must learn to do without the vacancy if she was to survive. She must be cunning. She must learn to *think* in bus queues, in buses, in lavatories, between table and sink. It was hard. She was tired. She yawned. Time moved on.

Marcus handed William speechlessly to Mrs. Orton, who squashed him against her breast, turning his shrieks into choking sounds, and patted his bottom. Marcus hovered, half afraid William might suffocate. He was equally alarmed by William's fragility and Mrs. Orton's bulk. He was repelled by the swollen shine of her artificial silks, her crimson and purple hands where they issued from cuffs with little globular buttons like drops of melted fat.

William, as well as the choking noise, now made another noise, setting his gums, his face scarlet, vermilion, hyacinth, suddenly pale, his padded butt quaking with explosive sounds, wet sounds.

"*Now* you are going to have to change his little botty. Then he'll feel better, won't you, lovely?"

"I can't."

"You can't expect me to get up them stairs again with me rheumatism, now can you? Get on wi' it. I'll tell you what to do and you can get on and do it."

"I—I—"

"*You* told his mum we'd be all right. I heard you. Now you can just do something for once. Go and get t'things out. You'll want clean nappies—a muslin and a toweling—and cotton wool, and baby powder, and a jug o' warm water. Go up and give us a shout if you can't find owt."

Marcus trailed upstairs. He found the rubber sheet and towel on which the baby was changed and laid them on the bed. He found the other things, neatly packed in a plastic bowl. He went down, step by step, for William.

Some yellow matter had made its way past the elasticated rim of William's uncouth sky-blue bloomers, and trailed across the plum silk.

"It's coming out," Marcus said, in a small voice.

"Get me a screw of cotton wool. Put the rubber apron on. Get a move on."

He went up. Pulled white fluff off the soft white cylinder. Put on the rubber apron, white toweling over the backing. It had a rubber smell, a witch-hazel smell, a female smell, maybe Stephanie's. He saw his thin sexless figure in this frilled garment in her dressing-table mirror. He felt silly, and worse than silly. He came down.

"You look a right idiot I must say. Tek the babby—go on—it's nowt but digested milk—won't hurt you. I've never met such a useless gowk. Never."

She grabbed the cotton wool and began to rub the side of her huge breast with it, sniffing, muttering with pursed lips, not prepared to evacuate the chair.

Marcus took William again, holding him at arm's length from his own towel skirt.

"You'll be dropping him. You're not fit to be let loose, I sometimes think. You've not got t'nous you were born with. Now get *on* wi' it."

"I am."

Stephanie remembered other libraries, still woolgathering. Principally the Cambridge University Library in the summer of her finals. She remembered the sensation of *knowledge*, of grasping an argument, seizing an illustration, seeing a link, a connection, between this ancient Greek idea here and this seventeenth-century English one, in other words. Knowledge had its own sensuous pleasure, its own fierce well-being, like good sex, like a day in bright sun on a hot empty beach. She thought of these various lights, Plato's sun, Daniel's body, that first moment of Will's separate life, herself in sunlight, and thought, as she had not thought clearly for some long time, of "my life" of the desired shape of "my life" as it had seemed so clear and so bright in that earlier library. She thought: this will not do, I must think about the "Immortality Ode," I have no time, any more. And saw that she *was* thinking about the "Immortality Ode," that the poem was about all these things, the splendor in the grass, the need for thought, the shape of a life, the light.

She was about to be able to think. And, as always at that moment, all her perceptions sharpened too. She saw the gray frosted windows of the library on Beastfair, the battleship-gray metal shelves, the pebbly polished concrete floor that jarred with the crazy formica of the table she sat at. One of the old men was secretively tearing up a piece of bread and a lump of perhaps cheese under the library table, popping little gobbets into his mouth when the librarian seemed to be looking away. The little man with the magnifying glass had moved on to *Leviathan*. He pleased her; it all pleased her. She turned to the poem.

Marcus put the baby on his rubber sheet and undid the bottom buttons of the bloomers, impeded by some aimless kicking. Inside the bloomers were transparent plastic pants filled with pale yellow runny stuff, and somewhere in the crotch, an embedded pin. Marcus, gagging, rolled down the pants and dropped them on the bedroom carpet where they left a stain. The pin troubled him for some minutes. It had a safety catch, obscured by excrement, and came only with skidding difficulty out of the wet toweling. As he released it the baby kicked again and Marcus, watching the roll of thigh waver at the pin end, felt tears rise to his own eyes. He could not. He could not. He pulled at the nappy—he had not troubled to observe the trick of lifting the baby by the ankles—and left a further yellow trail on the back of the child's vest, the bedspread, the carpet. He realized that he had now mislaid the pin, which might be under the child, and had also not thought how to transport the warm water from the dressing table without turning his back on the baby, who might then roll or slide off the bed. So he danced uselessly for some time, one hand on the baby's belly, one outstretched for the water, before he made two rushes, rescued the baby, slopped half the water over the carpet, and had to go back for the cotton wool.

The next bit was worst of all. He wiped and swabbed and gagged and polished and discovered yellow trails in the creases of the scrotum and open sores in the buttocks. He dropped a circle of used lumps of cotton wool on the carpet. He sweated. He found the pin, pointing scimitar-like into the baby's spine. He had another dance to fetch the powder.

He could not understand how a nappy could become underwear, using only one pin. He folded, refolded, tucked visible ends, desperately stabbed, waited for screams and did up the buttons, forgetting to replace the plastic knickers. Long pointed trailers of superfluous nappy dangled from his pinning. However, it was done. Returning to the top end, he found the baby looking at him. The peaked lips wavered, and the mouth and eye corners went up. Marcus, stepping back, wondering if that was a real, intentional smile, trod on the dirty nappy and gathered up his largely cleaned charge.

The "Immortality Ode" is, among other things, a poem about time and memory. As a schoolgirl, as an undergraduate of eighteen, Stephanie had been skeptical of Wordworth's valuation of the perceptions of early childhood. She had not felt that little children were particularly blessed or particularly blissful.

Now, feeling old at twenty-five, she was more interested in the distance and otherness of children, having a son. She read the epigraph "The child is father of the man" and thought of William, the light that had bathed him, the man he would be. She then read more attentively those passages in the midst of the poem about the Child which, as a girl barely out of childhood, she had read more perfunctorily, feeling them thicker and more ordinary, less magical, than the paradisal vision of the rainbow and the rose, the waters on a starry night, the one tree, the one flower.

There were two successive stanzas about the Child. The first describes him learning ceremonies and parts, from his "dream of human life," acting wedding and funeral, the Persons of Shakespeare's seven ages of man. This stanza reminded her, on this occasion, of Gideon's sociological sermon. The next stanza, the one Coleridge had found frightening and unsatisfactory, is a run of metaphors describing the life of the soul in terms of depth and confinement. The child is, to Coleridge's exact distaste, an "Eye among the blind / That deaf and silent read'st the eternal deep." Stephanie saw suddenly that the reiterated, varied "deeps" of this stanza were part of a Wordsworthian vision of a darkness that was life and thought, a contrasted image as true as the human habits and roles of the preceding description of the Darling of a pigmy size. The two came together in the final lines of the second stanza where the poet assures the child that "Custom" shall

> lie upon thee with a weight
> Heavy as frost and deep almost as life.

The "eternal deep" of the waters of Genesis has become the depth to which the root reaches, just beyond the constrictions, the weight of frost. She was only just old enough to see that "custom" could so bear down. The lines moved her, as her own earlier idea "I am sunk in biology" had moved her. And yet her mind lifted: she had *thought*; she had seen clearly the relation between the parts played by the child-player and the confinement and depth. She felt a moment of freedom, looked at her watch, saw that there was no more time to write this down or work it out. Indeed, even as she looked, what had seemed a vision of truth settled into a banal, easy insight.

Marcus came down with William. Mrs. Orton sat up and spread her thick knees.

"Here. Give him over here; let's see what sort o' job you've done."

"He's all right. I've got him. I'll walk him."

"Give him here."

"No, really. I'll just walk him."

"You've got no more idea how to mek a babby comfortable than t'doorpost. Look at you. All elbows and thumbs. I've never seen such a deedless body."

Marcus retreated to the stair foot. He didn't want her to have William. She had a large brooch of imitation china roses in the middle of her modesty front and the pin protruded. He didn't want her to see what he had done with William's nappy. He didn't want William to be clutched against that pin.

"He's okay, I said. He's okay."

"You really are a stubborn little tyke, aren't you? You waft round where you're not wanted, putting on airs to mek yoursen' interesting, upsetting them as lives in this house and mekking a right commotion about a clarty nappy. Why don't you go back to your own mum, you great booby? I reckon she'd make you do sommat, that's why. If this was *my* house you'd be out smartly I can tell you, and earning a decent living. All white and ladylike and soft; a real softy, that's you. And spiteful. Now, give us that babby, before you do him a mischief."

"I didn't do him a mischief upstairs. You could have gone up and changed him. I've seen you go up and down when you think no one's here. You *can*."

"So we're answering back, are we? I see I s'll have to come and tek him."

To Marcus's horror she did in fact raise her bulk from the chair and waddle slowly in his direction. He stood uselessly against the newel post; it was not in his nature to clutch William tighter. Mrs. Orton rolled up at his side and the little bulging hands pulled at William's shoulders. Marcus more or less hung on. Mrs. Orton, still clutching at William, skidded on a rug and went down on the stone floor. So, between the two, did William. Marcus sat down on the stair. The baby lay still at his feet. Mrs. Orton began to scream abuse, wallowing like a beached whale.

Stephanie, her mind on the platonic aspects of the "Immortality Ode," her body extremely anxious about William, came through the front door.

There was a terrible silence and then Stephanie, books flung down, had scooped up her still son, who, simply winded, began to scream. Mrs. Orton cried that she was sure she'd broke a bone again, it hurt something terrible, they must get the doctor, it was all the fault of that daft boy who wasn't fit to be let loose, who expected to be waited on hand and foot, hand and foot, the pain was something terrible, get a doctor.

"Marcus, please help her up."

"I can't."

"Oh, for God's *sake*. Hold William, then."

"I wouldn't trust 'im wi't babby, not after what's just happened . . ."

Stephanie gritted her teeth and said, "Can you get up if I pull?"

"No. No."

"I'll get a cushion. And the doctor."

After she had done these things, she took William from Marcus. She sat down, holding him close, shivering with fear and shock and guilt. Her hands were soaking.

"He's got no nappy on, either. Well, not to speak of. Where are his rubber pants? Who changed him?"

"I did."

"Oh, *Marcus*. Really. Oh, *Marcus*."

She began to cry.

Marcus went upstairs and shut himself in his room.

Mrs. Orton lay, moaning and muttering vituperation, until the doctor came and pronounced her bruised but not broken. He and Stephanie assisted her up the stairs, where she took to her bed. He checked the baby, who had a grazed temple but seemed otherwise fit and cheerful. Stephanie kissed the graze and wept. There is something peculiarly distressing about the first wound on new skin.

13

THE MUMMIES

"Do you dream?" the psychiatrist asked Marcus, routinely.

"I had a bad dream after I dropped the baby."

"Can you describe it?"

They had been sitting in a circle, on upholstered chairs, their knees touching. It was a party game; his labeling mind more or less captioned it "party game," though it was not clear whether it was "pass the parcel" or "musical chairs," or one of those obscene ones where you pass something with knees, or noses, or tennis ball between ear and chin without dropping it. All the people in the dream had been stiff, upholstered, with clumsy skirted knees and thick aprons. Their knees had been touching. He had been one of them. He had lost what they had been passing.

And then he was what was lost, crouched in the midst, and they were closing in on him, aged female players of The Farmer's in His Den who had reached the point of "We All Beat the Dog," only they were kneeling heavily on him on the floor, shuffling together. They had faceless heads wound wholly in white cotton-wool hair like those cactuses woven in soft gray filaments.

They were spinning and unwinding themselves into strip after strip of bandage and noisome cloth, and with the cloth came their flesh, deliquescent. And he labeled them the mummies. They were covering him in what they wound off the squat bobbins of themselves. They were busy, busy.

"I was in a circle of people. Well, women. They were squashing me. Their clothes came off. I called them mummies."

"Perhaps you don't like the idea of mothers?"

"Perhaps I don't."

"Can you say why?"

The next week, Marcus went home. He appeared one day in his mother's kitchen, and said simply, as he could always have done, "I've come back." She cooked a chicken in his honor, and Bill shook his hand for a long time on coming in from school, but no more was said except "I like the white paint, it's nice to come home to white paint." Stephanie reflected distractedly on the fact that her gentleness, Daniel's patience, Mr. Rose's expertise, Winifred's love, seemed inconsiderable moving forces compared to Mrs. Orton's bloody-mindedness and a dirty nappy. She felt that Marcus was in the world again, as much as he ever had been. Meanwhile, who would hold William if she were ever to try to finish the thought about the "Immortality Ode"?

14

FIGURES OF SPEECH

These were Alexander's Bloomsbury days. He worked in Broadcasting House where, for the first time in his thirty-seven years, he was part of a noneducational organization, with an office, a secretary, a salary, a hierarchy, a gentlemanly code of conduct. He was called an advisory producer but did not exactly produce talks or drama. He was expected to have "ideas." He drank with poets, gentlemen, and peripatetic dons in The George.

He was living as a temporary paying guest in a mansion flat rented by his friend Thomas Poole, who had moved from a Yorkshire training college to the Crabb Robinson Institute. His parents had kept, still kept, a hotel in Weymouth. He had gone from prep school to public school to Oxford to schoolmastering, returning temporarily to the hotel and whatever room was vacant and convenient. He was used to being limited to one room in an institution administered by someone else. Life with the Pooles, even in the early days of tea chests and too-brief curtains, was the nearest he had come to ordinary domestic life.

The block of flats was between Tottenham Court Road and Gower Street, made of red brick, with stone-framed sash windows and mahogany doors with polished brass. It was Edwardian and solid, designed as city homes for families with perhaps one or two servants. When the Pooles came the kitchen was still equipped with a system of electric bells and lights for summoning these people. Little discs oscillated in a glass box above the legends: drawing room, master bedroom, nursery. It was not clear which rooms were which and the bells no longer worked. There were four large rooms and four small ones, opening off a long dark corridor. The servants' quarters—kitchen, pantry, small box-bedroom—looked out onto a white-tiled well, spot-streaked, punctuated by window boxes, in which, on hot days, music and voices echoed. The Pooles were at the top of the building, on the sixth floor. The bigger rooms fronted the street, and through their glass bays could be seen the tops of London plane trees, flocks of pigeons, and in later years, the mystifying discs and cylinders of the post office tower as it rose over opposite roofs, stage by geometric stage. Alexander had a room at the end farthest from the kitchen. It was airy and bare and quiet. He had few things in it because he was only temporarily there. On his white walls he had his old posters, now under glass, the Picasso *Boy with a Pipe*, the Saltimbanques, the advertisement for his own *Buskers*, the Rodin Danaïde. To these he had added a poster from the London production of *Astraea*, the Darnley portrait in a border of Tudor roses. He also had smaller prints of the Van Gogh sunflowers and the Van Gogh yellow chair. In Cambridge Frederica was reading in *Brideshead Revisited* how Charles Ryder shamefacedly took down his sunflowers and turned them to the wall. Alexander was daily more puzzled and delighted by the sunflowers that he had seen without seeing for years. The print was a greenish yellow, unlike the paint it reproduced. Alexander had brought back a Provençal bedspread, a geometric floral print on a dark yolk-yellow ground, and he and the Pooles had chosen plain yellow curtains, a near-enough match. So the room was yellow and white, with a gray cord carpet.

He had come to London as successful writers did, or successful characters, at the end of those exploratory novels that analyzed and celebrated working-class values and virtues in the north, whose authors and heroes hurried down as fast as they could to the busy capital. The Pooles, too, were very deliberately leaving the provinces, making themselves metropolitan. They had left almost everything behind— the three-piece suite, the Wilton carpets, the glass-fronted bookcases, the family silver. Elinor Poole said to Alexander that the exciting thing was that the flat was *flat*, the rooms, all in a row, just rooms. You could sleep or eat or work in any or all of them. They furnished it with fitted cord carpets in silver and grays, with white paint, geometrically patterned curtains. Carpenters fitted streamlined shelves and cupboards. The children had bright Finnish blankets, scarlet, blue, yellow. They put up a Ben Nicholson print, a Matisse poster. Alexander liked it.

He also liked the new richness and ceremony of their cooking. His first vision of Gower Street had been Henry James's Glower Street, an unbroken dark gray line of Georgian terrace bordering wailing cars. On his daily walks to the BBC he discovered the glories of

Goodge Street and Charlotte Street, Italian grocers smelling of cheese, wine casks, salami, Jewish bakers smelling of cinnamon, and poppy seed, Cypriot greengrocers overflowing with vegetables unobtainable in the north, aubergines, fennel, globe artichokes, courgettes, glistening, brilliant, green, purple, sunshine-glossed. In Schmidt's amazing *delikatessen* you could buy sauerkraut from wooden barrels, black pumpernickel, wursts cooked and uncooked, huge choux pastries and little cups of black coffee. In Schmidt's you paid for everything with little receipts at a central caisse presided over by an erect, moustached lady in black dress and lace. In Belloni's, tall Luigi spoke rapid Italian and rapid Cockney, and weighed paper cones of black and green olives, a tiny bag of sharp-scented twisted scraps of mace, a mozzarella in cool, wet, straw-tied paper. It was urban, it was international, it was, or seemed, timeless. It was also a village, his village.

These were the early days of Elizabeth David, who taught a whole generation, dentally healthy, sensuously deprived, to see and smell and taste and make food.

A civility of Alexander's life at this time was the discussion, the repetition, of the detail of these cookery books with Elinor Poole. He shopped for her, emptying from his briefcase in the kitchen a packet of fresh ravioli, a bag of soft parmesan, a vanilla pod. Every day there was something new: mackerel with fennel, a stew of small squids, fresh-risen pizza. There was something splendid about this earthy life in the middle of a city. T. S. Eliot had observed austerely, in *Notes Towards a Definition of Culture*, that a people needs not only enough to eat but a proper and particular *cuisine*.

He gave up his early tactful attempt not to eat with the family. He observed that the Pooles were conducting their daily lives carefully and ceremoniously because they were afraid.

Thomas, like Alexander, had been clawed by love, or sex, during the Long Royston *Astraea*. Anthea Warburton had been quickly and quietly relieved of Thomas Poole's child in the summer of 1953. During the time Alexander had spent with her at the Mas Cabestainh he had never heard her express pain or regret. He had never heard her refer, explicitly or implicitly, to Poole. By the time Thomas and Alexander came to discuss the lodging plan, Poole's own period of articulate misery was over. He and Alexander drank a couple of pints in The Little John in Lower Royston where Poole remarked that if Alexander could see his way to lodging with them a bit he'd actually be doing them a favor, an outsider would help things along, things were a little sticky with the best will in the world. Elinor hadn't really got over that business last summer. Alexander felt unable to ask what Poole himself now felt. An English tacit decorum prevailed. They spoke to each other of Dr. Leavis and the common pursuit of true judgment, of how they would miss the Yorkshire moors, of the possible future use of television in education. Poole was nevertheless the nearest thing to a close friend Alexander had.

At first he thought that the ceremoniousness was initiated and largely conducted by Elinor. There was a way in which it could be seen as a placating of her husband, a daily, consciously renewed offering of herself as wife and housewife. If it was to Alexander that she talked about new discoveries—a mandolin in Madame Cadec's Greek Street cookery shop, an Italian pudding made of cream cheese, rum, and fine, fine ground coffee—it was always *for* Thomas that things were said to be made, acquired, or done. She would show Alexander Dolcelatte, creamy but not ammoniac, exactly as Thomas liked it. Or anchovies from a dark wet cask in a Greek shop. "I don't like anchovies myself, but Thomas has a taste for them."

Alexander saw that this solicitude could be read as aggression or reproach. This showed in the way in which the children were removed, gently and firmly, from areas of the flat where Daddy was said to be, or to be about to be, working. There were three children, Chris, Jonathan, and Lizzie, eight, six, and three, the boys with Thomas's square brow, blond hair, straight mouth, the girl with fine colorless curls so that Alexander thought of mouse fur and its shadowy paleness and only then remembered that that word, for hair, was rubbed clean of any lively associations. The children, having no street to run in, also lived ceremoniously. They were accompanied to school and nursery school across Russell Square. They were accompanied to Bloomsbury Square Gardens, where they rode tricycles purposefully and collected fallen leaves. Alexander knew too little about children to realize how little these quarreled. He remembered, seeing their artwork, that Elinor had been an art teacher. A collage they had made—a glittering dragon, with fleshy elastoplast nostrils and a brilliantly sequined, beaded, sinuous body—ran the length of the kitchen wall, woolen smoke twined above him. Things they had made—a cake, a papier-mâché dolphin—were ceremoniously shown to Thomas for his approval. "Look what we have done," she would say, setting him apart with the pronoun. And to Alexander, differently, constituting her audience and witness, "Look what we have done."

Thomas's responses were also ceremonious. He thanked Elinor for the good meals, thanked with care and specificity, making it clear that he knew what work had gone into sieving the soup, timing the sauce, arranging the salad. He discussed the children's works of art with them, and proposed expeditions to London things, the zoo, the clocks in the British Museum, the crystals in the Science Museum. The children's lives were full of startling and interesting *things*.

One morning over breakfast Alexander put it to himself clearly that communication in that flat was centered in, conducted through, things. He had no real idea what Elinor thought about Thomas, or Anthea, or indeed himself, but he knew exactly what she thought about potatoes, coffee, wine. He himself was so much in the habit of rendering things into language that he found them hard to see or touch without some kind of mental naming and comparing, in words.

He had a dim sense that it was possible to conceive of a state of affairs where this busy naming and comparing might not seem as much of a biological imperative as an unreflecting man might suppose. Working with words on a painter who was also an articulate writer had taught him that; you could see things before saying them, indeed without saying them.

Breakfast was muesli with fresh fruit, fresh coffee in a dark green French filter pot, gold rimmed, croissants, unsalted butter, homemade jam. The fruit changed with the seasons: dark burgundy cherries, gold-green greengages, wax-gold spotted pears, plums misted on purple-black. He watched Elinor arrange the fruits and then watched the fruits. Elinor grew her yogurt in a white bowl with a beaded muslin cover; these were days when the English had not in general seen any yogurt, let alone taken to having it delivered in

sterile painted plastic pots. Alexander thought about its being a
culture. It grew in the white bowl, differently white, a curded, sharp-
tasting, glistening mass. It was alive—more than the not-yet-dead
plums, with their breathing skins, were alive, though there was the
germ waiting inside the stone. The breakfast table was a still life,
with the easy life of vegetables and culture. Thomas offered Elinor pale
yellow butter. Elinor lifted the coffeepot; Alexander slid yogurt into
the dusty seeds and flakes of his muesli. There were two lemons
among the plums, to intensify the color.

How would one find the exact word for the color of the plum-
skins? (There was a further question of *why* one might want to do so,
why it was not enough to look at, or to eat and savor the plum, but
Alexander did not wish to address himself to that, not just now. It
was a fact that the lemons and the plums, together, made a pattern
that he recognized with pleasure, and the pleasure was so fundamen-
tally human it asked to be noted and understood.) There was a
problem of accurate notation, which was partly a problem of sufficiency of adjectives. Do we have enough words, synonyms, near
synonyms for purple? What *is* the grayish, or maybe white, or
whitish, or silvery, or dusty mist or haze or smokiness over the
purple shine? How do you describe the dark cleft from stalk pit to
oval end, its inky shadow? Partly with adjectives; it is interesting that
adjectives in a prose or verse style are felt to be signs of looseness
and vagueness when in fact they are the opposite, at their best, an
instrument for precision.

A writer aiming for unadorned immediacy might say a plum, a
pear, an apple, and by naming these things evoke in every reader's
mind a different plum, a dull tomato-and-green specked Victoria, a
yellow-buff globular plum, a tight, black-purple damson. If he wishes
to share a vision of a specific plum he must exclude and evoke: a
matte, oval, purple-black plum, with a pronounced cleft.

You may use the word "bloom" for the haze on this plum, and it
will call up in the mind of any competent reader the idea that the plum
is glistening, overlaid with a matte softness. You may talk about the
firm texture of the flesh, and these words will not be metaphors,
bloom and flesh, as the earlier "cleft" was certainly not a metaphor but
a description of a grown declivity. But you cannot exclude from the

busy automatically connecting mind possible metaphors, human flesh for fruit flesh, flower bloom, skin bloom, bloom of ripe youth for this powdery haze, human clefts, declivities, cleavages for that plain noun. The nearest color Alexander could find, in his search for accurate words for the purple of the plum, was in fact the dark center of some new and vigorously burgeoning human bruise. But the plum was neither bruised nor a bruise nor human. So he eschewed, or tried to eschew, human words for it.

On the other hand, he was mildly pleased with the pun he had happily found in the conjunction of the yogurt culture, the breakfast table, and his own reflections on T. S. Eliot and Elizabeth David. Language related, and then he reflectively related, bacterial culture, organic culture, human artifacts in culture, the life of the mind. He did not have, as Romantic proponents of the organic metaphor might have had, a sense that the "culture" pun was a profound insight into the necessary growth and life of any single being, bacteria, human language, life. But analogy was a way of thought and without it thought was impossible. Nevertheless, he was troubled by the sense that it was possible for, say, Vincent Van Gogh to get nearer to the life of the plums than he ever could. Both metaphor and naming in paint were different from these things in language.

Language might relate the plum to the night sky, or to certain ways of seeing a burning coal, or to a soft case enwrapping a hard nugget of treasure. Or it might introduce an abstraction, a reflection, of mind, not mirror. "Ripeness is all," language might say, after observing, "We must endure Our going hence even as our coming hither." Paint too could do these things. Gauguin made a woman from two pears and a bunch of flowers. Magritte made bread of stones and stones of bread, an analogy operating a miracle. Van Gogh's painting of the Reaper in his furnace of white light and billowing corn said also, "Ripeness is all." But the difference, the distance, fascinated Alexander. Paint itself declares itself as a force of analogy and connection, a kind of metaphor-making between the flat surface of purple pigment and yellow pigment and the statement "This is a plum." "This is a lemon." "This is a chair." "This is a breakfast table." Brushstrokes, skill, the signature of the one mind that said, "This is *my* plum, lemon, table, chair," were also connecting links, little lines of power, one man's vision of the world. It is impossible *not* to think about the distance between paint and things, between paint and life, between paint and the "real world" (which includes other paintings).

It is not at all impossible, it is even common, not to think about the distance between words and things, between words and life, between words and reality. A *trompe-l'oeil* painting is admired for its skill in mimetic deception. You cannot have *trompe-l'oeil* in writing, or any other form of pleasurable mimetic titillation and deception. Language runs up and down, through and round things known and things imitated in a way paint doesn't. No one ever *painted* "Put those apples in the basket and help yourself." No one ever imagined the house at Combray, the dwelling of Père Goriot, *Bleak House*, or Fawns with the *same* sense that they were seeing them and they were not real and not there that one has seeing the Yellow House, Las Meninas, or Vermeer's still women, bathed in silent light, forever reading letters forever unfinished. Even those who have fallen in love with Mr. Rochester or despaired with Mme. Bovary have not grasped those phantoms in their imagination as wholeheartedly as they have—separately—imagined Rembrandt's Saskia or Manet's Berthe Morisot. We have always known that these creatures are made of words as the sunflowers are made of paint, but words are our common currency. We all have words. We may not be able to paint an apple, but we can certainly utter a view on why Elinor liked live yogurt or the young Proust was neurasthenic—they are less real and more immediate.

We know paint is not plum flesh. We do not know with the same certainty that our language does not simply, mimetically, coincide with our world. There was a cultural shock when painters shifted their attention from imitating apples to describing the nature of vision, paint, canvas. But the nausea Jean Paul Sartre felt on discovering that he could not, with language, adequately describe a chestnut tree root is a shock of another kind. (It should be noted that though he failed to describe the thing mathematically, or with nouns and color adjectives, he did at least evoke it with metaphors, sealskin, serpentine, a tree root connected to the world by a man describing a vision of unconnectedness.)

.   .   .

He had trouble with the disposition of color adjectives in his play.

He tried to contrast the domestic visions of the early black *Potato Eaters* and the domestic hopes of his paintings of the Yellow House in Arles. Van Gogh the painter had feared and fled the domestic and had also idealized and desired its order, its ceremony. *The Potato Eaters* is painted in the black light of the north. The characters in it, painted "in the earth in which they were sown," do not meet each other's eyes but are firmly linked, breaking bread, pouring coffee, in their dark hut, individuals subsumed in a common life. The painting has a moralizing intention; it is a sermon in paint about the basic necessities of human life. Alexander respected it but became obsessed with a small painting of a breakfast table, on which Van Gogh painted the household things he bought for his artist's house, a clean, bright paradox, still and very much alive, held together by the contrast and coherence of blue and yellow. Vincent described it to Theo:

> A coffee pot in blue enamel, a cup (on the left) royal blue and gold, a milk jug checkered light blue and white, a cup (on the right) white with blue and orange patterns on a plate of earthenware yellow-grey, a pot of barbotine or majolica blue with red, green, brown patterns, finally two oranges and three lemons; the table is covered with a blue cloth, the background yellow-green, thus six different blues and four or five yellows and oranges.

In Alexander's mind these color words sang like a poem, though not like any poem he could have written, in or out of his play.

Some days he worked at home, partly editing BBC scripts, partly on his own struggle with color words. In those days there was something shadowy about the other inhabitants of the flat, which was intensified by its layout, since his room, in which the sunflowers burned in miniature and the yellow house stood pale and vanishing against the cobalt weight of sky, was well lit, and the main corridor, windowless, was always dark, even if the dark was graceful and cool. He would come out in moments of restlessness, blinking from light, and see the long rectangle almost smoky. On one of these journeys he

heard an Elinor he didn't recognize, talking crisply on the phone to
what he deduced was a female student of Thomas's, saying that she
herself did not take messages, that she preferred Thomas *not* to be
rung at home, that there was an Institute number with a secretary
whose job it was to take such calls, thank you.

On another occasion, in the early afternoon, he came out and saw,
at the other end of the corridor, but advancing toward him, a naked
woman, shadowy and pale, with flowing dark hair, a woman whose
rounds and triangular planes were differently lit as successive open
doors cast columns of light across her and then the shadows closed
again. It was a full and confident body, balanced lightly on fine feet,
large breasted, generous in the hips, but narrow and contained at the
junctures of waist, wrist, and ankle. The breasts, the palest things,
were high, with large, dark oval nipples. His eye, perhaps because his
mind was preoccupied with surfaces, saw lovely repeating ovals and
rounds, the gleam on the shoulder, the light on a lifted round knee,
the fall of the inner thigh. And the bright ovals and circles advanced,
moving, melding, reforming with their contrary shadows, the deep
purple inverted T between the breasts, the incurved arabesques of the
collar bone, a brown-black velvet curved triangle in the depth of the
neck, the flat triangle of dark hair between the thighs, thinning and
widening as she stepped. He watched the bare feet rise and fall, the
muscles of calf and buttock contract and swell, the bright hair swing.
He truly did not see that she was Elinor until she had advanced half
along the corridor.

She came directly up to him and stood close enough. "I'm sorry. I
was having a bath. I forgot the shampoo."

"I'm sorry."

"Oh, no. It doesn't matter. I don't mind."

She stood and smiled at him. She was more, and more varied, than
he would have suspected from her aproned trimness with her hair up.
She smiled, perhaps ruefully. She walked, close, past him toward the
bathroom and her left breast touched his arm. He put out a silent
hand and touched it, at which she caught a breath and stood still again.

"You were a vision," he said. "Going through those shafts of light,
from the doors."

Upon which she stepped past him, into his own room and stood, just inside his door, among the papers on the floor in the yellow light from curtain and prints. He followed her in and closed the door and then touched those surfaces, the rounds, the lines of muscle and tendon, the jutting padded bones. He thought fast and inconclusively about Thomas Poole, his friend, about the ceremony in that household, about his own not very great interest in sex, about the courage she must have to stand there, so decorous, so upright, so positive. Civility almost required of him that he take what was offered. He could hardly face her again if he did not. He could hardly go on living in the flat. What would happen if he did was even more baffling.

"Are you sure? ..."

She put a hand over his mouth. He took off his clothes. They lay down beneath his yellow bed cover, the dark head next to the geometric flowers. Gently and very slowly he touched the surfaces that had lit and shifted in the shadows, and gently and very slowly she touched him, everything silent and almost lazy, almost absentminded. So that when Alexander went in, it was as if it was only to make everything even more close and comfortable, more complete, the final knob of flesh tucked into the final soft space. It was the first time in his life that Alexander had even felt that this act made him biologically complete, that two had found some missing space or part, become one, moved together. He was more than usually given to finding the act of sex ludicrous, popping buttocks, squeaking sounds of flesh slithering or air groaning inappositely outward, but with this silent woman it was simply a question of a peaceful repeated bending and rocking until she closed like a vice, shivered again, and again, and again, still silent and smiling, sweating along the hairline, hardly to be called discomposed. Alexander saw and felt everything bathed in gold, and gave, finally, one cry that broke the silence and heard the woman sobbing. He thought both: this is what I am *for*, and more distantly, this is not what I really want.

"Are you upset?"

"Oh, no."

"You're crying."

"Because I'm happy. I'm very happy. Keep still."

So he lay back, limp, one arm curled about the dark head, one touching the crease of her thigh, and for a time they half slept. And then she said, "Ah, thank you—" swung her legs sideways, and walked away, out of the door, and he heard her go into the bathroom. He felt peaceful and happy. He looked at his place, his papers and pictures, and thought of Vincent Van Gogh, who had written:

> Sometimes, just as the waves break against sullen, hopeless cliffs, I feel a storm of desire to embrace something, a woman, a kind of domestic hen; well, one must take it for what it is, the effect of hysterical over-excitement rather than the vision of actual reality.

Vincent had painted his bedroom in every color. "The walls pale lilac, the floor a broken and faded red, the chairs and the bed chrome-yellow, the pillows and the linen lemon-green and very pale, window green. I would have wished to express absolute rest by all these very different tones, you see . . ."

Very few people have found this painting, whatever its intentions, to be an expression of absolute rest. What the painter intended to do was no doubt to introduce *everything* into that small space, in the shape of all the colors of the spectrum, and by so balancing them confine the components of white light into his image of rest or sleep, which he said should be framed in white, since there was no white in the picture. He wrote also that the broad lines of the furniture must express inviolable rest, but the deliberate distortions of perspective make the walls and ceiling, the very paintings on the wall, seem louring and crushing. There are two pillows on the bed and two yellow chairs in the room, as though sharing it were desirable or possible. Alexander, lying on his own crumpled bed, naked, in the middle of the afternoon (he was courteously waiting for the bathroom to be empty), looked around his large room and spread his single body to cover all the space.

He thought also of Vincent's distress, however dissembled, at his brother's marriage, at the birth of his child. It is true that Vincent felt, or claimed, that the expenditure of sperm in coition weakened the power of painting, a naively reciprocal view of the relation between the two that Alexander supposed himself, without having deliberated, to be above. But he minded the sense of his own inhumanity.

Oh it seems to me more and more that *people* are the root of everything, and though it will always be a melancholy thought that you yourself are not in real life, I mean, that it's more worthwhile to work in flesh and blood itself than in paint or plaster, more worthwhile to make children than pictures or to carry on business, all the same you feel that you're alive when you remember that you have friends who are outside real life as much as you . . .

Over the next few days it seemed at first as though it had been decided that everyone should go on as though nothing had happened. Apprehensive at supper, he had talked to Poole about teaching and had complimented Elinor, perhaps slightly more formally than he would otherwise have done, on her *oeufs Florentines*. Over the next ten days or so he noted that a shift had taken place in the ceremony in the house. Elinor largely stopped doing or saying she was doing things to gratify Thomas. Indeed, she consulted Alexander more directly—but not with nervous solicitude—about his own tastes and desires. Poole, on the other hand, began to smile. He said things to Elinor like "You always felt I was inclined to overinvolve myself in pastoral work"—which were unusual only because no such personal things had been said at all since Alexander came. Alexander stayed out drinking in the Fitzroy with poets and came home with a headache. Two days later he found Elinor, naked again, sitting on his bed when he came back from a foraging trip to the kitchen.

"My dear, I don't know—I'm not sure this is possible."
"Yes, it is—"
"I'm happy here. I don't want to do anything to spoil it."
"You haven't. You won't. You make everything better.'
He was already taking off his clothes. When he had her in his arms he said, "What do I make better?"
"Everything." Evasively.

They made love. It was the same—slow, easy, harmonious, satisfactory, silent.
"I would never have thought you were so beautiful, undressed."

"You *really* thought I was?"

"I was overcome. I still am. You are."

"I ought to tell you. I—I couldn't—touch—Thomas. Not after—that girl—last summer. Not because that wasn't understandable, but because it made *me* feel old and ugly and unnecessary."

"Don't."

"I knew you wouldn't like me to talk. Only—now I don't. I don't feel old. That's all."

"That's good."

"I used you."

"We all use each other."

"The first time, I used you. I came back today because—"

"Because?"

"It was so *nice*, I couldn't bear not to do it again."

"Ah," said Alexander. "And now?"

"I hope—I wouldn't like to think—I may come again, may I?"

"Of course," said Alexander. "Please do."

Over the next few months Alexander's life became both more intensely pleasurable and more unreal. Afterward, he remembered this time in very bright, clear primary colors, but all softly muffled, or mobled, as if seen through white veiling. (His work too was pleasurable but unreal and seen, in its drab olive and gray utility colors, also through translucent mediums; cigarette smoke, frosted glass door panels, the aquarium screen between studio and cubicle.) He was being made to feel more "part of the family." The children kissed him good-night after supper, like a third parent, he was consulted and drawn into conversations about decisions that were strictly nothing to do with him—choice of secondary school, new kitchen flooring, the guest list for a dinner party. And yet he was more than ever aware that he was not part of the family, that he was watching, looking in, not with any acquisitive or hostile intention, at their lives, which they were living out, with consciously perfected gestures, for or in front of him, like a drawing-room comedy, or a parlor game as it might be seen in the black, white, and fleeting smoky glass box of the television screen. (There was no television in the flat. These were days before a child felt deprived or ostracized because he or she was not knowledgeable about Batman or Muffin the Mule.)

Alexander's room became more part of the household, too. Once, he found the woman in there with a vase of tiger lilies, and several times with cups of coffee. But also he heard, as earlier he had not heard, Thomas and Elinor talking animatedly behind their own closed door in a clear stream of indistinguishable chatter and laughter.

He was invited into the children's rooms. They had three, two small, bright bedrooms and a large playroom, in the center of the corridor. He was fetched to admire what they had made, or to hear them read, or to read to them. It was particularly from the playroom that his memory of bright colors came, though the color was in part, of course, a real function of the new, unfaded things in the flat, cushions, chairs, paint. The playroom had blinds and curtains in thick white cotton, stretched smooth, softly ruffled, spattered with a plain yet pleasing repeated pattern of little sprigs of recognizable English flowers—scarlet poppy, blue cornflower, dark-eyed golden daisy. Many of the children's artifacts stood in this room; a knight in armor with knitted silver-string chain mail and vermilion-plumed foil helmet, a peacock of pipe cleaners, embroidery silks and brilliantly sequined iridescent tail, a huge sweet jar full of tissue-paper blooms on green garden-stick stems, white, cream, lemon, butter-yellow, tangerine, marigold, and deep orange. Each child had an easel. The easels stood in a triangle in the center of the room, with a collection of bright plastic beakers for mixing powder paints and a scarlet tin tray containing the boxes of paint. The children were making their own alphabet frieze to go round the room. Lizzie had done some simple things—E for egg, a gold blob in a white oval stuck on violet paper, O for olive, pimento red on green on darker green paper, G for goldfish, a solid orange shape suspended on uncompromising blue. Chris, the older boy, the one with a passion for swords and armor, had done K for knight, H for helmet, silver shapes on crimson grounds, and D for dragon and S for snake, curving shapes in varying greens with red mouths and white teeth and overlapping penned scales (a speciality) on yellow fields. And Jonathan, the quiet one, had done gray and brown animals—F for falcon, P for platypus, Z for Zebra, softer things, in finger-rubbed chalks, mounted on yellow ochre or beige. Everything in the room was labeled; labels with names, in Elinor's neat, large black script, were attached to things with drawing pins: mirror, toy cupboard, fish tank, mustard and cress, Chris's easel, Jonathan's easel, Lizzie's easel.

Alexander took to sitting in the room with them in the early evening and reading poetry to them. They sat in a row on large cushions and listened—they were good listeners—and their mother sat with them, four dreamy, serious faces among the words and colors, while he read "How They Brought the Good News from Ghent to Aix" and "The Pied Piper," "Jabberwocky," and "Welsh Incident," rhymes and riddles. It was as though the wholesomeness of the room and the enchantment of the extravagant rhythms of those early poems were complementary parts of each other, as the dragon was both fearful and homemade. Once, they were all eating freshly baked scones and redcurrant jelly and Chris had on his easel a half-finished painting of a green-and-white spider plant: Elinor did not believe in neglecting mimetic drawing for creative invention. Alexander thought that in this room one could see the beginnings of the thing that now obsessed him, the human need to make images. A stickleback may be misled into attempted slaughter by a red and flashing piece of metal; the wonderful goldfish in Lizzie's tank, with tail, fins, scales, vents, swiveling eyes, retracting round lips, fine dark trail of excrement, may see only horizontals and verticals, the glimmer of other gold, the green of weed, the circles disturbed in the plane surface of his world by grains of food. He may be seen by other fish only as a dashing gold threat or an irresistible sexual presence, or a mouthful disturbing a current. Yet we see so much of the fineness of his structure, and are impelled—why?—to measure the precision and limits of his vision. And to paint him. G is for goldfish. To write him, too. Alexander considered the stylized flowers on his Provençal bedspread and the stylized flowers on these English curtains, the tissue-paper blooms, Jonathan's difficulties in reproducing the creases in the folded green-and-white leaves, the sunflowers. F is for flowers. Did we make these images to understand the world, to decorate it, or to connect ourselves to it? The flowers on the playroom curtains stated that they were summer flowers; the flowers on his bedspread were geometry, recognizable as flowers because flowers had a geometric structure. The sunflowers were exact records of particular

dying flowerheads in 1888; they were named, in the confines of their
yellow vase, *Vincent*, they were, as Gauguin had said, Sun upon Sun.
He read:

> "In marble halls as white as milk
> Lined with a veil as soft as silk
> No doors are there to this stronghold
> Yet thieves break in and steal the gold."

E is for egg. F is for flower. S is for snake.

He noticed that he thought of Elinor rather as though she too was
neatly labeled in different environments—"the woman" in his bedroom, "their mother" in the playroom, "Elinor" (part of Thomas-
and-Elinor) in the kitchen, over meals. He was being given sex as he
was being given food and light and color. He began to feel sometimes
as though these careful surfaces, like the unbroken shell of the
riddling egg, like the silk balloon with no door in which spiderlings
live and grow, were impenetrable. This may have been—he could
not tell—his own choice. He could touch, he could even, from
permitted distances in permitted places, penetrate, but once, in the
act of making love to the woman, he had the illusion that his penis,
long and slender like himself, was simply a pseudopodium stretching
this elastic pale veiling into the crevices, reaching blunted for the hard
barrier and narrow slot of the cervix. The inside was a surface too. A
lined cul-de-sac. It was the surface softness and muffled yet defined
form that he so enjoyed about making love to this woman.

He thought briefly and inadequately, thinking about linings, about
the more mundane matter of contraception, and dismissed it. She
knew what she was doing. His long tip caressed the dark inner
opening. It had its own life and purposes. There were times when he
thought of it as a separate being. The one-eyed trouser snake is a joke
this side of poetry. Wordsworth called the new infant an Eye among
the blind. You could say, in poetry straight from the nursery, that the
one-eyed snake had made its way into the doorless marble halls. Or
you could say that gamete was seeking gamete, genotype genotype, in
order that there should be zygote and phenotype. You could ask, as
Alexander so presciently almost asked himself at the moment of
flowering, what a man is for, what a man wants.

15

WIJNNOBEL

A curious light was cast on the *Breakfast Table*, by chance, at a BBC formal luncheon. I write "by chance." There are, I suppose, times in all lives when concentrated attention to one problem, human, abstract, practical, seems to evoke a more than randomly distributed series of "fortunate" encounters with related people, books, ideas. This may be a phenomenon related to the apparently concentric scratches on George Eliot's metaphorical mirror, which seem to gather round the candle and self-regarding gaze of the egoist as Van Gogh's brush-strokes gather round his self-watching eyes. It feels, however, like the opposite of egoism, a privileged insight into the order of things, in which all things are to be experienced as parts of a whole. It can feel like a magical assertion of mind over matter, a telekinetic arranging of the contents of a library or at least of one's own track through it. In such moods, blandly or vacantly surveying shelves, even the catalog, we discover an unsuspected book, or argument, or set of facts wholly relevant to our problem and yet unsought. Some such revelation came to Alexander from some chance remarks of Professor Wijnnobel, in whose honor the lunch was being held.

It was not chance that Alexander found himself talking to Wijnnobel. The professor was there in two capacities. He was the author of a series of precise but wide-ranging talks on the representation of light in Western painting. He was also vice-chancellor designate of the new University of North Yorkshire. The university was already moving into the house at Long Royston on whose terrace Alexander's *Astraea* had first been presented. Alexander had read, but had not presumed to meddle with, the texts of the talks: one on Leonardo, Raphael and Platonic ideas of mathematical order and truth, one on Vermeer Van Delft, seventeenth-century optics, the camera obscura, the telescope and the microscope, one on post-impressionist icons and the painting of light, which included Van Gogh. The BBC controllers had felt that Alexander could properly talk to the professor about both his new post and his aesthetic interests.

Wijnnobel, a Dutchman, was one of the European intellectuals who had come to the British Isles in the war and had stayed on, writing and speaking in English. These émigrés—Wijnnobel was unusual in not being either central European or Jewish—were possibly the last of the polymaths. They were also the last generation, it later seemed, who were agreed on what human culture was, on what it was essential to know, preserve, and hand on. Wijnnobel was both a grammarian and a mathematician, was said, indeed, to be interested in some description of human cognition and notation that should combine the two. His interest in painting had something of the same progression from the elementary particles of vision and light to the complexities of metaphysics and ideas of reality. The broadcasts were illustrated with fine details, which Alexander, who was becoming a connoisseur of the rendering of the visible and tangible in the strange disembodied language of the radio waves, admired greatly. There was a description of the tiny beads of white paint on the dark brown forms of the boats in the *View of Delft* that was wholly memorable.

The voice heard on the radio was thin and clear and perfectly English, the consonants articulate, the vowels a little too plangent. Alexander had imagined a small, fine man and was alarmed to find himself face-to-face with a columnar giant, a man maybe six foot five in a dark suit, with a long square face, a full but not extravagant moustache, a square-cut head of black hair, and a pair of thick eyebrows over cavernous dark eyes. Long, rigorous lines were carved down from nose to mouth corner and along the other side of the cheeks. The surroundings, like the BBC itself, were a mixture of the austerely utilitarian and the civilized. The room was bare, a board-room with dusted windows letting in a gray street light, the chairs gaunt, the table angular. The lunch was laid with white napery, cut glass, heavy silver, and posies of flowers, incongruously set down like those feasts that appear in deserts as hallucinatory temptations for saints or travelers. The other guests were the Dean of St. Paul's, a Brains Trust Oxford master of a college, and a lady novelist who spent much of her time abroad lecturing on contemporary fiction for the British Council. Her name was Juliana Belper, and her face, above her rosy silk shirt and black tailored suit, was long and fine and distracted, a shade of Bloomsbury. They ate crab pâté, tournedos

Rossini, and poire Belle Hélène. The claret and the Stilton were excellent. The steaks were hard to chew. They were served by waitresses in starched white caps and aprons over black stuff dresses. Everyone's voice—apart from Wijnnobel's overlucid accent—was the same, everyone's combination of self-deprecation and unspoken certainty that there exist moral, tasteful, and conventional norms of behavior was the same. They knew what everything was—education, good art, good taste. Wijnnobel explained the idea of the new university, his face and body rigid, giving the impression, with a slightly military rasp in the way he stated objectives, that he was a retired or furloughed colonial administrator. He was against English early specialization, he said. Knowledge was not sealed in self-contained little boxes. His students would be required to have a foundation in science and mathematics, in more than one language. Also, the university would teach techniques, skills—architecture, engineering but also painting, radio, film. There would be communication between the disciplines at all levels. He was courteous, a little abstracted. He had explained all this before, many times.

In the 1960s, after pitched battles on the North Yorkshire campus, among others, after Satire and the mockery of the BBC and its Reithian precepts, after education had changed out of recognition, Alexander thought back with wonder to the shared certainties of that lunch, with nostalgia to the even grayness that had at the time faintly irritated him. He remembered also its one moment of violence, which came, surprisingly, in the form of an attack by Wijnnobel himself on Juliana Belper. She had not been listening too carefully to the talk about the new university, had picked up vaguely some remark of Wijnnobel's about the necessity for an educated man to know about the general and special theories of relativity, and had said, in words Alexander was sure she used in her lectures, that it was very true that great changes had taken place in the arts and sciences, that everything was now relative, we had lost our sense of certainty and absolute values, we perceived the world as fluid, random, and chaotic, and that our art forms *must* reflect the fragmented and subjective nature of our perception of the world . . .

Wijnnobel drew himself up and said, to the grouped wine bottles in front of him, "That is the kind of very silly argument with which I have no patience. That is the kind of simplistic nonsense I was hoping to avoid. 'Everything is relative.' It can only be relative to *something*. We are relative, it is true. Our measurements depend on our biology, on the skill of our toolmakers, on the geographic source and chemical composition of their materials. But even you must be able to see that there would be no theory of relativity without the absolute, immutable idea of the velocity of light—which in this theory becomes an invariable. We cannot have the idea of random happenings or chaotic conditions without simultaneously—indeed previously—having had a concept of order, an order of numbers, of form, of law."

"But our human *experience*," said Juliana Belper, "is chaotic." She was not interested in numbers. "We don't know our own nature—Freud showed us we don't know our own unconscious lives. We receive random impressions . . ." Her big eyes brimmed under a haze of soft hair escaped from a loose chignon.

"Sigmund Freud," said Wijnnobel, "like Johannes Kepler, was a scientist and believed in truth. Kepler observed that the apparently irregular variations in the motions of the planets were a function of the form of the lens of the eye. This does not mean that we cannot study the planets, only that we must also study the eye. Freud believed that there were laws of human behavior that could be truly observed and understood. His results are harder to verify but his intentions were exact and honorable. Your hazy concept of chaos and vagueness depends on ignorance and feebleness of intellect. Good art cannot come from it."

He had changed from a conventional, soldierly, stiff figure to a rigid, prophetic one, putting Alexander in mind of Freud's Moses, and reducing Juliana Belper to brimming tears and mottled-vermilion cheeks.

"I am intemperate," he said, without appearing sorry. It was a word to be frequently used about him during the student revolution of the 1960s, of which there was no foreshadowing at this table, where he appeared to be authority itself.

After this lunch Alexander took Wijnnobel to his office to discuss the last talk, on Mondrian. His office was on the top floor of Broadcasting House, lit by a sloping skylight, under which his desk fitted.

On his desk was the little print of the *Breakfast Table*, to which, after dealing succinctly with Mondrian, Wijnnobel turned his attention. Alexander explained his play, and said that he liked the picture because of its stillness. How could one dramatize stillness? Wijnnobel drew on a large pipe and laughed.

"I have a friend—an excitable friend—who could make a psychic drama of your picture, Mr. Wedderburn. He sees the erect male in every lone bottle and the receptive female in every round pot. What shall we make of the coffeepot? A blue French *cafetière* in two parts. My excitable friend would say that the upper male portion is fitted into the globular female and the lemons nestle at its foot, like the eggs Van Gogh painted in youth. A complete fertility symbol?"

"That spoils its quiddity as a thing."

"Even the touch of light has been read erotically. Vermeer's ladies are solid, remote, and untouchable, and held in a warm light which is a kind of love, isn't it? Sigmund Freud, of whom we were speaking, in *Beyond the Pleasure Principle* equates light and *eros*. Light is what makes our stony, inorganic world stir with life; light calls up and holds together complex forms. A curious work, that, which begins with bad dreams and decaying nerves and ends in a vision of Genesis and the origin of our divided nature. In Freud's myth the peace of the inanimate came before the striving of life, and the peace of the Aristophanic hermaphrodite before the constructions and cell divisions of Eros. In Freud's vision things secretly resent the calling to life of light. They wish to return to the state in which they were— instincts are conservative, 'every organism wishes to die only after its own fashion.' Maybe we could see our fascination for still life—or *nature morte*—in these terms? Maybe the kind of lifeless life of *things* bathed in light is another version of the golden age—an impossible stasis, a world without desire and division? I have made your coffee pot into the unfallen circular hermaphrodite of Plato's symposium. Is that dramatic?"

"Vincent thought," said Alexander, "that if he abstained his paintings would be more spermatic."

"What a graphic and unpleasant word. Is your breakfast table 'spermatic'? I think not. *Nature morte*, Mr. Wedderburn. Thanatos."

He paused. "Poor Vincent. A most disagreeable person I have

always thought. A combative, overcharged person. A man you would move quickly away from if he sat next to you in a café. Have you dramatized *that*, Mr. Wedderburn?"

"I have tried. I can't get it all in."

That night he dreamed a fearful and comic dream. He was pursuing, down the long and now infinitely extended dark corridor of the flat, what seemed to be a ball of furious flame that bowled over and over with irregular motions and a jerky speed. As Alexander came closer the burning creature hung arrested in the air, as though for him to get a good look at it, and at first, since it seemed like a multiple bird coiled in an eggshell of flame, he identified it as one of Ezekiel's winged creatures, flaring Cherubim, and then as it rolled away again it changed and became an almost hedgehoglike spherical creature, bristling with small human limbs and genitalia, the Aristophanic androgyne, tumbling like an acrobat from foot to foot with its two faces on its cylindrical neck, burning, burning. Alexander followed this absurd and yet menacing creature, and found that toward the distant kitchen corner it made another metamorphosis, becoming a midnight-blue bumping, banging thing, elongated on one side, still bristling with arms, legs, spouts, a coffeepot demon. And it made a hissing, spitting, threatening sound, and still in its ball of flame lurched around the kitchen door and vanished.

16

FIRST IDEAS

Frederica's extracurricular intellectual life was somewhat haphazardly arranged by men who invited her or escorted her to things. In this way, propelled by Alan and Tony, and by Owen Griffiths, she attended in one week two serious meetings in King's, one on the desirability of introducing a sociology tripos, the other on Cambridge humanism. She had no real idea what either sociology or humanism

was. Twenty years later she was startled how much the two had
seemed then to overlap. This was the quiet, forgotten, static time of
the middle fifties, after austerity, before affluence, also before Suez and
Hungary which were for next year. A time when political and
sociological thinkers were saying there were no great issues left, only
practical problems of economic and social planning, no ideology, only
a broad consensus, no class conflict, only, within reach, equality of
opportunity. A time when most British people believed modestly
and without excitement in better things to come as better things had
come, bananas, oranges, butter, the Health Service, the Butler Education Act, plans to expand higher education, motorcars for working
men. It was a dull and vague time to consider critically those large
words that had not been part of Frederica's narrow education: liberal,
just, human, free, democratic. All she had been taught to do was
rooted in the specific, the close literary reading. She knew only enough
to be *careful* about those large words, to see how they were used by
whom, out of a kind of residual tact. She had been taught suspicion,
not as a good Marxist would now teach suspicion of the self-
perpetuating uncriticized ideology, but in a worrying, nagging literary
way, suspicion of one word at a time, in a sentence.

The humanist meeting got itself, to her surprise, intricately and
circuitously enmeshed in an argument about whether humanism was
a religion. Should there be a creed, ceremonies, a hierarchy? It seemed
to Frederica self-evident that there should not—wasn't that what it
was all about? Humanists, they said, believed that the source of value
and the guide for behavior was the human. Each individual human
being and his welfare were of paramount importance, and these could
best be promoted in a democracy where all were equal and tolerance
was the major social virtue. It all sounded so easy, so self-evident,
so slippery. They agreed that they believed in planning; one young
man advanced an analogy between a central planning bureau and the
human cerebral cortex. It was King's; someone quoted G. E. Moore—
"Personal affections and aesthetic enjoyments include *all* the greatest
and *by far* the greatest goods we can imagine." There was nothing in
Frederica's behavior at that time to indicate that she did not hold that
belief and yet she could not have said that she did. Her attitude to
language precluded it. Marius Moczygemba said that St. Paul and

Christ had commanded human beings to love one another. Did we need God for that command to be meaningful? Oh, no, they all said hastily, though one added that Forster had felt that tolerance was the most you could *enjoin*—humanism could only create a society where love was possible for all. Alan Melville said, "But without God, or without a creed such as Marxism, where is the authority for our moral injunctions?" "In human nature," said one. "In the individual," said another. "In reason," said a third. "We *know* what is right and decent," said a last, paraphrasing the others.

"Do we?" said Alan Melville. "How do we?"

Frederica considered him, as he said this, with love. He sat on the edge of his chair, as though he might need to be free to flee. His expression was politely questioning, and yet she felt in him, debonair, amiable, a kind of contempt for all of them. He had told her a little about his childhood and youth: the comfort of the gang clustering in bombed sites, repeating phrases of common hate and bodily glory, the virtue there had been in whirling a chain, or holding a knife steady to slit to the bone, to mark, or worse, forever. He knew, he knew, that to be human was not simple. Where was the authority?

Most people at the sociology meeting did not know what sociology was. They assumed it meant the study of man in society, and that that must be a good thing, and moreover that it would lead to efficient planning which would lead to virtue and to freedom, as humanism had been at the earlier meeting equally expected to do. Frederica observed people here too. What "class," what "culture," what "elite" meant, she found harder to see as they agreed about it, but she could see that there were differences between, say, Tony Watson and Owen Griffiths when they spoke of "working-class culture." To Tony the abstract words were living forces—working-class culture was good, against mass culture, which was bad. Working-class culture included handmade artifacts, songs and tales, eating habits, cooking habits, sacrosanct because they had grown to be as they were. Mass culture was radio, pop song, television, packaged food, pulp magazines. Whereas for Owen working-class culture was the force of men like his father, who had organized other men into tight fighting groups to obtain better pay and better hours, which meant televisions and time for leisure. Owen said, often enough, "My father," as Tony never did, though Tony's father's abstract words were forces in Tony's life as Owen's father's burning ambition, hortatory eloquence, desire for power, were in his. For both men, "working-class culture" *was* their father. But it was quite clear that Tony did not see in Owen, aggressive, musically fervent, and mocking, those working classes he spoke of. And yet what else was Owen? And what of Frederica?

Bill Potter believed that Christian faith produced an untruthful and harmful view of the world, human beings, society. Frederica, in direct succession, believed that too, but had developed a skeptical mistrust of her father's undue respect for Leavisite "values" and the "life" located and propounded so easily in D. H. Lawrence. These things, values and life, seemed in certain lights to be morals and god without name or authority.

Frederica found herself in the common and difficult position of disliking the parts of the culture to which she felt she belonged rather more than those to which she felt antagonistic. She saw herself as shrewd, classless, free from artificial desire to climb an illusory ladder, or romantic identification with what was good about what had gone before. She was naturally in revolt against "authority" and yet she was happier with T. S. Eliot's hierarchical certainties than Dr. Leavis's *Scrutiny* utopia where she belonged, as she was happier with the wit and wickedness of *Brideshead* than with the minor spites and decencies of *Lucky Jim*, which might be said to have given literary form to the world she best knew. At least Eliot and Waugh involved the whole of things, fought it out, however absurdly, on a cosmic scale. She had been taught to dislike messy slurring of concepts. She had no clear concepts to like.

There remained Love, for which she was looking. She was taught about eros and agape, *caritas, amour*, self-love, and loss of self, and desired quite simply to be "in love." She continued not to believe in the love protested by men she slept with or talked to, and took a certain pleasure in the company of those who had interests other than herself, who could be subsumed too quickly in the embarrassment of fending off. There was Marius, who meant to be an artist. And there was Owen, who had an idea of his destiny.

Marius painted her, in his basement digs, producing a Modigliani pastiche with plum-colored eyes that annoyed Frederica, whose eyes were not that color. When the painting—which later became a kind of Jackson Pollock abstract—was done, he sat with Frederica on his bed and fondled her, occasionally asking her why she allowed him to do this. He had had a Catholic upbringing; he wanted sex to be sad and dangerous. Practical Frederica was becoming used to this male ambivalence. Owen Griffiths took her to dinner in the Union, where she was only permitted to go, being a woman, as his guest. He talked about the future of socialism, the reasons why the Attlee government had been elected and rejected, and said the best thing Frederica could do was to marry him, Owen Griffiths. He said it over a tough steak and a watery grilled tomato, as though that settled the matter. Frederica was characteristically unwilling to admit that the idea was a serious one and replied, as she often did, that she was sure that when he thought about it he wouldn't want to face anyone as argumentative as she was over meals every day. Owen assured her that this was the attraction—he told her to think of the future. He assumed that Frederica knew, as he knew himself, that he had an extraordinary future. The only extraordinary future in which Frederica was interested in that way was her own, but it is doubtful whether he saw this, as it is doubtful whether he ever began to imagine the extraordinary blankness and paucity of what passed for Frederica's political ideas. In this slightly self-centered obtuseness they were perhaps similar, as in a tendency to talk a good deal when excited. Owen Griffiths saw Frederica as a very clever girl who would make an ambitious man a good wife. Frederica recognized the ambition, and saw it as threatening. He was threatening in another way too: he had a tendency to force his way into her room to repeat his proposal at times of day when men were not allowed in Newnham, and once caused Frederica to be reprimanded—not for the first or last time—by her tutor. That she did not get into more trouble was partly owing, her tutor told her, to the fact that she might be expected to do well in tripos. Later—not at the time, when the judgment seemed perfectly natural—Frederica wondered at their priorities. Down the corridor a quiet brown girl who never spoke to anyone, a geographer perhaps, or a mild theologian, Frederica was unsure, was found the same term to have quietly married a restaurant proprietor, a Sardinian, who sang in the church choir and cooked, gossip said, like an angel. This married woman was indeed sent down—not for having gone to bed with her husband in her room, not for being out at night, for she did neither, but simply for being married. (Unsuitably married.) And yet what are we really being prepared for, Frederica asked herself, thinking of her tutor, a formidable woman with a rasping tongue and as sharp an eye as sweet Freddie's for the cheap garment, the ersatz glove, the incorrect phrase. They had no idea what it was to be a woman. In later years, in the light of that indiscriminate loving interest lavished on all female activity, all female uses of the self, which is the most unequivocally agreeable result of literary feminism, it became possible to see both Miss Chiswick and little brown Signora Cavelli née Brill as heroines of some kind, upholders of differing principles. Miss Chiswick had sacrificed something at least for the life of the mind: Miss Brill had had it taken from her against her will. In 1955 Frederica felt contempt, mixed with fear, for both of them. Surely, surely, it was possible, she said to herself in a kind of panic, to make something of one's life *and* be a woman. Surely.

17

FIELD STUDIES

Those who do not make natural social ties are liable to have artificial ones made for them. Marcus found himself on a long weekend course organized by Gideon Farrar at the Centre for Field Studies on the moors south of Calverley. Marcus now spent his days, clothed in a long brown cotton coat, wheeling trolleys of books through Calverley General Hospital, along the narrow passage between the long rows of beds, up and down in the grinding iron lift with trolleys bearing the unconscious from the operating theater, or wheelchairs on their way to physiotherapy or radiography. He managed to dispense books without talking to his customers. Nor did he talk to his parents, though he could feel them anxiously waiting for him to say something, and then, when he did not, to go back to his room. He went where Gideon told him to go because it seemed easy, and because it was a weekend away from Bill's nervous politeness. When he got to the Centre, he thought he had made a mistake. It was a group of creosote-smelling wooden huts round a central whitewashed concrete building. His first shock was to find that he was sharing a bedroom, as he had never done, with three other boys.

They took a shy tea on their first evening, maybe sixteen boys and girls from various schools and churches. Tea was poured from huge aluminum pots; there was bread and quantities of margarine and cochineal-tinged strawberry jam and pieces of square cake from a mass baking. Marcus sat down between two empty chairs, one of which was then taken by a girl with long brown hair tied in bunches and largish glasses who seemed to know him. She acknowledged equably that he failed to know her.

"You don't remember me. I'm Jacqueline. We sat next to each other at one of Gideon's family lunches. What are you doing now?"

"I push books round the hospital on a trolley."

"You must meet some interesting people."

"Not really." He made an effort. "What happens here?"

"Well, on this visit we experience each other." Marcus hunched his shoulders over his plate. "That's what Gideon says. I come because I like the place, I like the moors, I like the project work."

"Project work?"

"The big thing is the long-term study of ants. We have several artificial colonies, and some we observe outside. Christopher Cobb—next to Gideon at the top of the table—is a world authority. He's *fascinating*. You must hear him talk."

"I don't know."

"Perhaps you don't like ants? They are amazing, really. I'll show you."

"I don't like or dislike them. I'd like to see them."

They went for a walk in the late light, after tea. They trooped over a piece of moorland, down a cliff path, and ran and shouted on the

beach at the Boggle Hole, a small, funnel-like cleft in the cliffs where
a beck runs down to the sea out of the peat, brown-stained, tea-leaf
and gold, and slowly washes into the incoming tide, chill and gray,
salty and clear. The place is remarkable for an odd rock formation,
heaps and cairns and fossil bowling greens of almost-circular pieces
of heavy stone, rough to the touch, or smoothed by the sea, like a
cache of primitive cannonballs. Flat terraces of rock, crisscrossed in
their dully sheened green and black by little crevices and runnels,
lined pink and sandy with lichens and weeds, ran out to where the sea
moved back and forward, a fine layer of investigating water, over
them. Marcus balanced a stone in his hand and listened to water and
wind. Jacqueline reappeared. "Look at it all coming to life. Look at
the sea anemones. So much going on."

Marcus balanced his stone and looked, obediently, at the blobs of
dark brown and ruddy and occasionally goldish jelly, glued by their
one foot, a few fronds or tentacles wavering at the orifice of the belly-
button depression in the center. Jacqueline said, "Look, there's Ruth."
A gull called harshly.

"Ruth?"

"You know, Ruth; we *all* met at Gideon's Meal."

Marcus watched the Young People perambulating in small groups.
He had no idea which was Ruth, which he had seen before. They all
looked the same. Rainproof jackets and sensible boots.

"You don't notice much, do you?"

"No." He hesitated. "I have great difficulty in recognizing people.
Especially telling people apart in groups."

"They fascinate me," said Jacqueline. "None are the same, that's
what is odd, none. Ruth is the one with the long plait and the big dark
eyes. And the red jacket."

Marcus located the—or a—red jacket, but failed to recognize Ruth.
Jacqueline stayed with him, pointing things out, a mermaid's purse, a
hermit crab. He wondered if Gideon had appointed her to draw him
out. He liked her, in any case, because she liked the things. He shifted
his heavy stone from hand to hand and wondered why she should
find the world full of excitement and he see it through a haze of
unreality and fear. On the way back, as a small flock of moorland
sheep trotted, swaying on their skinny black legs toward them, he
tried a joke.

"And the sheep. Can you tell the sheep apart?"

"Of course. There's an old one—look at the knobs and hollows on her skull. That's a fierce one—the fatter one at the front. No two the same. She'd butt you with half a chance. Look at their beautiful eyes."

Their eyes were yellow, with a barlike vertical pupil. He looked for beauty, and registered the amber color.

"What do you think they *see*, with slits for pupils?" he said.

"I don't know. But one day I will. You can see their skulls so much more clearly than ours; that's interesting." She turned her face to him. "Can you imagine my skull?"

Threads of brown hair on an open brow; the warm muddle of the center-parted tea cozy of hair and the long bunches behind the ears, the solemn windows of the glasses that reflected his own, the thin, smiling mouth.

"No. No, I can't. No."

"Or your own?"

He touched the corner of his jaw, the apex of his cheekbone.

"When I have asthma or hay fever. When it hurts. The sinuses. But only from inside. I couldn't *draw* it. It feels long and sharp and inflamed."

She put one hand on his jaw and one on hers, calibrating. "Yours is longer than mine."

The sheep wheeled away, their gray woolen rumps swaying indistinguishably, trailing mats of heather and knotted wool, old blood and accrued tar.

"Can you tell them apart from behind, then?"

"If I try. They're a flock. One trots humpier than another. That one's dirtier. That one's skittish. You can tell if you try."

He tried to fix the black crisscrossing pattern of the trotting legs before they vanished.

After supper Gideon gathered them round the hot stove, a black tank with an acrid-smelling pipe chimney. Hot milky drinks were made and distributed; drops of milk that fell on the metal swelled, blistered, went coffee colored, umber, black, and smelled of rice pudding and then of disaster. Warmth itself, the mixture of drowsiness and choking in the smells pulled them together; they sat, mostly on the floor, and looked at Gideon. Who was saying that he proposed that they play a game that would not be a game, but a way of breaking through the cocoon of shyness and convention that separates every man from his neighbor, a game of Truth. Everyone should tell a story, a true story, a story about him or herself that he felt would really enable the others to know him—or her—better. He himself would kick off. The story he told was the story of a battle—a weeklong battle as he described it—with his adopted son Dominic, who had rejected Gideon's care, had run away three times and been found, once in a workman's hut, once under a tree in a park, once hiding in a school shed. Gideon described how on each occasion he had brought the child back, kicking and screaming, abusing him, Gideon, for not being his real father; the point of the story was how hard he, Gideon, had found it to come to terms with being apparently hated where he had hoped to give love, rejected where he had wanted to make harmony. "I could only act in the end," he said, "when I *admitted* my feeling, to myself, stopped being gentle, turned on him with *real* anger, and told him, 'I love you, but I won't put up with this; I grieve for you, but I myself am hurt.' " And then, the story ended satisfactorily, the child had been reassured, it had been a sense of his father's omnipotence and perpetual even temper that had so oppressed him; he had come home and climbed onto his knee and punched him playfully and they were a family again.

Some of the Young People were used to Gideon's methods. One boy told a story that followed pat upon, a story told not for the first time, of how he had been an evacuee in the war, of how his mother had been killed in the Blitz, of how his foster family—who didn't like him any more than he liked them—had taken him on, and he had not been grateful, had not known who *he* was, didn't feel right, a Cockney Yorkshireman, afraid he was tolerated and would not be really loved. Another boy told how he was the only one in his family to fail the eleven plus and his parents didn't want to know him, were interested in nothing he did. If there was a common theme to these well-shaped little outbursts it was one of parental inadequacy, failure of vision, absence. Gideon orchestrated the telling. He would ask a question—"And *then* what did you feel?"—elicit a sharp image, and tidy the narrative toward the discovery of the teller's true independent identity, his or her capacity to see the failures of others as inevitable. He made the stories *exciting*, and also acceptable, full of dramatic import. A cross dark girl told how her mother lived upstairs in her house and her father lived downstairs with another woman, and she herself negotiated between the two, carrying written messages, begging for money, fetching back borrowed pans. Gideon managed to offer this back to her both as though she had seen the situation with a sort of desperate wit and as though she herself was the only sane, only humane, person in the building. What had begun as a series of grim one-sentence statements became a rollicking account of banister-edge repartee. She was followed by the boy who had seen his father set upon and slashed by angry workmates for petty tale bearing to management. Gideon again managed to make a tale of sick fear into a tale of seen tragedy, to suggest, with the full force of his silken smile and leonine attention, that the boy was somehow heroic, had acquired wisdom. He turned to Marcus and asked if he had a story. "No," said Marcus. "Not really. Thank you." "Later maybe," said Gideon amiably, and turned to Ruth.

This time Marcus noticed Ruth a little. She stood like a child called to attention in assembly, her long plait between her shoulder blades, and looked straight ahead of her, at Gideon, clasping her hands in front of her, still, not twisting. She had a composed, Nordic little face, with straight blond eyebrows and very blue eyes: her mouth was straight and soft and peaceful. She said she would talk about her mother in hospital and began, without any preamble, rather flatly, saying how hard it had been for "us" to accept that things were not being done for them at home, that everything was dirty, and the shopping wasn't done, how they hadn't been able to help being angry with "my mother" and how that now hurt them. "What I want to say is how badly we treated her for how long. She got thinner and thinner and wasn't *the same*. And she still wanted to talk to us, she used to look at us sort of—hungrily—and we were scared of her, we didn't want to know her, we had nothing to say. She was in there lying and I was doing the shopping and cooking and cleaning and trying to do my homework and look after Daddy. Then we saw she would die, there wasn't any help, and we wanted it to be at once, not to go on, we wanted her to be gone, if she was going to go, and she kept trying to talk to us. She got upset when I got Christine's hair cut, but it was an awful nuisance, all knots. Then one day we went up there and they said she'd died peacefully and gave us her things in a bag. I didn't feel anything. I just kept thinking of things to do, cleaning the cooker, the under-stairs cupboard, getting rid of broken toys, things like that. Then one day I was going through a drawer and found half a sweater."

"Go on," said Gideon.

"A stripy one I'd once asked for. She was knitting it, before . . . Then I cried."

"And now you feel bad because you felt let down and angry—which is perfectly natural, inevitable," said Gideon.

"No, no, I don't. I—"

"Yes, you do. You kept everything going and now you feel bad because you were afraid, as well as being very brave."

Ruth said nothing. Gideon said—did he know the answer?—"And now your father relies on you, you carry the burden of the house and your A levels . . ."

"No," said Ruth. "Not any more. He married Mrs. Jessop. He." She sat down, neatly. Gideon left her and moved on. It was as though all the stories were one story: a father, a mother, a child, or children, an ideal pattern that turned out not to be so. Jacqueline threw away the story of the gift of a microscope to a favored brother, and her own final acquisition of one, which Gideon treated perfunctorily, as though it was somehow cheating. Marcus sat abstracted; he was beginning to fear bedtime. He had never had to share a bedroom with other boys.

The boys in his room were quite reasonable boys, strangers to each other, excited by the emotional electricity in the air. Gideon had gathered together the threads of stories, had spoken of the fragility of life and relationships, the need for something secure, stable, un-changing, the knowledge of Christ in each of us. The boys discussed Gideon with approval. "He makes it seem to *matter* what we do," one of them said. They went off to the washroom with sponge bags and came back bright skinned and peppermint smelling. Marcus sat on the edge of his bed, hunched. A boy said, "You don't talk much. Are you okay?"

"I've got—asthma. Can't breathe. Hope—doesn't—disturb."

"Feel free," said the cheeriest boy. "That stove makes a right stink. Get anyone's lungs. Hope you feel better."

He took an ephedrine capsule and put a tiny half-moon of adrenaline under his tongue. The boys in the room settled; two of them wrestled briefly over the theft of a spare pillow and Marcus, supporting his rib cage on his knuckles, saw their pajamas come apart as they swayed, fingers interlaced, shoulders and hips wriggling. A fuzzy dark belly button, a momentarily exposed penis, squarer and stubbier than his own, slightly lifted with excitement. Trailing white trouser cords. How could they touch each other? How? He breathed, whistling. He was ashamed. He watched them all get into bed, pull up sheets, and gray blankets, hump and settle. He breathed shallow, trying to be quiet. He had the fantastic idea that they were using up all his air. His right lung was particularly painful; a deep breath would rasp its matted rawness. The idea of the boys in the room swelled—peppermint breath and hidden pale and dark boyflesh and the smell of feet after running bulged everywhere. He wheezed. He put his feet down on the board floor. The boy in the next bed opened his eyes and flung out an arm. Marcus's overactive nostrils followed the swing of the armpit.

"Are you okay?"

"Can't breathe. I'll go out a bit."

"Want any help?"

"No. Just can't lie down. Hurts." He wheezed.

"You sound awful."

"It's not as bad as it sounds."

He crossed from his hut to the main building where there were still some lights. The night air, though painful, had a pine and heather smell. There were small sounds in it—a squeak, a whisk, a chattering ending abruptly. He went toward where he thought the kitchen might be, feeling his way along the wall, measuring his rattling, hissing breaths. He came instead to one of the big lecture rooms, with large laboratory benches, a lectern, glass tanks gleaming in the dark round the walls.

Someone spoke. "Who is it?"

"Marcus Potter."

"What are you doing?"

"I can't sleep. I've got asthma."

"This is me, Jacquie. I'm looking for Ruth. She was crying. I'll put the lights on."

The lights were under conical metal shades and cast round pools onto the tables. The bare, large windows reflected their white circles in another shape, from another angle. Marcus saw Jacqueline in the smeared velvet black of the glass, under what seemed to be an infinite procession of white globes, a gray ghost in a long woolen gown. He saw himself, too, pale pajamaed shoulders hooped and heaving, pale hair flopping, his glasses reflected reflecting diminishing white balls. The tanks round the walls of the room were the ant colonies.

"You look terrible. Sit down. Shall I get you a drink? Have you seen the ants? I'll put their lights on."

Shaded strips of white light appeared above the tanks. The sides of the ant colonies had a golden refulgence, which was explained by a neatly lettered label attached to them.

This is a colony of common British black ants, *Lasius niger*. The glass of the observation nest is yellow-red, as the ant is blind to rays in this range of the spectrum, although it is keenly alive to the range of colors towards the ultra-violet. Unlike the jet-black ant, *Lasius fuliginosus*, which follows a scent-trail, *Lasius niger* navigates by sight. Its large compound eyes can form erect images of moving things. It is thought possible that the insect at rest is blind, since the unlidded eye seems designed specifically to see movement.

Marcus considered the ants, with that still, slow observation that is a result of the immobility of asthma. The adrenaline, besides giving his heart a noticeable and irregular bump, also imparted a sense of urgency to what he was doing. The ants were invested with significance. They were, or appeared to be—the glass was yellow-red—in a reddish kind of soil, on the surface of which were scattered pieces of fruit—orange and apple—and tired edges of salad. The surface swarmed with various sizes of ant, running vigorously, casting about, turning, running, returning. The side of the tank was the wall of layers of corridors and cavities, in two of which the oval pupae were arranged, pale, whitish, neither in orderly rows nor in a haphazard heap, but in—to Marcus—unreadably organized clusters. Ants ran in the corridors as on the surface, shifting small grains of earth with fine feet, carrying pupae raised before them like huge processional candles. It seemed, to his distress, random and swarming. Ants appeared from nowhere, a knot of fiercely struggling bristles out of an invisibly fine tunnel. An ant carrying an ovoid much larger than itself abandoned it in the face of a crumb of soil, whereupon several other ants rushed out, acting in concert, though not without impeding each other, and carried it along another passage. Marcus stared at their furious, incomprehensible life. They ran and ran and bristled and waved and communicated. There were so many. More and more, as he stared. He did not know whether he was watching seething chaos or incomprehensible order.

Jacqueline reappeared with two mugs of steamy tea. Marcus said, "Did you find Ruth?"

"No. I will. I expect she's okay. She gets worked up. Gideon works people up. He thinks it does them good to be shaken up."

Marcus's mind's eye saw a large stick breaking and stirring the agitated corridors.

"Perhaps it doesn't." He wheezed and drank. "He doesn't stir you up."

"I have a humdrum personal life. Nothing to talk about. Let's look at the ants."

Part of the wall of the colony was a circular magnifying glass. Through it Marcus did not meet, but saw, the unseeing huge eye of a worker ant in a cavern lined with spun cocoons. The eye was like a huge apple seed. The ant itself was three glittering black, carapaced, pointed, and rounded segments and six finely jointed limbs. The form repeated itself, seed shapes, wherever he looked. The ants stroked the cocoon wrapping.

"Where is the queen?" said Marcus.

"Somewhere in the middle, in the dark. You can't see her. There's a photograph of her."

There she was, in her chamber, blown up to the size of Marcus's two hands, a mountainous distended belly with feeble head and feet poking from it, climbed over, as a grounded air balloon or beached ship might be, by diligent, tiny attendant daughters.

"Horrible," he said. "Horrible."

"No, why? Look at these—these are "repletes"; these are ants who just hang up as honey pots for other ants all their lives." There they hung, also as large as Marcus's hands, their swollen abdomens forcing apart the plates of their skeletons, living jugs and receptacles for plant-lice nectar poured in by the busy and mobile.

"Isn't it *interesting?*" said Jacqueline.

"Yes. But I don't like it. Them."

"That's because you see them as human. If you *don't*, they're simply amazing."

Marcus considered the swollen egg layer and the incessant motion in the dark tunnels.

"I don't see how you can't—see them in relation to us."

"You must try."

Marcus and Jacqueline went softly and companionably back to the kitchen with their mugs. There was a light in the kitchen and a small sound, the sniff and bursting splutter of someone crying. Jacqueline put her hand up to keep Marcus quiet, which was unnecessary; together they reached up to look through the glass panel of the swing door. Ruth was there, sitting at the table, her back to them, her yellow hair spread unconfined all over her blue shoulders. And Gideon Farrar was standing over the stove, stirring milk in a pan. They watched him make cocoa; they watched him hand her a cap and draw a chair up beside her, putting an arm around her shoulders.

"I hate her," the clear voice said, telling its fairy-tale story of dead queen and wicked stepmother, repeating a repeated human cry. "I hate the woman my father married. We were all right till she came. We *were*. We were clean and tidy and happy in our ways. And now we're filthy and messy and all hostile to each other and split apart. I hate her. I'm so unhappy."

"Don't, little one," said Gideon. "Don't. Don't take on. Live *your* life. Begin *your* life. You can bring so much love and happiness . . ."

He took her chin in his fingers, turned up her face, folded her into his arms, rested his smiling face on the captive golden head. Marcus felt stirred, ill, and quite disproportionately moved, not by what was said, but by the physical certainty of comforting of this gesture. Even seen through the glass door square Gideon was grandly sure that he, Gideon, was the answer to the cry, the love wept for in the dark, the one to turn to. Marcus felt small fingers steal into his. "Come away," said Jacqueline. "Come on. We oughtn't to be here." Her hand was dry and warm and firm; she did not pat or squeeze. He held on to her. He wheezed. He felt he had seen something important and not understood at all.

The next day, Christopher Cobb lectured on the ants. He was a man with a rounded and billowing woolly beard that had the density and curl of southern sheep wool: in nutmeg brown, a lively unfaded color, inside which his rounded lips were red like haws but appeared small, secret, and hidden, like an obscure sexual organ. His head was thick with a brown mattress of wool, a different brown again, a brown of indigenous animal fur, the sandy fringe below a hedgehog's bristles. It was a beard that Edward Lear would have populated with parasitic life, a plump thrush, a few quails, a titmouse. He had a tubby trundling body inside an oiled-wool Norwegian sweater. He spoke of the social life of the ant. He warned against seeing ant life in terms of human life—though the language he spoke was colored and informed by anthropomorphism. We have named the ants for ourselves: queen, worker, soldier, parasite, slave. We name their social behavior for ours; we talk of classes and castes. What interested Cobb was the problem of the guiding intelligence of the ant community. How does it assess, as it does, he asked, how many fecundated females it needs? How does it choose whether an egg or larva shall become a worker or soldier or queen? There is evidence that these choices lie in the genetic inheritance of the egg, but also in the nature of the food fed to the larva by the workers in its very early days. There is determination and some communal choice, but what chooses? A whole colony of ants has sometimes been compared to the aggregation of cells that compose one human being. Is this comparison helpful or distracting? Where does intelligence inhere?

Is it more helpful to see the nest as a machine—like a vast telephone exchange, said Christopher Cobb, in the days before the computer—or as Maurice Maeterlinck did, as a community of cooperative virgins, practitioners of an extraordinary altruism, ready to die for the greater good of "the ideal republic, the republic we shall never know, the republic of mothers?" T. H. White had seen them as inhabitants of a totalitarian labor camp. Now, in 1984, biologists have taken to referring to all organisms, men, amoebas, ants, songbirds, giant pandas, as "survival machines." They measure the statistical likelihood of altruistic behavior in baboons and partridges with computer analyses of degrees of kinship and the perpetuation of particular genes. They account for self-consciousness as a product of the self-images the computing brain of the survival machine needs to make in order to be efficient. Can an anthill be said to have self-consciousness? Christopher Cobb urged on the attentive young the need for objectivity (a word now fallen out of fashion). For imaginative curiosity without preconceptions. As though this were possible.

And Christopher Cobb, seen with imaginative curiosity? He was genuinely very much more interested in ants than in boys or girls, young men or women. He was a natural bachelor—a novelist may make that statement with authority, though another human being, with the curiosity proper to another discipline, a post-Freudian human being, would seek for, and within the discipline find, a reason for Christopher Cobb's choice of celibate solitude on the moors with glass tanks full of uncommunicating myriads. What bent of the libido caused Christopher Cobb to be fascinated by living, inhuman things, and within that large domain, by the ant? Or, to shift disciplines, what social pattern predisposed him to this role? Why was Christopher Cobb not interested in freshwater pearl mussels, or in radio waves, or in transformational grammar, or in the manufacture of fine needles, or in the alleviation of kwashiorkor?

How little we know. Marcus was interested in Christopher Cobb, and fascinated by the ants, in ways that were to change his life, and about which Christopher Cobb was to know nothing at all.

They went for a nature ramble. Marcus found himself observing the Young People as in the wakeful darkness he had observed the apparently pointless meanderings of the ants. They spattered the moorland, they made little groups, broke formation, joined other little groups, rushed and rested. Gideon, a great strider, made long loops and reverses, bursting from behind between two doggedly plodding boys and clapping his arms round their shoulders, crushing a girl's head briefly against his breast. Ants greet and recognize each other by vibrations and touches of the antennae—to be more precise, through the olfactory sense, which resides mainly in the last seven segments of the funicle, which is the process at the end of the antennae. Moreover, each joint recognizes a particular odor. The final segment recognizes the odor of the nest. If a curious worker amputates the segments in order, the ant's bewilderment and disorientation, or sudden battling with disturbed sisters, will reveal that the penultimate segment discerns the age group of workers in colonies consisting of various families of the same species; the last but two recognizes the scent with which the ant impregnates her own trail. Further segments recognize the smell of the queen mother in the nest, the smell of the ant's own species, which is different from the smell of the nest, and the hereditary maternal odor, not necessarily that of the queen of the nest, which the ant carries from the egg to the moment of its death. Whether the gamboling and slapping of the handsome clergyman was a considered human substitute for some such species contact and communication it is hard to say. Stephanie, hip squashed by him over the washing up, had recognized, she believed, a crude, old, and adequate existing form of human bodily communication. Marcus hoped simply to avoid being touched himself. He raised his coat collar and shoulders above his body and tucked his head into this shell in order to signal that he was not there. Jacqueline, however, came and walked with him, accompanied by Ruth.

He saw Ruth's plait, one fat tapering form between her shoulders. He saw with the thinly expanded clarity of the asthma, ephedrine, and adrenaline. One effect of these three is to define outlines of forms while somehow thinning textures. The painter Samuel Palmer, an asthmatic, managed both to contain a visionary stook of straw, a tree full of fruit, a bright moon, and a white cloud in a cage or net of dark outlines and to suggest that these things consist only of differing brilliances of pure light, defined by the eye in the linear mapping of their periphery. So Marcus saw Ruth's very glossy hair, its interwoven round and tapering segments repeatedly curving into the one plait, shining. She was clean and orderly and glossy, who last night had been wild and scattering. She did not say much; she looked composedly down. It was Jacqueline who talked. He heard Jacqueline's voice and saw Ruth's plait sway. "Look," Jacqueline said "at the bracken coming . . . at the shape the wind has made of the thorn tree . . . at the curlew . . . at rabbit droppings . . ." Her talk was informative.

Marcus went home infected both by the communal frisson of excitement and by an automatic, inculcated Potter skepticism about Gideon's preaching. He lay in bed, safe in his white room, and thought about God, which he had not done since he gave up trying to comply with Lucas Simmonds's visionary messianic explanations of his own gifts. His mind swarmed with a dangerous yet lively pattern of repeating forms, as it had at moments he had earlier been tempted to define as the onset of madness. Everything could be recalled, envisaged, as repeated ovals, as the world might be divided by looking through the regular-raindrop dimpling of some kinds of bathroom glass. White ants' pupae piled in layers, sheep rumps trotting, the weaving glossy segments of Ruth's plait, thorax and abdomen, white faces turned up to Gideon's firelit brilliance. He fingered the oval of his own cheek and through the window saw the irregular lump of a gibbous moon. There was a God, he suddenly knew, a God of overflowing order and intricacy, ovals and ants. He saw two Gods, side by side, Gideon's God, who was like Gideon, a golden man opening his arms to comfort, and a God of fine bristles in dark corridors, of segments and interlocking threads and forms, of force taking shape, innumerable shapes. Lucas had been mad to think that any channel of communication existed with this God. He was in and about Marcus and the world. That was dangerous. But it had been his function. He thought of Jacqueline's curiosity and the beauty of Ruth's plait. Adrenaline, his own, not the half-moon pill's, began to run.

18

HIC ILLE RAPHAEL

In Frederica's second year in Cambridge she became famous, or infamous, for her ornithology. The idea came to her when she was talking to Edmund Wilkie about experimental pigeons at a party of sweet Freddie's where she learned the word taxonomy, a moment—the learning—which was to remain sharp in her mind long after the faces and furniture surrounding the learning had faded into an indistinguishable mosaic-blanket Cambridge party. Wilkie was enthusiastically recounting a series of experiments on the migrations of birds. It was thought, he said, that they could follow magnetic fields. Wilkie was talking about how far allowances had to be made for variations from pigeon to pigeon and Frederica's mind was filled with an image of clattering flocks of them, all the same, heading the same way, differently feathered, at differing speeds. Just like the men at Cambridge, wanting one thing, if not only one, lavish, nervous, posturing, inhibited, bright, brilliant, manipulative, vanishing behind protective coloring. The ornithology was a fairly usual undergraduate joke, redeemed on Frederica's part by a certain chilly exactness in her identification of stances and amatory ploys, chameleon, fake, rhetorician, Lucky Jim. Marius Moczygemba illustrated these sketches, which were amiably published by Tony and Alan in their magazine, with a series of pen-and-ink drawings as proficient as his oil paintings were uncertain and dubious. This was before the arrival of what we in the sixties liked to call "satire." The best that can be said for Frederica's taxonomy was that it avoided school-magazine jokiness: indeed, it remarkably lacked any assumption of complicity with its readers. It was only much later that Frederica, rereading a run of these pieces in a lazy moment, said to herself that what she seemed to remember as having been written with a mixture of exasperated love and aesthetic excitement over her capacity to *notice* so much could, seen coldly, be read as withdrawn hatred. She had not meant it so, but it could have been read like that. The other odd thing was that although part of the ornithology's impetus had been a retort to male classifying of tits and thighs in bars and common rooms it did not occur to her until the series was nearly ended that the young men referred to girls as birds, or chicks. When she presented this discovery to Marius he said, "But I thought that was the point." Frederica said truthfully that she had thought of ornithology because of Wilkie's pigeons, and Marius said, "A likely story," and drew a swirl of greasy hair in two economical lines. "I *like* men," said Frederica. "Oh, yes, you can see that you like men," said Marius impassively.

In the autumn of 1955 Frederica met the poet Hugh Pink, accompanied him to the University Library, a place she visited rarely, where she fell in love. She fell in love, for all her sexual experiments, for all her canny prevarication, quite childishly, with a face and a concept.

Hugh Pink had knocked on her door with a sheaf of poetry magazines called *Fine*. He was thin and slightly stooping, with pale blue eyes and crests and troughs of wavy red-gold hair, which looked at first glance as though some 1930s perm had gone badly wrong, and could then immediately be seen to be inexorably what it was, growing as it did, with only one possible shape. Frederica bought a magazine, offered him coffee, asked about its title. It was called *Fine*, he said, as a kind of pun. It was interested in a poetry of precise images, clear-cut not sloppy, and it hoped not to be narrowly English in its orientation, so *Fine* could be taken as Italian for limits. He had a poem in it of his own, describing a Fantin-Latour painting of a white cup and saucer in the Fitzwilliam Museum. He showed this to Frederica, who liked it. It was written in short lines, not in the conversational-lyric pentameter then already usual. It described Fantin-Latour's description of a cup. It had no apparent emotions in it and its words were memorable. Also in that issue of *Fine* was a translation of Mallarmé's *"Ses purs ongles"* which was signed Raphael Faber. Frederica could make nothing of this at all. But she took to Hugh Pink, who drank her Nescafé and disarmed her sharpness by saying wryly, with his full mouth, that Pink was an impossible name for a poet, especially a poet who had, as he was aware he himself had, rather round pink cheeks. He said, "I feel it's an obstacle I've got to overcome. I feel a name is a *donné*; one has to accommodate what's given. Don't you agree? If I even had a few more initials it'd be better. You could sign a poem H. R. F. Pink, and that'd be better than two monosyllables. But my parents kept things simple. One name—less fuss in banks."

"I've never thought Potter had much of a ring to it."

"You could marry and change it. You could even become Frederica Pink."

"No. I want a name like Bowen, or Sackville, or Middleton, euphonious but plain."

"Pink isn't euphonious. I had a girlfriend once who called me Rosy. That wasn't good either."

"You must make Pink distinguished."

"My father's a distinguished surgeon."

"Distinguished for literature. So that people don't think about colors or flowers or cheeks but about Yeats and Eliot and Pink."

"A pink is a pink is a pink."

"If you say it often enough it sounds like skink, or drink, or even think. Just a word with a k on the end."

"It's not even a color I like."

"Oh, I do. I liked it a lot as a little girl, until they told me it didn't go with red hair."

"You liked it because pink is for girls. Now *I* have red hair—or reddish—*and* I'm the wrong sex."

"I like your little gray-and-white poem, Mr. Pink."

Hugh Pink wrote a frivolous ballade for Frederica—"Song for a redheaded woman." He bought her a curry and a chop suey and took her to the University Library. He showed signs of falling in love, which Frederica did not acknowledge, and offered her, meaning to share something he valued, a vision.

The basement coffee room in the library is a pleasant place, smelling of warm baking. They sat inside a glass wall and door, which opened out onto a high brick well that dwarfed the little quadrangle inside it. Two figures in M.A. gowns were standing next to the magnolia, then only a low bush, in the middle of the grass, arms clasped behind them. Hugh Pink said, "There is the cleverest man I know."

"Which one?"

"The dark one. Raphael. The Mallarmé man."

"I don't know him." The two men began a slow circumambulation of the grass plot.

"He's a Fellow of St. Michael's. Absolutely brilliant. A marvelous teacher. And a poet. A *real* poet. He has poetry evenings in his rooms —just for a few of us. It's hard to get invited. We started *Fine* because of his ideas, because we wanted to write in his sort of way."

The two men had come round so that they were now facing the glass between them and Frederica. One, short and balding, Frederica recognized as Vincent Hodgkiss, the philosopher of the distant Camargue beach party, who had talked of Wittgenstein's color theory. The other had a face that had haunted her dreams and daydreams from childhood until it was partially replaced by, or amalgamated with, Alexander Wedderburn. It is hard not to describe this face in clichés, for it was in clichés that Frederica had discovered, invented, fantasized, constructed, read, and written him, so: ascetic, saturnine, a little harsh, melancholy, black-browed under fine black hair over black eyes. Also a real, unknown man.

"Oh, dear," said Frederica.

Hugh Pink half rose from his chair as the two came in. His voice shook with respect. "Raphael."

"Hugh," said Dr. Faber. "Good morning." Clear. Not quite English.

"This is Frederica Potter."

Raphael Faber failed to notice Frederica Potter. He passed on, his head inclined to his companion.

"*What* did you say he worked on? What does he lecture on? When?"

A peregrine for the ornithology.

"Mallarmé. He lectures on the symbolists in Mill Lane. Tuesdays at eleven."

"How do you get invited to the poetry evenings?"

"You write a poem he likes. At least that's what I did. What is it?"

"I've never seen such a handsome man."

"You aren't supposed to *say* things like that."

"I would if we were two men and he was a girl."

"But we aren't two men, and I thought girls weren't supposed to care about looks. It isn't looks that matter about Raphael. It's quality of mind. I shan't introduce you to him again."

"Then I'll have to find some other way," said Frederica before she could stop herself.

"It wouldn't do any good."

"Probably not," said Frederica, recovering her equanimity, summoning up her considerable resources of willpower.

Raphael Faber's lecture audience was fit, though relatively few, confined to the two front rows of a large, steeply raked lecture theater. The only two people Frederica knew in this unusually intent gathering were Alan Melville, the chameleon, and Hugh Pink, who visibly hesitated over whether to make room for her beside him, and then did so.

Frederica was not a lecture goer. She preferred books to talk, and in any case most of the lectures at the university were already, or were to become, books. She had seen performances: Dr. Henn weeping with his head on the lectern over the fate of *Lear*, Dr. Leavis, with two fastidious fingers depositing a copy of *Early Victorian Novelists* in the wastepaper basket and exhorting his audience to do likewise. Raphael Faber was not exactly a showman, though he might have been thought, by a detached observer, to be making deliberate play with the impromptu, the understated, the unfinished sentence. He said he was lecturing on Names and Nouns: les mots et les noms. He was talking about a poet who believed that the world existed to be summed up in a book, a poet who referred everything to some final ideal book that was, and in Raphael Faber's view must necessarily remain, unwritten. If the poet was Adam in the Garden naming the things that grew there, what language did he speak?

His physical beauty was quite as startling as Frederica had remembered it, a beauty that could have supported a series of theatrical gestures or impassioned recitals, neither of which he indulged in. He paced, evenly and regularly, from side to side of the dais as he talked, his eye fixed, not on his audience but on empty air, arguing passionately and quietly with himself, as though he were the only man in the room. This should have been dangerous but was not; his hearers were rapt.

Language, he said, had once been thought of as Adamic naming; words had been thought of as somehow *part* of the thing they named, the word rose flowering on the rose as the rose flowered on the stem.

Then later—he gave examples, a neat and brilliant history of words unfitting themselves from objects—men had become more self-conscious about language, had seen it as an artifact, torn loose from the world, a web we wove to cover things we could only partially evoke or suggest. And metaphor, our perception of likeness, which seemed like understanding, could be simply a network of our attempted sense making. We were a long way from Plato and his hierarchy from the painted flower to the real flower to the form of the flower. He quoted Mallarmé who would, in one stanza, name rose and lily, in another evoke them poetically, unnamed, metaphors, pourpre ivre, grand calice clair, whose words pointed more and more precisely to an area of vagueness, absence, silence. He seemed to be celebrating and mourning a garden once full of imagined blooms, colors, lights, solidity, now inhabited by the ghosts of these things. Frederica was actually afraid—as though what she most cared for was being most beautifully, most lovingly, abstracted and whisked away. She wrote a note on her notepad to her neighbor Hugh Pink. "Heard melodies are sweet but those unheard Are sweeter." "Be *quiet*," said Hugh Pink, though Frederica had barely rustled and had not uttered a word. Raphael Faber came to the front of the dais and seemed briefly to see them. He quoted: "Je dis: une fleur! et hors de l'oubli où ma voix relègue aucun contour, en tant que quelque chose d'autre que les calices sus, musicalement se lève, idée même et suave, l'absente de tous bouquets."

He allowed himself this one moment of rhetoric, a magician conjuring in the empty air what was not there, a word, a thing, absent from all bouquets. She was to discover that he always allowed himself this one last moment, and that its words were invariably not his own. He made them a little bow, gathered his gown about him, and neatly absented himself.

"That was beautiful," she said to Hugh Pink, who looked unhappy.

"I thought you never came to lectures," said Alan Melville.

"I wanted to see what he was like."

"And why would that be?"

"Curiosity. Why do *you* come?"

"For the good of my tripos. And because the man thinks on his feet. Wi' passion. I respect that."

Frederica was temporarily at a loss about how to get to *know* Raphael Faber. She sensed that Hugh Pink regretted ever having drawn the don to her attention. She returned to the University Library where she borrowed his writings, two thin books of poems and a very brief novel, *Exercises, The Hothouse, Foreign Parts*. She discovered that he worked regular long hours in the Anderson Room and took to doing the same herself, sitting circumspectly two tables away, with a clear view of the smooth black back of his head. The poems, and indeed the novel, had a look of what might be called great purity on the page—a few, usually not very long words, mostly nouns, surrounded by generous white margins. *Exercises* was a series of brief images—a dinner table after a meal, a patch of oil on a main road, a rustling grain elevator, a used-car compressor, some no longer than *haiku*, some put together in two neat four-lined verses. *The Hothouse* was, for so austere a writer, torrid: it contained a series of interlinked poems on the heating system, propagation, growth, and death of plants in a greenhouse. Both collections were bleak and menacing beyond what they should have been, Frederica considered. (The poet himself would surely have disliked words so directly "evocative" as bleak or menacing; these were Frederica's own words.) She could see where Hugh Pink's detached little teacup poem had originated. The strength—which was there—was that of an exact vocabulary and an ear for rhythm that Frederica could recognize, though her own ear could not approach it. (That is another mystery about our innate capacities and power of learning—where does an exact ear for quantities come from? Is it born or is it bred?)

Foreign Parts she liked less. Its protagonist and sole character was a nameless explorer who journeyed through imperfectly apprehended landscapes and violent atmospheric changes, reiterating alternately, rhythmically, that he must find the source, that he must go on. After reading it twice Frederica came to the conclusion that the title concealed a somewhat vulgar pun, of a kind she was reluctant to associate with the fastidious Faber. The macrocosm was a microcosm, this man was his own island, he never journeyed beyond the bounds of his (or her) body. (Both views were possible.) The best bits were about indefinable frontiers: the edge of vision, touch and double touch, echo, far away, inside the head, air on skin. "There is nothing

in it," Frederica noted after the second reading, "as witty as Marvell's
'mine own precipice I go.'" Love, or what is gloomily named love,
did not preclude, indeed exacerbated, the critical faculty.

She pulled at his sleeve after a lecture on Herodias and Narcissism.
She said, "May I interview you for *Cambridge Notes?* I so enjoy the
lectures. I—"
"I do not enjoy interviews," said Raphael Faber. "I have never not
regretted an interview. Forgive me."

She wrote. She said she wished to write a Ph.D. on metaphor and
had been particularly interested in the connection between what he
said about some of Mallarmé's visionary images and his own figures
in *The Hothouse* particularly, the flowers. She said she had read all his
work several times and had been struck by it. He wrote back. He
would agree to the interview.

> Dear Miss Potter,
> Thank you for your interest in my work. I am always to be
> found in my rooms on weekdays between 12 and 12:30 if you
> care to call.

She had her hair dressed and read several periodical articles he had
written about metaphor at the turn of the century. She was excited
and afraid.

I wrote that Frederica fell in love with a face and a concept. This
was the way in which she put it to herself. She then tried to think out
what she meant by it. Part of the joy of falling in love—for the
intelligent, the watchers, the judicious—is the delicious license to set
something above thinking clearly, the pleasure of being driven, taken
over, overwhelmed. Frederica, despite her clumsy rushes of tactless
fervor, was doomed to be intelligent, a watcher, judicious, and as
she recognized this doom she desired proportionately to be let off, to
feel incontrovertibly. There are moments of biological terror between
two people when they realize that they cannot keep their hands from
each other, that they cannot, temporarily at least, touch, smell, taste,

hear, except in terms of the other, which are also love, and also immediate, and also incontrovertible. Frederica had not experienced such terror or such abandon, and indeed her careful fleshly experiments made it, in one view, steadily less rather than more likely that she would know or provoke it. Nevertheless she fell in love with Raphael Faber. How? Why?

There were many reasons and many kinds of reason. A good sociologist would have noted how many of her abstract criteria for a mate he fulfilled. She had told Alan and Tony she meant to marry a don. She was predisposed to fall in love with anyone Hugh Pink could describe as "the most intelligent man I know." Part of her, though only part, wanted his life, the library, the solitude in the Renaissance tower, the life of ideas.

There was a psychoanalytic view. The man was older than she was: a teacher and a good teacher, in a position of authority. Frederica's father was a teacher and a good teacher. She had already loved Alexander, who worked with her father, and had been seen as authority to be subverted or seduced. She was a good pupil.

On the face of things, Raphael Faber was as "suitable" as any of Jane Austen's well-endowed bachelors with country seats, with something of the fatherly spice of the protective Mr. Knightley added in.

If this is too reasonable, there is the question of the face. Alexander had been—was, indeed, but he was busy with Van Gogh and the lineaments of gratified desire in Bloomsbury—very handsome. This had a social value, quite apart from any sexual compulsion either party might or might not feel. Frederica used the word "beautiful" for both Alexander and Raphael with none of the irony with which she spoke of "beautiful Freddie," who was, as she knew, more accurately categorized as pretty. How do we choose a face? There are faces in history that have attracted an inordinate share of devotion. Makers of film stars know the powerful geometry—the breadth between the eyes, the proportion of length to width, the shape of hard bone under soft flesh. Helen's face, or Maud Gonne's, or Marilyn Monroe's. Biologists tell us that we choose our mates for numerous small congruities—like selects like but not too like. We choose people whose finger joints, vertebrae, mouth width, voice timbre, height, almost certainly smell, are closer to our own, much closer, than a randomly selected human body would be. Not wholly close—narcissism and incest are intimately related, and wise songbirds choose mates whose sequences of notes resemble their progenitor's except in one variation or shift.

Bill Potter had fine red hair. Frederica had inherited fine red hair. Frederica was incapable of finding fine red hair acceptable in men. She would not have liked Hugh Pink to touch her, not because he was unformed and insecure as an animal, though he was, but because his gingeriness and pinkness, his skin color and blue eyes, came inside some boundary of taboo she was not then, though later, aware of. But she was inclined, because of some subliminal identification with Pink, to take his word for the merits of the olive-pale and dark, fine and brilliant Raphael Faber.

Was it sexual attraction she felt, "recognizing" that face by the library magnolia, learning its nervous hauteur from the lecture-theater bench? She had fantasies about Raphael Faber. They were slow daydreams, delaying daydreams, complicated situations in which proximity was very, very slowly achieved, barely acknowledged, in which he might brush against her on the narrow stair down to the coffee room, might see her sitting in the library and come to stand near her chair, might then feel, notice . . . ? (There are fast daydreams —rolling in the grass in the sun, swimming naked, straight bed-work—in which she had earlier cast Alexander, and some unknowns —Moczygemba for an odd, randy week—but never Raphael Faber.)

Beside the sociological and the psychological and the aesthetic, the mythic.

As a girl she had put herself to sleep at night by telling herself an endless tale, living a myth. In this myth she walked endlessly alone in a wild wood, accompanied by the animals—lions, panthers, leopards, wild horses, gazelles. The animals were her people. In the myth she was the one who turned bush fires and found water, solved disputes, bandaged wounds, ran at the head of the gracefully bounding pack through dappled clearings. She wore always a floating pink garment and white veiling with roses, the original of which she was to discover, shocked, at the age of thirty-five, on a hand-painted plate that was one of Winifred's few heirlooms and depicted a buxom blonde nymph suspended on a crag with her hand resting on an exiguous bush, and behind her blue sky and flowing clouds. This enabled her to date the time of the animals as very early—when she was three, or four, when no one had told her redheads should not wear pink. Later, maybe, when she was eight or nine, the male figure appeared in the forest, with Raphael Faber's fine, dark good looks and an incompatible set of character traits, derived from Mr. Rochester, the sad and sinful Lancelot du Lac, Athos the mournful Musketeer, and other fictive innocent rakes. The Knight was beautiful but fallible and often in need of rescue. When rescued (as Lancelot was rescued by the Lily Maid of Astolat, as Artegall was rescued by Britomart), he would become strong again, a little cruel, intent only on his own purposes. The Lady would grieve: the Knight would be ambushed, by Morgan Le Fay, by Irish peasantry, by wizards, and would again helplessly need rescue. The composite Knight of Frederica's early myths, even more than the Renaissance-Georgian rake of her adolescence, had Raphael Faber's face. How had it been called up or constructed? Was it the male version of her early solipsist self, the same and yet different clichés. It was dark and lean because these qualities went with a delightful wickedness, they had Satanic and Byronic overtones. It was also "sensitive." Its opposite was square blond good health, honor, steadfastness, which formed no part of Frederica's female dramas. It is amazing, when we stop to contemplate the variety, the devious differences, the secret predilections, and emotional histories behind or under individual faces, that a culture should so steadfastly ascribe one physiognomy to one habit of mind, or morals. But we have done, and do, and this must affect the innocent lords and owners of archetypal faces. What if Hugh Pink had had Raphael Faber's bones? And is that a thought about chance, or crazy determinism?

She knocked on the door of his room with her heart knocking deliciously; he opened it, looking ready to retreat and close it in her face, and then smiled when reminded of her business and name.

"Come in, come in, Miss Potter, please have a chair. This chair, I think, the big one. Sit down. Will you have a glass of sherry?"

"That would be lovely."

The room looked out into the pale watery light above the river; it had an angle on the polite wilderness where the philosophical cow grazed. It was a dustless, impeccable, colorless room, apart from a pale cubist collage over the mantelshelf, a sky-blue bottle, a violin of old newspaper, a rosette of scarlet thread gummed and pinned along fine ink lines. The walls were lined with books, which had an unusual air of geometric neatness and coherence, partly, but only partly, conferred by the uniform habits of French publishing houses. There were square armchairs covered in unbleached linen. The desk was spotless and empty. There were some white freesias in a smoky glass vase on the table at which Raphael Faber was neatly pouring sherry into plain-stemmed glasses. Nothing was red or yellow or green or blue; it was all gray, fawn, brown, black, and clean white, even to the linen curtains. Frederica brushed at her skirt before sitting down. Raphael Faber brought her the glass of sherry and, surprisingly, a piece of dark, crumbly, spicy cake on a white china plate. Frederica watched him close the cake tin carefully, and brush away a few crumbs from his table. He then sat down in his desk chair, between Frederica and the light, and waited. He looked first at his feet, and then out of the window, and then, briefly, dropping his eyes almost immediately, at Frederica, who was aware that there was a pin in her brassiere strap, that her stocking seam might have slipped, that her neck was too hot. He waited, courteously and distantly, not helping her.

It was Frederica's first interview, and she rapidly developed a retrospective sympathy for Alan and Tony's hashed version of herself. She asked him about whether he felt any strain between writing, reading, and teaching. Was Cambridge a good place to be a writer?

"Why should it not be? I don't see the difficulty you are making. Good writers should be good readers. Writing is a civilized activity. Cambridge is a civilized place."

Frederica persisted. "I've noticed that a lot of my generation find it hard to write here. Too much criticism going on, maybe. They dry up."

"Perhaps they are not really writers, or not yet."

He was very polite, but there was something a little—hostile? sharp? destructive? about his answers, which always contained a faint suggestion that the idea that had inspired the question was silly in the first place. She was afraid of him. And his beautiful face pulled at her belly, sending distracting needle thrills up it. She asked rather desperately about influences on his work.

"I hope my taste is catholic enough for there to be no overwhelming influence. I admire certain modern French writers. And certain underestimated Americans. William Carlos Williams."

He spoke as though she could not possibly have heard of, or read, William Carlos Williams. When she asked about early reading he said that he had read in German largely as a boy and now did not. He stared out of the window.

"I am a refugee and an exile. I have forgotten German. I am a man without a native tongue."

This last sentence, but not its tone, intrigued Frederica, who sensed that he was saying things he always said, things he had fined down to precise statements to deal briskly with the curious, and no longer needed to feel as he said them. A journalistic instinct she hadn't known she possessed mixed with the female anger of the unnoticed woman. He must be stopped; he was bored and slipping away.

"The poems in *Exercises*—" she said, "are poems about things which extend the human body. Tools, and machines we get in and out of. I don't know quite how they manage to be so menacing when they seem so exact."

"There was a review," he said, "which said these poems expressed a modern distaste for industrial civilization."

"Oh, *no*. Nothing so crude. It is—they are—about the extension of our bodies into these things—calipers, grips, camera lenses—about *boundaries*. Like *Foreign Parts*, only quite different."

"Maybe." He sat up. "Have another glass of sherry. They are also about the laying waste of Europe, by factories and by war."

"The poem I like, the one I see as central, is the one about the oil on the macadam."

"How so?"

Frederica said a lot of things she didn't know she had thought.

"Because it's the *fluid* one. And the metaphoric one. You do the oil with images—the rainbow colors, the reflected sky—and when you talk about the darkness and wetness of it I think of spilled blood—I don't know why—am I wrong?"

"No, no. You are quite right." He poured more sherry and turned to her, his face transfigured by a smile. "None of the reviewers mentioned that poem. It is the one I like."

"It is so *exact* and means so much more than itself—"

"Precisely. So I tried to do in *The Hothouse*, but none of those poems, in my view, work as well, do you think?"

Frederica was surprised, as she should perhaps not have been, by the kind of alert gaiety that came over Raphael Faber after her praise of his reflective poem on spilled oil. Her later career was to provide her with many opportunities for assessing the extravagant warmth, the sudden efflorescence into speed, of those who see that something complicated, or obscure, that they have thought or made has after all been noticed and understood. At that moment she was more concerned with her own social emotions. There is something both gratifying and humiliating in watching a man who has taken you for a routinely silly woman begin to take you seriously, Frederica thought. It was always happening to her; her social life was a battle to establish the idea that she was intelligent, was capable of intelligent talk, in the minds of others. She took charge of the interview, said that the machines in *Exercises* were related to the mechanical environment in *The Hothouse*. Raphael Faber ceased to sit poised or posed in his armchair. He walked and talked, volubly, sharply, excitedly, about pumps, boilers, calorifier, glass panes, telephone box, motorcar, fountain pen. He told Frederica the history of metaphors of grafting and propagation, said he meant to write an essay on the human heart as a pump, literally and metaphorically. He gave her more sherry. There was an awkward moment when he became suddenly irascible at the suggestion that *The Hothouse* and *Foreign Parts* were related microcosms.

Frederica hit another more arcane and interesting embarrassment of the literary interview at this point. It concerned the roots. It was the uncanny prominence of the roots that had caused her to link the body imagery of *Foreign Parts* back to the trapped organisms in the earlier books. A plant in Raphael's hothouse had blindly seeking aerial roots, ugly-skinned, raised up. Some of the word patterns, a part of the description of the sac of the fountain pen in *Exercises*, breathily consuming air and ink, had made her hazard the idea that pen and roots were connected. The most unpleasant, and also the *thingiest*, the central, thing in *Foreign Parts* was a giant banyan tree, putting out more and more suckers which created tangled arches, a swollen hiding place of a tree, a series of organic traps, nets, snares. The traveler had been drawn into its multiple cavern and seized with Lotos-sloth. It was not nice. Frederica sat and listened to Raphael talking freely and with sophisticated pleasure of the intricacies of his work, and felt possessed, in her reading of the roots, of knowledge she wasn't sure he knew she had, or would like her to have. Or even had himself. She was much less sure than she had been that he knew consciously all that was going on. He did not appear to be a man who took kindly in practice, however much he must acknowledge theoretically, the idea that there were important things in his work of which he was unconscious.

Intellectual revolutions take a long time to affect us, and never stay still during their work. That Freud showed us something new, liberating, and alarming about the relation between the sources of energy and our own irredeemable sexuality is indisputable. (Irredeemable is a word from a quite different intellectual revolution, a much earlier one, now only intermittently recognized or acted on.) It is now fashionable intellectually to write of Desire and the Other, of the desire of a text for itself, or for another, of language for an ungraspable referent. When Stella Gibbons wrote *Cold Comfort Farm* poor appalling Mr. Myburg saw every cloud, bush, and bee as phallic, every softness of the earth as breasts or mount of Venus. Professor Wijnnobel tantalized or irritated Alexander Wedderburn with phallic or maternal bottles, jugs, and coffeepots. When Frederica was an undergraduate, thinking—run-of-the-mill thinking—concerned itself with "images." And images were read as Freudian by men and women who had never read Freud but knew that fountain pens, hats, and keys were penis symbols out of late Viennese dreams, but also universal, as corndollies and golden boughs out of Frazer were universal. The side-piercing lance of Longinus and the grail full of blood were male and female symbols of fertility, and this was known, as it was no longer known what was redeemed and what irredeemable. Roots too. "Stirring dull roots with spring rain." Frederica knew next to nothing about Raphael Faber but she knew what to think of roots. So now, considering the banyan thicket in *Foreign Parts*, she saw it as a knotted clumps of sexual organs of which the writer himself had used the words gross and swollen, impenetrable and dangerous. (Since he used adjectives sparsely this was the more surprising.) Frederica had moments of wishing to see pens as pens, hats as hats, keys as keys. Once sitting knitting with the newly invented double-knitting wools, she had stabbed the blunt, thick needle rhythmically in and out of the knotted mesh of wool, thought of sex, and felt resentful, unnecessarily delimited. But she could not do it. She thought of literary analogies; she imagined, concrete and various, the exemplars of the male organ with which she had come into contact. Thin limp white ones, narrow veined rods, blunt, dark cylindrical ones, rosy retroussé ones, shiny, crimson and violet ones, raised and angry, concrete universals. Did this imagination cause her to imagine the individual tucked into Raphael Faber's neat gray flannels? No, though it caused her to note the thickets of brushwood smelling of decay and dead leaves around the banyan, to register fear and distaste in the writer, about which she felt she had no right to know or speculate.

"The banyan tree," she said to Raphael Faber, "is particularly impressive."

"It is the tree of Error from *Paradise Lost*," Faber surprisingly replied. "Not the tree of life, or the tree of the knowledge of good and evil, but the Indian fig from whose leaves Adam and Eve made their garments. It is associated with the barren fig tree, cursed by Christ. 'The fig-tree, not that kind for fruit renowned . . .' "

"Go on."

> "But such as at this day to Indians known
> In Malabar or Decan spreads her arms
> Branching so broad and long, that in the ground
> The bended twigs take root, and daughters grow
> About the mother tree, a pillared shade
> High overarched and echoing walks between."

"Error because it is a multiple tree—truth is One, like the Tree of Life—this produces her daughters from herself like sin and the hellhounds."

"In the Mallarmé lecture you said that we can't reproduce—le bois intrinsèque et dense des arbres."

"There is Sartre's tree also in *La Nausée* which can't be named or described—horribly other, excessive."

"I haven't read *La Nausée*. I *am* reading Mallarmé."

"I will lend you *La Nausée*. Would you care for some lunch? I usually have cheese and radishes in my room, and a glass of wine. Would that be acceptable?"

It would. Raphael Faber brought out these things, and, relaxed now, talked happily and sharply about the cultural insularity and narrowness of the English. Frederica tasted crumbs of cheese and agreed happily that they were indeed narrow; she adduced the excessive admiration of English decency that annoyed her in *Lucky Jim*. Raphael had not read *Lucky Jim*. He gave Frederica wine and said, "Yet the English have no sense of roots."

"I have. I have a very strong sense of roots."

"Ah, but you, I take it, are Jewish."

Frederica stared at him. She saw her red hair and sharp freckled face, her intellectual greed, briefly as he saw it. They met each other's eye and blushed, both of them.

"No. Oh, no. Pure Anglo-Saxon, *echt* Englisch, as far as is known. *Northern*, you know. We are very conscious of our roots in the north. Northern lower-middle-class. Nonconformist."

All the labels she half hoped to evade. He looked uncomprehending and puzzled, as though these things were inconceivable.

"How strange. What an odd mistake for me to make. I don't usually make that mistake—mistakes of that kind. I wonder why I assumed you were Jewish?"

She could not answer this. He frowned. He did not like to be wrong.

"You must have a very different sense of roots."

"I was born in Lübeck. Thomas Mann's hometown. Do you know Thomas Mann?"

"We did *Tonio Kröger* for A-level German."

"Then you will know about German roots, a little. I did not have a very Jewish upbringing—my parents were not religious—but we were Jewish. I came to England in 1939. With nothing. A Quaker charity sent me to a public school in Suffolk."

"Just you?"

"I have a mother. And some sisters. My father—and all the other men, my grandfather, my uncles . . . my elder brother—were killed in Belsen."

There was something challenging in this last statement. Also, she thought—she could have been wrong—something hostile, not exactly accusing *her*, but accusing, and she felt guilt, with her ignorant northern nonconformist roots, though she could not have said how, or for what.

"And your mother and sisters?"

"They live in Cambridgeshire now. In a cottage." He thought. "East Anglian people are said to be particularly unwilling to accept strangers."

She had a very precise vision of a dark, sad queen and a bevy of dark, sad princesses in white aprons and lace caps. Tending a cottage garden, on alien soil. She wanted to say, tell me, tell me, and his experience was so far away, so strange that she could not find the right question. He did tell her, a little, precisely and expressionlessly, things she had read of elsewhere, about others, the terrified child hiding in a cupboard while the inhabitants of the house were rounded up and dragged away, a journey, on foot, hidden under horse blankets in carts, sleeping in barns, to a traveler that had handed him and others over on a cold night, out on a black sea.

"People were incredibly kind and incredibly cruel, and I was always afraid, *always*," he said. Frederica knew she was imagining it wrongly, but tried to imagine, produced B-film clichés, could not even touch at the fear. He asked about her roots and suddenly she could not imagine those either, all the minor details of small Yorkshire houses, nagging rectitude, driving ambition faded and could not be told. There was such a gulf between Bill Potter and his flights of fury and what had happened in Belsen. Haltingly, she said a little, watching him sharply, seeing that he could not even define "lower-middle-class," would never know how a thick or refined accent shaped your life. She said rather desperately, "It was like D. H. Lawrence. I have roots like D. H. Lawrence; my people better themselves a little, like Lawrence's ambitious women."

She had never had occasion to say "my people" before, like that.

"I can't read D. H. Lawrence. I dislike his hectoring tone. And I find his characters incredible. Art surely can't any longer be thought of as inventing people and giving them names and social backgrounds and amassing descriptions of clothes and houses and money and parties. All that is over."

He was really angry. He hated Lawrence. That also was new to her. She asked meekly what he thought she *should* read, as one by one the lights were put out, Tolstoy, George Eliot, Jane Austen, dead detail. Books full of people she knew and loved, inside and out, Prince Andrei with his little wife and his duty and his doubts, Dorothea theoretically choosing an arid man for moral reasons, Henry Tilney who loved back for no better reason than that he liked to be loved. It was an odd conversation, that first one with Raphael Faber. He was meticulously considerate of her feelings; he offered her, with nervous determination, little fragments of information, things about himself that she was simply not equipped to imagine as she could imagine Birkin or Pierre. His mood shifted from sentence to sentence, flashing out in theoretic passion against stories with characters, against whimsy, against insularity, against verbal sluggishness, and then suddenly gentle. It should have been, it had elements of, those early conversations between lovers where a life story is exchanged for another life story. (He was never again to be so easily, so deliberately, *open* with her about himself.) And Frederica felt her language heavy in her mouth. He had no native tongue: she had never questioned the efficacy of her own until he taught her, only her own skill with it. But her words meant nothing to him and he despised her kind of story on principle.

He gave her books to take home. *La Nausée*, Beckett's *Murphy*. Also a carbon of a poem in typescript.

"I should like to know what you make of this. It is called 'Lübeck Bells'; it is concerned with the bells in the Marienkirche in Lübeck. I went back there in 1950 to see—my place of origin. The bombing there was terrible. They buried the church treasure under the bell tower—to be as safe as possible—and the bells fell and are embedded in the paving—tons of twisted metal, like discarded pastry cuttings. They are keeping them and building a chapel round the hulks. I wanted to write about European history. It is not yet achieved."

She was not clear whether this last sentence meant the poem or the history.

She wandered back through clear gray Cambridge. He had made her head ache. He had lent her books—that was a beginning, lending of books was a universal sign of the beginning of something. To borrow implied to return. As soon as he was not there, love flooded her again like an easing of pain. She named what she loved: sadness, exact thought, remembered fear, a furious inner life. She remembered meeting his eyes when she explained that she was not Jewish. They were strangers. She loved a stranger. The world was larger than it had been.

Frederica selected the moment for the return of *Murphy* and *La Nausée* very carefully. She did not return the poem, because she did not want to use up all her reason for going back, and because she did not understand it. The only line she was sure she understood was Ophelia's: like sweet bells jangled out of tune and harsh." The words of the poem occurred in little blocks, without punctuation, arranged on the page in patterns of rectangles and steps like a visual code or intelligence test she couldn't break. There were German names, and what looked like Hebrew; distances, in miles and kilometers. There were some verbal patterns: Grimm, grim, grimmig, grimoire, a word she had looked up when struggling with Mallarmé's *"Prose pour des Esseintes."* "Wizard's book of spells: book of gramarye: gibberish, nonsense." There were gray seeds of umbellifers like light ash, a recognizable metaphor, but she was sure the ash was sinister. There was Mann, man, many, manly. She recognized Faustus and Adam Kadmon. She knew the poem was about the gas ovens and the bombings, the churches and the camp, but she could not tell what principle organized it. She worried at it, took back the novels, knocked on his door.

He opened it and looked at her with the genuine blankness of nonrecognition.

"I brought back your books," said Frederica.

"Thank you," said Raphael Faber, holding out his hand.

"I didn't understand the singing at the end of *La Nausée*," Frederica began, instancing something she had in fact understood, could go on talking about, if necessary.

"Please excuse me. I have a guest."

He stood, barring the door. In the pale room, stretched untidily in the chair, was the philosopher of the Camargue, Vincent Hodgkiss.

"I'm sorry. I'll go."

"Some other time, maybe," said Raphael with studied vagueness, taking a step back.

"I still have the poem."

"Poem?"

"It's hard to read."

He smiled, mocking, distant.

"That will be good for you," he said, and then, "You really must excuse me." He closed the door.

Love is terrible. Frederica analyzed and rethought these courteous sentences of retreat. Had he meant "some other time"? Was "You really must excuse me" designed to hurt as it had hurt? The simple explanation, that Raphael Faber preferred talking to Vincent Hodgkiss, simply did not satisfy the rage to know how he felt about Frederica Potter. It did not occur to her that there were men equally painfully analyzing her own awkward or complacent or muddled reasons for breaking appointments, or filling, with other men, rooms in which they had hoped to be alone with her.

A week later, she tried with the poem. Again he held his threshold against her. She was gallant.

"I'm returning your poem, which you kindly lent me. There's a great deal I don't understand at all, and I'd be very grateful if—"

"What poem?"

" 'Lübeck Bells'."

"I didn't lend you that."

"It was after we had lunch, and you told me about coming here from Lübeck . . . after we talked . . ."

"Why did I do that?" He looked angry and distressed. "Please give it back to me. It is unfinished and still private."

"Of course."

He almost snatched it and leafed through the paper.

"I'm sorry. I really was very excited by it. I can't follow all the references, but I—"

"The fault is mine. I can't think how I came to lend this. It is quite unready for reading. I am glad to have it back. I'm sorry to have troubled you with it."

"No, no, I—"

"Thank you for its safe return."

"I did want to talk."

"Of course. Not now. Some other time— How is your article?"

"It will be out in the next issue."

"I look forward to it."

"I—"

"Good afternoon, and thank you."

She discussed this episode with Alan Melville. Alan seemed unsurprised by Raphael's denial of his own gesture. One step forward and two steps fast backward, that was Raphael Faber, he said knowledgeably. "You must have alarmed him."

"Don't be silly."

"There's no point in loving Raphael Faber, unless you've a vested interest in unrequited passion."

"I might have," said Frederica, seeing sadly that she might, half aware of the importance of this.

The interview duly appeared: "Poet and Scholar," a portrait of St. Michael's don Raphael Faber by Frederica Potter. Frederica had spent hours on it. Tony and Alan had then snipped out paragraphs and crushed together critical commentary and personal description. Frederica wrote well on the poems; compared Mallarmé's language flower of the mind to D. H. Lawrence's highly sexed and anthropomorphic ones, and talked about the shock of talking to someone with no native language, with severed cultural roots. (This last metaphor had made her shiver a little. She replaced the word roots by "ties.") She described also his lecturing style and his austere room; this was what interviews did.

She received another letter.

Dear Miss Potter,

I feel I must write to say that I am strongly displeased by your references to my personal life in your essay in *Cambridge*

Notes. Had I known you intended to write in that style I should have confined my observation to technical poetic matters, with which you deal considerably more tactfully.

Raphael Faber

Frederica showed this to Alan and Tony. She was indignant.

"I put in *nothing* that isn't common knowledge. I don't know anything that isn't. I wrote it because I *admired* him so."

"People tell you things," said Tony. "They tell you things, and then, they hate seeing them in print."

"What can I *do?*"

"Wait," said Alan.

"What for? He hates me."

"At least he knows who you are."

She continued to haunt the Anderson Room. She watched him work—and read a fair amount herself. She was unsurprised, but horribly hurt, when he passed her, on his way to coffee or lunch, without answering her smile, without any visible sign that he recognized her. Once, when she judged he must be gone for a good quarter of an hour, she stood up and went over to see what he had been reading. It was not very helpful; there were volumes of Hebrew and some Greek, Mallarmé's correspondence, Rilke's correspondence, the *Duino Elegies* (not a library copy). His note-taking was like his printed poems, fine and black and small and clear amid spaces of white paper. Some of the black lines were Greek and some were Hebrew. The human sign was a series of little drawings along the bottom of one paper: vases, jars, bottles, urns, fat, tall, lipped, spouted, squat. And above these, framed in a neat black square, the words Concrete Universal. Raphael's handwriting to Frederica was magic. Seen on an envelope it made her startle; here it was, being turned out, line after line of it, with ordinary ease. Raphael came up quietly behind her and asked in a chill whisper if there was anything he could help her with. She moved her hand away from the white sheets as though it had been stung.

"I am *so* sorry. I suddenly wanted to know what you were reading. I want to know . . . I was thinking about your poems, and I just suddenly wanted to know . . . What a terrible thing."

"Reading and writing are private matters, Miss Potter. Or so I have always taken them to be."

"I am *so* sorry."

"Did you find your investigations illuminating?"

"I can't read Hebrew or Greek. And I don't know what a Concrete Universal is."

"Then you must find out, mustn't you?" He sat down. "Let me know when you have done so."

"About that interview, Dr. Faber—I—I wrote it out of such—*admiration*—"

"Silence is requested," said Raphael, quoting a notice on the desk. He turned to his books. "Think no more of it, Miss Potter."

19

POETRY-READING

She received, to her surprise, another letter.

Dear Miss Potter,

I wonder if you would care to come to a small gathering which is held in my rooms on Thursday evenings to read and discuss poetry. We begin at 8:30 sharp. Yours sincerely, Raphael Faber.

She thought of discussing this invitation with Hugh, or with Alan Melville, and decided against it. She would simply go there. She would not be stopped. At eight-thirty on Thursday she knocked on Raphael Faber's door, which was opened by Hugh, whose rosiness increased when he saw her.

"I'm *invited*," said Frederica, rapidly and roundly. She had her letter of invitation in her pocket, in case.

"Then you'd better come in."

She added her gown to a heap on an upright chair just inside the door. There must have been fifteen to twenty people in there, sitting in chairs, curled against the bookshelves on the carpet, side by side politely on the college sofa. Apart from herself there was only one other woman, a postgraduate she vaguely knew. The young men were of the elegant, rather than the baggy kind. Frederica had the illusion of briefly meeting a series of pairs of evasive, clear, almond-shaped eyes, as though the room were full of Siamese cats. Raphael Faber was serving white wine from a chilled tall glass jug. On his desk was a plain silver tray with green-stemmed glasses. The lighting —mainly from high ceiling fittings—was sad and harsh. There was an incongruous perfumed smell that Frederica traced to three white china plates of circular cakes covered with cracking white glacé icing. Raphael stepped over and among the semi-recumbent young men to welcome Frederica, to lead her to a high armchair. He gave her wine, and offered a cake, which, when bitten, proved to be light, dry, and very spicy. "My mother and sisters are always sending cakes. They believe, I think, that I am perpetually undernourished in this college."

It was not an easy evening. Various young men read poems, one on anemones at Paphos, one on parting from a lover, one on his old nanny in a geriatric ward. The discussion was sharper and more focused than the poems; there was a kind of savage glee to their critical competence that their verse quite lacked. They worried and dissected each other's images: nobody liked the metaphor used by the deprived lover of a dressing pulled away from a wound, and they were most ingenious in saying why it wasn't appropriate.

Frederica failed to notice the import of Hugh Pink's poem, which was, he said defensively, about "a snakeskin I had in my boyhood, a whole empty viper skin."

The initial impulse for Hugh's poem had been the visual resemblance between Frederica's crumpled, transparent brown stocking, with its dark seam and embroidered heel, wound in a semblance of life or agony round the leg of her chair, and the transparent, papery integument abandoned by the snake. But he had not had the courage, or, he would have put it, the bad taste, to put the stocking in. He was not a wit; he could not call it "On Her Stocking Left Empty." He had noted that a dead shabbiness was what stocking and snakeskin had in common. He had written about the snakeskin, leaving out the stockings, and thus had deprived his poem of the objective correlative so exhaustively discussed in essays at that time. He had compensated by putting in references to the snakeskin in *A Midsummer Night's Dream* and to Keats's "Lamia" and her shifting silver moons and spots and stripes. He had tried to put in, and then take out, brilliance, color, sleekness, leaving something "brownish, and stiffly fragile, left behind." Raphael Faber said, justly, that the Keats references overloaded the poem. Pink could not say, and only half knew, that they were the nearest he could get to its sexual content. "Is it nostalgia for childhood?" said one. "The pleasures of boyhood?" "How can it be," said another, "it's about a snake. Snakes are bad." "Not in little boys' pockets," said a wit at Faber's feet. "Maybe it's about masturbation." "No, it *isn't*," said Hugh, hotly, red blood meeting the fiery line of his hair. There was a discussion about the denotations and connotations of snakes, or what they called always "snake imagery." Hugh said his snake was his own snake, and the wit said that that was very naive, and that the poem was *unconsciously* about masturbation. Alan Melville said the poem was about absence. "You could argue that all poems are about poems, just as much as that all poems are about sex. It's about the *absence* of Keats and Shakespeare, that's why their presence worries Dr. Faber. It's a view."

"Is it a view you hold?" said Raphael.

"I never know if I hold a view," said Frederica's chameleon. "Only if it's a possible view to hold."

He was asked to read his own poem. He introduced it in a mannered and elegant way.

"This is a poem about mirrors. There are a great many poems about mirrors. This one began partly under the inspiration of Dr. Faber's brilliant lecture on Mallarmé and Herodias and her mirrors, and narcissism. My poem uses two images. One of them I got from George Eliot's mirror in *Middlemarch*. The other I got from a book of Chinese poems; apparently there is a Chinese belief that there is a world behind mirrors which might one day break through—shadowy warriors, dragons, huge fish. I thought of calling this poem "Narcissus" and then decided it sounded too pretty and floral and mythical.

So I called it "Narcissist," which I'm also not happy with; it's a little brutal. I wanted to include Narcissus's mirror without naming it in the poem. Anyway."

How *clever* he was, Frederica thought, so authoritatively pre-empting, warding off, dictating the terms of discussion for his ideas, as Hugh Pink had not been shrewd enough to do.

The poem was a series of clear visual images: a framed mirror on a chest in a dark room with uncurtained windows, some panes show-ing the night sky, some reflecting candlelight, silver blotches on the glass that became silver blotches on a dangerous water beast as the mirror became water surface. The face and unlit shape of the rising beast grew together out of the patterned matter of glass or water. The circles. A curious line as the beast broke surface. "For they are all concentric to this snout." Alan's voice was pronouncedly Scots as he read this, with panache, like someone finishing a Hallowe'en story, which was perhaps what prompted Raphael Faber to say, whether with approval or finical distaste was not quite clear, that the poem surely owed as much to the Gothic tradition as to Mallarmé. Fred-erica had by then tracked down the echo that was worrying her.

"It's John Donne, that's what it is, it's 'Love's Growth.'" Alan smiled his sharp smile. "So it is. Tell us about it."

It was from the same poem whose beautiful "root" image had haunted her during her meditation on the banyans. "Gentle love deeds, as blossoms on a bough / From love's awakened root do bud out now." The circles were the next metaphor. Frederica recited it.

> "If, as in water stirred, more circles be
> Produced by one, love such additions take
> These, like so many spheres, but one heaven make
> For, they are all concentric unto thee."

No one could pick all *that* up from that poem, said another, voicing the objection that is always voiced to any unprinted writing, not yet a canonical text, and Alan Melville offered the standard Raphael. I must work on it, said Alan. Frederica thought again: who response: people can sense, can feel, what they don't consciously know is there to think about. Only if the poem is achieved, said does he love?

After coffee Raphael read part of "Lübeck Bells." Like Alan Melville and with more need, he prefaced his reading with enough information to guide his audience's responses. He explained about the bells and his birthplace. The puzzling figures were incoherent scraps of information: the estimated number of dead in Belsen, bombed in Lübeck, kilometers between the two . . . The names were scholars, rabbis, unknown names of the dead. He had taken scraps from Thomas Mann: a description of a bourgeois room from *Buddenbrooks*, a sentence about Adrian Leverkühn's intolerable music. There were also bits of *Faust* and the brothers Grimm, meditations on roots of German folklore and language, as well as bits of Hitler's speeches. He had written, he did not quite say, in disconnected fragments because such things were apprehended in disconnected fragments. He read out his brief lines and echoes in a bell-clear monotone. This time Frederica noticed a repeated reference to the small white stones, or breadcrumbs, pointing the way home, which, associated with the word oven, made her think of Hansel and Gretel. It was an art of material reference rather than evocation. Armed with Faber's nonguide you could construct in your mind civilities and monstrosities, daily life and daily death, orders of language and human ceremony that were painfully *not* in the poem. What had, on a first reading, seemed impenetrable now seemed impalpable. Absence again. Private and public, animal and culture, evoked in such curtailed and evanescent ways that their order remained unconstituted. Another unheard melody. Frederica was alert and afraid. She preferred, naturally, plenitude, the too much John Keats in Hugh Pink's snake poem. This art was like those pictures that in childhood, on roughly pulped paper, had presented themselves as a swarm of inconsequential numbers. "Take a pencil and join all the numbers from 1 to 89 and you will see what frightened John and Susan on the beach/at the picnic/in the cave." An octopus, a bull, a huge bat. A lost childhood, a piece of a war, a horror, a deformed bell in a blasted bell tower. It was not there, it was ugly, it was beautiful. The young men turned their cats' eyes up. When he had finished he looked directly at Frederica, a private look in a public place, cautious, tentative, hoping. Surely? *He* was there, in the flesh, a real man in Cambridge, smiling. She smiled back.

As she was leaving he said, "You will come again, I hope."

"I can't write poetry, you know."

"It doesn't matter."

"Hugh said it did."

"Ah, Hugh. He is attached to you."

"Oh, not really, I *hope* not—I—" Too much.

"Good."

"Your poem—your poem is marvelous."

"Thank you." He was excited from having read it. "I value your judgment."

"You didn't seem to."

"Oh, I was oafish. You *must* forgive that. I don't really like to let it out of my hands. I can't bear to be separated from it. I can't think what—led me to lend it to you. Or perhaps I can." He took a step back. "There is no excuse for my rudeness. None."

"It doesn't matter. Nothing matters. I—"

"*Do* come again. I count on you."

Hugh caught her up in the dark streets, and then Alan. They cycled dangerously, three abreast, along Silver Street, over the river.

"What did you make of it, Frederica?" (Alan).

"How horribly much we enjoy *criticism*," said Frederica. "How clever and brutal and self-satisfied we are, doing that. But some of the poems were poems. Both yours were."

"I'm flattered," said Alan.

"It was a love poem," said Hugh. "With the crucial bit left out."

"How horribly much we enjoy love," said Alan. "The room was swarming with it. Everyone loves Raphael."

Frederica swerved and righted herself. She said, "I sometimes wonder who you love."

"Me?"

"You."

"I wouldn't tell *you*, Frederica Potter. It's a terrible business, love."

This time Hugh Pink swerved; all three clanked, disentangled themselves, circled on.

20

GROWING THINGS

William grew, stretched, changed shape. This seemed to happen in the twinkling of an eye and with the luxurious slowness with which he himself would examine the progress of a caterpillar. The feeble hands that clutched became square, gluey exploring fingers that could pick up the smallest crumb. The jerking bowed legs became massively creased and then, used, grew to muscle. Stephanie watched his vertebrae expand. He sat on the ground, and beat it with a skittle, a blue beaker. He lay grounded for weeks on his Buddha belly and then one day was up, swaying precariously like Blake's Nebuchadnezzar on purposeful hands and untouched, soft-skinned knees. He went rapidly backward, focusing on a coal scuttle, butting against a bookcase on the other side of the room. He stood, with wavering hands and jackknifing knees. He walked, from skirt to chair, moving slowly round the room, clutching and puffing, raising his plump foot high and planting it. She thought she would never forget any of these moments, these points of development, these markers in time, and forgot all of them as the next stage seemed to be William and eternal.

He was a frowning child, with changing striations of skin over a smooth, more slowly expanding skull. He would frown with concentration, trying to make a pinching thumb and forefinger meet around a yellow plastic disc, and he would resemble Daniel, considering ways and means. The sooty brows, the large dark eyes, the definite lashes, predisposed his frowns to look like Daniel's. But there was another frown, a gathering, pursing frown preceding a howl of rage or frustration, which was accompanied by the most amazing changes of color in the skin, from creamy marble to flushed rose to flooding crimson to veined violet, and this frown resembled Bill creating, Bill thwarted, Bill wholehearted in wrath. As fast as the colors rose they could ebb and pale, leaving again the unformed face that was nevertheless Will's face, not any other face. He had also a learning, thoughtful frown that barely creased the skin above his nose. He would sit on her knee and look at her face, testing her contours with fingers that in the early days, judging distances, jabbed at a bright eye or clawed at a lip corner, and grew rapidly skilled at caressing, patting her cheek, tangling her hair. She saw herself in him: the learning face was her face. They looked into each other's eyes and she saw herself reflected, a looming light, a loving moon, part of himself? His flesh was her flesh, but his look was not her look.

He used his new voice, organizing mouth and tongue round strings of primitive syllables, ba, ga, da, ma, pa, ta, varying and connecting them into chains of differently repeated patterns, bagabaga, ababababa, pamatamaga, a combination of elements, abracadabra, seeds of speech. Once in the early-morning silence she heard his ruminative voice making a long and complex statement, with intonations of question and affirmation, a lesson, a sermon, all constructed of rising and falling strings of syllables. These rhythms reminded her of the odd fact that she called half-remembered poems to mind, not with nouns, as might be expected, but with syntax and rhythm, placing conjunctions, prepositions, verb endings, before she could call up nouns or even the main verb. But if he murmured sentence shapes he learned nouns. She would hold him up, when he cried, to window or lamp, saying, "There, Will, look at the light, look at the light." And very early in his life he would repeat "igh, igh." She taught him also early book, cat, flower, and he applied these names extensively, using "boo" of pictures and newspapers, "cat" of all animals, and "fowa" of vegetables, trees, feathers, and once of his grandmother's modesty front, poking out of the neck of her dress. He sat regally on Stephanie's knee and named farmyards and jungles of pictured beasts, cow, hoss, gog, en, zeb-a, effunt, nake, raffe, whale. These things are banal enough and it is hard to write the wonder with which, in a mood of distance from the everyday and the solid, a woman can hear a voice speak where there has only been a wail, a snuffle, a cry, a mutter of syllables. Will's voice was a *new* voice, speaking words that had been spoken generation after generation. Look at the light. I love you.

She became obsessed with growing things. The cottage had a muddy little back garden, two tablecloth-sized patches of lawn each side of an asphalted path, and two ugly cement clothes poles. In the spring and summer of 1955, when Will was one, she tried to make this mud patch flourish with bright flowers for him to see, and with fresh vegetables and herbs for him to eat. She planted carrots and radishes, lettuce and rows of peas and beans. Will sat or crawled on the grass behind her as she scraped and pierced and hoed and dropped the tiny seeds. Now and then he clutched fistfuls of earth and stuffed them into his mouth. "Oh, no, dirty," said Stephanie, whose thoughts had been running on the extraordinary richness of ordinary earth, or the amazing growth of feathery green fronds and long, sweet orange roots from brown scraps. Will cried, "No" angrily, and then, as she wiped out his mouth, repeated mournfully, "No, dirty."

The radishes grew—some grew monstrously—and were served for Daniel's tea, red and white, hot to taste, cool to bite. The carrots were decimated and stunted by carrot fly and the peas and beans were straggling and random. Stephanie found it hard to be ruthless. She found it hard to kill things that coiled and ran in the earth, and harder still to thin out her seedlings properly, to pluck out some so that others might live.

The most successful thing was the climbing nasturtiums. She planted the little, round, ridged, tripartite seeds in compost in wooden trays; the kitchen was cluttered with them. From these, in due course, rose the blunt heads and double, umbrellalike leaves, veined and delicate. Her first tray, not pinched out early enough, wilted and died on long stringlike stalks like tangled spaghetti. The second, thinned out, produced seedlings that she planted out along the house walls and around the base of the clothes poles, fixing bright pictures of nasturtiums on wooden stakes to show where they were. Will staggered after her, uprooting the markers, tearing the paper, muttering "fowa." Some of the seedlings, too, he dismembered. But enough grew. That summer the wall of the back of the cottage was patterned with green discs, twining cylindrical stems, and fringed silk trumpets of scarlet and orange, ivory and mahogany-red, deep chrome and buff, with black lines inscribing the entrance for butterflies, with stamens quivering dark and powdered in their throats.

Stephanie watched them lift in the early light, fold into limp triangles at night, and was put in mind of Jack and the Beanstalk, the prosaic and angry mother who had been given a few seeds in exchange for a cow and had stood at the foot of a brilliant ladder into the sky.

Marcus, who called occasionally, sometimes with Ruth and Jacqueline, brought the cat. It had been found, Jacqueline said, in the gutter outside her school, having been hit a glancing blow by a car. The RSPCA was ready to dispose of it humanely. Jacqueline's mother, whose goodwill had been relied on, noticed that the cat was, lopsidedly, pregnant, and said that the RSPCA had the right idea. Jacqueline had carried the cat as far as the hospital where she had arranged to meet Marcus, who, unused to being appealed to, said Stephanie would know what to do. The cat cringed and moaned and spat. It was a tigerish tabby, with a cross glare in its eyes. "I don't want a cat," said Stephanie, cleaning oil from the creature's fur with William's cotton wool and baby lotion. "Daniel won't want a cat." "You shouldn't have a cat in the house wi' the babby," called Mrs. Orton from her chair. "We'll all fall over it and break us necks."

Daniel came in to hear an ululating howl, and to find his wife on her knees beside a clothes basket in which the cat squatted in blood, and glared at a pullulating, glistening dark package. "Go on," said Stephanie. "Go on, *help* it." And the cat lowered its yellow eyes and snapped with sharp teeth at the caul, and licked out the blunt-headed, stump-legged fish thing that squealed and moved blindly toward the cat, who began a low, rasping purr.

"Stephanie," said Daniel. "*Must* you?"

"I can't let it die."

"When I first saw you, you were trying to save all those kittens."

"So I was."

"I fell in love with you when I saw you being so bloody-minded about those kittens."

"They died."

"I know."

"These won't. This cat's helping. This cat's all right. Look."

And between bloody howl and primitive purr five more packages were propelled into the world, and all but one, a wet, gray one, licked into life. Two black, two striped, a white with striped blotches, a pale, unfinished-looking thing, late born, that tramped sturdily and wailed shrilly for some minutes, raising its bloody snout and earless head above the working rumps of its siblings, until the cat made space

for it. The gray kitten's neck was twisted right round, like a paper
bag. Its pink eyelids were closed. Stephanie, suddenly squeamish,
begged Daniel to do something. He picked up the tiny body in newspaper and carried it out, leaving her still sitting over the basket,
with overbright eyes. Behind her, Marcus and Jacqueline looked on.
Jacqueline said, "Look at them breathing," and Marcus, who could
have been repelled, who would earlier have been repelled, said he
was glad they were all right.

The cats, like the nasturtiums, flourished in the light of her attention. She wooed the mother cat with scraps of fish and bits of chicken;
later, she arranged the wandering, tremulous little ones around a dish
of warm milk, dipped their noses in, watched them sputter, wash, and
lap. If William grew fast, these creatures expanded daily, from eye-
less embryos, like miniature hippopotamuses, to climbing, running,
tumbling, soft things with pricked ears, rayed whiskers, cold little
pink pads on coin-sized feet. She thought about learning, watching
the cats grow. William practiced, picking up crumbs, directing a
spoon to his mouth, returning it to his plate, putting small things in
large containers, attempting to put large things in small containers,
weeping with frustrated concentration. One day, no cats had left the
box. The next, one black one could jump, and not only jump but
cling, and not only cling but overbalance and fall on his feet. The
next, three could, and the next after that, all. What staggered on
Monday ran and pounced and was halfway up the curtain on Saturday. She was ready to cry with pleasure one day watching the small
white kitten wash itself as cats have always washed, licking a curled
front paw, curving a hind leg round like a ham bone, the new pink
skin rosy under the thick, soft, short white hairs in its groin. Inside its
new white ears, the naked skin was pink and cold, like the Atlantic
butterfly shells that are scattered across Filey beach at low tide. Will's
movements were fumbling and random by comparison. He neither
ran nor leaped. And yet he had speech. She sat on the lawn amid tumbling cats and watched him progress toward her, three steps and a
heavy descent on his backside, three steps, his plump hands working
like acrobats', at arm's length. "Fowa," he said. "Cat." "Wottit," he
said. "Wiwottit." She interpreted. "Will wants it." "Un," he agreed.

"Wiwottitcat." When he managed to seize one, which was often, for they crawled toward him like wasps to a honey jar, he would clutch, and the kitten would go limp, and Will would lift it ruminatively to his mouth, a giant grinding flesh and bone, an infant exploring everything orally, and the mother cat would pace, mewing, and Stephanie would release the little cat and kiss her son. Mrs. Orton said they were unhygienic. Stephanie said to Daniel, "Look how *alive* they are." Daniel put up a notice in the church porch. "Homes wanted for healthy kittens."

Vegetable, animal, human. Stephanie slowly became host to a motley collection of strays, the more helpless and passive of Daniel's misfits, old or weak-minded wanderers who came and sat for hours at the kitchen table, or in armchairs, rumbled at by Daniel's mother, occasionally scowled at by Daniel. Stephanie gave them cups of tea, and small tasks to perform, colanders of beans to top and tail, peas to shell, lentils to pick over for small stones. They sorted jumble and labeled jam and fixed price tags with shaking fingers to knitted cardigans for infants, kettleholders, bootees. There were two or three regulars. There was watery, pallid Nellie, who had always been looked after by her eldest sister, who had just died. Nellie was forty and had the mind of a child older than William but constrictedly aware that she could not do things that would come naturally and easily to him, in a few months or years. Nellie's sister, Marion, had seen Nellie as a cross, a burden, and an infant. She had done everything for her: buttons, feeding, cooking, shopping. It was Daniel who had organized a chain of helpers to save Nellie from being put in hospital; it was Stephanie who taught her things she was half grateful, half frightened to learn, as though learning might in some way remove her from the human world entirely, remove those hands that now touched her at least to do up a brassiere, settle a cardigan, tie a shoelace. There was Morris who intermittently lost his memory since a head wound at Dunkirk, who could not hold a job and had twice attempted suicide. There was also Gerry Burtt.

Gerry too had had trouble with holding jobs, even when they were found for him. For some time he had returned with increasing frequency to the church in search of Daniel, to whom he repeated, as though repeating would exorcise it, and always with the same combination of blunted rage, desire for judgment, and horror of Barbara, the story of the killing of his daughter. One day he came to the cottage, without invitation, and found Stephanie, Will, and the cats playing in the garden. He stood on the patch and watched them. Stephanie looked up from a daisy chain and asked if she could help.

"I were looking for Vicar. Well, for Mr. Orton, rightly."

"He's not here. He'll be back at supper time. Have you been to the church?"

"Aye. I've looked there."

"Is anything wrong? Can I help?"

"My name's Gerry Burtt," he said, portentously as to Daniel. Stephanie, unlike Daniel, recognized his name from the newspapers, which she now read with a sense of urgency because she now lived in the world they described, a world of human events, births, accidents, marriages, deaths. She had wept for Gerry's daughter as she had wept for the woman whose two children had been found drowned in a flooded quarry, who had been transformed between morning and evening, and in five lines of print, from a woman, any woman, with two children, to a woman whose past pointed toward this terrible present, whose future was the afterlife of this absolute accidental blow.

"Have a cup of tea," she said to Gerry Burtt, moving William out of his shadow on the grass. "I was just making one."

"I wouldn't mind," he said cautiously.

One could not live on the assumption that misfortune, or worse, was infectious, although there is a profound human instinct to do so. Stephanie's flesh shrank away from Gerry Burtt, to whom she nevertheless gave tea, scones, a corner chair, and talked coolly and equably about the weather, the garden. He burst out suddenly in the middle of one of these murmured platitudes, "You've got a lovely boy, Mrs. Orton. Just lovely." She could feel his emotion, boiling and helpless. "I know," she said. "I'm lucky. So lucky, it makes me afraid." William threw a plastic swan from his high chair and Gerry Burtt retrieved it, handing it carefully back. Will banged it down on his tray, crowed, and hurled. Gerry Burtt retrieved. Stephanie watched. "He likes you," she said, false friendly. "Here, baby," said Gerry Burtt, intensely, and Will grandly took the swan again and brandished it, crying out, "Da-da-da-da-da."

One day, when they were all there, Nellie, and Morris, and Gerry and the perpetual Mrs. Orton, Stephanie put Will casually and deliberately on Gerry's knee while she made toasted tea cakes. Daniel came in unexpectedly and found them like this, with a frightened smile on Gerry's face and a dubious look on Will's more or less acquiescent one. He resisted the temptation to snatch his child, but said that night to Stephanie, when they were alone, that she didn't have to have Burtt in the house like that. Nor Nellie, nor Morris, who could be eccentric and frightening. She replied equably, "I do what I can. There's a lot of your work I can't help with. But I can put up with these and help a bit. They don't bother me. I do what I can."

There was something a little disingenuous in this reply. Partly at least she allowed the lost ones to sit in her house in order to neutralize Daniel's mother, who sat among them, one of many. They were a clear case, the lost ones, of the inadequacy of the theory that language is primarily communication. When they spoke, it was in closed monologues. Poor Nellie, who felt, and occasionally tried to say, that her head was inside some soft thick casing through which she saw and heard dimly and muffled, used speech to describe what she was doing, in a third person reminiscent of a repeated command. "Now pick up the peas, pick up the peas. Now press with thumb, now out, here they are, how many, six, a good lot, six is a good lot, no maggots." Morris in good moments spoke grandly and hurriedly, stabbing the air, in abstract words of the injustice of life, the bad deal we got, some worse than others, no rhyme or reason. In bad ones he repeated himself, describing terror of shells and seawater, noise and blood. Mrs. Orton described food long since consumed. Gerry Burtt spoke baby talk to Will, sounding not unlike Nellie. "Nice soft banana, put on brown sugar, milk, lovely, hunh?" Repetition, recapitulation, a kind of static seeking of a way out of the muffled, the painful, the intolerable, voices in a room. And through them Will hooted and sang his syllables and words, in ever more complex rhythms, for his own aesthetic satisfaction, it appeared. They played a game where Stephanie stood him on her knee and jumped him at random and he laughed, deep and surprisingly low. "Ha. Ha. Ha-*ha*, ha-*ha*, ha-*ha*. Ha. Ha. Ha-*ha*, ha-*ha*, ha-*ha*." Once she came into the garden and heard him, sitting in his pram, cry deeply and tragically, "Oh, *God.*" And then, in a crescendo, "Oh, God. Ogodogodogodogod O *God.*" And then a cackle of laughter, like the horse among the trumpeters. "Ha-*ha,* ha-*ha,* ha-*ha.*"

Daniel was discontented, and ashamed of his discontent. He felt he had lost things, which he should perhaps have been prepared to lose —his solitude, his absolute dedication to his work, and in some way his wife. He had brought about, through strength of will, a situation in which he now felt there was no place for that will. Gideon's abounding energy depressed him. Gideon, like Daniel, was a creation of social ties, responsibilities, where they had not been. But whereas Daniel operated in the realm of the practical—food and laundry, transport and company—Gideon created people's emotional lives. He inspired the young. He stirred up the sad. The people in the parish to whom he was drawn were the seekers, the disturbed, those hungry for feeling. He gathered them in groups and "sparked them off," on each other, on himself. Daniel felt that much of this was dangerous and wrong; this caused him to question his own intentions, his use of his own energy. He remembered that he had wished to give up, to clear away, to channel, his life. He had not meant to give it to jumble sales and coffee mornings, cubs' outings and marrying other people. Custom lay heavy on Daniel, too. He wanted things to happen. When he was little, he had said to his mother, "Why doesn't something *happen?*" And she had invariably replied, "Let us alone. Don't go bothering me when everything's nice and quiet." Her presence in his current niceness and quietness only exacerbated his impatience.

Stephanie's bodily placidness irritated him. It had initially both attracted and irritated him. He sensed her strength; he feared her inertia; he meant to stir her up. He had made their marriage happen. He had made her love him. He had trusted his own sexual fury because it was unique in his experience. He had launched himself into passion and had aroused a reciprocal passion. He was innocently unprepared for postnatal failures of interest or energy. He put his wife's tendency to avert her face from him in bed, to turn to one side, curling her knees to her chin, down to a variety of things. Encroachment: his mother snoring, Marcus creeping, the child roaring.

Fatigue. In the first few weeks, blood and soreness. He did not allow for the ebb and flow of hormones, though he was, at some animal level, very well aware that her sensual interests were dissipated over the variety of food, cleanliness, earth and watering, cat fur and flower petals, and his son's new skin, milky smell, malty hair. To see Burtt holding that was a violation of his territory that raised imaginary hackles down his large spine.

When he went to bed that night she was rolled away from him, reading *Good Things in England*. He stood and looked at her, and then pulled on a sweater over his clerical shirt, and his duffel over that, and went out, not slamming the door, and walked. Through little streets of workmen's houses, with lightless windows, and a cold smell of extinguished coal fires, across his own dark churchyard, smelling of cold earth, box and yew, down dark Thoroughfare, its shop windows sheets of shining black, along the dark canal. Smelling rotting vegetables, gas caught in billowing weed, more cold coal. He walked, and in his way prayed to the God who drove him, for patience in inactivity, for a reordering, for quiet sleep, by which he meant, and knew he meant, some response from his wife. Praying was not asking; praying was loosing these knots of care into some dark running stream of energy between It and himself so that things were delivered from him, to It, to deal with. He walked on. He breathed better. He came back cold-cheeked and cold-handed, bringing the coal smell with him.

She was not asleep.

"Did someone send for you?"

"No."

He undressed.

"Is anything wrong?"

"No. I went for a walk. For air. To think."

"Something is wrong."

"Not particularly." He hated this tone. This childish tone. A married note.

"Come to bed."

She was facing him, at least. He got into bed, a lot of cold flesh at once, subsiding. She put out her arms.

"Is it Gerry Burtt?"

"I don't like him near Will."

"He does no harm. He's sad."

"He let his kid get killed."

"He won't hurt Will."

"I saw the social worker. A Mrs. Mason. About his wife. They're talking about letting her out. In a bit. I don't know what he'd do if—"

"What's she like? Barbara Burtt?"

"I've not seen her. He talks about her. Scared stiff of her. Not surprising. He scares me in some way; I can better understand people who go berserk, you know, than people who just can't *bother* to keep a kid alive . . . I think he might give up on me too, if I saw her. So I haven't. Don't talk about her, not here."

"Someone must care for her—"

"Mrs. Mason does. A lot. Don't go on about her."

"Daniel—"

"What?"

"Do you want me to stop him coming?"

"No. It's not that. Forget it."

"What *is* it, Daniel?"

"There's no life in things."

She thought over things: house, garden, church, Gideon, Will. She put out her arms.

"Don't say that. *You* never say things like that." He had put life in things, for her.

"This isn't what things are *for*," he said, but his flesh was rising. She was holding him against her, the ballooning nightdress up under her armpits. They quickened.

"It comes back, Daniel, it *does*," she said, with such surprise that he laughed.

"So it does," he said.

And along that awkwardly hard, protruding bridge-piston of flesh they poured in their myriads, the gametes rising and hastening and swimming to their extinction or death in an inhospitably acid environment, to brief afterlives, connected to protective host cells, to culs-de-sac, to the cervical passage, the blind heads seeking, the flagellant tails whipping and rippling, all lost, all but one that was, some hours later, to embed itself in the wall of the female cell, to break in, feed, unite, divide, change, specialize. Daniel, suddenly lightened, kissed his wife's eyes and mouth and felt kinder toward Gerry Burtt. Stephanie, lazily warm and wet, touched Daniel's hair, smoothed his wet thigh, thought that things were getting better, that they were free after all, they loved each other, they could make space for some months of comfortable closeness and communication. She had a husband as well as a son. Her mind planned peaceably, reorganizing priorities. Charles Darwin, it appears, tried not to personify the force that chooses egg-cell and sperm, embryo and offspring, mate and victim, not to use of it verbs of conscious intention, as I have just used "choose" in order not to write "select." Language is against us. The classic novel would have taken man and woman to the marriage ceremony or, say, in *Roderick Random*—which Frederica read among bookworms and cicadas in her Provençal vine furrow— to the lifting of the silk nightshift and the entry between the bed curtains. We now go beyond and beyond, novelists and moralists both. But where do we stop thinking, about chance and choice, force and freedom? We do not need Dame Nature to decide whether the egg's presence in the fallopian fronds, rather than Gerry Burtt, or *acedia* or personal will, dictated Daniel's movements, Stephanie's movements, the degree of warmth, acidity, softness, energy in those dark places. We can resist personifying sperm or compulsive force, against the grain of the language we have. But we cannot resist the connecting and comparing habit of the mind.

These events have now been microscopically filmed from inside. We can see on our television screens, as large as life, meaning on a scale accessible to our perceptual apparatus, our sense of our own space in the world, the sprouting of the seminal particles in the testes, the sudden constriction and explosion of the orgasm, the primitive half-cells flowing toward the flowerlike ovum, the seaweed fronds that arrest, that trap, that guide, that select, that nurture. There are heat photographs of the blood stiffening the penis to an inverted South Africa with burning deserts and green oases. What conceits would Donne and Marvell have made of this vision? Or of the flow of sperm filmed on delicate duck-egg china blue, moving to the dark red womb and its human flora, unseen, unrecognizable, yet familiar. In the film, the head of the sperm rests in the circle of the egg wall as

Daniel's head rested on his wife's breast. Biologists have speculated that male forms repeat male forms as female repeat female. As the sperm is mobile and invasive, so is the organ that deposits it; as the ovum is large (relatively) and still and receptive, so are the inner vase and cavern forms that nourish and contain it in its turn. Container contains container; invader emits invaders. Emanuel Swedenborg thought all parts of the body and of the world were made of smaller units of the same nature: the tongue of myriads of minute tongues, the liver of smaller livers, for the world corresponded and was orderly. Goethe knew and discovered that the various forms of a plant, the stamens, the sepals, the ova, the pistil, are modifications of a primary leaf form, the Ur-form. There is a theory current now that the sexual function is an aberration from parthenogenetic herma-phroditism, the product of "parasitic DNA," which puts out a pilus, a "genetic syringe" to impart, cuckoolike, a factor of its own into the nucleic acid of another organism. While they slept with their heads together on the pillow, the cells pullulated and divided, boiled and extruded, arranged genes, chromosomes, proteins, plans, patterns, another life, the same life in another form. And as the immortal life of the genotype is transmitted, some say, so the phenotype, the individual body, becomes redundant, dispensable; it is economic for it to age, cease to function, die.

The germ of this novel was a fact that was also a metaphor: a young woman, with a child, looking at a tray of earth in which unthinned seedlings on etiolated pale stalks died in the struggle for survival. She held in her hand the picture of a flower, the seed packet with its bright image. Nasturtium, Giant Climbing, mixed.

Will sat on the lawn, while the blackfly clustered below the necks of the nasturtiums, a sticky dark band of small bodies, and inside Stephanie the cells hurried and informed each other. He had dis-covered that if he turned his head very rapidly from side to side and then stopped suddenly the world moved, brilliantly streaked with mahogany red, scarlet, rosy red, orange, gold, cream, green, and black, none of which he could of course name, but the colored ribbons of movement delighted him, humming and shivering, settling slowly like ripples in water when he ceased waving his head. The colored ribbons of his head movements had long floating tails, at his eye corners. If he put his head up and down it was harder to achieve this bright giddiness. Human cognition has been called "order from noise," or it may be, contrariwise, the patterning of the world with a constructed map, crystallized in the genes, repeating laws already informing the growing mind. Will made confusion and let it settle to form. He could name the rose, the iris, the sunflower, the tiger lily, the daisy, though all with one name, "fowa." Later, when he began to draw, he would draw five flat loops round an approximate circle until he learned the pleasures of the compass-constructed overlapping arcs that make up, in their way, a Cartesian flower—a Platonic flower?

21

A TREE, OF MARY, ONE

Marcus caught himself from time to time feeling happy. This feeling frightened him; he was unused to it. He was happy when he was with the two girls, Jacqueline and Ruth. Jacqueline tended to ask personal questions and press for answers—"What will you *do?*"—as well as giving him glimpses of what it felt like to work at what one wanted to work at, with enthusiasm. Jacqueline was normal. She was the first normal person with whom he had had an extended dialogue. She showed him things, slides of leaf sections, diagrams of plant cells, the breathing stomata, the chloroplasts. She asked for help with maths. Ruth he almost never saw on her own; she came sometimes with Jacqueline. Sometimes he thought they formed the usual pair of leader-innovator and devoted follower. Jacqueline watched to see that Ruth was happy. Ruth agreed with Jacqueline, on the whole. Sometimes Ruth's placid silences reminded him of his own strategy of reticence and silence; he recognized in her an analogous policy of noninvolvement, even fear. Yet he was also aware that both he and Jacqueline watched Ruth as though it was what *she* felt that mattered, as though things were valuable if she approved them. There was something a little autocratic in her manner. He remembered particularly one speech of hers directly addressed to him. Jacqueline often admonished him not to waste his brains. Ruth said nothing about his brains; she told him to try to be ordinary.

"You don't do enough ordinary things, Marcus. You don't like cinemas and bike rides and fish and chips and—"

"Gossip," said Jacqueline.

"That's right. You can't *imagine* him gossiping."

"I don't notice things the way you do."

"You're human, Marcus Potter. If you don't do ordinary things by nature, you've just got to learn by practice. I know."

"You know?"

"When my mum died, I didn't care—for anything. But I had to keep house for Dad and the kids, and it was *ordinary* things . . . shopping, doing the wash . . . I found I was human. Then *she* came and took over, but I'd learned."

"Ordinary things," said Marcus. "I'm no good at—'

"We've noticed. You can practice, with us."

Also, he found her attractive. He liked to think of her when she was not there, the spiral of her plait, the oval face, the eyelids dropped, the small closed full mouth, her joints at rest, the distance between shoulders and breasts, breasts and waist. Mostly, though, it was the image of that thick glossy tail, snaking between her shoulder blades. He wanted to touch it. He would have liked to unwind it, twist by twist, and shake it free, as he had seen it through the little glass door panel in the kitchen, that night.

He had done nothing about his ant vision of God at the Field Centre—what could he have done? He had pushed his book trolley along corridors. Then one summer day he was cycling the long way to Blesford, past Long Royston, where Frederica had played Elizabeth two summers ago, where the bulldozers were grubbing up pastureland to make the new university of North Yorkshire. Along the grass verges the cow parsley poured its greenish-white dust from lace umbels, there were moon daisies, little lemon-yellow wild snapdragons, lavender-gray-blue scabious as well as the stiffly thin scarlet silk of the poppies. Marcus had what he recognized from earlier experience as a dangerous sense of physical well-being, which simultaneously induced and fought against an increased sensitivity of his nasal passages, throat, and lungs to the flying pollen. There was the accustomed visual clarity: he took in the balancing patterns of the dry stones in the long gray wall; he saw threads connecting red and red poppy and poppy, in triangles and loops among the haze of blue and white and green. The cavity behind his nose bones felt both larger and more vacant, more oxygenated and more irritable, ready to prick, swell, itch, like a chilblain or a carpet of closely planted stings. He turned aside on a track across a field, up a hillside path among new corn, glass-green ears with delicate hairs. At the top of the rise was a knoll, on which stood several elm trees, maybe seven, one old tree and some younger ones, rising out of rough grass with random cloudy crowns and circling branches. He sat down at the foot of one of these and put his handkerchief across his breathing. He registered happiness, which was in its way as dangerous as the physical well-being; both presented themselves as empty patches of bright light on the inner eye, ringed by a prismatic flaring of color and danger. He tried to keep still. He considered the tree.

It had a dense, disorderly sheaf of twigs and suckers round the base of its trunk, and between these, and indeed under them, for many of them were attached above ground, the great, rigid, gripping lumps of the roots grasped the earth and went into it. He looked up the trunk which rose, scarred, cracked, knobby, and yet essentially direct into the air, a deliquescent trunk that forked and forked again into many repeated trunks, reaching or traveling up. This solid fountain had multiple crowns of thick secondary limbs, dividing into long twigs, fine twigs, leaflets, leaves, shoots. Its history traveled with it, solidified in the immobile bole, healed wounds, split skins, broken limbs, new angles and turns.

He touched its thick hide, neither flesh warm nor stone cold. Most of the form of a tree is dead cells, standing, contained in a thin sheath of living, dividing, watery cells below the bark, with the pushing exploratory cells shape-shifting at the questing ends of twigs and roots. The leaves were alive; he plucked one from the suckers, clear gold-green, strongly veined, saw-edged, rough surfaced yet shining, asymmetrical at the base. The veining pleased him. He looked up at the crown again, thinking initially of it as amorphous, on a huge scale, and then as he looked, revealing an order in its massed clumps, thrusting limbs and layered planes of green leaves. He knew there was an inner geometry—Jacqueline had showed him drawings of the cambium layer—but he began to see an outer geometry.

Carefully contemplated, the growth of leaves from twigs, twigs from limbs, limbs from bole, showed to a geometric eye a persisting regularity in all this gnarled idiosyncrasy. The leaves grew out of the twigs in alternate ranks, at 180 degrees from each other, and the twigs too could be mapped—given broken ends, scars, variations in girth, blemishes—as growing out of the branches on a regular spiral at the same angle. Marcus stared and mapped, stared and mapped, learning the tree. He took out a notebook and made a sketch of the principle of the spiral. This abstract, linear tree sketch gave him considerable pleasure. Always before, Marcus had thought of geometry as something spun from his mind across the threatening, shapeless mess of the world, reducing it to his order.

He looked back up at the leaves. Briefly, his eye confused figure and ground, seeing a mosaic of green on blue, a tracery of bright blue on green. Where those colors met gold lines flowed, as though each leaf, or sky segment, were outlined in yellow light like a converse of the unifying dark lead network of stained glass.

When he had become ill, he had had a time of terror in a field of pouring light, had felt himself to be some kind of funnel through which the light must flow, his eye a burning glass. He had then devised a kind of geometric scheme to make the thing safe to think about, two intersecting cones, at the center of which his eye, his mind, almost accidentally were. He now held his hand against the tree skin, working out that he was back in the same place, seen differently. Only he was not afraid. He was not afraid, moreover, for two clear reasons. One was that the tree, the tree itself, was the intersection, the meeting cones, between light and earth. (The word "earthed" came into his mind with a kind of silly coherence.) The other was that he was now, however imperfectly, equipped to *think* about this, to map its order.

The tree seen was solid geometry, meeting light. The tree, thought about, was contained and moving force and energy, stable yet changing, consuming and not consumed. Its leaves were patterned, canopy above canopy, to turn all their faces to the light, to make spaces and tangents for all of them to take in the light. They drank and ate the light. They breathed out water and breathed in air and light. Water rose uninterrupted from dark roots to dancing green. Jacqueline had said apple trees drank four gallons per tree per hour. The water rose, not through suction, nor from pressure, but because it was an uninterrupted cohesive column, drawn up from base to crown. For a moment he saw the geometric fountain of rising water, a twisting and branching rope, the inner figure—no, *an* inner figure; there must be many—of its life and shape.

Light traveled from the sun at 186,000 miles per second, and the green he saw was refracted light, for the chlorophyll absorbed the red and blue-violet waves from the sun. The green was the light the tree did not consume. He saw in his mind's eye the drama of the tree, the undifferentiated light pouring, silently, at terrible speed, meeting the solid rising column of water in the living and dead form of the tree.

He himself was not there for nothing. It was his eyes, their rods and cones, that made the chlorophyll-light green on the elm leaves. It was his eyes that perceived, through a prism of water drops and dust particles, blue in the empty air above him. The ants saw unimaginable blues, but were blind to reds and yellows. So, it is said, are the bees, to whom a dandelion appears purple, to whom a world of floral patterns and signs are revealed to which we are blind. What would Vincent Van Gogh have made of this knowledge, making yellow pigments correspond to the whirling circle of the sun, to the petals and seeds and sun shape of the sunflowers, seeing the complementary colors, yellow and violet, as a fast principle of the union of opposites, sowing his ploughed violet field under a gold sky with green seeds of light? Marcus looked at the pink-brown buds on the suckers, the mix of bronze and a kind of dark rose, and felt that he had his place, he was part of something.

Geometry he *saw*. The water, the properties of light, he *knew*. He must learn more. Plain curiosity is simpler and clearer than desire, and closer to life. Parallels have been drawn by psychologists between all human desires and their consummations. Appetency creates tension, in feeding, in sex, in cognition. The human being feels a relaxation of tension not when the final goal—nourishment, fertilization, truth—has been reached, but when the organism experiences, aesthetically, a release. Consumption, orgasm, what has felicitously been called the "aha experience" when a structure felt to be defective or inchoate suddenly appears formed and harmonious. Some such peace came to Marcus, looking at the beautiful form of the tree in the sunlight.

An elm grove has other qualities of desired peacefulness. An English elm grove is one individual, reproducing itself by suckers. It is true that the tree has flowers, what are called "perfect" flowers, male and female in one, the male stamens protruding above the female anther, so that when the flowers open, very early, February perhaps, the pollen cells can be blown in the wind to cross-fertilize other trees. But the English elm propagates itself underground, and was probably imported by Stone Age tribes who valued its suckering habit for fences. It might be thought a peculiarly happy tree, a self-sufficient tree, a kind of single eternity. The lack of variation among the clones, however, makes them peculiarly susceptible to the same disease. But in 1955 the elm was a sempiternal, essential part of our English landscape.

22

NAMES

The winter of 1955 and the spring of 1956 were bleak. Even in Provence, the blossom blackened, the lavender failed, the vines shriveled. Stephanie, heavier this second time, cycled more slowly to the hospital, her mind dense with times, weights, measures, precautions, vitamins, blood sample, Will's diet, yeast, little cakes for the Mother's Union. Custom and frost, frost and custom. She made Christmas again, dusting Marcus's polyhedrons, polishing stored glasses. Frederica came back from Cambridge and talked about theatrical tours de force, humanism, people. She talked, rapidly and shrilly, Stephanie thought, to persuade herself these things were real in the Frozen North. She said frequently, "Raphael says——" Stephanie tried to remember, to sympathize, to hear. But she felt a chill, as though she, her house, good and bad, brilliant flowers and warm baking as well as grumbling and responsibility, were what Frederica dreaded. She did not always answer Frederica's literary questions.

Marcus, on the other hand, was encouraging, back at Blesford Ride, studying maths, biology, chemistry instead of his old human topics. He still saw Mr. Rose; she had no idea what was said. He saw Jacqueline and Ruth, and occasionally other Young Christians. He tried with Bill, telling him his weekly marks, which were good, without trembling, even, Stephanie sometimes thought, with an almost-insulting deliberate kindness. He was practicing normality. He would remark on the weather, or the bus service, or the school plan to build a swimming-bath extension with something of the same, dutiful and surprised kindness with which he offered Bill progress reports. He asked Stephanie if she wanted a boy or a girl and what its name would be. Stephanie could only imagine boys and had agreed on Jonathan with Daniel. About girls they were less sure. Stephanie liked classical names—Camilla, Antonia, Laura—which Daniel disliked. They agreed once on Rachel, rather vaguely. She, or he, was due on St. Valentine's Day. Frederica said Valentine would do for either. Mrs. Orton said that was a fussy name and, when asked (by Frederica) what her own name was, said it was Enid. Stephanie sat and knitted and thought about Enid, which for her had associations of barmaids and Edwardian petits bourgeois, and behind that the pale Arthurian beauty of Geraint's Enid, Tennyson's Enid, Welsh Enid. It was in fact a beautiful word but as a name encrusted with undesirable associations like a biscuit jar covered with varnished sea shells, a memento of Scarborough, or Brighton, or Llandudno.

A child was also expected in the Bloomsbury flat. Naming talk centered on Saskia, desired by Elinor. "I want her to be happy, to be *somebody*, happy like a fulfilled cat, like Rembrandt's Saskia." Thomas said such a name would make the girl feel odd and conspicuous at school. Elinor said you could always add Jane or Mary or

Ann. She asked Alexander what his names were. He recited them—
Alexander Miles Michael—and added as he always added that they
were very military, down to the military archangel. Thomas favored
Mark or David. Elinor tried unsuccessfully to think of a male equiva-
lent for Saskia that did not come out of Georgette Heyer or the
Forsyte Saga. There was Gerard, said Alexander. He had met a
Dutchman called Gerard Wijnnobel. This reminded Thomas of
Brigadier Gerard; he reiterated that he liked plain names. "Mark or
Simon or David." "*Everyone* is called David," said Elinor. "That
makes your David more your own," said Thomas. "Saskia will always
be Rembrandt's."

Elinor's son was born, with ease, on January 12, 1956, at University
College Hospital. He was born at six in the morning. Thomas was in
the hospital, though not in the ward. Alexander was left in charge of
Chris, Jonathan, and Lizzie, at least at breakfast time: later, a
Universal Aunt came to help out. He put an apron on and served the
yogurt, the muesli, the fruit, feeling that he himself was an insubstantial Universal Aunt. "The baby has been born," he told the three. "A
boy, a big boy. Everyone is well." The children chattered and asked
when they could see him; Alexander said he didn't know; Lizzie
climbed on his knee and continued her inexorable catechism. Where
would the baby sleep? Would he make a lot of noise? Would he want
her baby mug which was *hers*? Alexander said he trusted there would
not be much noise and escaped to the BBC as Thomas returned and
the Universal Aunt rang the doorbell, simultaneously. Thomas said
Elinor wanted to see him. Alexander said, later, when she felt restored.
He meant to go, behind a large bunch of flowers, in a day or two,
with Thomas, or with Jonathan and Chris.

His office telephone rang that afternoon. He was talking to Martina
Sutherland, a formidable woman colleague with a first in Greats, an
incisive mind, a sculptured face, and an impressive record as a
producer. She had a reputation for driving and harrying her subordi-
nates and a cool friendliness to her equals that attracted and alarmed
him. He picked up the telephone."

"Alexander Wedderburn."

"Alexander. This is Elinor. I wanted to talk to you."

"I'm so glad all is well."

"I've managed to get one of these plug-in phone trolleys. I just wanted to talk to you. I want you to come and see this boy."

"Of course. I was thinking of coming with Thomas. Tomorrow evening? Today, if you're up to it."

A pause.

"Alexander. Can't you come *now*, on your own? I want you to *see* him."

"What's he like?" said Alexander foolishly, stalling.

"Perfect. Himself. Not like anyone at all—a perfect individual." Her voice ran on. "He is so *beautiful*, I cry."

"I'll do what I can. There's someone here now."

"Oh, my dear, I'm sorry. Look—*please* come. You will, won't you?"

"Of course I will."

"My landlady," he said to Martina Sutherland. "Just had a baby. Quite excited."

"How interesting," said Martina neutrally. "Now—don't you think this script is too dense—too many unrelieved names of philosophers, too close together . . . ?"

"Would you be free to come out to dinner?" Alexander heard himself saying. "Tomorrow, perhaps? To celebrate the end—well, almost the end—of my play?"

"I should be delighted."

So he went to see the boy on the day he was born. He was very agitated. Elinor had sounded unlike herself, overwrought and pre-cariously joyful. It was because of this tone of voice that he went alone, before Thomas and the children. He bought a large bunch of mixed spring flowers, daffodils like furled umbrellas, iris spikes, squat green-petaled tulip buds, edged with flame, all cased in creaking cellophane. He knew nothing about babies. The only one he knew well was the unfortunate Thomas Parry, in Blesford, who had, with reason, objected to Alexander. He had foolish visions of his own face, marmoset small. It was a small, light ward, with four women in it; he stepped across its width. Elinor, in a sprigged nightdress, put up a tired and shiny face, under dull hair, to be kissed. She smelled milky, sour milky. He tried to give her the flowers and a huge box of bitter-mint chocolates and she tried to direct his attention to the small crib, canvas slung on metal, containing a bundle wrapped tightly in flannelette, stiff as a pencil, mouth and eyes pursed, skin crimson, blotched with eczema. This head had a few, not many, blond hairs.

Elinor leaned over and lifted. "Hold him. Take hold of him."

"Oh, no."

"They're surprisingly resilient."

"They terrify me."

"I want to see you hold him." Overwrought, insistent.

"No, I can't. I just can't. I've no idea. He's better with you."

"Look, he's opened his eyes. Isn't he lovely?"

The child had, Alexander observed, a long pointed head and a broad brow. His eyes were a dark, indeterminate color. He was all shapeless, even the bones. They got squashed, or molded, didn't they, in the unthinkable process of being extruded from that tight hole? His mouth was all curls and droops. He was pitifully *small*. Almost anything could hurt him. He was barely there. Alexander put a finger out and touched the soft cold cheek.

"Elinor—let us be uncharacteristically plain. Are you, or are you not, trying to tell me that this is my son?"

This question had to be enunciated in a close, conspiratorial whisper. Elinor hissed back.

"I honestly don't know." She gasped and giggled. She bent over the boy and said into Alexander's ear, "I made sure—I always made absolutely sure—that there wouldn't be any possibility of knowing . . . of knowing *whose* . . . if by any chance . . . I thought I might tell when I saw him. Or her, I was sure it would be a her, Saskia."

"He doesn't look like anybody in particular to me."

"Well, look at the next baby and you'll see they're different. It's a myth. They aren't the same, and they don't look like Winston Churchill. Look at Mrs. Kogan's baby."

Mrs. Kogan's baby had a bush of black hair, full cheeks, huge eyes, a roundness. Mrs. Kogan bowed and smiled at Alexander who returned to his hissing.

"Chris and Jonathan don't look *unlike* me."

"Nor does Thomas, come to that. Big brow, thoughtful expression, blondish-brownish, straight mouth? You're a bigger man. Whose do you *feel* he is?"

"*Really*—" said Alexander, who felt nothing for the pink papoose but fear and trembling.

"The only way to tell would be a blood test."

"*No*," said Alexander, instinctively and loudly. As well as being bodily afraid of the baby he was embarrassed and apprehensive about this new, indiscreet, bubbling, agitated Elinor.

"Oh, my dear, I wasn't seriously suggesting . . . I feel all light-headed. Maybe it's the gas. And the strain of the last few months."

"Strain—" he repeated dumbly.

The ward doors swung and crashed. Lizzie and Jonathan and Chris burst in, with boxes of chocolates and bags of fruit.

"I'll go—" said Alexander.

"No, please—"

"I'll go. I've got to think."

"There's nothing to *think* about. Come tomorrow?"

"I've got a dinner engagement with someone from the office. I'll try to drop in. Thomas, how are you? I was just going. No, really."

"Isn't he lovely and little?" said Lizzie. "He held my finger."

"Very lovely and little," agreed Alexander, touching the colorless mouse hair of the little girl with the long fingers that had excited her mother. "You're a lovely family."

He sat in his yellow-and-white room and considered what he now saw as the furious activity of Elinor's mind over the past year. Until she had used the word "strain" he had not tried to imagine nine months' uncertainty as to whose child was growing inside her, alarm over a possible undeniable resemblance, alarm over his own response, which in the event had been less than gracious. He fancied that she had been so sure the child was Saskia because that way, a girl, the child, would be primarily her child, would resemble her . . . ? She had *used* him. He had known she was using him—to deal with Thomas and Anthea Warburton, with fear of age, stolidity, maternal invisibility. But it now seemed she had *meant* to conceive the child in their silent, civilized intercourse. Why? To punish Thomas? Or was she, like an actor he knew, compulsively in need of a child from every love affair? An expensive need, for a woman. Had he misjudged everything? Did she, as other women had, love him? She should have said, he caught himself beginning to think, disapproved of his own petulance and changed track.

Thomas. What did Thomas know, or guess, or think, or feel? Thomas was his friend, not the woman, Thomas he liked and respected and needed. It was possible that simply because they were English all would silently go away, because raising a voice, or commenting energetically, was in moral bad taste. The baby was Thomas's baby, and would remain so. Elinor might calm down. He himself would, of course, leave the flat as quickly as possible. This raised problems about the ending—now so imminent—of *The Yellow Chair*. He thought of Vincent Van Gogh and could raise only standard portrait images, a brown face glaring under a straw hat, a pale face enigmatically frowning among aquamarine whirlwinds and golden moons and stars. He was visited by a vivid memory of Frederica Potter, in the days of his Elizabeth play, wiry red hair disordered by explanatory hands as she offered him a lecture on Racine's metrics and a declaration of love.

Thomas took him to the Marlborough on his way to University College Hospital. On Thomas's way, that was—Alexander was meeting Martina in L'Escargot Bienvenu. When he told Thomas he wasn't going to the hospital Thomas said levelly that that was a pity, his presence meant a lot to Elinor, but she would, of course, understand. Alexander looked at his friend's face, which was a bland, unsmiling mask, and felt anger—as much as he ever felt—against the woman. He expressed this in his way.

"Perhaps I should move out pretty soon. You'll need the space."

"You've said that before. Elinor likes having you. Truly."

"And you, Thomas?"

Thomas replied, guardedly, "I've been grateful to you. I would have been frozen out, without you."

"But now?"

"I think you should do as you think best. Maybe we are using you."

Alexander, shocked by Thomas's plural use of the word he himself had found for Elinor's stratagem, drained his glass in silence.

"In any case, I hope you'll be a godparent to the boy. Elinor's very set on that, too."

"I can't. I'm not a Christian."

"A secular godparent. She believes in ceremony. There'll be a non-denominational ceremony in the University Church."

"I—"

"Think about it."

"I will. Have you decided his name?"

"Oh, yes. Simon Vincent Poole."

"Vincent?"

"For him. For your play. For Vincent Van Gogh."

"How curious," said Alexander.

Stephanie's labor began promptly enough on St. Valentine's Day. It was all that was prompt about it. Stephanie, orderly and brave, had dealt in her imagination with the distresses and discomforts to come. She endured the early stages better for this reason—the cold wet pull of the razor, the indignity of the enema. She even managed to hold on to a book, against the moment when she would be left alone with the rhythms of pain and the institutional crabbiness of the nurses. The book was *Our Mutual Friend*, of which she read very little, but with that curious agonized attention of pain that fuses images so that the slowly developing nightmare of a blocked labor, a twisted cord, arrhythmic grippings, suffocation, exhaustion, and finally the hauling forceps, coiled and coiled in her mind with Lizzie Hexam's coal fire, with the sluggish Thames and its cargo of dead bodies, with grappling hooks, ropes, lanterns, and nocturnal mutterings. There was none of the sense of a force with which she could work and cooperate; every contraction had its crosscurrents of negation, while her spine flamed and smoldered and her intermittent mind's eye saw the choppy black water under London Bridge as the tide turned. When she heard the child cry, after twenty-three hours, in the small hours, she thought it was crying with pain. She felt herself a numb sack of knotted and ripped and sagging muscles that would revive to hurt.

"It's a girl," they said, kindly enough. "She'll be all right."

"Can I see her?"

"Later. She's exhausted and so are you. Later."

They wheeled her away to be stitched. She thought they could not be aware of the cruelty of hoisting her fat, forked legs into their meat hooks and canvas slings. They called her Mother. "Breathe in now, Mother." "Is there any discomfort there, Mother?" They wheeled her back. There was Daniel, with dark-shadowed eyes, in some anteroom between butchery and communal sleeping place.

"It's a girl. Have you seen her?"

"No. They say she's doing fine. Really."

"That's all right, then."

"You look terrible. My love."

"Oh, Daniel. I'll be all right."

"You must."

"How's Will?"

"He cried for you. Your mum came. Mine's a fat lot of use. Yours wondered if to take him back with her."

"I can't think. He'd be frightened. You decide."

Bliss, when it came, was not the light there had been at Will's birth, no clarity, no knowledge, but the release, the warmth and unreality, of a shot of pethidine. Half a line of verse tapped at her fading consciousness. "Ease after pain . . . doth greatly please." Ease and sleep waned as she tried to remember the rest; she moaned, and tried to find a comfortable way of lying, without success.

When they brought the child she could almost smell their apprehension.

"Now, we're bringing you your little girl, Mrs. Orton. She's a lovely little girl, absolutely fine, a bit sleepy, but that's because she had a hard time . . ."

"But?" said Stephanie.

"But she's got a—a blemish on her face. Doctor says it's a hematoma—a kind of blood blister—and will almost certainly vanish in time, probably completely. It's just that it *looks*—you know . . ."

"I want to see her." I want to see her preferably not under the curious gaze of two prison wardens' wives, a bouncy girl married in a hurry, screwdriver-curious Mrs. Wilks.

"We're just bringing her."

They brought her. Wrapped from head to toe in a cotton sheet, pinned with a safety pin. The face in shadow . . . The left eye, closed, with an almost-imperceptible pale brow. The mouth curved up like a rococo Cupid's bow. The right eye, with a stain beginning at the outer corner. Stephanie received the bundle and turned the sheet steadily back. Jellylike, swollen, purple and red, the thing clung like a leech covering half the tiny brow and crown, flapping over the eye. There were marks on the side of the little skull where the forceps had gripped. The child did not stir. Stephanie felt pity—not recognition, as she had with Will, not wonder, but protective pity. She held on to the child. It had two long cat licks of hair beside the fine ears; the hairs were slicked down with waxy grains still, but they had a color.

"She has red hair."

"You can't really tell."

"She has red hair." Then: "She's all *right*, isn't she? Apart from this—she's all right?"

"She's a lovely, healthy little girl."

Stephanie held the child against her breast, turning the blemish onto her own skin, learning the feel of the little legs, the weak shoulders.

"I'll look after you," she said. "I will."

The child slept on.

At visiting time Daniel came, and Winifred, and Will. Stephanie handed the baby to her mother, who said they had been assured the blister would disappear. Will climbed, grunting and assertive, onto Stephanie's bed and put his little arms tightly around her. There was a trail of mud on the green bedspread. Daniel took his daughter from Winifred, and, like Stephanie, turned the damaged face into his own body.

"She has a very sweet face," he said, not inanely, meaning the word. The child opened a closed eye and appeared to gaze at Daniel's darkness. "She's very like you."

"I thought like Frederica. She's got red hair, can you see?"

"Nobody would call Frederica sweet. She's like you." He considered her intently. "Her name is Mary."

It was not a name that had been discussed. Stephanie said, "Why? We'll talk about it. I still like the idea of Valentine."

"She just looks as though her name is Mary."

And in some way it became accepted, without argument, that the child looked as though her name was Mary.

Will was untwined from his mother and shown his sister. He put his fat finger almost on the blemish and asked shrilly, "Why she got a slug on her head? Why?"

"It isn't a slug. It's a blister."

"I don't like her. I don't like her. I don't *want*—"

He began to howl, piercingly and steadily. Winifred removed him.

The pattern of the genes is biological, is chemical, is human history. Naming is cultural, also history, another pattern. Both Simon Vincent Poole and Mary Valentine Orton were received into their culture with the inherited ceremony of infant baptism, though Daniel had doubts about the efficacy of vicarious vows and Thomas, Elinor, and Alexander were at the least agnostic about renouncing the world, the flesh, and the devil. But rites there must be. Mary was christened in St. Bartholomew's by Gideon Farrar, in the absence of her principled grandfather and in the presence of two moved grandmothers. She did not cry; she was a preternaturally "good" baby, sleeping long hours, feeding efficiently and rapidly, despite Will's circular prowling round her meals, despite interruptions caused by his deciding to evacuate bladder or bowels just when she was calmly supping. Sometimes Stephanie thought the "goodness" might be lethargy induced by perinatal brain damage. This seemed less likely when she developed a sweet smile, sunny under the flushed dark cloud over her drooping brow. She was christened in a broderie anglaise bonnet, stitched by Stephanie to cover and shade the blemish. The grandmothers and Clemency Farrar all declared it "sweet." She did not cry, as I said, but Will did, beating his fists against his mother's collar bone, twisting and twisting Bill's father's gold watch chain she wore as a necklace, a kind of Potter presence, nearly strangling her. Mr. Ellenby was god-father; Mrs. Thone and Clemency the godmothers. (In Daniel's case, belief in the sacrament was a prerequisite.) There was iced cake, made by Clemency, and dry sherry, after. Will was sick. Bill came to the cake and sherry and commented on the names, William and Mary. "Like the Orange in 1066 *and All That*."

"Nonsense," said Stephanie. "Why not William and Mary Wordsworth?"

"Better his wife than his sister, if modern theories are to be believed. Better than calling her Dorothy."

"Mary was Daniel's idea."

"Indeed. For the Virgin Mother or the pourer out of precious ointment?"

"I haven't asked."

Daniel, who was in earshot, said easily, "Not *for* anyone. It just seemed the right name for a woman. She looked so like a small woman. I was so surprised. After Will."

"Mary's a good name," said the new conciliatory Bill.

The Bloomsbury University Church was built in the heyday of Victorian religious fervor, a pleasing piece of yellow Victorian Gothic, by the Irvingites, followers of the charismatic preacher Henry Irving, who founded the Catholic Apostolic Church, which depended on the laying on of hands. Unfortunately not enough hands were laid and the Irvingites are now only a scattered elderly body. The church, in Tavistock Square, is used by the university. A practical brisk chaplain, all things to all men, a phrase that originated with St. Paul but which Frederica, applying it to herself, wrongly believed to be a line of Shakespeare's Cleopatra, sprinkled Simon Vincent, who screamed furiously, with water from a warmed hand-beaten brass bowl. No one asked Alexander to make vows. There was a pleasant gathering of teachers and university teachers, and enough Poole and Morton relatives to make Alexander feel what he wished to be, peripheral. He had a civilized chat with the chaplain about continuities, and a pleasing one with a woman drama teacher from the Crabb Robinson Institute, who knew *Astraea* almost by heart. Elinor smiled and was graceful; she had recovered her good manners.

Vincent Van Gogh experienced some anxiety over the naming of his nephew, Theo's son, Vincent Van Gogh. He wrote to his own mother, "I would have much preferred Theo to call his boy after father, of whom I have been thinking so much these days, instead of after me, but seeing it is now so, I started right away to do a painting for him, to hang in their bedroom, big branches of white almond blossom against a blue sky." This gesture of love had done its maker no good. "Work was going well, the last canvas of flowering branches —you will see, it was perhaps what I had done most patiently and the best, painted with a calm and a greater sureness of touch. And the next day, done for—like a brute . . . I fell ill at the time I was doing the blossoms of the almond tree."

Was there, Alexander wondered, such a thing as an unlucky name? And who dare say Vincent was unlucky, given the still-existing brightness of the costly almond blossoms? Alexander gave Simon Vincent Poole a plain silver platter engraved with his given names, and went out to dinner again with Martina Sutherland.

Alexander put the last words to his play two weeks after the christening of Simon Vincent, who could be heard crying through solid walls and door as Alexander wrote.

He had got the language as right as he could. As he leveled and counted the pages he thought that a play neither came together nor achieved its own life in any way to which the comparison of childbirth was helpful. This had been put together as jigsaws are, as patchwork is, with a templet, not a germ cell, to guide its formation. Its scales were stuck on like the panoply of the Pearly King, not grown like fish scales or fowl feathers. It was made of language, which could still be jigged, adapted, reordered. It was *made*, that was the point, its "growth" was metaphorical. Wasn't it?

Anyway, it was finished.

23

COMUS

" 'Impostor,' " said Frederica to her mirror, " 'Do not charge most innocent Nature / As if she would her children should be riotous / With her abundance.' " / She looked threatening but insufficiently outraged. She was playing the Lady in a May Week garden production of *Comus* in the college of St. Michael and All Angels. The director of this *Comus* was an American postgraduate called Harvey Organ, who was enchanted by Cambridge, determined to master its shifting forms and fashions, determined to leave his mark. He came to Raphael Faber's poetry evenings, where he read poems of a greater technical proficiency than any of the regulars, and caused mirth by the use of long critical words. "I jest cain't conceptualize an image" was a catch phrase bandied between Alan and Hugh Pink and Frederica, none of whom had any idea that this difficulty might represent a serious problem, not a nonsense. He was also felt to be "insincere" because his poems were not about things he could be presumed to know about or have firsthand experience of (the Gobi Desert, clipper races, rat breeding). He was bull-necked, spectacled, not tall enough to carry his muscles with grace.

The Comus on the other hand was extravagantly and savagely beautiful, a creature with more color to his flesh and hair than Frederica had ever seen in a man. His skin was olive-tawny, his hair black and glistening like the raven down of the black bird to which, if he could ever have remembered his lines, he compared the darkness soothed by Frederica's chaste and nonexistent singing voice. His lips were red. Until she saw Harold Manchester Frederica had had no idea, she decided, about how red lips could be without carmine, grease paint, or lipstick. His nose was Greek, if his mouth was Oriental, as were the tresses—long for those days. And he had red cheeks, too, flushed darkly along the excellent bone. He was reading law in a desultory manner, had a blue in lacrosse, and played tennis for the college.

Unfortunately, he could not learn his lines.

Harvey Organ didn't mind this as much as he should have done, since it gave him a chance to recite immortal lines himself with transatlantic panache.

> "Wherefore did Nature pour her bounties forth
> With such a full and unwithdrawing hand
> Covering the earth with odours, fruits and flocks
> Thronging the sea with spawn innumerable
> But all to please and sate the curious taste?"

Harvey sounded like a sensual pedant, Harold Manchester like a clean-living sixth former as unaware of the appalling riches of the language as he was of his own baroque beauty. Alan Melville, playing the Attendant Spirit, changed accents most beautifully, from a Gielgud-clear Spirit *in propria persona* to a very Scots pseudoshepherd to a fairly military organizer of the final coup. Frederica did not appear with Alan. Her rehearsal time was spent with Harvey and Harold, a schizophrenic Tempter, the voice and the body. She did not mind this; she was distracted by waiting to see Raphael who walked in the garden in the evenings, trailing his gown, talking to groups of other Fellows.

The performances—there were three—were not a success. Frederica's costume—a sad falling-away from a pretty, vague sketch— was unbecoming. It was meant to look like a Jacobean masquing costume and looked, in the event, like a child's party dress from the 1940s, drooping sky-blue rayon, garlanded round hem, waist, and neckline with floppy pink-and-white rayon roses. Frederica was reduced to reciting both her own part and then Harold Manchester's, which he then repeated after her.

On the last night, when Frederica, distressed and lost in a dark wood, wandered through the warm evening between rows of chairs to the acting space before the river wall, she took in, slowly, and with alarm, that the front two or three rows were occupied by her friends, lovers, and close acquaintances. There, beside Tony, Owen, Marius, and Hugh, were, improbably, medical Martin and ADC Colin and the English faculty friends of whom she was later to think as the little band. There, farther back, was sweet Freddie Ravenscar with a group of his own upper-class friends and, smiling broadly, Edmund Wilkie with Caroline, and behind these and others, surely by accident, precisely upright. Raphael Faber and Vincent Hodgkiss. Her voice shook. When she finished a paragraph this unlikely claque clapped and chattered. When she invoked the "unblemish'd form of chastity," there was a boom of male laughter.

It might have been hoped that Comus would have his lines by now. Frederica gloomily doubted it. He simply had a deficient memory, and she wondered with asperity how he could ever hope to achieve a degree. The previous night he had been arrested for driving drunkenly and, it was said, at 100 mph along King's Parade, mounting a pavement and twisting two bicycles. This had elated and rattled him. He smiled from time to time and took his cues or clues more slavishly than ever from Frederica. You could recast the whole damned thing, she thought crossly, as a fantasy in the Lady's mind, a modern schizophrenic drama about echoes and divided personality. She hissed his lines and declaimed her own, and the male laughter increased and spread. The audience rocked and shouted and laughed. Frederica saw Harvey Organ with his head in his hands, beautiful Freddie *sniggering* next to a puzzled-looking black-avised man she didn't know, and beyond them Raphael Faber, his head thrown back, laughing as she had never seen him laugh. She thought of sending the whole performance up, guying her indignantly virtuous role, playing for laughs, and decided against it out of some silly loyalty to dead John Milton, "the Lady of Christ's," who had written to persuade another silly age of other virtues in unmatched iambics. She stared crossly at the mockers, the rout, the collective enemy, and wondered, *Who?* The answer came. It was Tony Watson, fake and journalist, false friend who had cast her to the lions. Had he done it because Alan had told him how comically it was going? She did not for a moment suppose he had ferreted out all these men in order to provide her with support or admiration. I'll *kill* him for this, she thought, muttering Comus's imprecations for him to repeat, and her own indignant patience, loud and sad. The curtain calls were long and vociferous. Flowers were pelted at Frederica, who glowered at Watson and gathered them up.

At the following party a surprising number of this audience turned up.

Harvey was talking to Edmund Wilkie and Vincent Hodgkiss.

"Brave girl," said Wilkie.

"What a shambles," said Harvey.

"You should be cast as Circe," said Hodgkiss. "You were wasted on that thankless prude."

"What I think," said Frederica, "is that chastity is—is personal *integrity*—that's what it's about."

"*Integer vitae.*"

"Do you know," said Wilkie, "that Vincent Hodgkiss here is going to your part of the world?"

"My part?"

"I've accepted the philosophy chair at North Yorkshire. I like the interdisciplinary idea."

"I'm thinking of going up there myself," said Wilkie. "I've been offered a lab and some money to do some work on perception and brain structure. I like it up there. The air's bracing. They have the inauguration in September."

Raphael Faber came silently behind Frederica. His voice was, for the first time, warm and personal.

"I admired you so much for just *going on*. Your courage appalls me. I should have cringed and crept away. I could never have stood there and gone on——"

"What else could I do? Anyway, I saw you laughing."

"It was so ludicrous. Forgive me. And then I understand, terribly humiliating. You are a brave woman."

"I was a cross one. It was a silly joke, by a friend."

"How, a joke? I don't understand."

She did not want him to understand.

"It doesn't matter. Just a joke."

Freddie Ravenscar's friends said it was all shriekingly comic and Frederica was jolly sporting and the plot seemed a bit daft anyway, and in need of livening up. Freddie introduced Frederica to the dark young man.

"Nigel Reiver. An old school friend. He came up for May Week, and when I got this note saying you'd like us to come and support this show I brought him along to cheer."

"I enjoyed it," said Nigel Reiver.

"You got a *note*," said Frederica. "I didn't write any note . . ."

"It wasn't your writing. But I thought . . ."

"It was a mean joke by Tony Watson."

"I liked the way you handled Manchester," said Nigel Reiver, who had not been listening. "He's a bloody good driver, when sober, but not cut out for this sort of caper."

"He looks the part," said Frederica. "He's extravagantly handsome."

"Extravagantly handsome," repeated Nigel Reiver, savoring the phrase. "Do you really think so?"

"Oh, yes. Not my type, but definitely handsome."

"What is your type?"

Frederica looked around the room, at Freddie, at Wilkie, at Hugh, at Marius, at Tony and Alan, at Raphael Faber talking seriously to Ann Lewis, and back to her interlocutor.

"I know when I meet them. I'm eclectic."

"Eclectic." He savored that word, too. "But you know what you like?"

"Don't we all?" She was a little drunk.

"Sometimes we get surprises."

He wasn't looking at her. Like so many men at so many parties, but more lazily, less nervously, he was scanning the company for interest, threat, attraction. He was solid and not tall, dark and a little sullen looking, with full blue cheeks. Then he lifted his head and looked her in the eye.

"Sometimes we get surprises. You must always make allowances for being thoroughly surprised, tomorrow or the next day."

She looked away.

"I shall. I'm sure I always do. I shall make allowances."

"Good."

It was Alan who took her back to Newnham. There, he said, "That wasn't really very nice of Tony."

"It was only really nasty if I'd conducted my life *furtively*, which I haven't. But it was a bit horrible. I felt like an *object*, made into an object."

"Sometimes you behave as though you were the only subject."

"All of us do that."

"You do it so obviously."

"Oh, Alan. I want to be part of things. You get shut out, as a woman."

"You're at the center. In a way most men can't be."

"Yes, but they're together and I'm alone."

"Newnham's full of women."

"Women don't live in groups happily."

"Nonsense. They would if they felt free to choose to. Don't cry, Frederica, you can't cry."

"I can, I'm humiliated."

"Nonsense. Come to our May Ball with me? We could have a companionable evening."

"So we could. I'm going to Trinity, with Freddie."

"That'll be glamorous. We'll have fun."

"Alan—you are my friend—forever—you are my *friend*."

"Do stop crying. Yes, I'm your friend. Not a wholly nice person, but your friend. Now, go in, and go to bed, and dream of—"

She dreamed that she was at bay, pursued and cornered by man-faced beasts, pards and libbards, Tony and Alan, Harvey and Nigel Reiver. She was trying to find Raphael Faber in the dark wood, and trees became men, and men became panthers and sports cars, but Raphael Faber remained elusive.

Frederica went to her two May Balls in the same dress. She had one cocktail dress and one full-length ball dress each year. The 1956 one was made by a friend who helped with the ADC wardrobe, to Frederica's specifications. The cloth was cotton, then a new cloth for evening dress. The color was graphite, with a slight sheen, like lakes in soft pencil on cartridge paper. Seeing this cloth Frederica had immediately known it was right. Not that it would do, nor that it wouldn't clash with pale gingery flesh and hair, but that it was right. The texture was crisp but not as solid as taffeta or poplin; it was capable of floating. Frederica profited from many lessons, including medical Martin's views on girls who took no account of their own bodies. She fitted the top to her thinness, with a severe round neck, not too low, and wide, with clean-cut, unfussy chemise shoulders. The waist was slightly dropped so that her long torso was straight and silvery like a pencil—from there the skirt, cut on the bias, flowed and floated over stiffened net. Those were the days of the boned basque, so that Frederica could both smooth her waist to her hips and push up her small breasts into neat decorous cones under the gray shimmer, their freckled division just, only just visible. From Freddie she had learned not to wear imitation-lace three-quarter gloves; she wore little white cotton ones. From Marius she had learned that her mouth was better painted paler and from the actors how to extend her eyebrows, draw triangles at the corner of her eyes, put her hair over a false doughnut to make a balancing knot. In the Newnham mirror before the Trinity Ball she looked at the lovely color her ginger had become against the graphite and gave a sigh of satisfaction. She packed a black cigarette holder in a black clutch bag and put on black sandals. It was the best moment of the ball.

She found herself thinking often and often, during the aimless hours that followed, of Jane Austen's balls, fourteen couples and an energetic pattern of set dances that made everyone part of one group. Freddie's dancing was anxious and Freddie was anxious about himself —the root of his criticism of others. They formed part of a group of six or eight who sat together for smoked salmon and champagne, strawberries and cream, at a card table in a hot tent. They talked almost entirely about common acquaintances, whom Frederica didn't know. "Did you go to Hep's funny party?" "Did you know Madeleine has now got a thing about Derek, which is ghastly for both Julian and Debbie?" They talked about clothes and where to get them; they wore strapless dresses with little pleated busts; none of the other women was an undergraduate. Someone called Roland trod on her sandal and laddered her stocking. Someone called Paul told a frightfully funny story about a noisy lavatory cistern in a country hotel where someone had gone for a dirty weekend. Balls would be all right if you were in a state of early total obsession with your partner's body —she had observed several cases of this, bright clinging pairs drifting among the jigging and trotting. Or if you were a professional ballroom dancer, though the floor space was inadequate for flourishes. Or if you were the sort of writer with an ear for limited repetitions of limited phrases, which she was not, and did not wish to be. About halfway through she was suddenly touched on the arm by a stranger who said, "May I have this dance?"

Freddie was talking to his neighbor. Frederica said, "I don't know."

"Tell Freddie just this dance."

She recognized Nigel Reiver, whose evening clothes fit him, who was not smiling. Freddie turned and smiled, and Frederica rose to her feet.

Nigel could dance. He could make Frederica, no natural but no nincompoop, dance too. He looked after her.

"Two little steps, *slide*, come inside my arm, turn, there's the corner, lovely. You follow very well, for an independent woman."

His pelvis pushed hers. His hand was cool and light and hard on her backbone. "*Swoop*," he said, negotiating a corner, "turn on the spot, I'll do this, lovely, now let's do it again."

"How do you know I'm an independent woman?"

"You are, aren't you? Besides, I've asked around. You're somebody."

"And you? What are you?"

"Oh, I have a house. In the country. I put a lot into the house. Family's involved in shipping. I do things for my uncle, with the ships. Mark time, don't go forward until I—*now*, slide, step, step— wonder who invented dancing."

"Human beings have always danced, surely."

"Take the English to make it embarrassing and unnatural." That was out of character, as she had read him. "Prefer Greek folk dancing. That's my foot. You could do with lessons. Glad you can't do *everything* perfectly."

"All I *can* do, I assure you, is exams."

"Oh, no. I can't tell people who can do exams, not my field. But I can tell people who can."

"Can what?"

"Never mind. I'll wait and see if I was right."

And the abrasive and padded pelvis, wholly intimate and politely distant, butted her own, and she felt a quiver of excitement, noted and suppressed.

"Take you back to Freddie," said Nigel. "See you around."

Freddie's pelvis fell away like a tired feather pillow. Freddie's hand was clammy, however well cut his hair, well polished his shoes. Flowers on the tables between silver bowls of punch wilted and were deleted by theft and accident. The long night ground slowly on, punctuated by walks to the lavatory, where, on the fifth visit, she discerned the gray dawn through a high window. Then, too late, dejected, they walked ritually along the Backs and saw the willows in the first pink and yellow of the morning, and went back to Freddie's room and yawned their healthy young way through a real breakfast— kidneys, scrambled eggs, bacon, mushrooms, coffee, toast, the second sensuous pleasure of this long night of pleasure, Frederica thought grimly, the first being of course the satisfactory sight of herself in her gray dress in the mirror.

There was twenty-four hours to recover before the ball at St. Michael and All Angels, and Frederica slept, catlike, for twelve of them before panicking about ironing and freshening her one dress. If the view in the mirror pleased her less—there was gray under the eyes to match the slaty cotton—the ball was better.

Trinity's tent was green and white. St. Michael's was deep rose; people eating in its light looked warm and fleshly. In the gray hall the lighting was also rosy, deepening wood brown, fleshing the gray skeleton fans of pillars and vaulting with light. Jiving with Alan Melville was a matter of courteous and dubious fingertip contact, of harmonious untouching parallels of movement, divorced and peaceably solitary circling. Dancing with him was like dancing with the fan vaulting, with a cool bone structure covered in air and light. His touch was dry and warm and minimal.

They sat in the tent and ate smoked chicken.
"Does Raphael Faber come to May Balls?"
"I doubt it. Can you imagine him dancing?"
"Oh, exquisitely. If he wanted to."
"But he wouldn't want to. He's probably gone away. For peace and quiet. A lot of the dons do."
"Where would he go?"
"To his mother and sisters."
"Shall we look?"
"What else did we come for?"
St. Michael's was a small closed college. Raphael's rooms were at the top of a building that looked down onto a cobbled courtyard on one side and out over the Backs on the other. Thus, both from the courtyard and the sloping lawn or the walled garden you could see

the illuminated frame of his window if he was in. During rehearsals, visiting Hugh, or Alan, or Harvey Organ, Frederica always lifted her head to look for that rectangle of light. Tonight, there it was, yellow in white on gray. The scholar's lamp. The inside she was outside.

"Let's go up."

"Will he mind?"

"If he does, he'll say."

It was unclear whether Raphael had sported his oak, closed the heavy second door whose civilized presence ensures privacy. It was very slightly ajar. Alan pulled it farther open and knocked on the inner door. No answer. He knocked again, and, hearing some inner sound inaudible to Frederica, made his way in. Raphael was alone, stretched on the sofa, in gray high-necked sweater and trousers. He sounded irritable.

"Who is it?"

"Alan and Frederica. We got tired of enjoying ourselves and came to call. Throw us out, if you're busy."

Music swirled up from the courtyard, a din and melodic hum.

"How can I be busy in this racket? Would you like tea or coffee? I was trying to read Pascal. And failing."

He went into his little kitchen. Frederica went to look at her face in the mirror over the hearth, pushing stray wisps of hair into the knot. Alan came and stood beside her. Raphael came back from the kitchen and stood between them, one arm on each shoulder, the black male, the naked female with its silver strap. There were their three faces: Alan, triangular, a little sly, above his slanting bow tie, herself white, eager, hungry looking, above her naked chest and peeping breasts, and behind, the third, dark Raphael, meeting his own eyes in the glass. In the mirror Alan's reversed eyes met Frederica's, and both smiled at Raphael's intent look at Raphael. It was the first time he had touched her. His woolen arm was light on her skin, his fine fingers briefly, briefly smoothed her upper arm, pinched a caress, fluttered away. They sat down and talked, about Pascal mostly. There was no urgency to talk, the coffee was good, there was, as always, spiced cake. It was the quintessence of Cambridge, music, dance, closed courts, and, high above, civilized talk about Pascal. When they left Raphael touched her again, briefly, more certainly. "Do come again, you are always welcome." He added, "I hope you'll be here during the Long Vac Term." And Frederica, immediately, said, "Yes. Of course."

Frederica traveled back to Blesford with Edmund Wilkie, who had business at the new university, and obligingly pushed her across Calverley station on a luggage trolley when she became overtaken by nausea and dizziness. The family doctor diagnosed German measles. "A good thing, young woman, to become immune to that before you want to marry and produce a family." Frederica tossed her raw and flaming face from side to side and did not say that she had, partly, no desire to do these things. Stephanie and her family did not visit for fear of infection. Frederica was partly glad. Will and Mary disturbed her. She did not want to dandle them but the fact that they were there, and living, gave her a primitive pleasure. German measles damaged embryos. She considered the mess of semen and contraceptive jelly that had worked its way in and out of her and thought embryos unlikely. She believed in her own "luck." Luck being the non-engendering of embryos.

Winifred came up with soothing dishes, chicken soup and beef tea, and in the evening warm bread and milk with a dusting of sugar, a sickbed dish known in Frederica's childhood as "pobs." Winifred did not ask about Cambridge and Frederica did not tell her. She did ask if Frederica was comfortable, and did plump pillows. Frederica felt her presence there as a tolerated continuity. Winifred, good cateress, was doing what she had always done. Frederica did not discover, then or ever, that the silent female form, bearing dish and napkin, was in fact burning. Winifred loathed the sight of the young leggy body, sprawled in its damp nightdress, where once her child had been. She stood in the kitchen with the dry, bloodless fire rising in her and drove herself to wait on this least needy of her children only through pride. Her days for child care were over, her body no longer fit to bear more. And here was this creature, the length of whose limbs was some kind of insult, acquiescing briefly in being waited on. I am like a dried-up stick, Winifred told herself. I should be left alone. She knew as well as her daughter that this was no homecoming.

Bill himself came too, pained for her and embarrassed by her hot red tossing. He congratulated her on her First in Part I, somewhat routinely, as though he had expected no less of her, and asked how it had gone. She told him crossly that she had learned so much, so much by heart, and hadn't written it down in the papers, and now daily remembered less and less of it. Pages and pages: *A Tale of a Tub, Piers Plowman, A Death in the Desert, Empedocles on Etna*. To what end? This interested Bill. A good memory, he said, was a priceless possession, an essential part of human culture. He himself, he confessed to his feverish daughter, increasingly forgot names. "Why do *names* go first? I spent minutes yesterday looking for Leslie Stephen, panicked, lost Virginia Woolf too, and the DNB, and ended up idiotically referring to "the distinguished father of the author of *To the Lighthouse*." Absurd. You inherited a good memory from me. You all did. Look after it. Train it. It's our link with our kind."

Frederica thought she had inherited it in the form most like the one it took in him. She had inherited greed for learning, greed for knowledge and information, as surely as she had inherited red hair, sharpness, and something that could euphemistically be called impatience, from him. Where do inherited characteristics cease and acquired characteristics begin, she was to ask later. The life of English literature lived in her like genes for red hair and irritable movements of the hands and mouth. From Bill she had learned to learn poetry, to shape an argument, to recognize forms of thought. Where is the borderline between nature and culture? Gerard Wijnnobel believed that the neural links of the brain itself in all probability provided the material fusions and connections that allowed all human creatures to recognize certain grammatical structures as certainly as they are born with a geometric capacity to organize perceptions into horizontals and verticals, round shapes and cubes. Was it possible to inherit an ear for language as one might inherit perfect pitch or mathematical intuition? And did this bear any relation to inheriting Shakespeare's vocabulary and rhythms, Lawrence's pugnacity, Milton's artifice and self-assurance?

She talked also to Bill about Marcus. Bill said, "He seems to be getting on. I feel he only does so on condition I show no interest."

"That's a bit extreme. He has to make his own way. That's normal."

"I do know, Frederica, contrary to what you all seem to believe, that one's children are not brought into the world to do what one has left undone. But I care about a sense of continuity. A handing on of values."

"I don't know. You *are* your present and your future. And I am mine. Like Napoleon, being his own dynasty."

She wanted Bill to say, "*You* are the one like me, the one who will carry on," though she would immediately have disputed this had he said it. But she had carefully made this sentence impossible for him. And he was discouraged by Marcus's retreat, and Stephanie's withdrawal from the race.

"You'll be all right," he said, in fact, not with his old cocky fire but with an apprehensive assertiveness, as though for him to say it increased the chances of its not being true. He looked down at her thoughtfully, seeing perhaps in her infested face, with its whorls of deep rose stippling, its hot and gritty skin, an unacceptable mirror image of himself. Frederica supposed, and intermittently minded, that Bill cared more in his thwarting, passionate, pedantic way about both Stephanie and Marcus than about herself. Part of him responded to Stephanie's acquiescent womanliness as he did, she supposed, to his silent wife. Marcus he had tried to drive as he drove himself. As though immortality of the body ran through the daughter and the life of the mind through the son. And she, Frederica, more like him— surely, surely?—impressed him less as woman and as mind.

Her mind played tricks during this illness. She savored the pobs and wondered if they could be a Yorkshire version of Proust's madeleine. They had what she always thought of as a white taste, the different whites of soft bread, glistening sugar, creamy milk. She did remember earlier Fredericas, supping with sore throats in blackout wartime nights, being coaxed by Winifred to get her strength back after whooping cough. But there was no revelation, partly because, Proust would doubtless have said, she was willing one too consciously, partly because she did not want her brief past, she wanted her unknown future, which weighed on her as the vast unread expanse of *A la Recherche*, undertaken for Raphael, weighed on her sense of form. During the worst days, she read neither Proust nor anything else. She floated delirious, separate from herself, thinking clearly that someone in the room was hot and wet and uncomfortable. She heard herself, from a distance, reciting over and over the whole of *Comus*, chanting expressionlessly and rhythmically all the words, with no change in pace or emphasis between temptation and riposte, display of excess and plea for temperance. Everything came together. Raphael's gentle pinch, Alan's distant dancing, Hugh Pink's rosy fervor, the crew of suitors in their rows of chairs, the Lady of Christ's, Marcel Proust and the half-learned order of Italian grammar jumbled together with the doubleness of her feeling for Cambridge, her desire to be let into its closed courts, her sense that it was a dangerous bower of bliss, like Comus's magic structures. Feverishly she recited and thought about the young men, the beautiful, the lively, the intent, the scrupulous, the soft, the strutting, the randy, the hot-breathing, seed-spilling, urgent young men. (She did not say, the loving, the hurt, the fearful, though she could have done.) The false seducer's rhetoric of too much associated itself with the too much of male Cambridge, thronging the seas with spawn innumerable.

She saw young men round the bare walls of her small room, like the cut-out friezes of dancing figures, hands and ankles joined, that she had made as a child, or, more palely, like a satyr dance on a Greek vase. Language gripped and drove her.

> "If all the world
> Should in a pet of temperance feed on pulse
> Drink the clear stream and nothing wear but frieze
> The all-giver would be unthanked . . ."

The word frieze indeed perhaps called up the frieze of dancing youths on whom her imagination pinned or painted the various individual pricks or penises her intuition of a concrete universal had detected in Raphael's mangroves. Somehow Marcus's pollen and Proust's garden of girls, *les jeunes filles en fleurs*, added themselves to this vision, the young men danced in the Fellows' Garden among pink cups and tall blue spikes. The excess gold dust sifted onto passing soft-winged creatures. They did not shade, they shone. By the light of young men in flower. What could be the right French word? Lumière, brilliance, luisance . . . The earth cumbered, and the winged air darked with plumes . . . Who would be quite surcharged with her own weight . . . And strangled with her waste fertility . . .

24

TWO MEN

Most of her friends were not in Cambridge over the summer. They were in Stratford and Orkney, Basingstoke and Athens, Dublin, Bayreuth, and Perpignan. Raphael, seen in the University Library, expressed benign approval of her learning Italian in order to read Dante, and invited her, irregularly and with varying degrees of warmth, to come to tea. She felt neither that she was making progress, nor that it was entirely hopeless and silly. He told her to read things, and she read them. He discussed her progress with Proust. And one day Nigel Reiver surprised her by simply turning up and inviting her out for a drive in the country.

"I was working."

"It's a lovely day. I've got a new car. We could have tea at that place where people have tea. Or somewhere else."

She said yes, because the idea of being outside Cambridge, outside its laws and passionate priorities, attracted her. He had a black sports car with an open roof. Frederica sat beside him in the airflow and did not look at him. His hand moved on the gear lever, his legs decisively teased and drove home accelerator, brake, and clutch. He took corners fast, sharply, and in a way that always shocked her, so that she had to brace herself with a hand, recover her balance. He did not apologize for these inconveniences. They had tea, not in Grantchester, which was impossibly full of tourists, but in Ely, under the shadow of the cathedral. He asked polite questions about Cambridge, her holiday plans. Frederica asked, after a time, why he had asked her to tea. He replied that he liked a girl with more in her head than clothes and grabbing the nearest male. Frederica felt that his attention was not on this chat, though she also felt that his attention was directed toward her, in a way she could neither sum up nor respond to. He revealed a little more about himself. His father, now dead, had been a colonel in the regular army. His mother lived in Hereford. He had two sisters. He had inherited a listed dwelling, an old place in the West Country, Tudor and later. He described it, giving this his full attention—the little hall, the parlor, the winding staircases, the gallery, the dairy, the flower garden, the herb garden, the orchard, listing varieties of apple and plum. "And there's a moat," he added. "A good one. It had no water in, only green slime and old clods. I've seen to that." Frederica imagined a scaled-down Long Royston, a history of generations of private lives. The stables needed a lot of work, too, Nigel said, but were now spick and span. Did she ride? No, said Frederica. She had had no opportunity. Nigel Reiver said he was sure she would do well, if she had a go. He said this seriously, not mockingly, and again she noticed the disproportion of his face, the slight coarseness of the dark lower jaw, the quickness of hand and eye, the attention in reserve for something else.

They looked around Ely Cathedral where he revealed unexpected characteristics, though Frederica caught herself up sharply on this word later, asking herself what could be "unexpected" about someone about whom she knew next to nothing. He was, as a sightseer, an intense observer of minutiae, turning back misericords and studying them with eye and fingers, laughing over a woman beating a fox, commenting on the mixture of woodenness and living shapes in an owl with a mouse, drawing his finger along the yowl of a tortured demon, or around a plump acorn, adding no historical or aesthetic information, simply seeing and taking pleasure in representation. Frederica was reminded of Alexander Wedderburn's finger tracing the shoulders and haunches of Rodin's Danaïde. She would not have caressed wood and stone so. Her sensuality was to find a word for the shape; "plump" was her word, also "yowl." What Nigel said was "Look at this, the, this is *right,* hunh?"—but his finger knew, as his responding grimace acknowledged, the medieval artist's knowledge of the pull of lips and throat in agony.

He took her to see the *Seven Samurai* at the Arts Cinema, in an uncut version. Frederica began watching this in a Cambridge mood, looking for structure, recurring motifs, moral form. Nigel sat very still, absorbed. After a time something strange happened to Frederica, which, being Frederica, she observed, without impeding the happening. She began to believe the film, to suffer with its people, to feel fear, hope, love, and hatred as she had not simply done since childhood, since *Robin Hood* and *David Copperfield, Redgauntlet* and *Ivanhoe.*

It was perhaps for a perpetuation of this willing suspension of disbelief for the moment that those like herself committed themselves to the study of literature. Afterward Nigel talked with exact recall and entirely as he would have talked if the men they had watched had been real soldiers, not actors, not celluloid shadows of actors disposed in a square, deployed in a narrative frame. "That was the tensest moment," he said. "And you saw the bit of grass so clearly, it's funny how that happens at those moments—" Or, "You could tell he could hurt anyone at all and think nothing of it." And Frederica, dazed by poetic faith, dazzled by the clarity of her perception of the innocence lost by study, found his language the most appropriate language that could be spoken, direct, discriminating, enthusiastic.

He took her to dinner out of Cambridge, in a restaurant she'd heard of but never visited, and bought delicacies with the same exact and judicious pleasure he'd shown over the carved mouse or the description of the trees in his orchard. "Let me order for you," he said. "I know the menu." And introduced Frederica to a smoked trout mousse, a steak in flaky pastry, an apple crêpe, none of which she would have chosen for herself, all of which she remembered and savored.

He told her about an expedition he'd been on, up to the source of the Nile, with five other men who'd been in his regiment in the army. He was not a perfect storyteller. Frederica formed no very clear impression of any of his companions, a bastard in his way, a decent enough chap, pigheaded devil, glutton for punishment, and could not take in the details of the assembly and dismantling of collapsible boats. Nor did she vicariously see the clear and bright-pointed heavens over white sand, or dark vegetation—"The stars were very close and clear; they are out there," said Nigel. Nor did she feel the bursting thorax, the dehydration, the heavy legs and flooding well-being of fit men relaxing used bodies after battles with boiling rapids or long hot climbs. He said, "It was all right, out there, it was real, all right, you knew what you *were*," and she could feel that he was telling a truth, without knowing what truth. She liked him when he was telling this threadbare tale of great effort in an alien world. She liked him less when he told her a story of his school days, about a silly bugger they'd locked in the fives court all night in the freezing cold to punish him for some indecency of dress or comportment. "That wasn't very nice," said Frederica. "No, I suppose it wasn't, looking back," said Nigel Reiver. "But it was damned funny at the time, listening to him roaring and bellowing for help, I can tell you, damned funny." He put back his head and laughed, happily and alone.

He left her outside Newnham in the dark. She offered her face, in payment, out of curiosity, out of habit. He touched her cheek as he'd touched the yowling demon, brushed warm dry lips over the bridge of her nose and cheekbone, and said "Not yet" with the authority of some code she didn't know and was almost sure was irrelevant anyway.

Next time she went to tea with Raphael, Vincent Hodgkiss was there. He was often there, and usually left when she arrived. She was not quite sure—despite talking to him after the *Comus* debacle—whether he remembered exactly who she was, or the circumstances of their first meeting at the distant sunlit lunch at Les Saintes-Maries de la Mer. Today, he suddenly addressed her directly, showing that he knew perfectly well who she was and how they had met.

"We shall see you, I hope," he said, "at the inaugural junketings in North Yorkshire? Crowe tells me he hopes to reassemble the cast of Alexander's play. Rather pleasant. I'm trying to persuade Raphael here to take an interest. There's a chance to change the face of university teaching. They could do with a poet who speaks many tongues and is no mean aesthetician. But I think I shall fail. I think it hurts Raphael to move outside Cambridge—outside this lovely college—for any reason, ever."

"That's not true," said Raphael, "I am not irretrievably attached to this place. I don't believe one should care too deeply about one's surroundings."

"Then come out of them. Come north and use your imagination on concrete and girders and an Elizabethan hall of great beauty. Come on, I dare you. Come and stretch your legs on the moors. Invigorating, isn't it, Frederica?"

"Oh, yes, it is . . ."

"I should very much like to. Very much."

"But you won't," said Hodgkiss, too sharply. "Will you? At the last moment, there'll be a reason, you won't come . . ."

The two men looked at each other. Frederica was aware of a tussle of wills whose roots and form were not accessible to her. She waited patiently.

"Crowe would put you up."

"By all means ask him."

"Perhaps I will." It sounded threatening. Hodgkiss turned to Frederica. "I rely on you," he said, not making it clear whether he relied on her to persuade Raphael, or to present herself at the inauguration.

When he had gone, Raphael seemed unsettled. He paced up and down, asked Frederica brief questions about the north, and didn't seem to listen to the answers. He said, "Do you think Cambridge unfits one for the world?"

"Of course it does. It's more real—and less real—"

"Mallarmé came here. He wrote an essay on cloisters. He said the idea was repugnant to the democrat in him, the privilege, the separate towers going up, the past . . . And then he said, perhaps these old institutions were an image of an ideal *future* . . . He saw the towers as arrows rising into this time—but really he didn't like it. I tried to quote his words about towers and silence in "Lübeck Bells" but it defeated me. I couldn't link this retreat with what we—they—went through, in Europe. Fairyland. Vincent knows I— He knows I can't —he ought not to . . ."

"I feel—about Cambridge—one is either shut in it, or shut out of it—"

"I think I must be shut in. I am terribly unfitted for any life but this."

Frederica put out a hand. She said, "There *must* be men like you in the world—"

And Raphael took her hand, and said, holding it, standing beside her, looking down on lawn and river, "Vincent is right. I am afraid of the outside world. Of the inside world too, of everything, but of the outside differently. I might even say—he is right to think I have an almost phobic fear of going as far as the railway train and the journey to this new university . . ."

"Ah, no, you *can't* be like that, that you *must not*," said Frederica. "Listen—up there, the north, my country, is beautiful—well, that bit is beautiful—it's real in a different way—I can't bear you not to have seen it—*you must come*—"

And she put her hands up to his shoulders.

"Ah, you care," said Raphael, and slowly, incredibly, he bent his head, put out his own arms, drew her toward him, and kissed her on the mouth. Frederica was not Marcel Proust dissipating Albertine's kiss in pages of cross-referencing psychology, aesthetics, self-analysis, comparisons with other kisses. She breathed hard and took it in; she put up a hand to touch the dark hair and found it harsher than she had imagined it. The kiss she characterized as "thin"—it was nervously given, and drawn back birdlike immediately. Frederica said, "Oh, *please*" and clasped his thinness firmly with both arms— another surprise here, the fragility, the weakness of limp bones and chill, uncertain hands. The bird head came tentatively down again, eyes closed like some suffering saint, and again the thin nervous mouth rubbed hers, this way and that, not purposefully. Frederica thought of saying, "I love you," and thought this would certainly be too much for him, would cause him to draw back, so said his name, her own voice booming in her own ears, Raphael, Raphael.

"It's no good," he said. "I can't . . ."

Can't love? Can't get involved? Don't know how to make love? Can't like women? (A clear possibility.)

"Please—" she said, "please—don't go away, don't."

"Frederica," he said, and led her, or was led, it was unclear who initiated their tottering progress, to his sofa, where they sat side by side, holding hands. Raphael thought.

"You looked lovely in your evening dress, with Alan. You are not a beautiful woman, of course, but when I saw you . . ."

Whereas you are beautiful, Frederica wanted to say. I love you. Such directness would be like blows. She stroked the passive hand in hers. One might release him from this sleepy-frozen apprehension if one was older, or wiser, or cared less? She had never known what to do with men who did not know what to do. She remembered someone saying to her, "You know how to follow," on the dance floor, and was annoyed later to remember that it had been Nigel Reiver. She thought she might go home. She turned to Raphael and kissed his suffering face, at the eye corner, at the mouth corner, which twitched —with what? Revulsion overcome? Passive pleasure? She stood up.

"I must go. May I come back?"

"You must. You must." Eyes closed. "I'm sorry. Something upset me."

"Please don't be *sorry*. That's the last thing I—look, you are what I care about—"

"Thank you." Unshifting.

She more or less fled.

25

CULTURE

The inauguration of the new vice-chancellor took place in September, during the week when Parliament was recalled to discuss the growing Suez crisis, the Suez Canal Users' Association was set up, and President Eisenhower told the world that the United States would not be involved in a Middle East war. The new university at that time consisted of three completed buildings and a courtyard, set into the moorland at some distance from Long Royston House, reached by a partly permanent, partly temporary paved way over churned mud and harrowed fields. There were various approach roads, over which lorries and cement mixers rumbled, in dust, in peaty sprayed mud. There were half a dozen prefabricated buildings in which under-graduates would be taught and, in a basic fashion, fed. The three buildings were hexagonal heavy towers in a darkish concrete slab; they stood around the one courtyard which was paved in a bluish engineering brick. Two of them shared one wall; the other stood alone. They were and were meant to be reminiscent of northern keeps and millstone grit, older than the pleasant long, low front of Long Royston, as well as rawer and newer. At first sight their lighting was odd, at least from outside. Huge expanses of glazed window, revealing staircases winding, or even large spaces, the width of the tower, alternated with deep eyelet slits, closed and secret. The architect, a Yorkshireman, Stanley Murren, had said that the large windows were inspired by the grand and heavy front of Bess of Hardwick's monument, Hardwick Hall, more glass than wall. Stephanie and Frederica walked along country lanes to Long Royston, pushing Will and Mary in pushchairs, peered into black and watery pits or peeped through protective boarding. There was a good view of the finished tall tower from a lower lane that made it appear to stand alone on a ridge of moor, almost windowless, crowned with a bronzed dome. In Calverley Public Library and in Long Royston House plans of the whole project were displayed—clusters of hexagonal towers of different heights, moving out into the landscape, joined by covered walkways, concealing cloistered hexagonal courtyards. A honeycomb: a model of a complex molecule. Frederica liked it. Stephanie did not know what it would do to Long Royston, which it dwarfed, or to the moors, which it was eating into.

The ceremony took place in the theater, which had been built high enough in the solitary tower to be lit only from above, through a glass roof that admitted daylight or could be closed out with curved hatches like the aperture of an observatory. The stage was almost entirely surrounded by circular banks of midnight-purple upholstered theater seating, set on concrete tiers; the cemented walls were unrelieved by windows or decoration. On a raised dais on the raised stage were two very new formal armchairs, Scandinavian in inspiration, upholstered in blond leather, with the crest of the new university embossed on them. Music was played—a shrill, clear, trumpet fanfare—and the new professors and vice-chancellor proceeded to their seats and welcomed the princess who had come to present their Royal Charter. There was a nicely medieval-seeming flutter of silk and velvet hoods among the professors, scarlet, cerulean, ermine. The royal person was clothed in a perfectly matching old gold coat and jaunty feathered hat. She was attended by a lady-in-waiting in chocolate brown and cream; their two handbags glistened in the shaft of daylight in the dark upright cylinder. In the center of this shaft stood the new vice-chancellor in black silk with violet hood and violet linings, decently rich. This was Frederica's first sight of Gerard Wijnnobel. She found something slightly perplexing in the spectacle of an unusually tall and imposing figure of a man in the guise of a scholar, as though he should have succumbed to occupational hazards and ailments, the stoop, the shuffle, or perhaps found some other use for so much body as opposed to mind. His hair was dark and neat, winged with silver. He took off his tasseled cap, put on silver-rimmed neat square glasses, and gave a professional twitch to the silver microphone, which gave a mechanical cough that sighed and ran round the interior of the tower. The idea of a university, he said, was a theme to which scholars had addressed themselves and would address themselves. He intended to speak briefly of the founders' idea, his own idea, of this new university in this old place. His voice was not exactly English, and by no means transatlantic. It did not have the limpid clarity of Raphael Faber's colorless English, like water in a glass. It was a thicker medium —isinglass, in which crystals might grow. Not guttural, not explosive, nor even incorrect—only where Raphael's was appropriately elided, Wijnnobel's was all, even what the English lose, pronounced.

He talked about the education of the complete man. Of the breaking of rigid molds of study or métier. The idea of this university was embodied in its architectural project. Its buildings, which would be arranged in similar, but never identical groups, radiating along paths that joined them repeatedly and variously, recalled both the history of human culture, of human life in buildings, and the order of science, with repeated functional patterns.

The emphasis was on links. In the nineteenth century history had been a major linking force; the life of the mind was peculiarly involved in the search for origins, of species, of tongues, of societies, of beliefs. In modern realignments of old studies history became an easy and inevitable point of contact. But there were other ways. In the Renaissance both artist and scientist investigated the laws by which the world moved. Leonardo believed the artist perceived directly an immutable, if energetic and infinitely varied, order of things. Kepler had discovered the laws of planetary motion and expressed intense aesthetic delight in their beauty, and a belief in their correspondence with the Platonic-Pythagorean music of the spheres. "Beautiful" and "elegant" are adjectives commonly current among mathematicians to describe a proof and the relative value of a proof. Einstein himself described the hunger of the human soul for law as analogous in artist, scientist, philosopher, and lover. He had said, "Human nature has always tried to form for itself a simple and synoptic image of the surrounding world. It tries to construct a picture of what the human mind sees in nature. All these activities are reconciled by acts of symbolization."

Symbolization. The forms of thought. As a grammarian, Wijnnobel said, warming to his subject, he was himself a student of one of man's most powerful systems of symbols. There was research being done into the relations of natural languages and man-made languages, on the one hand, and on the other, into the forms of brain activity and perceptual development. One might go on to meditate on the fact that our cognitive capacity appears to be well matched to truth or reality only in some areas, particularly numerical and spatial forms. Human inquiry in many fields fails signally to attain any intellectual depth. Wijnnobel himself would instance our apparent incapacity to discover a scientific theory to account for normal use of language or acquisition of linguistic forms. There appears also to be some barrier between man's biology and any complex or rigorous study of the function of his memory.

Picture forming seems crucial. The physicist Max Planck believed his quest could not be carried on without some concept of a real world we shall never know, but must perpetually strive to map and discover. He speaks of the "world picture" habitually, and describes what he calls "the continual abatement of the intuitive character and ease of application of the world picture . . . The immediately experienced sense impressions, the primordial sources of scientific activity, have dropped totally out of the world picture, in which sight, hearing, and touch no longer play a part."

We cannot perhaps picture our picture making. Even with all our windows we shall only catch glimpses of the real world. I believe, with Planck, said Wijnnobel, that it is real, it is there, that it is our need and our duty and our delight to picture it. We shall not answer the question What is man? nor the harder question What is real, what is true? But our plurality of windows should surely protect us against, rather than inducing, solipsist despair. Trees in the quad grow, observed or unobserved, that is my faith, flowers bloom and apples fall. I trust we shall grow apples. A girl crosses the courtyard in a yellow dress and can be seen, optically, amorously, medically, sociologically. She is a system of mass and energy; she is pullulating with cells growing and dying; she is a motif in a Dutch painting or a modernist analysis of color and vision, she is a native speaker of Dutch, or English, she is a student of engineering, she is a member of social class A, she is an irreplaceable individual, she is an immortal soul. What Kepler discovered about optics Vermeer applied and exemplified in the light and color of the *View of Delft*. And from that painting Marcel Proust picked out the patch of yellow wall and associated it for all time—or all imaginable time—with an exact, irreducible vision of truth, order, and likeness. Great intuition—in all fields—perceives order and likeness in the differences and multitudinous movments of the universe. Intuitions of order fail, and are succeeded by others, but we persist in seeking. A university is, or should be, a model universe with many orders and intuitions. Our separate faculties make up one man, one impossible, yet imaginable man.

An anonymous donor had given the university a pair of large figures by Henry Moore. There was local argument as to whether this anonymity masked Matthew Crowe. The gift, at this early stage, had its inconveniences; the bulldozers and tractors churned what would be terraces and courtyards. Stephanie and Frederica went to see these statues in their temporary site, accompanied by Will, a trotting and taciturn two-year-old, and Mary in a folding pushchair. At the back of the one tower, through the one courtyard, they stepped out over boards to a rough terrace over the moor. The figures were incorporated into a kind of stage set of a slightly curved piece of wall, and a flight of steps abutting heather and cotton grass.

The figures were male and female. The female, hugely bulky, broad of base, fine at ankle and wrist, sat lightly poised on the steps. Her center of gravity was the base of her spine in a wrapped, layered expanse of hip and pelvis. Her small head was round eyed, like a powerful staring doll, or even a sitting bird on the nest. From knee to knee the stony, paradoxically fine folds of her garment were stretched, like lines left in sand by a receding tide. Behind her the male stood erect, like a chess piece, partly constructed of balanced cubes, with the suggestion of a breast plate or squared shield. His cleft head was raised to the sky—a helmet, an alert, staring crested bird, a reptile from which the bird was descended, its gape of mouth or comb open to the sky.

Will, on hands and feet, scurried up and down the steps, between and round the figures, picking up a pebble, a snail shell, a feather. A compulsion to belittle the female figure came over both women. Stephanie said she reminded her of how her own hips had spread since childbearing. Frederica said an earth goddess with a bird brain was hardly an inspiration to a generation of female undergraduates. Will rushed horizontally across a step and clutched the stone knee, as at home, in the kitchen, to his and her great danger, he clung to Stephanie's legs as she fried or lifted joints from the oven.

"He knows what she is," said Stephanie. "Stability."

"If, just for once, women could be fire and air," Frederica said to her sister.

"Not till they die, if you're quoting that," said Stephanie placidly. "We are earth and water; it seems to fit." She thought. "Anyway I like the earth. Rocks and stones and trees; I like the earth."

Frederica, restraining Will from climbing into the huge, receptive stone lap, was put in mind of Dame Nature, hutching the all-worshipped ore in her loins to deck her sons. From above a voice hailed them. The Long Royston party descended: Matthew Crowe, Alexander Wedderburn, Edmund Wilkie, Vincent Hodgkiss, Thomas Poole.

"A princely gift," said Crowe, waving at the figures. "Good morning, ladies."

Frederica was struggling with Will. Alexander asked Stephanie how she found the work. Powerful, said Stephanie, and Frederica, from above, cried out that they found the female threatening.

"The male," said Wilkie, "has aspirations. He erects the bulk of stone in an ingenious upward spiral. He is not content, as she is."

Thomas Poole admired the baby. He had, he said, one of his own, a boy, more or less the same size. A delightful age, they noticed everything. Mary spread wide arms and rotated her little hands on her fat wrists, seeming to sift and clutch the air. There was a little moorland breeze in the soft red silk on her skull; she murmured syllables, ba, ma, da. Will's little hand, firmly grasped in Frederica's, was dry and warm. His body was still an awkward cartwheel of reluctance.

Alexander offered to push Mary. Thomas said he was practiced. Alexander bent over Mary to hide his face and saw for the first time the red stain on hers, no longer bloated and jellylike but almost painted over the invisible fair eyebrow, a rosy-russet, flecked with golden-brown.

"They say it will go," Stephanie said. Mary puckered her face suspiciously at Alexander, who touched it, gently enough, and Frederica watched the baby weigh matters and decide against howling. They all walked back to an accompaniment of Crowe's evocations of buildings yet to be. Here, where sand and muddy girders soughed in a wet pit, would be the language tower. There, behind a run of gray board fence, padlocked and posted with warnings of danger, would be the life sciences.

"And Professor Wijnnobel's apple trees?" said Frederica, haunted by the concrete imagery of the inaugural lecture, the windows, wide and narrow, looking in or out, the girl in the yellow dress under apple trees, Max Planck's paradoxical world picture of a reality measured not by the sensual ear, eye, or touch but by instruments she was quite unable to picture.

"I have my orchard still," said Crowe. "My russet apples and Ellison's oranges, Reinettes and Laxtons. I do not know where the vice-chancellor envisages his trees. Eventually he will have a lodge with a garden. For the moment he is lodged in the guest rooms in the west wing. I entertain him to dinner tonight in my antiquated turret. I hope you will all join us later for coffee and drinks. Do come."

Frederica went, and listened to talk of the future and gossip about chairs and wrangles. Raphael was not there. She had had to ask Hodgkiss, in the theater tower, and Hodgkiss had said, "He could not bring himself to—I knew he could not. He goes up and down between St. Michael's and the library. An ideal life, frightening in its monotony."

Stephanie was also absent. She had surprised herself by feeling acute social fear at the thought of an evening of talk in Crowe's hothouse. She had grown used to the mumblings of the dependents, the life stories of Daniel's Mum, the babble of William, the murmur of Mary. She would have been surprised to know that Alexander noticed and regretted her absence. He had fleetingly thought, very vaguely, that she might be the person to tell about Simon Vincent Poole; she was judicious, she took things in, she did not fling out. But she was not there, and Frederica was. He talked to Frederica about Vincent Van Gogh.

26

HISTORY

Frederica's final year in Cambridge began with the Suez crisis, and contained other incursions from, excursions into, the world out there. Later she saw this year emblematically in an image of the isolation of this fenland town on the way to nowhere, with its carved white colleges and inviolate lawns under a threatening sky such as loured over El Greco's Toledo, or Turner's diminutive Hannibal crossing the Alps, a cosmic battle between light and dark. Someone had told her there was no high ground between the winds of Siberia and this flat patch of England, only the cold North Sea. In the year of Suez, which was also the year of Hungary, the outer world intruded not as telegrams and anger but as troop movements, sunk ships, men gunned down, a sudden urgent need to think about national identity, fears of violence, responsibility. It was not of course truly new, but Frederica, like many of her politically placid contemporaries, was unaware of revolt in East Berlin or rumblings in Poland. The Hungarian revolution, like Suez, *news*, in every sense of that word. They were—we were—a generation who had characteristically (one must immediately except Raphael Faber and Marius Moczygemba) innocently and unwittingly lived through a convulsive and exhausting piece of history. Most had felt creeping terror about human nature itself, faced with the pictures and documents of Belsen and Auschwitz, Hiroshima and Nagasaki, from which some parents sought to protect their young and to which others had thought it necessary to expose them. Frederica had correlated these terrible images with unlived knowledge acquired from literature to form a belief that human nature was dangerous and unstable. *King Lear* expanded petty spite, usual filial resentment of domineering parental folly, into a universe of mindless cruelty and grim hopelessness. Courage and prowess in the *Oresteia* met blind passion and hatred and produced a mess of horror. The companionship of men in Owen's trenches ended in frothing lungs and mutilated limbs. I record these usual images of the unspeakable in order to wonder at what kind of knowledge they were to Frederica, powerful, secondhand, undeniable. Because it is true that the beliefs from this knowledge coexisted in her with a half-disappointed, half-bourgeois unthinking certainty that a Prufrockian comfort and tedious good sense would prevail, in public, in private. (When I write "bourgeois" I mean the word in the sense in which Frederica had learned to understand it as a term of opprobrium from reading *La Nausée*.) Boredom, to put it crudely, boredom, complacency, and stultification, were the actual enemies to be fought, not folly and ruthlessness on the grand scale. "The boredom, the horror and the glory," Eliot had written. It was no accident that Cambridge discussed the sin of *acedia*, that the word found its way into endless undergraduate literary letters, along with "bad faith," "relevance" (to what, in those apolitical days?), and other unfocused anxieties. When the first Hungarians arrived in the university in December, with their tales of street fighting, tanks, and the brave extinguished single voice on the radio, the outside world came in like an occupying army. More than one young man was called Attila, and there were Ildikos too, who seemed to have ridden in on those sweeping, uninterrupted winds. (Frederica's geography was hazy.)

This was Frederica's first experience of passionate public feeling. Friends divided, often unexpectedly, over Suez, into those who believed in the British as a "responsible" people, who were afraid of the implications of the word appeasement, and those who saw the "action" as cynical opportunism or the product of an outdated vision of imperial glory. Owen Griffiths, Tony Watson, Alan Melville, received, with degrees of derision and anxiety, military letters instructing them to hold themselves in readiness for recall. Others, including Freddie, offered their services. This may suggest that support or outrage for the government's actions divided along class lines, which was not quite true. Ideas of national honor, mild or furious xenophobia, pragmatic judgments of economic advantage, exist in blank oppositions in all parts of English society. In later years Frederica was to think at length about how matters of outraged principle, infringement of liberty, life, death, the finance of the Aswan Dam, the survival of Israel, and the perpetuation of the satellite one-party state in Hungary had become in Britain inextricably involved in matters of cultural style. Her own judgments of the Suez events were as much judgments of style as of morals. She had learned from *Passage to India* that the British empire, even if narrowly and locally just, was insensitive, overweening, and wicked through its lack of imagination and vision. She had learned that the First World War was a product of the disproportion between gentlemanly ideals of honor, courage, and patriotism and the realities of the big guns, mud, and the slaughter of conscripts. It was known then, whatever we may think now, that Kipling was a bad artist because blinkered by jingoism and boyishness. The playing fields of Eton were there to be mocked, not idealized. (Frederica hated sport.) Such learning led to seeing the Anglo-French intervention in Egyptian affairs as schoolboyish arrogance, and Frederica did. Those older than she was, working from other models, saw Colonel Nasser, demagogue and nationalist, as another Hitler, a potential enslaver of his neighbors. Frederica and her kind saw him as a spirited rebel against the exclusive *mana* and protective we-know-best of the school prefect.

But even then, and increasingly in retrospect, Frederica found it distasteful to be aligned with the equally boyish grumbles and ranting of Jimmy Porter and Jim Dixon. Imitators of these wanted to bring down the hereditary, the culturally pretentious "establishment," the prefects, and did this—in art—with a mixture of jokey brutishness and virile appropriation of the prefects' complaisant women. (It is true that a Polish politician found Lucky Jim's bizarre gestures a very just approximation to the impotent gestures that were all that was available to his own young and intelligent compatriots.) It was not easy for Frederica to sympathize with these differing assertions of British masculinity.

The Cambridge Union, where women were not admitted, held an emergency debate. Owen Griffiths went there and cried out, in incensed and well-made Welsh paragraphs, against tattered flag-waving where the needs were clean air and educational opportunity. Tony Watson went there and recounted later, gleefully, to Alan and Frederica, his experiences of a kind of rugger-scrum of exalted duffel-coated ex-officers all issuing agitated orders that went unheeded since there were no other ranks. In Newnham itself passionate advocacy of anything at all had been restricted, in Frederica's experience, to the evangelical Inter-Collegiate Christian Union, who approached strangers courageously over coffee after lunch, and the serious followers of Dr. Leavis's culturally exclusive idea of English and the university. Yet she witnessed a screaming match between two gowned women, standing on tables in Hall, and saw in this, again in retrospect, her first close study of a real clash between opposed political visions. She could not later remember what had been argued or who had been screaming on what side. Only words—"naive," "megalomania," "criminal irresponsibility," "puerile flag-waving"—flew in unaccustomed shrillness over the heads of a passionate if tentative audience of young women whose major concerns might have been assumed to be—were—love and marriage, homemaking, nebulously, just possibly, "my career."

Frederica also had a brief conversation with one of sweet Freddie's elegant relatives who had become involved in a committee that met over tea in The Blue Boar to arrange futures and housing for Hungarian refugees. This girl, a china-skinned Belinda Something, had not voluntarily spoken to Frederica except over salad at the May Ball. She now solicited her support for this new work, slightly flushed, bending forward in her eagerness, and said, "This has changed my life; this has given me a reason for living."

There were tears in her eyes. Frederica was shocked and moved. She was used to world-weary youths, but Belinda had seemed so sure that the party world, the marriage mart, were important and subtle, full of life and value. Frederica thought how little one knew about people. How easy it was to associate a certain baying vowel sound and lips-only smile with complacency. All the same, if you thought of Bill, of Alexander, of Raphael Faber, of Daniel Orton, it seemed a little absurd to need a central European revolution to reveal a purpose in life. Her own problem was the existence of too many, and conflicting, purposes.

To suggest that Frederica's life or consciousness were profoundly altered in this year by Suez or Hungary would be nonsense. She was preoccupied by the tension between Cambridge and the outside world as it affected herself. And she was in love with Raphael. She had given up so much else—including both acting and the random sexual adventures, whether because of Raphael, or as a consequence of a pregnancy scare, or out of a rudimentary awareness that she was distressing people, men, was not clear.

There were two hypothetical future Fredericas—one closed in the University Library writing something elegant and subtle on the use of metaphor in seventeenth-century religious narrative, and one in London, more nebulous, writing quite different things, witty critical journalism, maybe even a new urban novel like those of Iris Murdoch. The trouble was, she sometimes thought, that the two Fredericas were really indissolubly one. The Ph.D. writer would have died of aimlessness and spiritual vertigo without the drive of the worldly one; the worldly one would have felt like a creaking, varnished carapace without an abundant inner life. In the world of the fictive and hypothetical future, they could coexist, and Frederica took steps to promote the careers of both. She wrote an application for a Ph.D. And, at the suggestion of Alan Melville, she wrote an entry in January 1957 for the *Vogue* talent competition, consisting of an 800-word autobiography and two shorter pieces.

One of these was a travel piece on Provence, the Van Gogh landscapes, aïoli, boules, mistral, unchanged Saintes-Maries and wooden Sarah le Kâli. (Frederica liked this inadequately supported mythical identification.) The other was a list of "Hurrahs" and "Boos" for 1956 in which she included Iris Murdoch, *Waiting for Godot*, brilliantly colored shoes in variety, and the new voices of the Hungarians, under Hurrah, and Porteresque rudeness, newspaper headlines about Suez, pleated skirts that crumpled, and the U and non-U debate under Boo. "I feel," she said to Alan Melville, "as though I'm writing lists like Eliot's *Notes Towards a Definition of Culture*, beetroots and grey-hounds, Elgar and sliced cabbage. What is it about lists that is so compulsive?"

"His is a very feeble *foreigner*'s list," said Alan, the cosmopolitan Scot. "He saw what obtruded itself. Boiled cabbage doesn't *mean* much, when all's said and done, except that it tastes nasty."

"It might mean the English don't care about taste."

"Aside from the ambiguity of the word taste there," said Melville, "it doesn't give much purchase? Not as it would to say why we queue so patiently for buses without angering and beat each other up in football stands, conversely, or why we suppose the police are benign when I know as a fact from my misspent childhood that they can tear your ears off and make you throw your breakfast up, if you had any, as well as any thug."

She consulted Raphael Faber about the Ph.D. application, which went in the same week, the week in which Raphael had a long and troubled conversation with Vincent Hodgkiss about the ambivalence he felt toward Israel, the sense he had that he should be there, with other survivors like himself, fighting for survival, and the fear he had of that sense of community, the overriding need to stay where he was and think as he did, European, international, intellectual. That conversation is not part of the stuff of this novel, and Frederica was not aware of its substance, nor that it had happened, as she was unaware of the history of the foundation of Israel, the ugliness and triumphs, having been offered only a scanty biblical narrative and a simplified map of that indefensible (militarily speaking) land by an enthusiastic Scripture teacher at Blesford Girls' Grammar.

Frederica did not tell Raphael about *Vogue*. She was sure he would hold precise and prudish views about the worthlessness of that way of life. She used the word prudish, not "puritanical," because Raphael was Jewish. Fastidious also, but that wasn't quite strong enough.

Like many other projects of the time, Frederica's hypothetical thesis derived from a dictum of T. S. Eliot, in this case the one about the dissociation of sensibility that occurred between Shakespeare and Donne, who felt their thought as immediately as the odor of a rose, and Milton, who did not. It was almost as difficult in 1956 not to believe in this cataclysm, akin to Ice Ages and the consumption of the fatal apple, as it was not to believe in the Freudian unconscious, even if one essayed a proper skepticism even if one had been nurtured, as Frederica had by Bill, to approach all such assertions with a doggy, worrying opposition. So powerful was the myth of this divorce of names from things that it was almost impossible not to see Shakespeare's verse as qualitatively different from Keat's in this way, not to read Tennyson as though he failed to be Donne. Frederica had, over and over again, authentic experiences of sensuous immediacy of thought when reading Donne, and not when reading Tennyson. (This is not, in my experience, true of modern students, who see Donne as a cryptographer, a philosopher of desire, or a narrator of fictions, who do not see with the mind's eye a bracelet of bright hair about the bone, nor the bright air that clothes angels, nor gold to airy thinness beat, who do not shiver at the mind's capacity to call up a sun in a bedchamber, a star in a tomb.)

Nevertheless, Frederica told Raphael, sitting beside him on his sofa in the clear, wet Cambridge light, she wan't sure what Eliot said was true. Especially about Milton. He had been cast as the villain in this century, but before that, he was the master. He was what people were rejecting, and people always seemed to go overboard when rejecting someone or something.

Raphael held her form between his fine hands and smoothed out her folds. It was a vast topic, he said. How would she restrict it?

Frederica said there were two kinds of metaphor. Comparisons between sensuous things—Wordsworth's marvelous sea beast and his stone in the sun. And the kind that compares a human abstraction to a sensuous experience: affliction to a blunted knife, love to compasses, desire to a crumb of dust stretched from heaven to hell. The seventeenth century had problems with the second kind because the sensual world was the fallen world, and yet you must make metaphors of sweetness or brightness to describe virtue and heaven, however corruptly. Somewhere here there was a real difference between Milton's metaphors and Marvell's. And then there was a problem with the Incarnation. Immensity cloistered in thy dear womb. Or *Paradise Regained* in which Christ was a *character*, in which, she rather suspected, the whole world was built up out of imagining infinite apprehension trapped in corruptible and limited flesh. Milton's Christ was the dissociated sensibility reassociated. Possibly. She would have to see.

Raphael said that what she was talking about was a work of incalculable theoretical complexity, a lifework, and that there had only been nine Ph.D.s awarded in English since the war. Frederica retorted, not wholly truthfully, that what she wanted was precisely a lifework, comparable to Raphael's own, and that there had to be a tenth Ph.D. someday, didn't there? She added that she had hoped it might be possible for Raphael to supervise this work.

"Hardly," said Raphael. He stood up, and stood in the hearth, his hands behind his back, smiling down at her. He had a habit of smiling —to himself—when he found himself in a position to speak sharply. It was not a nervous smile, but the smile of someone about to place a dart accurately. Frederica thought of it as his angelic smile, partly because it resembled an expression she thought she remembered on the face of the monumental St. Michael, pinning down the dragon in the Boul' Mich' in Paris.

"Why not?" she said.

"Well, in the first place, it's neither my faculty nor my period. You need a theologian."

"I've learned more from you than from anyone else here."

"That may be. It doesn't affect my professional competence. In the second place, there would be a clash of temperaments."

"Oh, *no.*"

"You are a very willful young woman. You would take neither direction nor correction easily. Whereas I like to direct postgraduate work very precisely. The English respect for amateur muddling through is a major reason for the few successes there have been."

"I *need* direction, I do."

Raphael smiled again, and told her, "You have no idea what direction is."

"I admire you. I can learn, from people I admire."

"You have strong feelings about me. I have no desire or pretension to experience a transference outside an analysis."

The word offended and hurt Frederica. She cast for an answer. "It *isn't* a transference" was feeble. An assertion of independent-mindedness could be categorized as willful. Willful was one of Raphael's words—always derogatory, it appeared in surprising places where Frederica could see nothing but indifferent exercise of free choices.

She remembered another woman saying, "Of course women are always making intellectual passes at him," and saw herself proferring her printed form as though she had extended naked legs along his couch, or swayed in like the cigarette girls in films, a tray slung on webbing protruding between jutting bosom and fanny. Raphael smoothed his coat collar.

"Thirdly, or maybe firstly, I find the subject antipathetic."

"How?"

"I am a Jew. A Jew whose upbringing has predisposed me for and against Milton. I was taught English by a Lutheran scholar who found his theology acceptable and his verse overwhelming and made me learn huge stretches when I was far too young to understand it. Partly, still, I admire the ambition. *Tout existe pour aboutir à un livre.* He had the impudence to try to rewrite the original Book. But then— he is so heavy-handed, so pompous, so absurd. Everything that shouldn't be, God and the angelic orders, made horribly concrete and trivialized."

"I thought—he set his mind against making things concrete. From *Comus* to *Paradise Regained* is such a long step. From a world teeming with *things* to such an austere vision of—of images, of the desert."

"Oh, he knew. Thou shalt not make any graven images. The Puritans were iconoclasts; they broke the lovely images the early Church was full of, the virgins and saints and angels. But—as I see it—the Christian religion itself is the final presumptuous image-making. I find the Incarnation absurd. I don't say you haven't got something, about the metaphoric difficulty of making a *character* out of incarnate Christ. But you can't expect me not to feel a little repelled. It's simply the final graven image, from my point of view."

Frederica felt a rush of understanding: in this prohibition, the reason for not inventing and naming characters. In this fear of the concrete image, the passion for the vanishing mind-flowers of Mallarmé.

"I've never for a moment *believed* it."

"It's your heritage, however, to take or reject. Not mine."

He was talking about himself. Their conversations—the good ones —occasionally took this form. First, the rebuff, then the small space for a personal statement, from a safe distance. Then occasionally a shy warmth. He hated, she believed, direct questions about himself.

(Not that, since the interview, she dared to ask them.) But now and then he told her things that she treasured up, memorized exactly. That he had once spent a holiday in Wales. That his sisters read every word he wrote. That as a child he had been afraid of the dark and of unopened bottles. This may have been something to do with genies (genius). Had he said that, or had she glossed it? That he worked—at his writing—from dawn to ten in the morning. That he disliked George Eliot very much. That he also disliked Merrydown cider. Tiny jigsaw pieces. And besides this patchwork, figures of vivid little quirks and curlicues, the colored and shining expanse of the Mallarmé lectures, ordered, intricate, flamboyant, controlled. What is a man? There was also the vulnerable imagery of the banyans in *Foreign Parts* which had become wickedly involved with the variable penises sprouting on the imagined paper frieze of *jeunes gens en fleurs* during her German-measles delirium. What is a man? How do we know?

"You could teach me how to look at the theology."

"I couldn't teach you how I see it. It's in the blood."

"But we can *talk* about metaphor, civilized talk. We live in the same world."

He smiled, a composed, benevolent smile.

"We could certainly talk about metaphors. We do."

"There are Old Testament metaphors that are part of the thing I want to study. The Song of Songs."

"Ah," said Raphael.

"You don't," Frederica said bravely, "like making images of things —naming unreal people—you don't like the Incarnation—but that— those are so very concrete."

"Ah, yes," said Raphael. "Thy navel is like a round goblet, which wanteth not liquor: they belly is like an heap of wheat set about with lilies. Thy two breasts are like two young roes that are twins. Similes, not metaphors."

His voice, reciting, had a clear twang, precise, musical, not pedantic, but fastidious and distant. His face still wore his angelic smile.

"Or the male," he said. "His hands are as gold rings set with the beryl; his belly is as bright ivory overlaid with sapphires. His legs are as pillars of marble set upon sockets of fine gold; his countenance is as Lebanon, excellent as the cedars."

How alien, thought Frederica, frightened, how alien in their chill richness, these comparisons. "A bracelet of bright hair about the bone" made her shiver; this too, but with fear of a sensibility she had no knowledge of.

"I like the plain lines between the rich concrete things. 'How beautiful are thy feet in shoes.' And 'Many waters cannot quench love, neither can the floods drown it: if a man would give all the substance of his house for love, it would utterly be contemned.' Raphael—*is* it a religious poem? I used to think it was obviously simply erotic, but now I think—"

"Of course it is religious. It is about the unimaginable fulfillment beyond the senses. You will find it at the center of your thesis."

The words were loose in the room, the bright ivory belly absurdly and dangerously shining beside the banyan penis and the flowering boys. I am sick of love, Frederica thought, and at the same time, there is no space for the imagination among all those minerals and prolific animals, teeth like washed sheep bearing twins. She looked at Raphael and laughed.

"It's exotic and sensual and very *cold*, all at once, to my sensibility," she said.

"And to mine," he said, sadly perhaps. "I like better its ghosts in Mallarmé's dreams and mirages—"

"Raphael—I wasn't asking—I didn't mean—I only wanted—"

"Oh, I know." He came near, walking in a swarm of ivory and gold, myrrh and breasts, silks and soft young creatures, a thin dark man in a very clean, softly shining corduroy jacket. He put a hand on her shoulder. "I know. You only want everything. You're a formidable girl, Frederica."

"But you will at least *talk* to me about the thesis."

He relaxed suddenly. "I really doubt whether I'll have much choice in the matter, don't you? We shall sit companionably and in silence in the Anderson Room, year after year, and argue about theology and aesthetics from time to time—"

"You can always kick me out if I just bore you."

"Oh, but you don't." He brushed her brow with his lips. "Boredom is the last emotion you inspire. I am—you know—a very timorous creature. Outside my own small habitat."

"Well, let me *in*."

"Where else are you but in? Sitting on my sofa, drinking my wine, discussing my ideas? Have another glass and then you must rush away, we both have work to do."

Nigel Reiver, like the Hungarians, came in with the air of the outside world wrapped round him like a cloak of extra-visibility. He came on a day when Frederica was confined to her bed with curse pains, lying curled self-protectively under a heap of blankets, clothed in a peacock sweater above the waist, and pants and padding below. There was a line of pain like a sword slash along the groin to the aching pubic bone, and sick knots of thicker pain in the lumbar and cerebral ganglia. Her room was as usual strewn and stirred with cast-off clothing, open books, used crockery. She was trying to read, some Proust, some Racine, some Plato, the lines of words becoming attracted to the floating waves of pain as tapes are held to sheets of cloth with the minute nylon hooks of Velcro sealing. She had discovered that in these circumstances short bursts of concentration were possible. The paragraphs themselves then too settled into fortuitous relationships: Proust's Berma performing *Phèdre* in a sea-green cavern while Frederica read *Phèdre*'s speech about the fire of the sun in her blood and the soiled light, and then turned to Plato's myth of the fire in the cave. Her own gas fire boiled and bubbled sporadically; she could feel hot gouts of blood welling out. In the window over the desk geometric fish shapes made by Marius Moczygemba danced and circled on their fine threads. Nigel knocked and came in and said, "You've got this room like a hothouse."

"I'm ill. I like to boil when I'm ill; it comforts me. I didn't expect you."

"How could you? I was in Tangier. Now I'm back, so I came up to see you. On the off chance, naturally."

"I ought to be at a supervision. I feel like *death*. You only caught me because I'm dying."

"What of?"

"Bleeding," said Frederica, who believed in calling things by their names.

"That's a natural thing; that shouldn't hurt."

"What do *you* know about it? Sometimes it does, and sometimes it doesn't. This time it hurts like hell."

"Where?" said Nigel, advancing into the room. He had on a large and rather formal overcoat, a camel wool, of a kind men in Cambridge never wore; this made him appear fleetingly vulgar, though the overcoat was expensive and simple. Frederica was disconcerted. Alan or Tony or Marius or even Hugh Pink she would have invited to sit on her bed to console her, or to make themselves coffee, or to consider themselves thrown out. But she didn't feel she *knew* Nigel Reiver, and had no idea what he thought their relationship was. She had discovered by her third year in Cambridge that women were not the only sex to have powerful fantasy lives. Men dreamed, or believed, they had a special relationship, an understanding, an intimacy on the most fragile bases, an intellectual confidence that could have been made to anyone who happened to be present, a good-natured drunken kiss offered as payment for escort from a party, a childish scribbling of notes during a lecture on Mallarmé. But what rules men like Nigel Reiver worked to she had no knowledge of. If there were other men like Nigel Reiver. Places she didn't know and thought vaguely of as the Home Counties or the Shires might be full of Nigels, professions like the army, or places like the City, might support them in numbers. But the men Frederica knew were all—even the unhappy ones, even the misfits—Cambridge men.

"Where does it hurt?" he said patiently, coming nearer.

"All over. Down here—across my belly—all along my back and up my neck. I feel awful. If I were you I'd go away."

"After I've come all this way to see you? Oh, no. I can stop a lot of pains. I've got good hands. Let me have a go."

He took off the overcoat and hung it rather carefully on a hanger on the door. Underneath he had a scarlet polo neck and black-and-white tweed trousers; he was muscled and dense and broad. He held out his hands.

"Come on."

"No."

She was afraid. She didn't want him near the sweet bloody smell or the messy sheets, or her unkempt hair or her hot pillow. She felt vulnerable, like a mermaid, in her half-clothed state, her naked legs cold in their hot blanket casing.

"Oh, no."

He smiled and came on. He had a grim and slightly scornful little smile, as though her "no" was a pointless gesture, better not even made. He picked his way across her debris, not touching any of it, lifted Proust and Racine off the pillow, and sat down at her shoulder.

"Now, turn over, on your face."

"No, I—"

"Go on. There's a good girl."

As though she was a horse, or a laboring sheep. She turned over. Blood welled. She closed her eyes, briefly. Nigel spread his hands, wrists together, fingers out, and plunged them down at her shoulders, like a water diviner.

"Don't tense up so. Feel this great knot. You're making it swell. Now, let me undo it. Let go."

He had, indeed, good hands. Frederica had never experienced anything like it. It was as though he had taken all the complicated web of muscles and nerves that held together her narrow shoulders, had fingered and smoothed each of them, and had laid them back in warm sheaths so that she could feel their directions and connections in a benign heat.

"You can't be reading all these books at once."

"Yes, I can. I've got tripos in a few months. I'm good. I shall do well."

"And then what?" His fingers, the regular warm friction, probing her neck vertebrae. She thought the word impersonally, and then wondered, was it? She closed her eyes.

"I dunno. Sometimes I think I'll stay here. And do a Ph.D. I've got a topic. I've applied. I also did the *Vogue* talent contest, just for fun."

"And what do you hope to do eventually?"

"I don't know." She would not say the word marry and would not, perhaps could not, think of a convincing future without it.

"That's marvelous, what you do. I didn't know it was possible—"

"What? What was?"

"To get rid of pain like that."

"I ought to do your back."

"No."

"Come on."

"No."

"Why not?"

"It's all in a mess. I've got no clothes. I—"

"You wouldn't be the first woman I've seen. I'm interested in your *back*. At the moment. I learned a lot from a farrier I knew. He could work his way along a horse's back—so—" he turned down the sheets —"loose all the vertebrae, give the spine a sharp tap with the side of the hand"—he demonstrated, without touching her—"and you'd see the old nag sigh with relief. Click, click, freedom. Go on. Let me."

"It's all messy."

"Doesn't bother me."

He worked. Frederica relaxed and glowed, skin and flesh and bone. He talked.

"I wouldn't stay here if I were you. Enough is enough, I'd have thought. What do you want to do *eventually*? You'll want to marry."

"I don't know."

"You'll be very odd if you don't."

"That's my business. I could marry a don, and stay here."

"And what about the real world?"

"This is real. As real as anywhere."

His hands were now hot and dry. He talked. "I've been with my uncle in Tangier. He knew this Suez business was coming—he's got friends in Israel as well as in Persia and Oman and Egypt. He got it right—knew Nasser'd close the Canal, sold a whole fleet of little ships that relied on the Gulf trade, made a killing on the stock market. Bit of an old pirate my uncle Hubert. Lives in style in Tangier. M'father left him in charge of our money, the girls' and mine; he looks after us, in his funny way. The house is mine, though. I shall need a wife, to care for my house."

"Maybe she won't want to have been married for the sake of a house."

"I won't marry her for its sake. It'll be for mine. I know what I want."

"What do you want?" Lulled and stretched out, the long line of spiked bones supple and throbbing.

"I want something *not boring* most of all. Sexy, of course, and warm and kind, but lots of women are that. Only most women are *so boring*."

"Maybe they find you boring."

"Possibly. That's not the point. I doubt if *you*'d even understand what I'm talking about. You aren't bored and you don't bore—you'd make your own amusement anywhere, I suppose. Wouldn't you?"

Not in Blesford.

"Yes. I would. On principle."

"I knew it."

She wanted to say, I won't marry you, you and your house; you shouldn't think it. But he hadn't asked her to marry him, and his manner of discussing her hypothetical lack of boredom made it very clear that hypothetical was what it was. He was not asking her to marry him. He explained neither why he had stayed away so long without communication, nor why he had now come back so sure of his welcome.

"You feel better now," he told her, and she agreed meekly enough, since it was true. He proposed that she get up and that they go for a drive, out of Cambridge, and she agreed to that too, for the sake mostly of the car, of speed, of the crossing of that invisible hedge between the garden and the world. She felt protected from him by the bleeding, and close to him because of the heat of his fingertips.

They drove out to Ely again, into the real world, which in that part consisted of a lattice of straight narrow roads across the tops of dykes, along which the black black fenny earth lay turned and beside which the water of the drains glinted darkly. It was a thin, unruffled reality, the same for miles through villages of impoverished cottages with a level crossing and a concrete drive with the look of a disused runway. These villages bore names like Stripwillow, names prettier and greener than they were.

When Ely's mound was distantly in sight Nigel suddenly spoke of Hereward—mostly he drove in silence. He said, "It all seems smaller than I thought of it when I was a boy, when I read *Hereward the Wake*. I really lived in that book, you know. Great stuff. Hereward the Berserker, the brain hewer, the land thief, the sea thief."

He stopped the car; it was the end of dusk; they looked along the gray road and the brown bracken-and-bramble dyke and the secret black water. She thought he would try to kiss her, but he said simply, "Look."

Round and soft, heavy in size, light in its silent carriage, a huge white bird floated up and over the dyke.

"Wait," said Nigel.

There was a low sound and then a kind of choked scream, and a second bird, creamy against the thickening light, veered across the path of the first.

"Barn owls," said Nigel. "I love their stubby butts and their way of turning those great heads. Gilbert White says how soft and pliant their wing feathers are—so as not to make much resistance on rushing. Now *he's* a great writer. I read him in our library. And Parson Kilvert. And W. H. Hudson. I can see the point in books like that. They make you see things better. Do you know Hudson?"

"No."

"Well, you should. I know a first-rate hotel in Huntingdon. Will you have dinner with me?"

"Oh, yes, please."

"They do good roast duck there, not fatty but crisp. And venison pasty. If you're hungry."

"I'm meant to be at a party in Caius."

"You were ill. If I hadn't cured you, you'd have been too ill to go."

"That's true enough."

The hotel was as good as he said; sipping brandy after a varied and tasty English dinner in front of a log fire in a paneled room, Frederica felt warm toward Nigel Reiver, who had given her a day in the outside world, had handled her spine, shown her an owl, reminded her of childhood reading. She had a vivid image of a small intent boy in a library with paneled walls and window seats overlooking a huge lawn with a moat beyond it—a secret, self-contained, imagining little boy.

"Which book did you like most?" she said. "In your library?"

"Are you laughing at me?"

"No. Why?"

"You sounded a bit patronizing. A bit *kind*. I don't take to that."

"I didn't mean that. I was just remembering reading things at that age—Sir Lancelot, and *Puck of Pook's Hill*, and *Tales of Asgard*—"

"Have you read Tolkien?" said Nigel. "Tolkien's a genius. In my opinion."

Frederica had not read Tolkien. Raphael had called his prose "nasty" and Tony had said that his social views were simplistic Wagnerian ideas of good and evil, master races and subject races, and a silly idolization of bucolic England and a nonexistent merry peasantry. Nigel Reiver leaned back with the Huntingdon firelight dancing on his swarthy face and said that in his view the books were alive like *Puck*, because they told a real story, because they were *simply* about good and evil, because there were lots of battles with the landscape and no machines, no politics, no sex.

"They make you feel clean," he said. "Now, laugh."

"Why should I laugh?"

"I told a girl in Oxford I thought he was marvelous and she laughed like a drain. Said I was a hopeless case. More or less kicked me out then and there."

"You got the wrong girl in Oxford," said Frederica. "Mostly they like him there. He's an Oxford man."

She was intrigued by the girl in Oxford. How many girls had dined with him in how many hotels and talked about *Puck of Pook's Hill?* His summing up of Tolkien was, she decided, shrewd and not naive. You could perfectly well feel refreshed by a story with lots of struggle, no politics, no machines, no sex. She studied Nigel Reiver covertly and found he was looking at her with a calculating amusement. There was something very like Puck in Nigel: his darkness, his muscular shoulders and stocky body, his large ears, something sly and humorous and evasive in his English practicality. Driving back to Cambridge she thought about his name. Nigel was a name she didn't like, a name belonging to respectable little boys from nice homes who didn't like her and whose sisters were called Patricia and Gillian and Jill. Now she suddenly saw it differently, a name from Sir Walter Scott, a name for a pirate or a border robber—Wordsworth had been going to call *The Borderers The Reivers* had he not?

"Is your uncle called Reiver, too?" she asked drowsily, through the brandy.

"Yes. Why do you ask?"

"You said he was a bit of a pirate. It *all* suddenly felt like Hereward."

"I don't quite catch your meaning," said Nigel, looming beside her in the thick camel coat, those firm hands clasping the wheel in leather gloves. When they came to Newnham he pulled up in the light, turned to her, and said, "Well?"

She did not move away. She was suddenly a little afraid. He reached for her, confident and firm. The smell of his skin was warm and dry and somehow familiar, a good smell, not like her own, but acceptable as her own.

"Mostly I don't like wet kisses," he said. "But you—"

Kissed, Frederica was even more frightened. She was not sure why this was; it was in fact because she had not, in her adventures, felt specific desire, but only a general need for sex, and had confused this, on occasion, with something more local, or had misled herself. She shook. Her hands and knees quivered. She thought she had better get away and then that she wanted him to hold her, even against the inappropriate overcoat. He sat rather stiffly and said again, "Well?"

"What do you mean, well?"

"I mean, what do you want?"

"What do *I* want?"

"Don't you?"

"I don't know what you mean."

"Hadn't you better be getting in?" he infuriatingly said. Frederica got snappily out of the car on some impulse of self-preservation. When she was around the front he called, "Come back."

She came.

"Don't be awkward. We had a good day."

"We did."

"Come here. I'll be seeing you."

She would not ask, when?

"Give me a kiss till next time."

She could not bear not to touch him again. They kissed, rather primly, through the car window, she standing, he leaning back in the driving seat.

"I'll be seeing you," he said again.

She walked stiffly back into the college, aching with all sorts of contradictory pains.

Characters are fictive and hypothetical. So too is the little sheaf of invitation cards on any Cambridge mantelpiece, moving from the future tense, which is a fiction, next Saturday, Friday week, Wednesday at eight, to the past, or the might have been, as in the case of the Caius birthday party—Jeremy Laud, twenty-one—which Frederica was forever absent from, having gone to Ely and Huntingdon with Nigel Reiver, or a serious gathering in Harvey Organ's rooms to discuss Empson's *Seven Types of Ambiguity* under the auspices of the Critical Club, which she had missed in order to discuss her Ph.D. application with Raphael Faber, or a card written in pale blue painted strokes depicting a hunched figure in a raincoat, a debonair long-haired poet, a slouching spectacled journalist, inviting Frederica to an evening of music with the three English students she now thought of as *la petite bande*. Shuffling these, putting the lost past, *paradis perdu*, behind the hopeful or fearful future, she wondered what she had missed—another conversation with Harvey about the word "image," guitar singing, a hangover, a new friend. It was the merest chance, Forster told us of Ricky's vision of Agnes embracing her love, that he had not been disgusted. But he was not to know that. Chance overseen by Forster, who proposed, disposed, and judged. It was by chance that Frederica did not meet Ralph Tempest at Jeremy Laud's formal gathering, at Harvey's debate, at Mike, Tony, and Jolyon's smoky talk with pasted mottoes on the walls. Who was Ralph Tempest? He was shy and clever. He did not talk easily, but when he talked he had much to say. He too could not decide whether to stay in the university or live in the world, and was to find his own way of bridging the two, teaching and traveling to research. He was an anthropologist with a gift for concise expression who read poetry for pleasure. He had a mouth that with a few years' certainty would become kind, and a wit that was in 1957 wholly private, shared with one old school friend in a voluminous correspondence. (He was an Old Boy of both Eton and Manchester Grammar School owing to vagaries of scholarships and his father's odd career, which included the army, advertising, and latterly the church.) He knew little about sex and would not have dared to touch Frederica, but he was to learn a great deal from the weeping wife of a professor of anthropology in Tripoli whom he was to love, briefly, tenderly, and hopelessly. He would have made her happy and left her free. Ralph Tempest, at Harvey Organ's gathering, dancing with an awkward grace with beautiful Freddie's Hungarian-obsessed cousin, Belinda, at Jeremy Laud's birthday celebration, sitting on Mike Oakley's in Christ's with his arm around the waist of a girl with an incipient double chin in a dark peacock brocade dress, a girl who, like Frederica, is writing an essay on blood and light in *Phèdre* but has not read Proust (neither has Ralph Tempest) and has her own reasons for not considering a Cambridge Ph.D.

27

NAMES OF GRASSES

In the early summer of 1957 Marcus sat his A levels in mathematics, additional mathematics, chemistry, and botany. (This idiosyncratic choice was dictated partly by his reluctance to dissect flesh. The school authorities, pleased to see him doing anything at all, anxious to console his father and restore him to some norm of human behavior, had accommodated him, with some difficulty and some extra botany at the Girl's Grammar, where he worked in the same class as Jacqueline but not Ruth.) In the same summer Frederica sat finals in Cambridge and wrote orderly booklets, brimming with quotation and cross-referencing, on tragedy, literary criticism, Dante, and the English moralists, who included, in those days, Plato, Aristotle, St. Augustine, and small slivers of Kant. Stephanie observed that the stain on Mary's brow was definitely paler and less outstanding. Will, aged three, had a passion for books. He knew his alphabet and would identify characters on billboards loudly from bus or bicycle seat. My W, Mummy's S, D for Daddy, M for Mary. Stephanie read to him tales from Grimm, old English fairy tales, ballads, and charms. There was no television, no prancing mule, no flowerpot men. There was a pleasantly loathsome East Anglian bogle called Yallery Brown and a skinless Scottish sea monster called Nuckelavee, to whom he was particularly attached, possibly because of the rhythm of their names. What he liked, and what Daniel was impatient with, was repetition, the virtuous acts of the Little Red Hen, the endless gullible relations of Chicken-Licken, three pigs or three princes galloping on three roads with three friendly animals to face three giants in three castles and bring back three brides of varying beauty and virtue, of varying capacity also to weave silk fine enough to pull through a gold ring, or spin straw into gold.

There was a clear moment, when he was writing his A level botany, when Marcus acknowledged that he was contented. He had written an exhaustive answer on various aspects of the sexuality of plants, and was moving on to his chosen area of special study, the Gramineae or grasses. The great variety of sexual forms and behavior of the plant world in their way did more to detach Marcus's attention from the idea that he "must be" homosexual than anything the psychiatrist said or elicited. (This was not because Marcus anthropomorphized the plants but, on the contrary, because he was interested in them, and an informed interest in something, anything, maybe, is conducive to moral calm.) He wrote quietly about the monoecious and dioecious households of trees and the extravagant mimetic capacities of the bee orchid.

He wrote about hermaphrodite flowers, categorizing them according to their elaborate arrangements for preventing self-pollination, which is desirable only as a last resort—better one's own seed than none. In this context he described the behavior of the cup-and-saucer vine, a creature he had never seen, usually bat-pollinated, which fertilizes itself with a final convulsive movement of the stamens just before the corolla falls. He described also, with pale, clear diagrams, the device of cleistogamy, the self-fertilizing of flowers that never open, but "marry closed." In this country violets and wood sorrel will fertilize themselves in this way if they develop too late in the woods to be reached by the sunlight and their pollinators.

Naming and distinguishing between the grasses gave him a pleasure that complemented the pleasure he took in his maths. Grasses, too, and naming plants, went far back in his life. His mother had taught him to name common wildflowers; the blown seeds of the grasses had entered and damaged the mucous membrane of his nose and throat; his inflamed flesh had wept and shuddered and pricked at their intrusion. Yet now they could be categorized, named, seen clearly. The Gramineae have "flowers either with stamens and pistils, or with stamens or pistils only, sometimes neuter, that is without either stamens or pistils, one, two, or more inclosed in two husks, or valves, called glumes. The whole collection of flowers forms a spikelet." The stem of the grasses is often called a culm; it is cylindrical, or nearly so (never triangular), hollow, and jointed.

From where does the intense satisfaction come that is to be taken in that kind of writing? Or more simply, in listing and drawing, as Marcus did:

Alopecurus—Foxtail grass
Phalaris—Canary grass
Phleum—Cat's-tail grass
Lagurus—Hare's-tail grass
Milium—Millet grass
Gastridium—Nit grass
Polypogon—Beard grass
Aira—Hair grass
Arrhenatherum—Oatlike grass
Hierochloe—Sacred grass
Panicum—Panick grass
Poa—Meadow grass
Briza—Quaking grass
Cynosurus—Dog's-tail grass
Triticum—Wheat grass
Lolium—Darnel
Anthoxanthum—Vernal grass

That summer Marcus had a vision of the world as a globe marked out not only by flowing stripes of water and huge nets of roots, sliding sands and towering rocks, but by a kind of human love, not grabbing, not consuming, not even humanizing but simply *naming* the multitudinous things to be seen, for the sake of seeing them more clearly. In bed at night he saw this globe specked and glittering with infinite points of naming, and also he saw himself advancing into a midsummer hayfield, seeing it neither as a sea of fearful undifferentiated light, nor as a place where he might persuade Ruth to lie at his side, nor yet as an obstacle to be got through, but as itself, with all the hollow stems of the named grasses glittering with their individual

difference, *poa, panicum, arrhenatherum, anthoxanthum, phalaris.*
He would now by no means have understood Jean-Paul Sartre's
existential terror at the formless otherness of the root of a chestnut
tree, and in that mood, at that age, he would not have understood
Sartre's sense that matter escapes our naming, bulges beyond it,
threatens to engulf, so that it is meaningless to say the sky is blue, or
to count chestnuts and distinguish them from plane trees. The
geometry seemed to him now part of the stuff of things: in his mind,
in the stems of the grasses (cylindrical, never triangular). There had
been a time when he had barely saved himself from the terror of the
churned mud of Far Field, which he connected with the deadly fields
of Passchendaele, by a geometry made of map-drawn white lines and
goalposts. Now he noted that poppies flourished excessively in
Flanders fields because the shell-torn soil exposed the seeds to more
intense light.

I had the idea, when I began this novel, that it would be a novel of
naming and accuracy. I wanted to write a novel as Williams said a
poem should be—no ideas but in things. I even thought of trying to
write without figures of speech, but had to give up that plan, quite
early. It may be possible to name without metaphor, to describe
simply and clearly, to categorize and distinguish, one specimen from
another, *arrhenatherum, les jeunes gens en fleurs.* There would be a
heavy emphasis on nouns, on naming, in such a hypothetical book,
and also I suspect on adjectives, those unfashionable categorizers.

Marcus, writing his A levels, was in a state when it was clear and
distinct ideas, not fusions of vision, that excited him. He liked
labeling specimens—representatives, that is, of their species. In the
world in which Frederica was writing her finals, wisely discussing
T. S. Eliot's idea of the poet as catalyst in the pseudochemical fusion
of images, or Coleridge's idea of the symbol (reflecting the general in
the particular, the special—or speci-al—in the general and the universal in the special), or Plato's metaphors of the Cave and the
Fire, or Racine's tropes about Phèdre's guilty blood and the darkened sun, it went almost without saying that to make comparative
images was to have great power, to be a small god making new
wholes. Frederica's friends would have pounced on Marcus's history
and the cleistogamous flower and thought they had understood

something because they had seen an analogy. Whereas, in fact, part of such an instant vision is the closing off of other ways of seeing.

Adam in the Garden named the flora and fauna (and the rocks and stones, presumably, and perhaps also the gases and liquids, atoms and molecules, protons and electrons). But even in the act of naming, we make metaphors. Consider the grasses, so carefully distinguished one from the other. They are little figures of speech. *Gastridium*— nit grass, from *gastridion*, a little swelling. *Aira*—hair grass, from *airo*, to destroy (a destructive grass). *Panicum*, or panic grass, from *panis*, bread, because the seeds of this grass can be milled and eaten. *Arrhenatherum* is from *arrhen*, male, and *athe*r, an awn. It was the natural grass for me to choose to put into a sentence with the shade of *les jeunes gens en fleurs*? And then the vernal grass, *anthoxanthum* —*anthos*, a flower, *xanthos*, yellow, next to *phalaris*—*phalos*, shining—and suddenly, do we have a description, or an evocation of the fields of light?

In the Renaissance there was a belief that language was a God-given symbolic system describing, or naming, objects that in their turn were a language, like the hieroglyphs, written by the Creator on the surface of things, so that flowers, girasole, heliotrope, represented, for instance, the spiritual truth of the soul turning to the source of light and life. Chance correspondences, correspondences depending on the narrowness or obsessiveness of our own vision, correspondences explored by scientists in search of the laws of growth, light, motion, gravity—all these were part of a divine language that was the Word informing inchoate matter. These small figures of speech in the naming of grasses are no such matter; they are obviously part of the overwhelming human need to make connections and comparisons (foxtail, cat's tail, hare's tail) even if they are also the stuff of poetry (Panic, Trembling, Shining). As Vincent Van Gogh said, in our world, olive trees may stand for themselves, maybe must stand for themselves, and so with cypresses, sunflowers, corn, human flesh. (Though he could not divest any of these of the cultural metaphors that come close and intrinsic as their shadows, replacing, as he almost said, the old halo.)

Marcus did not see that, either. But he was interested in resemblance, in something he called imitation, without knowing if, or where, there was a will to imitate. Consider the bee orchid, that trap in the form of a female bee that invites the agitated male to grasp, to penetrate, to shake on the flower flesh that then tips him into a vegetable prison where he must roll, for its fertilization, until it withers. Marcus, like most human beings, was constrained to see this as a work of intelligence, not of pure chance. If over millennia the form of the flower has more and more exactly approached the deceptive form of the bee, and the live mechanism has been perfected, it is beyond our intelligence to conceive of this happening without intelligence. Blind chance is so much harder to imagine, and bears little relation to what we usually mean by chance, the random blow of fate or stroke of luck, the falling of the coin, or rocketing of the billiard balls, this way or that. Through centuries we have believed that our minds mirror the order of things and can therefore apprehend it. The flower has no eyes to see the exactness of its parody. How it knows, if it knows, that it is exact is beyond the scope of our apprehension. Because of the bee orchid, because of that disturbing overexact trope (like Coleridge's marble peach in one sense, a copy, not an image), Marcus had come to extend his ant-god into a pervasive organizing intelligence. He still believed it had nothing to do with him. He struggled *not* to say, "It was designed to look like a female bee," but it was almost impossible not to believe in a Designer.

He took Ruth and Jacqueline to see his elm trees. He did not talk to them about light, or about design, though he did show them how regular the spiraling twigs and limbs were in their idiosyncrasy. They lay, all three, in the grass at the foot of the tree, chewed apples, and talked about their hypothetical futures. Ruth was set on being a nurse. Jacqueline and Marcus were applying for places at the University of North Yorkshire, Marcus because there he could do both the maths and the plant studies, Jacqueline because she was attached to North Yorkshire. Marcus was also, when it came to it, reluctant to commit himself to moving too far from the home he found so oppressive. Jacqueline put an arm round both Marcus's shoulder and Ruth's, pulling them to her; Ruth pushed back, out of fun, out of a desire not to be touched, Marcus could not tell, and they all rolled over on the spiny grass, legs mingling, palms touching, breaths close. During this pleasant scuffle he was able to run his hand down the length of that shining plait, and feel the spine under it ripple and shiver—with what? Pleasure? Irritation? Jacqueline's warm brown hands were on his shoulders, her face brushed his, and his hand reached again for the thick hair, cold even under the sun. Ruth rolled away, and sat up, pushing down her skirts. Jacqueline lay for a moment curled against insubstantial Marcus; then she too sat up and laughed. It was the first time Marcus had enjoyed touch as far back as he could remember. They were comfortable, the three of them.

Will had a small railway, given to him by Winifred, which consisted of a large figure-of-eight of interlocking pale blue plastic track, with points, a turntable, and jigsaw joints. On these loops trundled a scarlet engine, two yellow trucks, a green tanker, and a dark blue guard's van. Sometimes the cats—they had kept the she-cat and her blotched white kitten, now a slim, edgy ballerina cat—patted these trucks as Will propelled them round and they overbalanced, causing him to become very angry and to hurl bricks and other toys at the cats. Mary too would stagger across and sit heavily in hot plastic and toweling on the line, or grab the engine and crow. Stephanie's sympathies were with Will: she too had been an elder child from whom things had been taken by a single-minded younger one. But she was frightened at the range and extent of his fury at these interferences. His face set crimson, his teeth ground, his small brow creased and lowered. His passion was absolute. He would break up his own railway and hurl the parts about the room, he would bite, not only Mary's chubby shoulder but his mother's helping hand, and even on occasion his own. Or he would beat his forehead against the bottom stair until there were purple contusions and smears of blood. Stephanie found this hard. She could sing a sick child to sleep, or read a tale for the twentieth time with as much expression as the first, but anger daunted her. She responded to her son as she did to her father, dully and passively, picking up his missiles, moving Mary out of reach, offering neither chastisement nor unsought and unacceptable comfort. One day Will threw the scarlet engine at Mary as Daniel's mum came downstairs from the bathroom. The grandmother put one fat and knobby laced shoe on the engine, which spun away, twisting her body, as she parted her legs and fell, with a sound of ripping petticoat and a howl of agony. Her face was contorted plum-black; she screamed words, "*Now* you've done it," and "*No* consideration," and subsided into gasping. Stephanie ran forward and was beaten back by furious hands.

"That's no good. Me 'ip's gone. I know. It's gone where it went before. Don't touch me; it's agony. Get some 'elp, don't just stand there."

They were all screaming and weeping, Mary from fear, the grandmother from pain, Will from terrible guilt and anger. Stephanie fetched the ambulance; Daniel's mum, wet faced and snorting, was rolled on a stretcher, wrapped in scarlet blankets, carried out of the door. Stephanie, Mary on one hip, Will pulling the other arm, came out onto the pavement. The little eyes in their fat folds looked at her sideways and shrewdly.

"Well," said Daniel's mum. "You'll be 'appy now." She gasped and gathered herself. "Got what you want, now. You'll not be sorry to be shut of me."

"Oh, *don't*," said Stephanie.

The face that was lifted into the ambulance seemed to her to be glistening with the energy of spite.

"Don't think I don't know how you feel, girl. You're civil enough, but you've no use for me, I'm a cross you bear, a load on your mind, better put away. I've not had a cross word out of you since I come, and not one word o' real warmth or humanity either, not one. You don't care what I am so long as your duty's done, you cold fish. Mekking me sit wi' all them lunatics. So *good*. You don't know *what* I've suffered in this house, you've no idea, you . . ."

"Come on, mum," said the ambulance men. "Shock," they said to Stephanie, closing their white doors. "Think nothing of it."

But she did. It was true. She had borne with Daniel's mum, and had not known who she was. Mary wailed. Will dragged at her hand.

"Will they *mend* Granny, will they? Will you mend my railway? Mary took it. Grandma trod on it. It's—badly *damaged*." He was good with words.

"It can be repaired, can't it?"

So, for the first time since Marcus had come, Stephanie had supper alone with her husband. This was late, since Daniel had visited his mother and various other people. He sat silent in his dog collar and shiny black clothes, his thick hair ruffled, his face dark with beard-growth, at once overdressed and unkempt, uncared for. Stephanie saw him with detachment, as she might see anyone, and had no idea what to say to him. She did not want to begin with the usual names of Will or Mary, Mum or Marcus; she did not want to offer the common coin of rates or jumble sale, dependents or Farrars. She was married to this chewing, frowning fat man. *She* was married to him. A craziness rose in her, half inadmissable euphoria at the old woman's absence, half the sense of her unregarded self coming painfully to life like a numbed extremity. As so often, this formed itself in a kind of anger.

"You might talk to me. We don't often get any time to ourselves."

"What about? I'm not used to talking. It's been a bad day."

"I know. But we never *talk*."

"Can I have some more vegetables? The little beans are really good."

"I've been thinking. I suffer from having to use a limited vocabu-lary. All the time. How big do you suppose the average used vocabulary is? A thousand words? Two thousand? Will can't know that many, and Mary even fewer. And the people I see—in the shops—"

"And my poor old mum—"

"And your poor old mum," she said steadily, "and most of the people in this parish, wouldn't understand most of the words I really care about if I were suddenly to *say* them, right out, out of the blue. So the words become ghosts. They haunt me."

"Mebbe I wouldn't understand them either," said Daniel disagree-ably. "My own vocabulary has deteriorated since college days. Or since we were courting."

"Exactly. Have some more beans." Food improved the temper. "We learn to think and can't use our thinking words—"

"Like what?"

"Oh," she said, frivolously, desperately. "Discourse. Discourse of reason. Sophistical. Ideal—in a Platonic sense. Catalyst. Anacoluthon. Mendacious. Realism. The worst things are the words that do have meaning in the tiny vocabulary I do use, like real and ideal, words that lose half their associations . . . Don't you understand, Daniel?"

"I do," he said. He pushed away his plate. "I shouldn't have made you marry me. I thought *that* was real, God help me."

"It was." Quickly.

"Aye. And your great unopened volumes of vocabulary, they're *real*, too."

"Daniel—I can teach it to Will and Mary." She was afraid of what she had done. She had meant to say something loving, from her to him. Who was he? What did he care about? He was a good, a practical man. She loved him. Did she not?

"I don't understand. It wasn't what I meant. This." He gestured at the comfortable little room, where Will's things, including the red engine, were heaped in a clothes basket, where Mary's nappies hung on a clothes line by the fire. He laughed. "I can't find a word. It's all got—*muffled*."

"Muffled is a good word."

"Don't be *nice* to me, Steph. Don't patronize. That I can't bear."

"Daniel, I love you."

"I think you do. It was daft of you. I mean that."

"You can't choose, about love."

"Can't you? Mebbe you should. I never thought it that important, until . . . I hate *talking* these days. Gideon's a great talker; he gets talking things done, discussion groups and that, but not . . . It wasn't what I was meant—"

"You knew so clearly what you were meant for. Before you married me . . . You've lost something, too. As heavy as my vocabulary."

"Aye." He stared at the table. The best, she thought, for her solitary self would have been to go on talking, to make him talk to her, but she was too afraid of failure and too unused to words herself now, to dare that. So she did what she knew was second best and dropped to her knees beside his chair and put a hand on his, her bright head on his knee.

"I do love you. Now we *are* alone."

He stroked her hair, and put out blind arms, and they clung together. In silence they stood and climbed the stairs and tumbled into the new space of their bedroom. In bed they were happy, they knew each other, they loved each other. And the words wandered loose and unused. Peripeteia. Anguish. Morphology. Infinite in faculty. In apprehension how like a god. Men have died and worms have eaten them, but not for love, nor yet for constriction of vocabulary. She slept under the weight of his arm.

28

THE YELLOW CHAIR

Wilkie handed Frederica the *Manchester Guardian*. They were having coffee in the Friar's House, where the espresso machine was newer than in the Alexandra and the coffee tasted fresh and pungent through white froth, and flakes of cinnamon and bitter chocolate, not corrupt and washed up as coffee does through old grounds.

"NEW VERSE PLAY BY ALEXANDER WEDDERBURN. The team that brought off *Astraea* in the year of the Coronation, playwright Alexander Wedderburn and director Benjamin Lodge, are putting on something very different at the Dolphin Theatre, *The Yellow Chair*, an intense, claustrophobic drama about the wild and tragic events of the last years of Van Gogh. The painter himself, a demanding part with its lyric intensity and moody savagery, is played by Paul Greenaway, who will be remembered for his sympathetic television portrayal of D. H. Lawrence in *Look We Have Come Through* by promising 'angry' Jim Cobb. Gauguin is portrayed by Harold Bomberg, last seen as Laertes in the Stratford *Hamlet* and taking a break from Shakespeare. Michael Witter, fresh from filming *Hornblower in the Baltic*, is Theo Van Gogh. Rising young star, Debbi Moon, plays various parts, including the prostitute, Rachel, to whom Van Gogh presented his severed ear. Wedderburn says the subject 'more or less presented itself' to him on holiday in Provence, where he became involved in the 'electric arguments' between the painters. Benjamin Lodge says the piece is a marvelous vehicle for a versatile actor and Greenaway has the stature to carry it off triumphantly."

There was a photograph of Greenaway glaring over a Lawrentian beard, side by side with a gray-and-white reproduction of Vincent's last aquamarine self-portrait, glaring tight-lipped against a characteristic background of ascending spirals, here confused by the dotty veil of the newsprint.

"They make it sound rather *ordinary*," said Frederica.

"You must take to arts journalism," said Wilkie, who was in on the secret of the *Vogue* project, "and redeem it. When I have my arts slot on the TV, you can come on my program and pronounce on Alexander's artistic integrity without once using the words intense, brilliant, vehicle, or Christopher Fry. Shall we go and see *The Yellow Chair*? Shall we hire a charabanc and make up a Cambridge party to cheer his first night? Do you remember how staggered you were on that starry warm evening in Avignon to see him and me descending from the battlements like falling angels? Do you have a little warmth in your heart still for him? I've never been clear how things *ended* between you two."

Frederica ignored the personal part of this.

"*Do* let's have a charabanc. Do you know Raphael Faber? Do you think you could persuade him to come?"

"Yes I do, and yes I might well. He was seen at *Waiting for Godot* so it's obviously not impossible for him to get to London. The charabanc might be beneath his dignity. He's a lost cause, though, as you must know."

"Lost causes can be quite comfortable. They take up less of one's life."

"You should have stuck with me, for that. I'd take up *very* little, very pleasantly."

"No, thank you."

"All that blood," said Wilkie. "Oh, my God, all that blood. Better me than sweet Hugh Pink, though, don't you agree? I'm more resourceful."

"I don't go to bed with Hugh Pink."

"Why not?"

"It would upset him."

"What a *moral* girl you are, to be sure."

"Oh, I am, I am," cried Frederica with real indignation. Wilkie laughed.

The bringing to life of a theatrical idea is also always the small death of a larger idea, Alexander had already discovered. There was one miraculous moment, however, the lighting rehearsal with the finished sets. The Dolphin was a small, renovated theater in the City, near the river, away from theaterland, that housed experimental new plays that moved into larger, more permanent homes if they pleased audiences. The designer of Alexander's play, also responsible for the lighting and for various visual effects, was a young man called Charles Koninck who taught at the Slade and had understood what Alexander had meant when he said he wanted the stage full of light. There were three acts and in all three of them the stage was seen as a closed receding box, the backcloth, by various devices, made to seem small, bright, and far away. There were three objects on the stage: Vincent's yellow chair, solid wood and rush, Gauguin's more opulent curving chair, green seated, reddish-brown painted, highlit in violet, and an easel containing a large blank canvas on which, from time to time, were flashed magnified transparencies of various works, the huge black painted Bible of Vincent's father, the heap of yellow novels on a brilliant pink-and-white ground painted in Paris, the Breakfast Table.

There were three acts: during the first, everything was black and white, dark with highlighting, Dutch, wintry and somber. The backcloth was the cottage of the Potato Eaters with its black earth colors, its dark light, its claustrophobia. The wings, which were geometrically distorted to appear to diminish and recede into this cramped space, were designed from Van Gogh's early drawings of rows of willows along canals, tangles of roots on pollarded trees, frozen branches trailing networks of ice in the garden in Nuenen. Trees and roots rose like cage bars, beautiful and trapping. In the second act, color flooded in. Across the back of the stage was the purple-and-gold Sower; on the left wall were the Sunflowers, larger than the landscape, shining circles of gold on blue; on the right wall were the Irises, painted at St. Rémy, "the other violet bunch (going as far as carmine and pure Prussian blue) standing out against a background of shrill lemon yellow." He called this a terrible painting, Vincent, and said he was afraid of it. Koninck, a precise balding young man with steel-rimmed glasses, had devised ways of intensifying this image by projecting a second slide of it over the first one, or by flooding it with gold or violet light so that it could be got to radiate gold, or heave like a purple sea.

In the third act the flower pieces stood still, but the Sower had been replaced by the Reaper, the dark gold sun by the pale white gold of the burning sheaves. He had seen it through bars, from his asylum cell, and Koninck had made it possible from time to time to shine bars across its brightness into which the Reaper advances away from us, as the Sower strode from the sun toward us.

I saw then in this reaper—a vague figure struggling like a devil in great heat to come to the end of his task—I saw then in it the image of death, in the sense that humanity would be the wheat one reaps. So it is, if you like, the opposite of that sower I had tried before. But in this death, nothing sad; it happens in broad daylight with a sun flooding everything with a light of pure gold. My dear brother—it is always in between the work that I write to you—I am laboring like one possessed. I am more than ever in an insensible fury of work . . . It is all yellow, except a line of violet hills, of a yellow pale and blond. I find it queer myself that I saw like this through the iron bars of a cell.

"Pleased?" inquired Koninck of Alexander. "I hope so. I am, rather."

"I'm overwhelmed," said Alexander truthfully. "So dark and so bright."

"It's presented some interesting problems," said Koninck. "There are one or two tricks I want to try with lighting the actors, on the lines of what is done in ballet. If you light the stage with a red spot and a white spot and you have two figures, each blocking the light from one spot, you might imagine you'd have a red shadow and a white shadow on a pink ground. But the eye adjusts itself and sees pink light as white so that it sees the blocked red light as *white* minus red—cyan-blue. You can have a pretty dance of red and turquoise shadows on white. I've tried to get something of Van Gogh's complementaries to follow him and Gauguin around—or to cast two shadows of him on different screens. The terrible reds and greens of human passions we can do with the primary colors of light. The violets and golds are harder, but I've constructed some crossing beams. And we can have a whole drama of half-stage lighting round the two chairs, absolutely glittering with electricity, literally. We can marry the complementaries into a single white image. We can make haloes. We can change the color of his clothes and backdrop as he did in the self-portraits. You haven't got much action in your play, more talk—so we'll fight it out in light. Should be intriguing."

"It should," said Alexander. "It could be very irritating—his word, not mine—?"

"Irritating and harmonious by turn," Koninck said. He added, to Alexander's pleasure, "I'd forgotten what a very great man he was. I guess we'd got too used to him. Having to do these three-dimensional images makes you see him all new. You know painters nowadays learn their art through the color of slides, not oil paint? We live in a world of projected light. You've got a concentrated box of modern art light in there. Pouring in. It's a dream."

The first-night audience, like all first-night audiences, was both unusually benign and ready to be spiteful or condescending. Alexander, sitting retired at the side of the circle with Martina Sutherland, smiled abstractedly at Thomas and Elinor Poole and saw suddenly in the middle of the front row of the circle the red hair and sharp face of Frederica Potter, sitting between Wilkie and a thin, dark man he didn't know. The whole front row of the circle was in fact Wilkie's charabanc party, which had traveled, in fact, by train in reserved compartments with bottles of white wine and smoked-salmon sandwiches. There were Wilkie's Caroline and Ann Lewis, Alan Melville and Tony Watson, Marius Moczygemba and Hugh Pink, and, on the other side of the dark man, Vincent Hodgkiss, whom he suddenly recognized and smiled nervously toward. He preferred his audience anonymous. Frederica waved and he waved back. The curtain rose.

It was to be criticized as a static play, and also, paradoxically, compared to its disadvantage to *Waiting for Godot*, in which nothing happened, whereas in *The Yellow Chair* there was madness, destruction, and death. Greenaway remained on stage throughout, inside the screens, inside the flats with their willow cage or decorations of sunflowers or irises. He remained in the full glare of the bright light, or in the center of the dark haze of the black light of their Dutch youth. On stage also all the time, but outside the structure of flats and screens, was Michael Witter as Theo Van Gogh, almost always alone, on the apron, in the wing, but toward the end accompanied by his new wife, Johanna Van Gogh-Bonger and her child in arms, the newly named Vincent Van Gogh, a family. Twice during the play Theo stepped into the box of light, once in the second act, after the one violent scene when Vincent had threatened Gauguin silently at his bedside with a razor, and had rushed away intimidated, to slice off his own ear. At the end of the third act, after the final act of violence, he joined his dying brother, cheek to cheek on the pillow of his bed. "I wish I could go away like this," Vincent said, in life, on the stage, and died. Other silent people, the bearded postman, Roulin, the two doctors, Rey and Gachet, a series of women, all, like Johanna Bonger, played by Debbi Moon, appeared as half ghosts between inner screens and outer painted boundaries, lit by Vincent's attention and Charles Koninck's spotlights, through gauze.

Alexander noticed mostly what Lodge had done to his work. He had made several changes, subtle and unsubtle, in the direction of a sexual explanation of Van Gogh's derangement. He kept the silent "rescued" prostitute, Sien (again Debbi Moon), crouching naked and half veiled behind a screen, as Vincent had drawn her as *Sorrow*, for much more of the Dutch sequence than Alexander had meant, so that what Vincent said about love and solitude was thrown at this unresponding figure.

He had introduced balletic action into Act II where Gauguin and Van Gogh cohabited and quarreled. Alexander had written in one silent woman to receive the bloody half ear. Lodge had peopled a whole shadow night café with Toulouse-Lautrec whores to whom Gauguin in blue-green gloves demonstrated the art of the épée while Vincent played morosely with a cutthroat razor at home, seated on "his" half of the stage, on the Yellow Chair. Vincent had indeed written of himself as an ox and Gauguin as a bull.

Lodge had had difficulty persuading Greenaway to make Vincent as unpleasant as he must, in company, have been. Alexander had quoted Wijnnobel. "If he came and sat next to you in a café, you'd move away, wouldn't you, it would be most disagreeable." Greenaway had learned a very good trick of hectoring or lecturing Gauguin from very close up, speaking close to his face, infringing his body space. He spat words—Delacroix, Gethsemane—which landed in spittle on Bomberg's clothes and shone briefly. Lodge had given him Van Gogh's comparison of his own painting to acting. "Work and dry calculation, and where one's mind is extremely strained, like an actor on the stage in a difficult part, where one has to think of a thousand things at one time in a single half hour . . ."

Neither Greenaway nor Alexander's verse conveyed that which was the essential, the work, the dry calculation, the strain. If Alexander had thought less of Van Gogh's intelligence, he could have done his grubby, unprepossessing presence more effectively. He was interested in the isolated mind. Lodge was interested in failed communication. Greenaway conveyed the latter. He swallowed Alexander's words in a Method rush of feeling but his anxious pawing of Gauguin, and Theo, his abrupt backward rushes to break contact, were impressive and memorable. Alexander felt it was good, and that something was lost, a feeling to which he was accustomed.

Wilkie, assiduously rushing backstage, greeting Lodge, hunting down Alexander, somehow managed to get the Cambridge party invited to the supper for the cast and stage staff, which was in an upper room at Bertorelli's in Charlotte Street. Frederica traveled there in a taxi with Raphael, who said nothing about the play, but was very agitated about the etiquette of appearing at a party to which he had not really been asked, and made several attempts to divert the taxi to Liverpool Street, or to get out and send Frederica on, alone. Frederica said he *must meet* Alexander; it had been a dream of hers that he should meet Alexander. Alexander had written *Astraea*, in which she had played Elizabeth. Raphael had not heard of *Astraea* and seemed to suppose in advance that it was nothing he need trouble with. He expressed a brittle amusement at the idea of Frederica as Elizabeth, and asked if it had been anything like the ordeal that the

Lady in *Comus* had been. Frederica said, "I was most horribly in love with Alexander at that time."

"Did he know?" asked Raphael, somehow conveying the belief that the normal state of love was that it should be unspoken and unknown.

"I made sure he did."

"You would. Of course."

"It came to nothing," said Frederica hastily. "Or rather, it came to something horrible I won't go into."

"No," said Raphael. "Don't. I am *sure* we should not be going to this party."

They had a room with four long tables round the walls. On the whole, the actors sat at one end, and Cambridge and friends of the author at the other, though Elinor Poole had somehow managed to be sitting next to Paul Greenaway, who kept stroking her hand on the tablecloth. Frederica, arriving latish because of the trouble with Raphael, found herself sitting next to him on the inner circuit of the table, more or less opposite Alexander, who had put himself in a corner and looked tired. She introduced them.

"Alexander, this is Raphael Faber. He's a Fellow of St. Michael's. I go to his Mallarmé lectures. He's a poet."

Alexander introduced Martina Sutherland, who was sitting next to him. Dark-haired waitresses in black dresses and small white aprons brought moules marinière and avocado with prawns and smoked eel and pâté and they all ate. Frederica tried to tell Alexander how she had been moved by the light. Alexander said little, and Raphael nothing, until Martina leaned toward him in soft pink light over her prawns, showing the dark curve of two freckled breasts inside a black scooped neckline.

"And you, Dr. Faber. What did you think of the play?"

Raphael was looking at his plate, taking apart smoked fish with a knife and fork. He spoke, slightly choked, and did not look up.

"I do not have a great regard for Vincent Van Gogh," he said.

"That needn't matter. You could still admire the play. Why don't you like Van Gogh?"

It was Martina's profession to elicit opinions. Alexander knew she would be listening with a professional ear to the phrasing and cadences of Faber's reply, considering whether he expressed himself concisely, whether he had anything new to say, whether he said um, or er, or was a potential broadcaster. Alexander had by now almost developed such a professional ear himself and for some little way into Raphael's subsequent remarks noted how they were being delivered, rather than what was being said.

Raphael, still with his eyes cast down, put his knife and fork together.

"I don't think he was among the very greatest artists, perhaps because of an element of willfulness, of obtrusive self-regard, of *personality*—which would of course make him attractive to a playwright. Rilke once observed that the hypnotically readable quality of Van Gogh's letters militates in the end against him and against his art. He was always so concerned to justify—his behavior, his work—as though they couldn't stand alone. He was always striving to *prove* something. Rilke points out that—compared to Cézanne who is a much greater artist—Van Gogh is a man possessed by a theory. He discovered the relations of complementary colors but he had to create a dogmatic scheme, a metaphysical scheme, out of this, willfully. And his desire to make paintings that should be what he calls "comforting" is also willful, a rehash of the remnants of his preacherly concern, his religious obsession. He speaks of reflecting "that something of the eternal which the halo used to symbolize." He's a post-Christian Romantic in a world he hasn't come to terms with. And he obtrudes *himself* all the time—"Raphael's carved upper lip curled in perfect scorn—"he has one of the most *personal* styles in major art. He lacks that final clarity and selflessness. Rilke hit it again when talking about Cézanne. He was comparing Cézanne and Van Gogh when he praised Cézanne for painting not 'I love this' but 'Here it is.' Van Gogh never reached this insight. The play makes this abundantly—even distastefully—clear."

Frederica could say nothing. Martina was doughtier. She said, still with a professional eye on Faber as a debater, "Even if we take that point, we can hardly expect Alexander to write a *play* about 'Here it is' or the anonymity of great art. Plays are *about* personality, and striving, and conflict. What did you make of the play?"

Raphael appeared to be thinking crisply, without any reference to the men and women to whom he was addressing himself. One cold sentence drew out the next. In his room in St. Michael's Frederica loved this cool integrity, a man thinking. In Bertorelli's, among the wineglasses and smeared ends of pâté and heaped empty mussel shells, it was something else.

"I thought the play vulgarized what is interesting about Van Gogh. It was very slickly Freudian. Everything came back to the mother, the dead brother Vincent, the symbiotic tie with Theo. Many people have such problems and don't produce major art. There were so many missed opportunities. Heidegger wrote excellently about the quiddity and meaning of Van Gogh's boots; Artaud has a brilliant piece on his madness as a product of society's misunderstanding of art. But here there is no sense of large movements of thought or culture—just personal relations and stage lighting. I am afraid it is a very *English* piece. There is a kind of—how shall I put it—rather clotted English nature mysticism to which I am perhaps unduly unsympathetic, not being English. You have always found it very easy to appropriate and assimilate Van Gogh into this tradition. I think in painting of the school which takes its inspiration from the work of Blake and Samuel Palmer, and in writing of novelists I find almost unreadable, John Cowper Powys, Lawrence of course. Van Gogh knew Rembrandt and understood impressionism; he was not English. It is so *easy* for the English to get excited about corn and blossom in a rather intense way, without any vision of wider horizons. It is a provincial art.

"And there is the matter of the verse itself. I should have said it was almost impossible at this time to write well in a verse based on the iambic pentameter, I should have said one would almost inevitably be unable to avoid the pseudo-Romantic rhapsodies of the Georgian poets. I do not think the significance of Vincent Van Gogh is really to do with this kind of bucolic ecstasy. I may be wrong."

"Well—" said Martina somewhat breathlessly. And then, dryly, "You certainly put your case eloquently."

Raphael looked up nervously then, and could be seen shaking his hair from his brow, stiffening his shoulders into some awareness of his surroundings. He looked for a moment like a frightened child caught out in a prank, and then resumed the expression of thoughtful severity with which he had spoken. Frederica watched all this, and turned her attention to Alexander, who met Raphael's nervous and prickly look with a sort of weary patience.

"You may be right," he said. "I can't tell, at this stage, with a play. I didn't mean to do that—all the English gestures you point out—but I can quite see I may have. The Freudian bit got emphasized by the staging, somehow. But surely it does obtrude? I wanted to . . ." He could not achieve this sentence. "It doesn't matter," he said. Martina put her hand warmly over his on the tablecloth and gripped.

Frederica took some weeks to work out her reaction to this attack by one beloved upon another. At no point, to her credit, did she see herself as in any way central in this confrontation. At first, immediately, she was afraid for Raphael, fear of what he would feel when he realized how he was breaking the laws of the hospitality about which he had appeared so nervous in the taxi. Then she felt pure jealousy when she took in the proprietary movement of Martina Sutherland's hand. She looked at Raphael, to whom she had always been subservient, as she had not to Alexander, and tried to balance protectiveness for his gaffe with a strong desire to slap, scratch, or damage him. As for Alexander. She had suspended disbelief in his play, which recorded a wild battle with light and the earth. She said, "If you are like Van Gogh, Raphael, you have to go *through* 'I love this' or 'I hate this' to 'There it is.' Nobody has the right to criticize him who hasn't been there."

"And how do *you* know that?" asked Raphael. "Ordinary people mustn't suspend thought and judgment before genius, you know."

"I know partly from the play. So it worked, for me."

"You have a generous nature," said Raphael. It was this last, unthinking, unkind sentence that sent Frederica's eyes back to Alexander, who smiled. With no constraint, no anger, wearily and with warmth, he *smiled*. Frederica wanted to cry out "I love you, Alexander," but his hand was in Martina's, not inert, but caressing the fingertips.

Later, in Cambridge, when the reviews came out, she thought it all out further. The reviews—the serious ones—were on the whole hostile to Alexander, though kinder to Lodge and Greenaway. There were those, hooked on the new social ferment to be detected in *The*

Entertainer, who were prepared to blame Alexander for writing about art, the past, and even the individual. Van Gogh was the painter for ordinary men and women. Tony Watson wrote a long and eloquent piece along these lines for the *Cambridge Review*, cleverly looking up and using Raphael Faber's throwaway references to the views of Artaud and Heidegger.

She thought about Raphael's ideas. "Not 'I love that' but 'Here it is' " he had quoted, and there was something in that right and wise, and part of the Raphael she loved. But something had changed; she came, increasingly frequently over the end of her last year, to see Raphael himself without love. He had judged Alexander without *seeing* Alexander, and Frederica, who had loved him with the suspended judgment of the lover, the readiness to be infinitely interested and delighted, withdrew this tolerance. She quoted waspishly to him in her mind *dicta* from the New Testament he did not admit to his canon, "Judge not that ye be not judged," or the brief parable about the mote and the beam in the seeing eyes. He had disparaged Van Gogh for being in the grip of a theory—what else was he himself? He had spoken out against "personal" painting and writing, and wrote, secretly, most personally, most privately. And so on. Judgment, once loosed, ticks on, and on, and on, remorselessly. One effect of it was that when the letter came from *Vogue*, inviting her to a lunch in the Hyde Park Hotel for the twelve finalists in their competition, she accepted with enthusiasm.

For two or three weeks after *The Yellow Chair* she was in love with Alexander in the old way. She survived this as though it was a curse pain, or an attack of motion sickness, a visitation beyond her control. She remembered the twined fingers on the tablecloth. When the *Vogue* invitation came she thought of writing to him, of asking to see him, and might have done, had not Nigel Reiver turned up again at exactly the right moment, and proposed a day out in London, if she was going there. She arranged to stay with a woman friend the night before the lunch, and went up on the train, preoccupied with buying a hat, which she was sure she would need for the lunch, and apprehensive about Nigel Reiver. Alexander faded again into part of what she was and knew, lost his urgency, except as a point of reference.

29

LONDON

London excited Frederica. She knew little of it, and could not connect the parts she knew into a coherent map in her head. What she liked, being young and strong and curious and greedy, was the anonymity and variety of her possible journeys from territory to territory. She liked hurling in bright boxes among endlessly various strangers from Camden Town to Oxford Circus, from Liverpool Street to Leicester Square, or, after the *Vogue* luncheon, from Hyde Park to St. Paul's, to see Nigel Reiver in the City. Differences delighted her. She stayed overnight with Wilkie's Caroline in a flat in Camden Town, which was Wilkie's base during his negotiations with the BBC. This flat was the disproportionate cut-down first floor of a mid-Victorian terraced house with flimsy tall dividing walls making lobbylike little kitchen and bathroom out of the corners of what had been large bedrooms, leaving high gaunt boxes of rooms, not clean, the low furniture in the bottom eighth of them brightened by flung Scandinavian colored blankets and woven Indian rugs. Caroline's friends padded around in tight stretch trousers and ballet slippers. Frederica put on her luncheon dress, a navy poplin with too much gathered skirt to be severe and no white piqué, which she thought made her look secretarial. She journeyed to Oxford Street and bought a plain, schoolgirlish brimmed hat in John Lewis's, a fawn hat, which was not quite what she wanted, but the blues were wrong for her blue, and the grays too close in weight of color to her navy, making both gloomy. The hat was yellowish fawn. She snipped off its band with nail scissors and tacked on a navy ribbon that did match. She knew she looked undergraduate makeshift—the dress had been made by the theatrical home-dress-making friend. But she looked neat, and self-possessed and thinly shapely. It would have to do.

The lunch was a quite other world. They sat, twelve finalists, all women, among the *Vogue* staff in a huge room with plate-glass windows and heavy ballroom chandeliers, grouped in fours around friendly tables with heavy pink cloths and posies of pink and white carnations. The other contestants varied from the poised and expensive to the plainly frumpish, rather to Frederica's surprise. They had salmon and strawberries, and the magazine staff moved from table to table, in their good clothes and agreeable perfumes, assessing as she had seen Martina Sutherland assess Raphael Faber, listening for skills, for ideas, for originality, gently and toughly, with excellent manners and an edge of decisiveness she found she liked. She talked. She talked about *The Yellow Chair*. She talked about what one needed to know about a play or a film, about why a cutting review was almost always more amusing than an ecstatic one, about ways of circumventing this. She was still thinking of herself as the potential author of the definitive work on Renaissance religious metaphor; she was saving up the hats and speech habits of the other contestants for Alan and Tony. They were all arranged in a pyramid, like a school photo, like a bowl of fruit, and photographed for the occasion. "If you came to us," said a woman in a feathered cap and a cream linen suit Frederica could not have kept clean for twenty minutes, "we would start you on copy editing in the features department, I should think." Frederica said she would like that, and sipped cold white wine. It was all unreal, sharp and caressing, very pleasant. The winners were announced. Frederica was not the winner, but the honorable runner-up. The editors came and spoke to her, and said they hoped, they very much hoped, she would work for them for a year; she had a future in journalism. She saw Raphael's austere face, and Alexander's tired one, the image of the white town in the middle of the fens, the image of bustle and brightness of all these different streets. "I must think," she said. "It sounds marvelous. I must think." She wanted to live, to stop thinking, to have something immediate. Here, anything could happen.

Nigel waited at St. Paul's. He looked different in his dark suit— even more compact, more formidable, alien. He had been gathering information about shipping for his uncle, he said. He spoke to her from some sort of formal distance, bowing courteously, taking her elbow, guiding her. She had seen St. Paul's but had never really considered the City, and was surprised, and because she was ready to be, intrigued and excited by the difference of the people in these darker and heavier streets. Nobody was loitering. Most people, especially the young, of whom there were many, men in dark suits and women in dark skirts and neat blouses, were hurrying to get somewhere. She thought she had *no idea* where they were going, or how they lived, or what they did, and stared at every advancing young man as if to extract some sense of his habits, his slant of mind. All she managed to notice was that a cheap suit goes into wrinkles and creases at every point where the human body bends, and that Nigel Reiver beside her was soft and sleek in his. He wanted to show her the old city, the City of London, which was there before Shakespeare and before Dick Whittington, burned and reformed, the city of the guilds and the moneylenders, of civic pride and personal cut-and-thrust. He took her through narrow arched alleys and half-secret passages in and between buildings, in and out of courtyards, past bombed churches and churches still standing—so many churches. Past St. Giles Cripplegate, bombed in 1940, where Cromwell had been married, and where John Milton lay buried. These were days when the Barbican Centre was only a projection, a utopia in the minds of architects and planners in hope. They walked over the rubble of bomb damage, spattered with the pink-purple of willow herb, the tenacious mustard yellow of groundsel. Decay stood side by side with heavy-handled glass doors and gilded signs.

Nigel walked her on, down toward the river. He took her between warehouses and showed her pelts and skins piled and trussed inside windows black with grime. He said, "Now. Can you smell that?" and they stood side by side, and from somewhere, over the fish and mud smell of the river, over the dust and petrol of the road behind them, came a wind of spices, of old wood impregnated with spices, heavy and rich, pungent and sharp, cinnamon, cassia, nutmeg, cloves. It came in waves. Nigel snuffed and breathed it. Frederica associated it forever with his compact body in its soft, dark covering, furs and spices, a foreign mystery.

"I love the idea of the boats," he said. "Of the shipments coming in from all over the world. I love to see the commodity dealers work. Tea and coffee and pepper and cocoa. Have you ever tasted pure cocoa, Frederica? Bitten the nut? Smooth and bitter—a black taste on your tongue, very rich, yet very pure and light—"

They came to a place where a narrow alley debouched on the river, by a blackened wall and a landing stage where a barge was tied under a tarpaulin. Nigel sat on the river wall and she sat beside him, an incongruous pair, if there had been anyone to see them, he like a seal almost, with his dark hair and body, she holding on to her hat, holding down her flurry of skirts in the slight breeze. A few years later Anthony Armstrong-Jones was to photograph beautiful women in floating garments on fragile chairs half in and half out of this thick water at Rotherhithe. Frederica watched it lap at slimy walls and iron posts and rings, slapping the sides of the barge, turning in muddy little eddies out in the stream.

"Tide's changing," said Nigel Reiver. "I like it here. There's been a ford here since Roman times. Merchants crossed here for centuries—all through the Dark Ages, too, some people kept coming, bringing things in, taking things out. I like this river."

Never had Frederica found herself in such a gale of contrary perfumes: blown spice, decaying vegetables, pure mud, impure mud, a whiff of new-cured leather, the salt of the sea coming in, and closer and subtler, the smell of Nigel Reiver, compounded of sunlit cloth, faint, faint Old Spice, a touch of sweat, a warmth of acceptable skin. She had forgotten it, and now knew that he meant her to remember, and notice him.

"I come here by myself," said Nigel Reiver. "To think things over."

"And now with me," said Frederica.

"And now with you," said Nigel. "I like being with you."

He kissed her and she clung on to her hat. He put a black cloth knee into the flapping poplin and gripped her. He straightened her collar and rearranged her hat, and took her back past spicy air and dusty fur bales to find a taxi. She thought: he is a freebooter. The word gave her a thrill of romantic pleasure.

He had the use of a room in a flat full of young stockbrokers and lawyers in what from the outside looked like a graceful Kensington family home with huge windows and white-painted walls. As they let themselves in, two young men came out, tailored and brushed, clattering their polished feet in time down long front steps. They greeted Nigel with a courteous word and a knowing smile. They seemed not to see Frederica.

"Unfortunate," said Nigel. "There's usually no one here at this time. Let me scout round the kitchen. I could make you some sort of sandwich. Stand here a minute." He went and returned. "The coast's clear."

Frederica followed him into the kitchen, vaguely affronted that he should seem to need to be so furtive about her. The kitchen surprised her by being large, well-furnished, and filthy. The sink was full of burned pans, the vinyl stained with splashed soup or coffee. There was a calendar over the refrigerator displaying a blonde girl sitting on what seemed to be a goatskin in a transparent black shirt, by no means adequate to cover the shiny and shadowy bulges of breast and thigh, cleft of bosom, and shaved pubic mound. There were notices stuck to the refrigerator and cupboard doors with cellophane tape and drawing pins. "Will the sod who took Andy's sugar supply please Replace pronto." "Do Not empty butter dish without making sure there is another pack." "Toddy owes Vic half a jar of Nescafé and some milk." "Who has got my shortbread biscuits?" Frederica decided sharply against offering any help with all this, and watched Nigel, clumsier than he had seemed at anything, cut doorsteps of bread and slices of crumbly white cheese.

"Someone might have got an apple. Do you want an apple?"

"If you're sure we can—"

"Somebody nicked a good three-quarters of a bottle of my cognac last time I was here. I've got a right to a couple of apples. Come on up."

His room was dusty, a furnished-lodgings room, with a gatelegged table, a flimsy painted wardrobe, a vellum-standard lamp, an unmade bed, very churned up, and male clothes hanging from every protrusion, round the outside of the wardrobe, over the back of the one armchair. Male shoes ranged round most of the skirting boards and the bed was hung with towels. Nigel pulled out two old dining chairs and a leaf of the table, and they sat side by side and chewed the sandwiches, with glasses of a red wine that Nigel produced from inside the wardrobe. Their knees touched. Frederica knew what must happen and was, for her, nervous. She was nervous for two reasons. The first was that she had no real idea what Nigel thought was happening or would happen. Fun? A one-night stand? A preliminary to an invitation to become the mistress of his moated grange? The way the two young men had not seen her seemed to suggest that Nigel was—that they all were, perhaps—in the habit of arriving at odd hours of the day with unmentionable women. The second was that she was physically afraid. It might all, she thought with unfocused distress, be "too much." Nigel asked if she would like to go to the bathroom. He advised her to take a towel. "You can't leave them down there—they get nicked to polish shoes or mop up slops." The bathroom was again expensively fitted and overlaid with grime and smear. The washbasin had a rim of old foam and shaved whisker tips. The bath itself was full of cloth, which Frederica, staring at it from the lavatory seat, finally deduced to be a mass of tangled blue and white shirts in clouded water. Someone had obviously given up scrubbing the collar of one of these halfway; there was a nailbrush thick with soap, and the garment draped over the bath rack. Frederica suddenly realized why the house smelled familiar. It smelled like the changing rooms at Blesford Ride School, a smell of male sweat, male urine, old suds.

When she went back up, Nigel had made the bed, with remarkable competence considering his sandwich construction, and was sitting on it. In silence they undressed and got in. After a time the smell of sex, salt like the sea, shut out the other smells. After a time, Nigel shut everything else, Alexander, S. T. Coleridge, the gracious and clever *Vogue* ladies, John Milton, Raphael Faber, the shimmer of Cambridge, the puzzle of the undissociated sensibility, out of her busy mind. She had been right to be afraid. Her last thought before she fell heavily asleep with her head on his strange breast was that she had not known warmth could run right through, from two spines to meet in the stretched and relaxed triangles at the front. "Stop fighting," he had said, over and over, "Stop fighting," not aggressively, not censoriously, but with a practical gentleness of hand and hip and penis. She thought, poor Frederica, that she was a woman without the ultimate capacity to abandon herself, and several times, during this warm and patient battle, gave artificial little moans and tremors of pleasure that were ignored by the unknown man, inexorably searching her, handling her, knowing her. "No, not yet," he said, as she fought and stiffened and pulled away, "not yet, not now, *wait,* there's a good girl, wait." And when finally she lost her grip of herself, of separate Frederica, and rose to meet him, fell back to make space for him, cried out and heard herself crying, he said, "*There*," and, "*Now*," and turned his face away from her and stiffened and fell. She slept like a stone, not knowing who or where she was, and woke in a panic to unknown skin and the steady thud under her ear of unknown blood from an unknown heart.

In the moment before he pulled her over again, her greed now answering his urgency, she felt, "Oh, I am dying," and understood one of the oldest metaphors.

Hours later, over another hacked meal at the dusty table, she told him about *Vogue*. "I got a job today," she said. "A year on *Vogue*, if I want." Everything tingled in her; she could feel blood hot and pricking in odd places, the crease of the groin, the armpit, the breast muscles. "Congratulate me," she said. All her joints were weak, not only the obvious ones, knees and ankles, but wrists and pelvis and the knot of the neck.

"Okay, I congratulate you."

He was smiling. She had hardly ever seen him smile. He was smiling, but not looking her in the eye. As though staring into the distance, happily enough, through a leaf-patterned wall and a streaked mirror.

"I don't know what to do. Whether to stay in Cambridge or to get out and come to London. I'm not sure I'm cut out to be a journalist."

"Oh, come to London. We could have fun."

"Fun wasn't the primary consideration."

"Not the primary consideration," he said, repeating her phrase, as he had before. "Maybe not. But a consideration, wouldn't you agree?" He sighed with satisfaction. He was confident. Frederica picked up a wineglass with her jelly fingers and spilled it. Nigel mopped up after her with a white handkerchief as glossy as his table was dusty.

30

UNUS PASSERUM

There was a Saturday before Christmas that was a long day. Stephanie was, as usual, trying to put together the costumes for the small actors in the nativity play: she sat among cardboard boxes of toweling and hessian, rayon and taffeta. She found the oriental turban she had made from her old May Ball stole, peacock shot with lemon, pinned with a rhinestone buckle. It was dusty now and the feathers she had pushed into its folds were bent and tattered. She pulled them out, put a few stitches in where the cloth had come apart, and poised the curl of cloth on the head of her son Will. His dark eyes smiled out at her, seriously, under it. "Wait," she said; she would find the cloak too. She pinned this around his small shoulders and he strode off to clamber upstairs and look in the mirror. Mary pulled her skirt and said, "Me, me, me have." "In a minute," Stephanie said, stitching.

It was the day for Gideon's Young People's Group, which had swelled and increased in liveliness since its foundation. It met in the church hall, and there was dancing and cider as well as intense discussion of the problems of modern living. It had projects—the painting of old people's flats—and retreats—weekends spent discussing modern life and the difficulty of relationships in the secular world, usually at the Field Centre. To Stephanie's surprise, Marcus, now an undergraduate at the new university, living in one of the stripped-pine servants' attics in the old house at Long Royston, attended these fairly regularly. He also came to church on Sundays, usually sitting with Jacqueline and Ruth and a general group of Young People. In the days of his "illness" Marcus had come to church with Lucas Simmonds. Now he sat among the girls. She had no idea what he was thinking or what he believed. He talked to the sensible and lively Jacqueline, who was also now an undergraduate at Long Royston—the name persisted in the common consciousness. Perhaps he was in love? There was no reason why not—she did not quite know how she had come to think of him as forever incapable of usual passions. Perhaps Jacqueline? She was fairly sure he did not come because of the undeniable charismatic powers of Gideon Farrar, though again he had not talked to her about this. Indeed, since the days of dependence in her house he had kept her very much at arm's length, as was perhaps natural. His independence was precarious. She was part of what he was escaping from, what he was afraid of.

Daniel came in in the morning, accompanied by a girl with a pitted skin and greasy hair whom he did not at first introduce. He was very angry; she could feel it, moving like invisible heat at the red end of the spectrum. He asked if she had seen Gideon. Gideon, he said, had vanished again, leaving various unmade decisions about Christmas services and get-togethers. It was Gideon who was the man for get-togethers. Gideon was never there when wanted. He, Daniel, did what Gideon should have done yesterday, tekking *twice* the time over it since he hadn't organized it efficiently himself in't first place, and getting no thanks. Small Will presented himself silk cloaked and hatted in front of Daniel's legs, and said, "Look at me." Daniel said "Mind out," and said to Stephanie, "Can you mek us some coffee, then? This is Angela Mason," and pushed his son roughly, who cried out, clutched the stout pillar of his father's leg, and butted it repeatedly, damaging the turban. Stephanie got up to make coffee and said to Daniel, "Don't be like that to Will. He wasn't doing anything wrong. He was showing you."

Her voice was unsteady. Daniel clashed his fists together; he knew her susceptibility to anger, how she feared the raised voice, the aimless blow at anything or anyone. He picked up Will, who asked crossly to be put down, picked up Mary instead, who kissed him, and introduced Angela Mason.

"Angela's the social worker attached to Barbara Burtt. She's gone missing from that hostel. Gone looking for your Gerry Burtt, I shouldn't wonder. I thought you might have an idea of how to get in touch."

Stephanie said from the kitchen, "He sent a postcard. Months ago. From London. All it said was 'St. Bennet's crypt is a good place with good people. You'll find me here if you ever make a trip to London.' Oh, and he sent kisses to Will and Mary."

Daniel received this information in a rather grim silence. Angela Mason said that perhaps the clergy at St. Bennet's would be able to put her in touch with Gerry Burtt, to see if his wife was in touch with

him, or if perhaps he would now see her. Stephanie said she was sure
he had gone to London in order *not* to see her, and that matters were
best left that way. Angela supped Nescafé and absent-mindedly
twiddled her fingers at Mary, who hid her face, with its fading red
mark, in Stephanie's breast.

"I do think we ought not to be defeatist about this. Barbara has
been *very ill* and now wishes desperately for some normal human
contact, some return to ordinary life. She wants so very much to see
her husband and explain to him that she was ill, irresponsible, not
herself. She's rather a weak person, very dependent on others' good
opinion, very up and down. I've tried the parents—they're still living
—but they won't cooperate. The mother came once."

"What happened?" said Stephanie. Angela Mason resumed her
professional voice. "Barbara did try to make contact, but the mother
just couldn't take it, and began to abuse her, I'm afraid. Barbara
broke down. She couldn't say anything in the face of the rejection.
She doesn't feel she's anything to offer. She despairs easily."

"Gerry won't help," said Stephanie.

"I'd like to see him to decide that for myself," said Angela Mason.
"He must have cared for her once."

It was agreed that Miss Mason should write to the clergy at St.
Bennet's. Daniel went off and left her sitting with Stephanie, who
made more coffee, and listened to a perfectly proper and laudable
description of Barbara Burtt's loneliness and fear for another good
half hour. Despite Gerry's descriptions, probing hospital phone calls
before the release and now Miss Mason's psychological account of
trauma and inadequacy—"when I saw the Mother, I saw she had
never been given the chance to believe in herself as a separate woman,
Mrs. Orton, she'd been given frilly nighties but no self-respect"—
Stephanie had no idea of Barbara Burtt. She supposed vaguely that if
she were to meet her she too would come to be imaginatively
involved in the humanly inhuman miseries, fears, rebuttals, waves of
bodily panic that had led to the death of Lorraine Burtt in her dirty
cot. As it was, she had nightmares about Barbara, a dream figure with
blazing, flowing red hair and diaphanous frilly negligee, a cross
between Bill in a rage and the first Mrs. Rochester, who bent low over
Will's cot or Mary's, who tossed away the bedclothes and exposed

chill shriveled bodies, who brandished a lighted torch. She knew it was moral cowardice, but she did not want to have to imagine Barbara Burtt. It was just as well for her, however irritating, that Angela Mason spoke entirely in dead phrases, easy terms of her trade. *She* couldn't set a real woman in Stephanie's mind against the object of Gerry's panic terror and her own nightmares cultured from its contagion. She clutched Mary to her body, for comfort, and Mary rubbed a chewed handful of Marie biscuit into the front of her dress, not for the first time.

After Angela Mason had gone, the next arrival was Clemency Farrar, offering help with the nativity play costumes. Clemency's half-black son Dominic had played Balthazar last year in the silk turban and cloak—he was the last of the Farrar children to move from primary school to secondary school. Stephanie knew from schoolteachers in the congregation that Dominic, large for his age, had a reputation for bullying the little boys at St. Luke's, the church school where both he and Jeremy Farrar now went. (Jeremy, though much smaller, was two years older than Dominic.) The teachers had asked Stephanie whether to report these rumors to Gideon and Clemency—they were inhibited partly because Dominic was adopted and colored. Presumably they had not. Clemency opened today's conversation by saying how much appreciated Dominic's acting gifts were at St. Luke's—he was playing the Cowardly Lion in an ambitious *Wizard of Oz.* "He throws himself into parts, Stephanie. I thought he *was* the black king when he did it last year—such presence. Such *dignity*—didn't you think?"

Stephanie agreed, and waited to hear about the achievements of Daisy, Tania, and Jeremy. She made more coffee, and began to sort haloes for variegated angels. Clemency said, "Have you seen Gideon?"

"No. Daniel was looking for him, too. Isn't it his Young People this evening?"

Clemency nodded. She threaded a needle with gold thread, and wrapped and unwrapped yellow ribbon round a plastic headband.

"Your brother goes, doesn't he? Marcus. To the Young People?"

"He seems to enjoy it."

"Oh." Will put up a hand to the bundles of cloth and Clemency pushed it away. "Stephanie, dear—can I talk to you?"

"Of course."

"Have you—*heard* anything?"

"Heard?"

"About the Young People. About Gideon."

"No." But I have seen, she thought, and would not say.

"I don't know how to say this. I've had—complaints—complaints —from a Mrs. Bainbridge."

"Tom Bainbridge's mum."

"Milly Bainbridge's mum. Milly goes, now and then. To the Young People. Mrs. Bainbridge claims that Gideon—Gideon has been inter- fering with her."

"Mrs. Bainbridge is a very unpleasant woman," said Stephanie, truthfully and rapidly.

"But that isn't the point," said Clemency. "Is it?"

Stephanie remembered. She had gone up to the church hall to fetch something Daniel had forgotten—a book, was it? Sheet music?—and had gone quietly into the little office that took up one corner of the hall. All the lights had been off, in the body of the building and the office, but someone had, she thought at first, left the Calor Gas fire on, a major financial misdemeanor. She saw its incandescent dome of gauze, blue-green, red, white light, and then saw the two bodies in the desk chair beyond the firelight, Gideon Farrar with his shirt open to the waist, and the girl, her shirt also open and pushed back from naked shoulders. Only it had not been Milly Bainbridge, a bay-haired truculent Blesford Grammar sixth former. It had been the pale-plaited one of Marcus's two friends, the one who said little and looked quiet, the one who was training to be a nurse.

"Do you believe her?" said Stephanie to Gideon's wife, temporizing.

"Probably yes," said Clemency. "I mean, it wouldn't be the first time. I notice *you* don't sound exactly shocked or surprised. She could make an awful stink."

She stared defiantly at Stephanie, as though it was Stephanie who could or might make the awful stink. Stephanie remembered the early days of Gideon's incumbency, the knowledgeable hand seeking her own waist, the arm on the shoulder, the gaze on the opening of her dress. She had closed the door, in the hall, that evening, gone home, and said no more. Since then Gideon had avoided her. Clemency might have noticed and drawn the wrong, or even the right, conclusion.

"Gideon," she said carefully, "is a very *expressive* man. I've noticed. He likes dancing, and touching people in a friendly way, and making contact. It's part of his success."

"It's sex and lust."

"Energy *is* sex, in many ways, good and bad," said Stephanie, blundering on through her own platitudes. "Clemency—do *you* think —any real harm—is being done to Milly Bainbridge? Or anyone else?"

Clemency's handsome little face set. "Probably not, to those silly girls. They probably ask for it. Probably not nearly the harm he'd do himself if it got spread about. But to me, yes, to me, *to me*. He disgusts me."

She put her head down on the flimsy cloths and began to weep, dry and choking but abandoned, saying things Stephanie was sure she would, with her proper pride, her niceties, regret.

"He's a goat. I always knew. After Jeremy. Always on at me. My fault—no good, I've been, since Jeremy was born. I used to be half glad of the girls, because that way he'd leave me alone, not be always prancing up and fingering, *pushing himself* at me . . . You won't know what I'm talking about. You're happy. I've watched you and Daniel. You're happy. Nothing goes right for us. Well, that's not true. Gideon's *career* goes right, if he doesn't ruin it . . ."

"The children—"

"They loathe each other. They gang up on poor Jeremy. Dominic even—Dominic waves his—his *thing* at him and says there's something *wrong* with Jeremy because his is minute, and Gideon *laughs*. I've neglected Jeremy because the others were deprived, and now he *hates* me, he hates everyone, he wets the bed and can't keep up with his class—my little boy—I'm sorry, I'll shut up."

Stephanie tried to be practical. "You must speak to Gideon. Warn him. If you can. Or shall I ask Daniel?"

"He's scared of Daniel. He thinks Daniel *judges* him all the time. He plays the buffoon with Daniel. You talk to him."

"How *can* I?"

"You don't frighten him. He'd listen to you. You talk to Mrs. Bainbridge."

If you marry a man, you marry his job. This job more than most. All the same—

It was at this point that the white cat brought in the sparrow. It had never been a renowned hunter. It had had a phase when it brought in crawling things from the garden, laying them out on the rug in front of the fire, a row of pink wet worms, a small group of milky-brown slugs, two huge black ones, humpbacked and stippled. Will put them lovingly out again, curling them among the nasturtiums, balancing the smaller ones on sunflower leaves. "There," he said, "Good earf, nice leaves, all right?"

The sparrow hung limp in the soft white mouth and then flapped vigorously.

"Oh, poor *thing*, I can't bear it," said Clemency Farrar.

"A bird, a bird," said Will. "Get it, Mummy."

Stephanie advanced on the cat, which looked pure pale green evasion, and trotted under Mrs. Orton's chair. Stephanie reached under the chair and grasped odd limbs—a hind leg, a lashing tail. Her wrist was scratched and there was a muffled sound of growling and cheeping.

"Let *go*," she said, agitating the chair.

"Let *go*," said Will, uselessly commanding in his silks.

The cat and the sparrow emerged separately on the far side of the chair, the bird hopping, close to the ground, trembling.

"Get *out* of here," said Stephanie, kicking the cat, waving her arms. "Get out, get out, go away."

"*Bad* cat," said Will, advancing.

"She'll scratch you," said Clemency.

The cat made a sudden decision and plunged through the cat door, like a sulky tiger through a hoop. Stephanie pushed the coal scuttle across the cat door. Will stretched out his arms to the bird, which suddenly came to life and flew up onto the top of the bookcase.

"Leave it a minute," said Stephanie, breathless. "If we open the windows, it'll fly out, perhaps, when it can."

"It could be a pet bird," said Will.

"No, it won't like that. It's an outside bird; it wants to be outside."

"I'll be going," said Clemency, who had pulled together her self-control and rectory manner during the battle. "Would you—can you —have a word with Gideon?"

"Oh, can't *you*?"

"I daren't. I daren't. And he wouldn't listen. He wouldn't—he might even—I annoy him, that way, I make it worse."

"Can I talk to Daniel?"

"If you must. I'd rather you didn't, but if you must."

Daniel didn't come in. Some nativity mothers came and sewed a little. Daniel rang to say he wouldn't be in for supper, and Stephanie, who had cooked macaroni cheese, fed Will and Mary on it, bathed them, read to Will, *Hansel and Gretel*, and put them to bed. Will put his arms up twice. He said, "Will the bird be all right, Mummy?"

The bird was still up on the bookcase. Earlier in the day, at Will's insistence, she had climbed on a precarious chair and tried to grab it. It had flown in swooping circles, brushing lights and curtain rails, and had landed temporarily, with one defiant cry, on the cooker. From there it had flown back to the bookcase. The room was cold, because she had opened the window as wide as it would go.

"Daddy'll help it to go out," she said. "Sleep now."

"It isn't hurt, is it?"

"It couldn't fly like that if it was hurt."

"The cat isn't *bad*, is she?"

"No. It's her nature. Cats eat birds. But not in our house, do they, Will, if we can help it? It'll be out in the garden by morning. Now, go to sleep."

Daniel didn't come in, but Marcus did, at about eleven, after Gideon's Young People. She made him coffee and wondered whether anything could be learned from him about the extent or seriousness of Gideon's misdemeanors. Marcus seemed, she thought, uneasy and preoccupied. He sat in Daniel's chair and stared moodily into the fire.

"How was the evening?"

"All right, really."

"You don't sound enthusiastic."

"We talked about love. Different kinds of love. Eros and agape. Charity. Family love. Stuff we've had before. You know."

"Were there many people there?"

"Quite a few. Yes. Quite a few."

"Did you all talk?"

"Well—you know how it is. He—Gideon—he likes to get us to share our experiences. So we shared them. People told about their experiences of love. He thinks we're a noncommunicating society. We don't share. So we shared."

"It sounds terrible. That is, you *make* it sound terrible, Marcus. Was it?"

"I don't know. You know how he is. He's got a gift for making things seem—large—significant—you know."

"Did you talk?"

"Good God, no." Marcus was shocked. "I *couldn't*. That would be the last thing. Love is private. Or so I thought."

"What do you go for, Marcus?"

"Well, my friends go. You know. Jacquie. Ruth."

"Do they talk?"

"Sometimes."

He had wanted to tell someone, someone outside, what Ruth, answering Gideon, had said about love, and now suddenly did not. It made someone look foolish, himself, Ruth. Perhaps even Gideon, whose encouraging smile hung in his visual memory slightly demonic, encouraging Ruth to go on. And on. Outside there was a clatter and a howling. The cat was trying to come in. Preoccupied by love, Marcus had not noticed either the bird on the bookshelf or the draft through the house. Stephanie now pointed up at it and said, "We must get it to go out. It can fly. I've seen it."

"I'll get up on a chair."

The bird rose toward the ceiling and flew off, not out of the window, but farther into the house, into the kitchen. Stephanie ran after it and brushed it off the cooker. Go out, go *out*, you foolish thing. It soared, banged the ceiling, fell, and flapped wildly across the floor and under the refrigerator.

Stephanie, with Marcus hovering awkwardly behind her in the doorway, pulled the refrigerator out, away from the wall. No sound, no motion. She got down on her knees and peered under the exposed back of the machine. Its casing folded down and under, forming a ledge maybe an inch wide. On this, shivering in a corner, the creature was perched. She lay down on the kitchen floor and rolled back her sleeve, stretching her arm under the casing, reaching with extended fingers for the small shape, seeing in the shadow the live bright eye.

And then the refrigerator struck. She thought, as the pain ran through her, as her arm, fused to the metal, burned and banged, as her head filled, "This is it," and then, with a flashing vision of heads on pillows, "Oh, what will happen to the children?" And the word altruism and surprise at it. And then dark pain, and more pain.

Marcus was slow. Later he was to think it out, how, if he had been Daniel, he might have switched the thing off instead of standing there, smelling burned flesh, watching his sister's incomprehensible rigid drumming, hearing the gasp, and then the horrid relaxed silence, full of burning. He went to the door, opened it, and called, "Help," soundlessly from a dry throat. He went back, because the burning smell was increasing, and because of it, and too late, pulled out the refrigerator switch. He could not touch or look at her and wasted time pitifully in going up and down between kitchen and door before he finally thought of the telephone and managed to fetch an ambulance. While he was waiting for this, watching Stephanie's leg across the kitchen lintel, her shoe half off her foot, he remembered the children, asleep upstairs, and became possessed by terror that they might wake, might hear, or see, or smell . . . might ask him, Marcus, to do . . . to be . . . It became necessary to find Daniel. He could think only of asking Gideon Farrar where Daniel might be and made himself look up the telephone number on Stephanie's kitchen board.

Clemency answered. He coughed. No sound came.

"Speak up."

"It's Marcus Potter. I—Is Daniel there?"

"No, he isn't. I'll ask Gideon."

A silence. "Gideon doesn't know where he is. Is anything wrong?"

"There's been a—There's an accident. I think. Stephanie I think—"

"Are you all right?"

"No, I think she's dead."

And then, along the wire, Clemency became part of shock.

"Is anyone *there?*"

"No. I phoned the ambulance. Daniel—"

"We'll come over. Hang on."

The little house filled with people. Ambulance men turned Stephanie—Marcus did not look—and attempted artificial respiration. Gideon Farrar brought a bottle of brandy and gave Marcus some in a teacup. It was no good, the ambulance men said. They would get her to the hospital, but it was no good. A key turned in the front door, and Daniel came in, frowning with surprise, suspicion, irritation, at seeing Gideon and Marcus, over whose heads a sudden sparrow plunged into the night.

31

DANIEL

Daniel woke the next morning in a bedroom flooded with light. He thought of things he had to do, Holy Communion, Morning Prayer, and then the light struck him as terrible, as something that should not *be*, now, as things were. He did not, however, close the curtains as the light poured in, but looked resolutely at it, dressed, and went to wake his children. Last night Clemency Farrar had tried to take his children with her, or failing that, to stay with him, but he had refused both.

He remembered. This was the first time he had had to remember and therefore the brightest and rawest, like the indifferent sunlight.

He remembered her on the ground with her burned arm, and her mouth pulled apart and rigid in pain. He remembered the soft brightness of pale hair spilling over the skeleton, and a milky stain on the front of her yellow dress, a blemish, Mary's smeared Marie biscuit, though he did not know that. He knew and named what had happened fast and immediately. "She is dead." The shock produced in him not weakness but the opposite, a kind of access of mental clarity and physical energy, pumped adrenaline as in a man about to begin a long race, which he knew, in a sense, he was. For one long moment he felt all his gathered strength, like the seventh wave ready to break against the harbor wall, and had the foresight to see that his strength would be the source of his hurt, that it would take him a long time to know this and to suffer it, that he would think, and remember, and imagine, and that there would be no way of shortening this. Time ahead now was time after this. He bent down and touched her hair, briefly, her chill-warm hand, not that face.

He was a practical man. He thought, as they carried her away, of what must be done; indeed, the appalling and irrelevant nervous energy required action. We should tell her family, he said, and picked up the phone without hesitation to speak to Bill and Winifred. He was driven partly by some compulsive sense that if it was now true that Stephanie was dead it should be intolerable for anyone at all to be in the state of ignorant illusion in which he had walked home from the pub, come up the garden path, and turned the key in the door. One of the more distasteful aspects of his work was comforting mourners who refused to accept the reality of death. "There must be some mistake," the wisest and soberest too often said. Or widows, "I still wait for him to come home after work." He must *make this be true* for himself, relentless, no lies, no consolations of fantasy. Bill answered the telephone.

"Yes?"

"It's Daniel." He could not find even a mitigating preparatory sentence, could not bear to speak a few half-true words that might allow Bill to contemplate the possibility of death before its fact. "I have rung to tell you that Stephanie has been accidentally killed. In the kitchen. The refrigerator was not earthed."

He listened to the silence at the other end, intently, testing the other man's strength. Bill said, flatly enough, "Stephanie is dead?"

"Yes." How could he say, "I'm sorry." How absurd. "I didn't want you not to know."

"No. You were right. May I have a moment to—take this in?"

And was the adrenaline moving in Bill's older veins? He listened to silence in the receiver. Then the sharp little voice said, with a faint shaking, "I have told Winifred. She—wants to know if there is anything we can do. Immediately. For you and the children."

"No, thank you. I shall manage."

They listened to each other's silence. Daniel said, "I don't think I can talk any more."

"No," said Bill. "Good night, Daniel."

He spent some time trying to telephone Frederica, who now had a little flat in Kennington, but did not answer. She must be out, at a party, with a man. He looked around his living room, at the frightened, shapeless faces of the Farrars and Marcus. It was then that Clemency suggested taking the children and he refused. Gideon said, "Are you sure, Daniel? You know, it takes time for—for anyone to realize that things like this have happened. We can't leave you alone."

"I know perfectly well what has happened. I also know I shall feel worse later. But I should still prefer to be left alone." He looked around the room and saw Stephanie's unfinished work, the nativity costumes. "You can take all that stuff away. Please." He looked at Marcus, who sipped brandy from the teacup. He wanted Marcus, too, out of his house. Marcus trembled.

"I—I should have turned it off. I didn't realize what was happening. I—should have switched it off."

"She should have known it wasn't earthed. So should I. Accidents do happen. They are not our fault, but we find that hard to believe. We are frightened of things out of our control."

Clemency said, "Do you want to come with us, Marcus?"

Marcus looked at Daniel, who shook his head, like a tormented bull.

"I want to go home," said Marcus.

He went along the corridor in the morning to where his children slept. Mary in a large cot, Will in his bed. Mary was standing peering over the bars; he lifted her, smelling her night smell, baby powder and ammonia, and went over to Will. To Will too he wanted to tell the truth concisely and exactly without preamble. He was always to remember the small moment when the sleepy child smiled and stirred, ignorant, starting a usual day, and Daniel looked at him from the prison of his knowledge. He thought he must get Will up, give him some food, say something—what?—gentle, not frightening. Will said, "Where's Mummy?"

"Mummy had an accident. She's gone to the hospital."

"They will make her better, like Gran. Can we go to see her?"

"Oh, no, Will. It was a very bad accident. Mummy is dead."

Mary was wet against his shirtfront. Will's dark eyes met his and Will's breath went in, and in, and in. He said, "No."

"It will take some time to believe."

"No," said Will, and turned flat on his face, pulling the sheets over his dark head. "No. No. No."

It was a bad day. He finally persuaded Will, who said nothing more, to come down and eat breakfast. Mary ate some and threw some away, anxious and disturbed. People came, many people, Bill and Winifred, the Farrars, the dependents, churchwarden, wives. He found himself hosting a kind of perpetual tea party (of which he did not partake) that alternately sat in silence and talked briskly about other things, the nativity play, Christmas, how to make parkin (someone had brought some). Winifred took Will and Mary while he went to morning service, which was a mistake, since Gideon Farrar rose in the pulpit and said, "My heart is too full to speak to you this morning of the subject I intended. Most of you will know by now that Daniel Orton's wife, Stephanie, died unexpectedly in an accident last night. She was a beautiful and gifted woman, who was nevertheless unassuming and charitable to everyone who came her way. We all loved her, and must support those closest to her, her husband, children, and parents, in this terrible time of grief."

There was more: ordinary words, like stones, turning live Stephanie into remembered Stephanie, good-natured and distancing. Daniel took the words as another lesson of truth. She *was*; she *was*. She was going away. It was right. He had not begun to know that she would not come again, though his intellect clung to the task of repeating this statement to him until he knew it in fact. It was worse when Gideon came to anecdotes of Stephanie's parochial usefulness. Here for the first time he allowed himself to remember her plaint about diminished vocabulary, which he had silenced with sex, which he willed himself to stop short of remembering.

He began to move things, with the purposeful restlessness that characterized this time. He emptied her drawers and cupboards with extraordinary efficiency, folding the clothes away into large cardboard boxes for the Salvation Army. He felt a little mad, handling her underwear, her nightdresses, and something else, a choking, suppressed in the interest of order, when he came across the pink poplin dress she had worn when he had first loved her, in Felicity Wells's hot little room, in the old vicarage. The degree to which he had suppressed violent feelings, during all this activity, only hit him when he opened the linen basket in the bathroom, a week later, and found a brassiere, a pair of pants, a petticoat, coiled at the bottom like snakes ready to strike. That was the first time, taken by surprise, that he had tears in his eyes. Howl then, he told himself, standing in the bathroom with the ghosts of her bodily habitation in his square fingers, go on, howl. He could not.

In London, crossing Russell Square, Alexander Wedderburn cannoned into a weaving and wavering female figure he at first took for a drunk and then saw to be Frederica Potter, whose face was purple and red with weeping, still running with wet sheets of tears. "Stephanie is dead," cried Frederica loudly in Russell Square, so that pigeons flew up and indifferent walkers turned their heads. "Oh, Alexander, Stephanie is dead." He took her back to Great Ormond Street and gave her coffee, wrapped her in a blanket, and elicited from her the information that she had been out "on the tiles" at the time, sleeping "with someone." "I feel I should have *felt*, have *known*—" Frederica wailed, and allowed Alexander to comfort her, to tell her, as she already knew, that she could not have possibly foreseen this, that she was not guilty, that it was an accident. Alexander said that he would travel north with her, if he might, to the funeral.

He remembered Stephanie as she had been on the day of her wedding, standing in her white clothes in the sitting room in Masters' Row, still and rounded as he leaped up and down stairs in search of little gold safety pins. He wrote to Daniel, out of the pain this image caused him, but did not evoke it, imagining rightly that Daniel would not be able to bear at all, as he, more distant, could only just bear, the idea of her living. He wrote to Daniel an uncharacteristically grim little letter, saying that he did not know how one could come to terms with such things, but that men had, and did, and that Daniel was, he knew, strong. This letter, in its rather abstract, glancing way, spoke to Daniel as others, more loving, more evocative of the woman, the wife, the mother, did not. He kept it, unlike the others, which he answered quickly, quickly, and threw away.

He told Gideon that he would take the funeral service himself. Gideon expressed doubts about this. Daniel was being wonderful, but was he taking too much upon himself, the children, the house, the burial? Could he not accept consolation or support from anyone? Daniel glared at him pugnaciously. He could not bear, among other things, that Gideon should touch her again with his silly words, should presume to say anything about the woman, her, *his* wife, Stephanie. Her name was also becoming difficult for him to think or use. He said "she" or "my wife." "My wife" was to do with him, with Daniel, with the need for acknowledging loss and going on. He had to say, "My wife is dead." It was something people needed to know. But her name was hers, and to speak it was to tremble on the edge of the necessity and impossibility of knowing that *she* had been alive and was now dead, had been afraid and—He told Gideon that he was better if he was employed. He wasn't ill; he needed to be doing.

He decreed, also, to Winifred's alarm, that Will should attend the funeral. He remembered—in some way he was being made blindly to relive—the unreal days after his father's death, when he had been isolated, taken away from what was happening, made to "play." Will should not play, should not be confused, should know his mother was dead. Winifred, looking round the bare cottage, seeing how very thoroughly her daughter's presence had been stripped from this place she had lived in, her photographs gone, her desk tidied and bare, even her gardening basket vanished, said that Will would be frightened. It was very frightening at his age, to think of bodies under the ground, she knew herself, and he was only little. Daniel looked at her with his black anger, different from Bill's wild rages, and could be seen to be making himself remember that she had lost a daughter.

"When my father died," said Daniel, "I was kept away. No one ever told me anything. I didn't grieve. This did great harm. People do go under the ground and do not come back. Children in other times were allowed to *know* this. Will knows. One of Gideon's Young People will look after Mary. Mary does not know, not in the same way. Will must live through this."

"Don't make it too hard for him," said Winifred.

"He says very little," said Daniel, showing uncertainty, briefly. Then, "He asked if the *bird* was all right. He was worried about the bird."

"If I can help with Will . . ." said Winifred.

"I'd be glad if he could sit with you, then," said Daniel.

Most of the people who came to the funeral remembered Daniel at his wedding, brisk in his heavy body, smiling round at his church and his people. Most were discomfited by the way in which he spoke the words of his office. He was already standing in the chancel by the coffin, black and silent, when the church door opened and a final member of the congregation slid into the back. Bill Potter had been unable to bring himself to come to his daughter's wedding to a curate whose beliefs he despised and whom he could not welcome as a son. Now the two men looked at each other over the heads of the people: Frederica and Alexander, Gideon and Clemency, Marcus and Mrs. Thone, Winifred and small Will, clutching the pew shelf. Daniel spoke almost savagely, "We brought nothing into this world, and it is certain we can carry nothing out. The Lord gave and the Lord hath taken away; blessed be the name of the Lord."

The words were a thin defense between him and the pit. They were an action, customary and saving, not because he any longer believed any of the more comfortable ones, but because the terrible ones spoke some of the truth of things. For a thousand years in thy sight are but as yesterday; seeing that is past as a watch in the night. As soon as thou scatterest them, they are even as a sleep: and fade away suddenly like the grass."

.   .   .

If after the manner of men I have fought with the beasts at Ephesus, what advantageth it me, if the dead rise not?

All flesh is not the same flesh; but there is one kind of flesh of man, another flesh of beasts, another of fishes and another of birds. There are also celestial bodies and bodies terrestrial; but the glory of the celestial is one, and the glory of the terrestrial is another . . . The first man is of the earth, earthy: the second man is the Lord from Heaven . . .

What had he thought would happen? That the words would console as he had consoled others with them, that, however dimly, the resurrection, the change in a twinkling of an eye, the orient and immortal wheat, should seem real to him? He walked beside her boxed body to the edge of the pit, and his restless mind told him he believed none of it, none of it, perhaps never had, he was as *she* had laughingly once called him, of the earth, earthy.

Man that is born of woman hath but a short time to live, and is full of misery. He cometh up and is cut down, like a flower, he fleeth as it were a shadow, and never continueth in one stay.

He looked at the earth, at the foolish sheets of fabricated unnatural grass that he had forgotten to countermand. He looked at the wheels of flowers, autumn chrysanthemums mixed in with early forced spring flowers of winter, as happens at that time of year, white circles of unnatural perpetuity. He talked on, to the end of the committal service, looking down into that very narrow place, and thought, and tried not to think. When the words were over, he went on standing, looking reasonably and obtusely at the earth, while the others shifted on the pebbled path in high heels, or stamped cold feet on the clay.

It was Bill who took his elbow and said, "Come away, now, Daniel. Come away."

Under the yew tree Winifred and Frederica were trying to grasp a small, frightened, angry boy, who was whirling and screaming and biting.

.   .   .

A funeral, he had always said, was a drawing together of the living; it was a rite for the living. He had urged parishioners to let go, to let the dead be as they were. He walked along beside Bill, who stared at the paving stones as though learning them, and thought he had understood nothing. How could he be drawn together with these people? His place was out there, in the dark, in the wet, in the cold. He saw the winter trees, the gravestones, the edge of the church through a kind of sooty veil, on which danced little points of light that in a kind of giddiness he identified with the words he had just said.

Bill spoke. "Have you noticed how the old gravestones say 'Died' and the new ones say, 'Passed away,' or even, 'Fell asleep.' We're ill equipped for this, aren't we?"

"I thought I knew that."

"In the Middle East they put ashes on their heads, they tear their clothes, they scream and weep. We walk reasonably along together. I could say, I wish I had behaved differently to you, but that says nothing to what has happened now, does it?"

"No," said Daniel baldly, walking on in the black air. He did not notice when Bill fell back and joined the others.

32

VANISHINGS

The decorum of the novel, on the whole, requires that time not be given to grief. In detective stories, where deaths occur thick and fast, dropping into the text like leaves in Vallombrosa, no one is incapacitated by grief, no one's behavior changes; the text looks forward to the next death, if we are in *medias res*, or to the intellectual resolution, the revelation of who was responsible, if we are nearing the end. Detective stories, like the belief in original sin, console and comfort men for death, because someone always *is* responsible for bringing it into the world (of the novel) and all our woe goes out with retribution or atonement. One of the many unpleasant aspects of grief is the need to feel responsible or guilty—so that Marcus's grief for his sister turned partly on his folly over the electric plug and partly, irrationally, on his desire to tell her of his love for Ruth. He was unpleasantly shocked, on arriving at the Farrars' house for the funeral food and wine, to find Ruth there already, handing out glasses and carrying small Mary, who held the glistening plait with one hand and a chicken sandwich with the other. Daniel too felt responsible and guilty, though his reason battled against it, he told himself, as he told others, that his wife's life had been hers, that he must not take away her living of it, her own responsibility. Later nevertheless he was to spend long periods thinking of how she had been made dumb, by marrying him, about Wordsworth and Shakespeare, of how he had failed to come home an hour earlier, of how he had pushed Will that morning, wrapped in the remnants of her bright ball dress. In these early days he felt guilty only of having survived. This was the second stage, after the first flash of—can we call it joy?—when he recognized that he was a survivor, and about which he also, later, tried to avoid feeling unnecessary guilt.

There is a temptation to hurry over the next part of their lives, particularly Daniel's. It feels a little like discretion; it is both English and composed to turn away for a time, and take up the narrative again when there is something to narrate. Once novels ended with marriages. Now we know better, we lumber on inconclusively into the sands and swamps of married life, ending in a query, an uncertainty, a bifurcation of possibilities that allows the reader to continue the story with his own preferred, desired projection. Death is more of an end than marriage. Tragedies end with death. Watching the quietus of blind Oedipus, the multiplied nevers of old Lear upon the rack, we feel, Aristotle told us truly, something like relief, a slackening out of the importunities of pity and the tension of terror, a space for the flooding in of clear light, perhaps. But light hurts the waking eyes of grief. Tennyson knew that. On the bald street breaks the blank day. Shakespeare managed, it occurs to me as I write, to include the different pain of grief in the resolution of tragedy. The worst suffering in *Lear* is at the end, the accident after the resolution, the unacceptable.

Why should a dog, a horse, a rat, have life And thou no life at all? Cordelia's death, if we imagine Cordelia and not only Lear, makes that play too uncomfortable for the Aristotelian relief. We can let Lear go, gladly and gracefully, but not, if we have imagined her, Cordelia. Thou't come no more. Daniel had read *Lear*, pricked into it by Bill's scorn for his education. He had meant to read a lot more, to be able to talk to his wife as she was, and had not done so, because of the children and the Inhabitants, because of work, because he was afraid of Stephanie's mind as something that separated her from him. *Hamlet* too contains grief in tragedy—its sluggishness, its aimless protracted inactive suffering could as easily be ascribed to the workings of grief in Hamlet as to the more usual (and not incompatible) unacknowledged fear and desire for the mother. Hamlet comes to life in a startling way when he enters the world of death. It is not without reason that nineteenth-century portraits of actors depict him always with Yorick's skull, on the edge of the grave into which he will jump and from which he will emerge with an identity. This is I, Hamlet the Dane. And less than an act to go.

Surviving, in this sense, is exactly not resolution. Over the next weeks he retold himself his own story, backward from that moment, forward into a future of which that moment was the origin. The rest of his life was life after this death. And what had gone before became tormenting, lurid and unthinkable precisely in the degree in which it had been bright, significant, or simply happy. Memories were like spectral sunshine, painful on hurt eyes. They had walked along the beach at Filey in the roar of water and wind. They had clung to each other for warmth in his little room in the vicarage. She had sat up in the hospital bed, with his gift of irises beside her, holding Will in the circle of light from a high reading lamp. All these images were contaminated, superimposed on that other, the curled black lip, the wet teeth, the fallen hair, the stained dress, the burned arm. He was a man who had supposed his life to be a kind of solitary dedication to helping and he had loved once, and once only, a mild gaze, round breasts, full hips, and a peaceful lively movement—it was bearable to remember these fragmented aspects almost, but intolerably dangerous to call up, to reach out to, to name the whole living woman. His intelligence worked overtime, forging cunning maneuvers and survival plans for simultaneously knowing and not knowing what had gone. (*Who* had gone. Even the pronoun was part of a necessary diminishing.) He could not simply obliterate his past, or so he thought, so he must go over it, bit by bit, see it all, in this new cruel light, as leading to this, and to this only. But he must never lose hold of the truth, never relax into imagining or desiring her presence for a moment. Such a desire would, he felt, loosen his hold on the knot of will and biological continuity that was his self. He must continue to get up, feed the children, work.

He told himself that he would not even dream she would come back. It is possible, critics argue, that Lear died in the illusion that she *had* returned, look on her lips, look there, that his heart, like Gloucester's, burst smilingly in the illusion of a return. Daniel was possessed by fear of such an illusion, which was fed by the similarity of women walking at the other end of streets, blonde hair escaping under hat or rain bonnet, by a hallucination in which a bath towel became her nightdress, hooked on the bathroom door. He did not think he could wake from a dream of her presence or return and survive. So he did not dream. His will penetrated the shadows and drove out dreaming. At least, if he dreamed, it was in such dark that it never came to light in the morning.

Though in the morning, besides the intrusive light, there were other problems. A danger time was the time of half-consciousness on waking, when day after day he remembered, under his own orders, that there was a terrible thing he must know but not have to remember in detail, that he must not wake lazily, or confused or hopeful. If by any chance he forgot this, flash after flash the whole sequence of that time would play itself through in his head, his steps on the path, his key in the door, the sight of Gideon and Marcus, and then that which also had to be remembered, the soft hair, the burned arm, the fallen shoe, the stained dress, that face.

One of the things he had known, had had to know, professionally, was that other people are unaware of the slowness of grief, of the increasing difficulty of survival. At first, when he was nothing but numb will to know and wear through, they came often, bringing flowers, bringing food, asking to treat the children, begging him to visit for meals, which he refused. Later, when he had begun to think of her body—still not herself, her body—and occasionally could not bear to be contained by the walls of his house, they came less often, and seemed to feel that he must now be back to normal. They brought him their problems again, problems of sex and love and loneliness and money, and he said to them what he would have said if he had been truly engaged with what they brought, instead of sneering in his dark mind at its sameness, its smallness, the inevitable end it would all come to.

So quickly, so quickly the English stop speaking of grief, he thought, ungraciously, knowing that he had resented the inadequate words they had spoken, and sometimes worse than inadequate. Maybe Stephanie had been taken, a deaconess said, so young and so happy, because our Lord wanted Daniel to know the way of life without such love. Cordelia was killed, Christian critics argue, to effect the reconciliation of Lear with the heavens, to redeem him. Daniel thought for a terrible moment of Stephanie cycling off to the prenatal unit with her Wordsworth heavy in her bicycle basket. She had had *her* life. Who could believe in a God who killed that life to teach Daniel Orton a lesson about suffering? Shakespeare killed Cordelia to show that there are worse things in our world than guilt and atonement for guilt, that Lear's wisdom, painfully acquired and not very great, was of very little moment beside that cry. Why should a dog, a horse, a rat . . . And even *that*, Daniel thought, after he had abruptly terminated the deaconess's remonstrances, was self-referring. There were times when he was amazed that *anything* was alive, a greenfly or an early daffodil someone brought him, when he feared for its green silky weightless life as much as he feared for his children.

The children will be a great consolation to you, they said, they went on saying. The children were what he was for. That at least was clear. He washed and clothed and fed the children; he read to Will; he found girls to sit with them, or took them, not often, to Winifred when his work called him away. He had, perhaps, supposed himself that they would be a consolation. Instead, they were a source of fear. He feared for them, and he feared them.

His cooking was slow, limited, and unimaginative. They had a lot of bacon and eggs, many sausages, tin upon tin of baked beans. There would come a time when he would learn to cook, but not yet. He did not like even handling the, her, cooker. He stopped short of asking himself what they thought, seeing him struggling with her cooker. The liver was hard and bitter, the chops burned. They pushed away food, which Daniel made them eat, when he could. That he did not eat himself, subsisting only on broken toast and cups of tea, nobody noticed.

He was afraid for them as he was afraid for flies and small creatures, only worse, far worse. He had seen them as growing and separate, Will with his busy speech, Mary with her patting hands, resembling himself and Stephanie, but splendidly separate. Now they appeared primarily and monstrously vulnerable. He would not let Will open the door for the postman, nor clamber on the garden fence; he hit him once when Will tried to carry a jug of hot water from sink to dining table. Mary in the flesh had not been quite separate from her mother and now he cringed a little before picking her up, remembering *her* hands, her shoulder with Mary's head against it, her hair teased by sticky fingers. Mary, hitherto placid, did not like being picked up and rejected him vigorously with flat palms and whistling howls. This was not as bad as Will watching him across the meal table, a family not a family. The electric light itself seemed darkened and gloomy. Will's black little look was an accusation.

"Where's Mummy gone?"

"She is peaceful. With God. God cares for her."

"In a box. Will she come out of the box?"

"Her body rests there. She *herself* is free and with God, Will."

"Is God kind to her?"

"God cares for everyone. He loves them."

"Not us. He doesn't love us."

Staring.

"Will, eat your cornflakes."

"I don't like them. They taste funny. They aren't right."

"They're all you'll get. *Eat them.*"

"Supposing she wants to come out of the box?"

"She can't." He tried to say what he had said to his flock, that what was there *wasn't* her, Stephanie, Mummy, and because he didn't believe it himself couldn't force the words out. "Stop worrying, Will. Eat."

"She might want to come back to us, really—she might."

"No, Will. She can't. Dead people can't. That is how it is."

And Will, casually pushing his uneaten food to the floor, "I want her, though. *I want her.*"

"You have me. I'll try. I'll try to—"

"I want my mummy back."

No, the children were not a consolation. Feeding them was something to do, and he did it. He read *Hansel and Gretel* over and over, ignoring, because he was beyond comforting, Will's reiterated assertions that Hansel and Gretel had been all right though their daddy and mummy had left them in a wild wood, to a witch who tried to eat them; they had got away and gone home, and it had been all right; they had been all right, hadn't they? Daddy, *hadn't they?* They had been all right, said Daniel thickly, trying to cuddle Will, who beat with rejecting fists against his black male front.

He too was preoccupied with the box. It was not a preoccupation to share with Will, and it seemed unmentionable to anyone else. He was not fanciful, and had always rather enjoyed the way the burial service took cognizance of bodily corruption and set it against eternal light. It was not until it was this flesh—which he remembered piecemeal, the sight of her spine, walking away from him, of her ankles, cycling, of her hair, her hair on his pillow—that he found his mind would not leave the image of the cold and dark, the deliquescence, the softening and loosening, the liquidity, though after my skin worms destroy this body, yet in my flesh shall I see God? He loved his son Will, flesh of his flesh, flesh of her flesh, and he felt himself and his imaginings loathsome and dangerous to Will, who could still, perhaps, defend himself against the foul and corrupt nature of the face of things with the gruesome Grimm stories in which the young and hopeful returned, always returned, from castle and cavern, with the gold ring, the silk cloth, the toad bride who was metamorphosed into a lovely princess. As for Daniel, every head smote off, every felled monster, along with trodden beetles, fallen sparrows, the burned triangles of liver on his plate, revolted and perturbed him. He did not dream of Stephanie, but he dreamed most horribly of the head of the horse Fallada, live and bloody above the castle gateway, warm to the touch, too soft, too spreading . . . He tried reading Enid Blyton's *Little Noddy* and was castigated by his son who said, "Mummy doesn't like *that* book, we don't read that. We read *this* book, we do."

When did it come to him that he might not, after all, in the sense he had taken for granted, be going to survive? He had thought ahead in the brightness of that first terrible day and had imagined a time *after* this had got worse when he would again have to start living his life, doing accustomed things reasonably, thinking outwards. He had allotted himself, out of the normal strength of his energetic living, an indefinite time for suffering, almost resenting, with that part of himself that was still before death, still planning work, the interruption to his vocation. Then he said to himself, as he wrenched his past into this null present, that his very strength prolonged the learning of pain, as a strong bodily frame prolonged a mortal illness. In the startled beginning he lived forgetful moments in the equable past, moments of dogged purpose in the imagined future beyond knowing this. Then he came to think of himself as swimming, struggling to breathe, in an airless brown tunnel, lit with the phantasmagoric flashes he had first seen as the words of the burial service on clay, and the tunnel was narrow, he worked like a mole, and clogging, but he was strong, he worked his way along, to no goal, not even to rest in a cul-de-sac.

He must have wished to exhaust himself; he must have wished to be able to let himself off. In times of stress with his wife, in earlier moments of despondency or aimlessness, he had walked, mostly at night, soothing himself with the rhythms of his footsteps. In the long evenings when he sat alone, the children in bed, he came to feel his little house, which he had once seen as a fragile hut in a blast, as something thicker and more oppressive, heaped on him, like the earth in that narrow slit. He would look from chair to table to the kitchen door and the tiled kitchen floor, where she had slipped, had prostrated herself and stretched out her hand for the bird, and he could not be still there any longer without—without some unimaginable bursting into noise or violence that must be kept from the children. He would go out then, making short dashes to the church, the churchyard, the canal, always impeded by the heavy chain of his fear for the children, which increased with every step.

In the church, he did try to pray. Not to Christ, but to the old, thick, undifferentiated God who held together the stones of that place, who lived like electricity in its heavier air, whose presence he sensed only rarely but who had driven him. Thou turnest man to destruction: again thou sayest, Come again, ye children of men. Thoult not come again. It was not that the church was uninhabited: something was busy there, as it had always been, something that had incorporated and annihilated the small human voices that piped and sighed there. There was more in the world, and more outside the world, than men and their small concerns; Daniel could hear it, life, beyond the thud of his own heart, the snuff of his own breath. To think that people had knelt here and prayed to be relieved of the shame of acne, to have a girl in the choir smile in their direction, to pass an exam for which they had inadequately prepared, to have the vicar see their new hat, *now*, or *now*, or now. It had laws for these little things; unearthed electricity struck through flesh, wet blood, bone, to the tiled floor. But he could not stand there and shout to it to strike him, where he stood, nor yet to undo, to bring back. All he could ask it to do was what he could and must do himself: make him survive usefully. It was not exactly that he did not believe in it. It did not, particularly, believe in him. It had laws for him. Christ had said that the Father cared for the fall of a sparrow, but though it was clear Christ had cared, it was not at all clear that the powers did. The power struck, according to law. Men had fragile skulls, their hearts pumped efficiently, delicately, robustly, and an air bubble could stop them. The image of the hanging figure on the cross was a human cry for things to be otherwise, for human suffering to be at the center, for man to be responsible for his own destiny and for the destroyed to come again, to come again like the grass, like St. Paul's wheat sown in corruption. If after the manner of men I have fought with the beast of Ephesus, what advantageth it me, if the dead rise not?

Daniel thought the dead did not rise. Because he had brought fear to an unacceptable pitch he blundered quickly back through the cold night air to the cottage, thinking about the vulnerability of small skulls, the suffocating of small lungs, that drawn-up lip, the burned arm, the soft dead hair.

Gideon and Clemency came to call. Daniel did not offer them coffee, but they did not go away, and Clemency, without asking, went into his kitchen as though it were hers and made coffee for all of them. She had brought homemade biscuits and told Daniel that he was looking haggard and undernourished. She put the biscuits out on a plate on the dusty table. Daniel refused them by the simple expedient of not taking one. Will came up and took three, one after the other, stuffing them into his mouth as though he was starving. Clemency offered one to Mary. She sat in Stephanie's chair and coaxed Mary to trip across to her and have a nice biscuit with a sugar violet on it. Mary came, sucked the biscuit, leaned a rosy cheek against Clemency's yellow linen skirt, smearing it. Clemency wiped the smear in a businesslike manner with a little handkerchief. Rage rose in Daniel so that the room swayed a little and he saw two jittering window frames behind Clemency's head. Gideon said everyone was worried about Daniel, who had been absolutely splendid, of course, but must be feeling the strain. He wondered if a holiday? He wondered if the children would like to come and be part of their large family for a time? He wondered also if Daniel should perhaps speak to a counselor, someone experienced in dealing with grief . . .

"No," said Daniel.

"I know," said Gideon, "that it is hard for you to speak of dear Stephanie, but I think it might help. We are all too ready to tidy away our dead, to close them out of our hearts and minds. I wondered if it would help if we recalled—just sitting round the table as we are—something of the marvel of her existence, gave thanks for her life, for these little ones, for the happiness she brought to so many."

"Only the day she died," said Clemency, hardly faltering, "I brought her a personal problem, a delicate matter, and she was so *wise*, so gently patient with—with something rather disagreeable—"

Was it then that Daniel felt survival loose its coils? A wind rushed to his ears; dark bars, lit with fire, stood out before his eyes, bizarrely carving Gideon's benign face into burning sections, here an eye, there half a yellow beard-face.

"She belonged," said Gideon, "to all of us; we all mourn and wish to mourn with you. Let us pray. Dearly beloved Father who understands human mourning having given your own son for our sake . . ."

"Get out," said Daniel. He stood up and gestured at Clemency, who had seen Stephanie since he had, who had used up words she might have . . .

"I think you need *help*," said Gideon.

Daniel hit him. Something took possession of Daniel, his heavy hand crunched on Gideon's face, and came away bloody. For a moment he felt peace. And then the rage flared again.

"Get out," he said to Clemency. "Out of here. Get out."

"I ought to take the children," said Clemency, in her smeared skirt.

"Just get out," said Daniel.

Mary stood weeping behind Mrs. Orton's armchair. Will was in the kitchen, his body pressed against the wall, his cheek against the refrigerator's cold white side, his little face set white.

33
THREE SCENES

They had family tea again in the little house in Master's Row. The large brown teapot shone mildly on a blue-checked tablecloth. Toast was in the toast rack and bread and butter cut in overlapping slices on a willow-patterned plate. Winifred had brought out again Marcus's old heavy-rimmed dish inside which a faded Christopher Robin watched the Changing of the Guard with Alice. Mary had this dish, and Will had Frederica's Peter Rabbit cup, plate, and egg cup. Winifred made toast soldiers for Will to dip in his boiled egg. There were spicy gingerbread men. She had held Mary at the table to press currant eyes into the spread-eagled figures Will had rolled and cut. They smiled candied-peel smiles. She had made a coal fire again, where once she and Bill had sat in cold silence with one bar of the electric fire. Its light played on polished spoons and warm if battered wood. There were flowers on the table, extravagant spheres composed of rising flamelike segments of ruddy and gold chrysanthemums, for which Mary reached and from which she was lovingly held back. Winifred could not have said she was happy. How could she be happy? But she had a purpose, which had put life into her.

Three months ago she had picked up the telephone one night. He spoke sharp and fast.

"I want you to come now and get the children. I want you to have them and take care of them. *Now* you must come, do you understand? I have to rely on you."

"What are you going to—"

"Oh, nothing silly. I have my standards. But I can't go on. I shall damage someone. You must accept that."

"Yes, but I, but they—"

"They will be better with you. I'm going. I'm just *going*. Will you come?"

"Of course."

"Now. Promise."

"I promise."

"I'll be in touch."

She took a taxi. When she came to the cottage, they were both in bed. She had packed their things and taken them back. She had known she must do this but had not guessed how it would change her.

From time to time they got postcards. Never again phone calls. He appeared to be working his way south. Haworth, Nottingham, the Potteries, cathedrals, views of moor and fen, meaningless town centers with concrete road lights. Love to Will and Mary.

She had not understood what it would do to Bill, either. She had been a patient, tight-lipped mother; she was a cuddly, indulgent, gentle grandmother. He had, as father, roared, castigated, laid down his expectations. Now, he played. True, he had tried to play with Marcus, "creative" play, counting blocks, telling the story of Beowulf, or Siegfried, or Achilles, offering the child his culture, and had been rebuffed. Will liked stories. And Bill had lost his intent, driving aspect. In the early days Mary was pleasant and easy to amuse, and Will brooded darkly. But he allowed Bill to read to him, even to read poems, had responded to "The Pied Piper" and the "Jackdaw of Rheims," had made Bill repeat and repeat the tale of true Thomas wading in blood above the knee. They all four sat together over these firelit teas and kept back the dark.

Marcus came in, from time to time, and sat at the edge of the room, saying nothing, but present, looking at the children, Will in particular, with some fear, whether they fought with cushions or, as happened, wept wildly at the sound of a banged door.

The death of his sister had changed things between Marcus, Ruth, and Jacqueline. He had entered Ruth's world, what she thought of as her world, it seemed, in which the bearing of loss, patience, knowing gentleness, was central. Jacqueline had become afraid of him. Ruth came to see him in his student attic at Long Royston, gathered him into her cool arms, lay beside him on the bed—he asked no more—smoothing his hair, telling him it would pass, everything passed. So she must tell her patients, he thought, and for some of them it would be true and for some not, or not as she intended it. He could not tell anyone, neither Ruth herself, nor Jacqueline, nor Winifred, nor Mr. Rose the psychiatrist, how he had gone there that night to tell Stephanie about Ruth, Gideon, and love. He felt numb and too little; it was as though Daniel's furious grief had taken away his own right and volition to any show of grief or guilt.

He came home because it both pained and pleased him to see Bill and Winifred playing with the children, as they had failed to play with him. Will sat on Bill's knee, curled as Marcus had never curled, in the crook of that wiry arm, his little head erect and watchful under Bill's sharp chin.

Bill recited, mostly to Winifred, a poem of Hardy's he had found, looking up things to recite to Will. "He was an inferior novelist but a real poet," said Bill, "despite a shocking tendency to use secondhand language and tired phrases.

> "I am the family face
> Flesh perishes, I live on
> Projecting trait and trace
> Through time to times anon
> And leaping from place to place
> Over oblivion.
>
> The years-heired feature that can
> In curve and voice and eye
> Despise the human span
> Of durance—that is I;
> The eternal thing in man
> That heels no call to die."

He made quite a little occasion out of the reading, drew them together, held their eyes.

"Cold comfort," he said. "But something?"

Winifred was moved by this. Marcus was not.

Frederica sat in the little library she had imagined, on a window seat with a long, worn tapestry cushion, and looked out over mown lawns in spring rain to a little brick bridge over the moat with water in it. The room was beautiful and alien, furnished in green and dull gold and rose, with much-loved old mahogany, Chinese jars of pot-pourri, and the books, the unopened library of a dead gentleman, the letters of Lord Chesterfield, Gibbon, Dr. Johnson, Macaulay, Scott, Kingsley, and *The Lays of Ancient Rome* into which the child, Nigel Reiver, had dipped on wet days, like these days of her first visit. Nigel's two sisters, Olive and Rosalind, who do not come into this story and knew nothing of what had passed of it, had presided over the tea, of which the remnants were in front of them, on a low table. Georgian silver teapot, reflecting firelight and misty outside light, delicate Spode cups, a platter of fine sandwiches, a crumbled half chocolate cake, on a lightly starched damask cloth on a large dark tray. There was a silver creamer, and a saucer of sliced half rounds of lemon, glistening and acrid. The two sisters, wearing heathery tweed skirts and cashmere sweaters, were like Nigel, dark, and blunt, slightly sullen, and full of bodily life.

Frederica was not sure why she had been asked, just now, or why she had agreed to come. Nigel was the one person who seemed able to encourage her to cry out, to beat against him. But this was not her place. On the first day she had been startled by the size of it—unlike Long Royston, Bran House was an ordinary dwelling place, so that its dairies and conservatories, outhouses and stables, seemed endless, as Crowe's showier, more palatial ones had not. She had walked with Nigel through the fields to the home farm, surprised that a man could *own* so many free-growing trees, so much wild grass, part of the earth. She had not expressed this surprise. She had stood outside a pen of pheasants, bright birds strutting higgledy-piggledy inside wire, ridiculous in their confinement, had seen strings of drooping rooks and moles drying in death on a gatepost.

She had a pretty bedroom with a white-curtained four-poster and crocheted cotton cushions, all white. It was like a book. At night Nigel came in barefoot, silent and powerful from start to finish. She had envied Stephanie the certainty of her desire for Daniel, who, however improbably, had been what Stephanie *wanted*, in a way she,

Frederica, had managed to want no one. Confusedly she thought she had perhaps relied on Stephanie to do for both of them things she herself feared doing, perhaps couldn't do. Let me in, let me in, Nigel was in the way of saying, and she could not tell, it was true, sometimes, where he began and she ended, they were in a way joined. Was *that* what Stephanie had meant, had had? The idea of her sister was always monstrous, because always dying. If she remembered some good thing, cycling side by side, tea in Wallish and Jones, an argument about *The Winter's Tale* which Stephanie loved and Frederica could not swallow, the imagined Stephanie became rigid and horrible and then she began, sweating, to weep. She had not had the courage to see her in her coffin before she was shut away. She had thought she had a good courage, could fling herself at things, but she could not do that. Nigel was the only person to whom she had confessed this, and he had understood, as he understood, she believed, blind moments of terror or passion. She thought of this again in the middle of his long thrusts that night and began to cry, trying to be soundless, and he held her tightly, against the dark. He was very much alive. His house, and his watching sisters, were alien, but he was very much alive. In the night she clutched him, and in the day they walked in the rain over his ground retracing his ancient paths, noticing signs of life, a whirr of green wings, a startled jackrabbit, the tremor of a hawk.

Later than both these, Alexander answered his door in Great Ormond Street and had to go down a flight of stairs to the main front door, where his visitor kept up a steady, drilling ring. On the step was a figure, black and filthy, bearded and disheveled in an old raincoat and scored and grit-planed boots. Alexander took a step back and then recognized Daniel, who had lost much of his fat, whose black clothes hung on him under the raincoat.

"May I come in for a bit? I need a warm place. And a shave. And a phone. I thought of you. You wrote me a good letter, that was mostly why. Can I come in?"

Alexander let him in, provided a bath, and offered food. He would have offered clothes, but they would not fit, even now. He made a heaped plate of gammon and eggs, brown bread and mushrooms, tomatoes, all of which Daniel consumed, sitting at a low table in front of Alexander's fire. He had grown a vast matted beard, which he had trimmed in the bathroom but not removed. He spoke between mouthfuls in small bursts. The flat was pale and peaceful, straw and gold and blond wood; a lot of light came through high, fine-framed Georgian windows. Alexander had taken to housekeeping in a minimal but punctilious way. He made yogurt as Elinor had done, and had put a vase of irises on his desk, next to his little image of the *Breakfast Table.*

"I've been walking," said Daniel. "I walked most of the way. Sometimes I got buses. Slept out—sometimes—sometimes in transport digs and such. Won't bore you with all that. Don't think I knew where I was going, rightly—the idea was to finish myself off, tire myself out, like—go to nothing."

How could he say? He had fought his flesh, punished it, and spoken to no one for week after week, treading heavily from surface to surface, tarmac, grass, sand, heather, indifferently, realizing what "tramp" meant. He remembered his feet moving, and the regularity of the movement taking the life from his mind, from himself, from what had happened.

"Nearly did finish myself off. With walking. And not eating. Got as far as St. Bennet's. You know those people—they take anyone in, dossers, vagabonds, suicides, drunks. I knew a man who'd gone there. By the time I got there I was in a right state—filthy, wi' pneumonia, couldn't talk, might as well have had lockjaw. Put me dog collar in a pocket the second day—funny I went out in it at all, but I did, it was a kind of notice hung on, to start with, this is what I *am*, coming to nothing. They got me in hospital. I've been helping out a bit. Waste of public funds. Now I help out there. But it's time I came back to life."

On his walls Alexander had large images of the Sower and the Reaper, made for him by Charles Koninck, larger than life, or canvas, swarming with yellow and violet light. He knew very well that a casual visitor, most visitors, might see in them the usual bourgeois brightening up. He knew also that the painter had wished to make images that anyone, that everyone, could hang in their room to cheer themselves up. Daniel's gaze passed them indifferently. Alexander lived with them to live with the idea of extremities he didn't, perhaps couldn't, know. He looked at Daniel and didn't know him either, what drove him, what had almost brought him to nothing.

"What will you do?"

"I can't go back to housekeeping. Once, I wanted to—now I don't know. I hope I can go on working at St. Bennet's until something turns up. With the down-and-outs. But first I must square things with the bishop. They don't know who I am at St. Bennet's. I thought I'd try myself—my real self, you know—out on you, to see if it held together."

"Will it?"

"It might."

"I'm glad you came."

He pushed aside the debris of Daniel's huge meal and poured coffee from a blue enameled Polish pot into a golden Vallauris pottery breakfast cup.

"Coffee. To put some life into you."

Daniel was twisting something in his fingers. It was the dog collar.

"Thanks."